The Belle Of Linley Cottage

The Belle Of Finley Cottage

The Love in Lillet Series

J. J. Greenaway

To Mommy and Daddy,
Thank you for always believing that I could do this even when
I thought I couldn't
Love you to Infinity and Beyond

To anyone who has felt like they have to wait to be happy,
Don't wait
Start living your dream life today

Content Warnings

This book is intended for an 18+ audience. It includes explicit language and sexual content that is not suitable for younger readers.

This book also includes depictions of anxiety, depression, grief, divorce, and overbearing parental figures with mentions of fatal car accidents. Your mental health is important so please visit my website (authorjjwrites.com) for a full content warnings list to make an informed decision as a reader.

Playlist

Far Away | Tiffany Day	3:12
half of my hometown | Kelsea Ballerini ft. Kenny Chesney	3:52
You're on Your Own Kid | Taylor Swift	3:14
golden hour | JVKE	3:29
Unwritten | Natasha Bedingfield	4:15
Paradise | Carmody	2:56
Scared of Happy | Fifth Harmony	3:24
Bad Haircut | Stephanie Poetri ft. JVKE	3:42
july | Lyn Lapid	2:45
Canada | Lauv ft. Alessia Cara	3:04
Overloved | Raven-Symoné	4:12
Never Knew I Needed | Ne-Yo	3:37
making the bed | Olivia Rodrigo	3:19
Because You Live | Jesse McCartney	3:19
Art of Love | Guy Sebastian ft. Jordin Sparks	3:59
My Days | Joy Woods	3:42
Sweet Nothing | Taylor Swift	3:08
Mine (Taylor's Version) | Taylor Swift	3:52

May your choices reflect your hopes,
Not your fears

Nelson Mandela

May

Chapter 1

The fact that Zach had been voted "most likely to succeed" in high school felt like a slap in the face.

What kind of valedictorian graduated from college without a real job?

He probably should have thought more about what he would do with an English degree before choosing it because, at that moment, he was at a loss for what he wanted.

Well, no, he had thought about what he wanted for the future in the abstract. The big dream was to own a publishing company where he could publish not just his own fantasy and sci-fi novels, but also others that also showcased larger-than-life tales from a multitude of cultures, alongside a chain of secret library-inspired stores where they would stock those books and more.

That was the ultimate dream.

It had been something he was steadily climbing toward since the beginning of freshman year. But he was currently in free fall back down the mountain, because even with his course load of grammar and writing workshops, hours of reading books to analyze their themes, and summers of being the top bookseller at The Book Haven, Zach couldn't sell himself as an employee to any of the publishing houses he had been applying to for the last few months. He had thought that being paid to read books and help other novice authors get their stories out there as an assistant to a literary agent would be a way to show that he knew a good story when he saw it and that maybe he could write an amazing story himself. Not hearing anything back from any of the companies was discouraging, to say the least. They didn't even have the decency to tell him no. It just added to the overwhelming feeling of failure that he had been wading through for the past week, which was the last thing he should've felt then.

He graduated two days ago. His whole family had come up to celebrate this achievement with him. It was something to be proud of, and yet he didn't feel that way; it seemed that four years of hard work had accumulated into a worthless piece of paper. He indulged his family by going to dinner the night of graduation but was turned off by the idea of going back home right afterward. At Walker University (affectionately known as Walker U), most graduates would spend the weekend after hopping between bars and parties to celebrate their last moments of freedom before they went into the workforce, but Zach was already putting in for overtime with his job hunt.

Though, his family believed otherwise. His grandmothers, Mimi and Gigi, were always telling Zach to get out more. When they heard about this tradition, they told him that he should partake. They convinced his father to leave him on-campus with Mimi's car, and let him drive back down after he had his fun. Zach told them he would do so, but in reality, he spent the weekend in his bedroom, looking through job application websites, and eating takeout. The sounds of other grads wafted through the window, laughing and cheering as they ran from their apartments to the street of bars, restaurants, and convenience stores at the bottom of the hill. This had been a frequent occurrence every weekend since he moved in junior year, which was a small price to pay for an easy six-minute commute to his classes. In his final years of college, the last thing he wanted to do was worry about how he was going to get to campus without a car when the closest apartment complex that he could afford was nowhere near a bus stop.

Regardless, he truly felt at home when he was at Walker U. He would miss the large brick buildings and winding paths that covered the campus, along with the cafes and libraries where he spent hours doing his best work, both studying and writing-wise. The ability to go anywhere he wanted in the campus area was a freedom that he didn't want to give up. The thought crossed his mind to pursue a master's degree just so he could stay on campus and continue the life of an academic, but his scholarship had barely covered this degree, and he had no desire to spend all of his savings to get another.

Another yell of excitement shocked him out of the brain fog of his eighth application of the night, the twenty-seventh of the day. He groaned before shoving back from his desk and slamming the window shut. The rising temperature didn't seem as annoying anymore; he didn't need any more reminders of how everyone else was taking advantage of their last responsibility-free weekend before they headed off to their new lives while his throat dried up as the dread of what came next settled in.

He plopped back into his desk chair just as someone knocked on his door. It opened to reveal his roommate, Beau, dressed in his third favorite party outfit. He had already worn the other two this weekend.

"What?" Zach coughed as he started closing some of the tabs on his screen.

Zach could hear Beau lean against the doorframe, and he was certain that Beau was looking at him with his most judgmental gaze. "Your face will get stuck like that if you don't relax."

"I am relaxed," Zach replied through gritted teeth, making Beau chuckle.

"All work and no play makes Zach a dull boy."

"I'm not dull. Just frustrated," he fumed before slamming his laptop closed and taking off his glasses to rub his eyes. His phone buzzed and lit up with another text of congrats, this one from his friend Kit, who had sent him a finals care package two weeks ago. He knew he should probably text her thank you for that, but he just turned off his phone and sat back in his seat as he put his glasses back on, trying to find some semblance of calm.

"Because you have not relaxed all weekend," Beau reminded, tapping Zach's forehead to keep his attention. "Which is why you need to come out with me and Mateo tonight and let loose. Give your eyes the break they definitely need."

Zach looked up in time to see a smirk worm its way onto Beau's face before he suggested that he "maybe find a girl who can help release that tension in your neck."

Zach glared at him as that was the last thing on his mind. While he enjoyed spending time with both Beau and his boyfriend Mateo, he'd rather not spend his last night on-campus mediating their ongoing debate of who's the superior skateboarder or sitting awkwardly until a woman approached him. The fact that Beau was even suggesting it at that moment was way off, especially when he knew that Zach had pretty much given up socializing and hookups once he got into his job-hunting mode. Zach couldn't even fathom that they were friends at times. Though the two of them were practically twins with their warm brown skin, dark brown eyes, and coiled black hair, they could not be more opposite. Physically, the only thing that separated them were Zach's rectangular glasses and his decision to keep his hair short, while Beau grew it out into a proper curly 'fro. Personality-wise, Beau was the outgoing, always-in-the-know guy who wanted to drag Zach out of his cocoon and turn him into a social butterfly like himself, which was never going to happen.

Beau liked to say that they were "bound by a love of words" but, in reality, Zach just sat next to him in their freshman English class (and every class they took together after) because even though Beau was nosy as hell, he was easy for Zach to talk to and get along with.

Even when Zach said things like, "The only pain in my neck is you," Beau would just smile at him with unbridled joy in his eyes.

"Wow, tell me how you really feel," Beau snorted as Zach put his laptop into his brown messenger bag on the floor.

"The thought of going out with you two makes me violently ill and I would rather sit through a real-time video of someone putting together a 10,000-piece puzzle than be at a party right now," Zach looked up, saw the raised brows on his friend's face, and shrugged. "You *said* say how I really feel."

"Yeah, but puzzles? Really?" Beau said with a scrunched-up face as his Texan twang rang through his words.

Zach felt his throat get scratchy again. "They can be relaxing," he insisted before standing up and pushing past Beau to head to the kitchen. He needed a drink.

He could hear Beau's footsteps echoing behind him as he continued past their bathroom. "Only you would find a 10,000-piece puzzle video relaxing," Beau snorted, making Zach's eyes roll.

"A lot of people find them relaxing. Just like you find dancing in the middle of a sardine can of a club relaxing. Besides, I would rather not spend my last night here being a third wheel to you two."

"You're never a third—"

Zach raised his brow when he turned back at the end of the hall for a moment and Beau's mouth snapped shut. "Okay, maybe you were the last time," Beau admitted. Zach nodded, walking past the counter that split up the kitchen and living room. "But we were in the honeymoon phase!"

Zach scoffed as he stooped down to open the fridge. The only things left were Beau's leftovers from their Jade Dragon takeout order, and a single glass bottle of Zach's favorite orange soda, which he pulled from its shelf. "You've been in the honeymoon phase ever since I forced you two to get it together."

"Which I'm eternally grateful for," Beau admitted as Zach pulled out a bottle opener from one of the kitchen drawers, "but believe me, it's starting to wear off. We move next week and I still can't get him to tell me if he rented a moving truck or not. Do you know how annoying it is to deal with someone who is constantly giving you one-word answers to difficult questions?"

"No," Zach said as the bottle cap popped off. He turned to face Beau and smirked at the glare he gave him. Irking Beau with their sarcasm and dour attitudes was one of the things Zach and Mateo bonded over. After years of constantly being around an expressive character like Beau, finding someone else who preferred to stay in and have blunt conversation was a delight.

"How the fuck do I keep getting stuck with people like y'all?" Beau questioned. "Talking to either of y'all feels like pulling teeth."

Zach took a breath before bringing the drink to his lips, keeping himself from telling Beau to fuck off and leave him be. He knew that he should be happy for his friends; they had the opportunity to work at a news startup that they had been following the inception of for years. The moment the call for potential reporters went out, Beau and Mateo answered with a ferocity only those two journalism students could muster during midterms. Now, they were moving to New York City, and Zach couldn't help but resent them for having a much easier job search than he had. Not to mention, they were moving to a place where people were constantly working to be at the top of their game, while he was doing the walk of shame back down to Lillet, Maryland, where everything moved at a snail's pace. He had to go back to living in his childhood bedroom, under his father's warden gaze, while Beau and Mateo were going to be living in their own apartment in a city thousands of miles away, where they don't have to worry about their parents dropping in whenever they like. Zach had deliberately picked a school that was too far for a regular drop-in, but that didn't stop his father from calling or texting every evening to make sure he was in his apartment and not out partying, which showed how much he knew about Zach's personality.

Zach didn't even want to think about what his father would be like when he settled back in. He had contemplated staying in his apartment until mid-summer. The university had already forced them to pay until the end of June, so he could surely stick it out here for a while longer. But as much as he wanted to, groceries weren't going to pay for themselves, and without any classes to take, he surely would lose his mind trying to figure out what to do. Tomorrow, he was taking the two-hour drive down, but tonight he was going to wallow in his misery.

Apparently, this was written across his face. "I'm telling you. One night in a club could really turn that frown upside down," Beau suggested before trying to poke around his mouth, but Zach quickly slapped away his roommate's hand.

"You know I don't like clubs—"

"Or parties. Or the student union. Or anywhere that people are, in general," Beau listed off as he had a thousand times before. "Remind me again why you're trying to move to New York. It's literally a city known for being full of people, and you are known for actively trying to avoid people."

"Because that's where the major publishers are." Zach took another sip of soda. "And if I can get my foot in the door there, I'll have an easier time when I finally go to publish my book."

"Mhm. The book you won't even tell me the plot of? That book?"

Zach kept his mouth shut, making Beau groan. "Come on, you're saying you'd let somebody who looks through hundreds of manuscripts a week—only to approve three—have the chance to look at your book before you even tell me what it's about?"

"Pretty much."

Beau rolled his eyes while adjusting the cuff of his flowy burnt orange top. "Well, I hope you don't spend the next few weeks just holed up in your room writing this top-secret book."

Zach shook his head before taking another sip of soda, wincing as the carbonation burned his throat. "Can't. Gotta find a job in town to help pay New York rent prices."

"Any ideas?" Beau asked as he messed with his curls in the mirror magnet on the fridge.

"Probably The Book Haven. Des loves having someone competent working in the store that he doesn't have to train." Zach had contemplated calling him that day between sending applications but given that he was trying to sneak into town unnoticed the next day, he decided against it. He was a shoo-in for the job anyway.

Beau nodded as he turned back to Zach. "Hey, spending your days surrounded by books, that's your dream, isn't it?"

Zach hummed nonchalantly as he took another sip of his drink. Beau rolled his eyes. "Okay. I'm not letting you put any more of a damper on my evening, so I'll leave you here to sulk. Don't wait up."

Zach let him get near the front door before he called out, "Hey."

Beau turned around.

"I am going to miss you."

Beau grinned, "I know you will. Who else is gonna make you go outside?" Zach rolled his eyes, making Beau coo at him. "Aw, I'm gonna miss that eye roll."

"Don't get sappy on me."

"Don't worry, I'll save our grief-filled goodbye til morning." A ping rang throughout the room. Beau pulled out his phone and smiled at what was on the screen. "Mateo's downstairs. See you later."

Zach waved him off as the apartment door closed. With a huff, he walked back into his nearly empty room. Besides two suitcases, his school bag, his sheets, and the aloe plant that he bought at an Ecofest junior year, his room was back to the bland state it was when he moved in. His father took everything else back to Lillet after their graduation visit. He was not going to let Zach take multiple trips upstate to get his things when they were already there. He wasn't going to let Zach do a lot of things once he moved back in.

Zach placed his drink on his desk before digging into his bag to pull out his current read, or the book he was trying to read anyway. He was a quarter of the way in, but he could barely remember what happened in the earlier pages, and flipping to where he stopped only reminded him of that.

His phone buzzed on the desk, and he groaned when he saw a message from his dad.

Jedidiah

Are you in your apartment?

Zach rolled his eyes as he picked up the phone to reply. This was one message that he couldn't let go unanswered.

Zach

Yes

I told you I was staying in to work on applications tonight

Jedidiah

Good. What time are you getting here tomorrow?

Zach

Don't know, planning for 1, but you know how traffic is

Jedidiah

Okay, see you then. Good night.

Zach

Night

Zach groaned before tossing his phone and the book on his bed as he felt the frustration rising to his temples again.

He had to remind himself that everything was going to be fine.

He would find a job, and he would be moving to New York before the end of the summer.

He took a breath as he sat down at his desk and grabbed his notebook from his bag, flipping past the lists of book ideas and outlines he'd made to an empty page marked with his favorite ballpoint pen, and started to write out his new plan.

If he was smart to be valedictorian at a school where the average GPA was 3.79, surely he could figure this out.

Zach's Current Goals

1. Start Full-Time Job at The Book Haven and get a Great Recommendation from Des

2. Look Up Online Courses for Hard Skills needed for the Publishing Industry

3. Prep Answers for Least Common Interview Questions

4. Search for Cheap Apartments in NYC

Chapter 2

Lillet, Maryland, was one of those townships between real towns; a picturesque view from the highway that travelers never thought to stop at while they moved on to their real destination. Most people wouldn't know how to get there if they tried.

Zach, however, knew far too well how easy it was to turn off the highway a couple of exits back from the actual view, then venture a mile down the road before turning onto a maze of side streets, until veering left on the road that led downhill into the town. It was easy for anyone who had lived in Lillet their whole lives, not someone who just wanted to pass through. Most of the townsfolk wouldn't venture outside of Lillet unless they had to for their job or a grand event that wouldn't happen in the small community.

The problem for Zach was that everything in Lillet felt small. The postcard view lied about how big the town actually was. There was only one road into town, only one high school that everyone attended, only one grocery store to find food, the list went on. The city felt like its own little self-contained ecosystem that was broken off from the rest of the world, and Zach couldn't stand it most of the time, but it did inspire him to write his favorite story idea to date: Project Void, a tale about a small team aboard a ship in deep space surrounded by never-ending darkness. If Zach had a therapist, they would probably have a field day after reading it, but it was nowhere near ready for anyone to read. That was a long-term goal. He first needed to focus on getting his life back on track.

While Zach planned to be back in town by one, DMV traffic put him there closer to half-past two, which was probably for the best. The lunch crowds were back in their offices, and school kids were still in class, leaving Zach some time to sneak into town without being spotted by anyone. Even so, it was hard to blend in while driving his grandmother's Ford Mustang down Main Street, which hadn't changed at all.

It was still the same block of multicolored brick buildings it always had been. The bookstore, the thrift shop, the cafe, and the arcade were the main sights to drive by. Zach could still remember the weekends he and his friends had spent on that strip, making their rounds before heading to their favorite spot in town.

He pulled the car into the parking lot behind the row of buildings and let himself take in the quiet. After spending the rest of the night covering his head with his pillow to filter out the continued ruckus from graduation parties, it was actually welcome to hear very little going on for once. When he got out of the car, the heat of the day came on at full force. Perhaps wearing a sweater vest wasn't the best idea when Maryland was prepping for summer, but he did really like sweater vests.

He walked around, and entered the first cream-colored storefront that housed his home away from home: The Book Haven. The doorbell rang above him, and the familiar smell of paper and lemon floor cleaner comforted him immediately, alongside the hum of the air conditioning.

The Book Haven was a store designed for book dragons to come and begin their book hoard, something Zach had started to do once he'd saved up enough money. When he was younger, his family didn't go to the bookstore. His father was a librarian, so Zach got most of his books from there and found nothing wrong with that until he learned that he always had to return the books after he read them, which broke his heart. There were some books that Zach never wanted to part with, so he constantly checked them out again and again until he was told someone else had them on hold.

And then The Book Haven opened up.

He and his best friends, Kit and Joon, had been waiting for the next book in their favorite adventure series The Sea Guardians to come out when Kit's father surprised them by taking them to The Book Haven and buying them each a copy.

Zach had immediately fallen in love with the place.

At the time, he was only interested in children's books, but over the years he had managed to go through every nook and cranny of the store and picked up books from nearly every section. The wages he'd eventually earned from The Book Haven almost immediately went back into the store, and he started to build up his own little library in his room. He made a Bookstagram during his sophomore year of college to document his library growth over the years. Not that he let anybody in his personal life know about that—Beau had only found out about it when he looked over Zach's shoulder in the middle of him making a post—but through social media, he had found a plethora of new books that he wanted everyone to read and see on the Book Haven shelves if Des had the room to take his suggestions.

It was easier to suggest things to people who didn't know him well in real life. It was why Zach had the best track record of convincing customers to buy the books they came in for. He always reminded them that the more they read, the more they could hone their reading tastes and find their forever favorites, so Zach read a multitude of books to figure out his top recommendations for people new to different genres, leading him to know the store like the back of his hand.

The display of new releases was front and center as it always had been, with a sign of the store's book dragon mascot, Wyatt, showing them off as a new addition to his hoard, his yellow scales shining like gold when bits of sun came through the window. Behind the table was a maze of hardwood bookshelves of varying sizes that led to other tables of recommendations, and a small children's reading area in the back of the store. To the right stood the hardwood counter and the display of impulse purchases, and to the left, the selection of romance books— affectionately known as the Love in Lillet section after the lighthouse lovers— took up most of the wall, save for the front section near the door reserved for history books about Maryland and town lore.

Zach fell back into his natural walk through the store, strolling along the Love in Lillet wall before weaving through the aisles and finding himself in front of the writing and grammar books, looking for titles he didn't already own or read like he always did. He had just picked a promising title when he heard footsteps approaching him. "You know, I should really just get rid of that section."

Zach smiled. "Then why would I have any reason to come here?"

"Because you miss me," the familiar voice replied in his usual gruff tone.

"Nah," Zach chuckled, finally letting himself look up at one of the only people he didn't mind seeing: Des Davis, the proud owner of The Book Haven and more beanies than one could imagine. Many people thought he wore one to hide his bald head, but Zach was one of the few who knew it was because he wanted to look like Samuel L. Jackson in *Shaft*.

Zach didn't think it came across well, but he wasn't going to be the one to tell him, especially when he gave him unimpressed looks like the one he was giving now. "Don't play with me. I know you missed me."

Zach held his fingers up with minimal space between them. Des chuckled as he rubbed his bearded chin. Zach was trying to ignore the tan line where Des's wedding ring used to be when Des said, "Now, what happened to going to New York and changing the publishing industry forever?"

Zach bit his lip but then let out a breath and replied, "The plan got derailed, but it's a minor setback. I was wondering," he said as he put the book back on the shelf, "would you mind if I came back to work here again for the summer?" Zach paused when he saw the frown on Des's face. "What?"

Des sucked his teeth. "I'm sorry, Z. Not that I don't want you back, but I thought that you would be otherwise occupied by now. I already hired someone to take your usual spot."

"You did?" Zach said, trying to ignore his heartbeat revving up in his chest.

"Yeah, and I can't afford to take on anyone else full-time."

"Oh," was pretty much all Zach could say as another one of his plans was shredded into a million pieces.

Before he could go into a full-blown panic, however, Des said, "Hey, but I still need someone to do part-time on the weekends if you're interested."

"I can do that," he said without hesitation.

"You sure? Cause I know you usually can't do Sundays, and—"

"I'll make it work," Zach insisted. He was going to make it work.

Des nodded. "All right. Well," Des held out his hand, "welcome back to The Book Haven team."

Zach shook his hand with as much faux enthusiasm as he could muster before letting it drop. "Hey, if you want to, you can start using your employee discount now," Des chuckled.

Zach shook his head. "Nah, that's fine. I'm barely reading at the moment anyway. I only wanted to stop in to see what was here and..." *Try to get back a job that's already been taken.* Zach smiled at Des and hoped he couldn't notice the shaking of Zach's hand. "I'm good. Maybe next time."

"Alright." The bell rang again, pulling Des's attention. "Well, we'll talk later, and I'll have the paperwork ready for you on Saturday."

"Sounds good. See you then," Zach said before rushing past him to get out of the store before he did anything that might show the oncoming panic in his head.

What the hell was he supposed to do now? It should have been an easy comeback, but Des was right. He wasn't supposed to be in Lillet at all, so why would Des hold his old job for him anyway? At least he had a part-time gig, but that meant that he was still going to be in his house for most of the week, and knowing his father, he was going to come up with some job for him to do if he didn't find something else. Even when he was younger, his father hated the idea of his kids doing nothing during the summer. He came up with Camp Roberts, where they would do workbooks, write up reports, and make presentations, basically extending their school year until they started up again in the fall, and Zach did not want to give him a chance to make an adult version of that.

The sun and the radiating heat of the sidewalk nearly blinded him as he stepped back outside, taking him out of his spiraling thoughts, but he was so focused on letting his eyes readjust that he was completely caught off guard when something knocked him down to the ground.

"What the hell?" he groaned as he pushed against whatever

was on top of him. He tried shielding his face with his hands from whatever it was, and when he finally got a glimpse, he saw a furry behemoth of an Australian Shepherd attacking him with his tongue.

Zach grimaced.

He was not a dog person.

He heard something squeaky come closer before the mass of multicolored fur was pulled off of him. "I'm so sorry, he's usually not that aggressive with his affection," someone said above him.

Zach took a moment to breathe before he finally put down his hand and looked up. He was practically knocked down again when he took a good look at the dog's owner. It was a woman, a very pretty woman. She was the type of pretty that made people do a double take to make sure they hadn't imagined her beauty: Copper brown skin that shone in the sun; thick, curly black hair framed her face past her shoulders, along with rounded rectangular glasses with thick brown frames. Not to mention a smile that made her denim overalls and white long-sleeve combo look that much cuter.

She was just really pretty.

And Zach didn't do well when it came to talking to pretty girls.

"You okay?"

And he had been staring at her for far too long to look anything but creepy.

He quickly lifted his head off the ground but regretted it when he got a bit dizzy. "Do I look okay?" he grunted as he used his hand to stabilize the oncoming headache, and that's when a wagon came into focus. She was pulling an honest-to-God red wagon behind her that was filled to the brim with floral packages. Zach's mouth worked faster than his brain when he groaned, "Who pulls a wagon around anymore?"

Her brows raised above her glasses frames as she looked down at him. "I do," she said in a firm tone.

"What are you, five?" he questioned, again without thinking, eyes widening when he realized what he said.

The woman's head tilted. "Excuse me?"

Zach cringed. This was not a new thing. Whenever Beau dragged him out to bars to try and integrate him into college nightlife, Zach had no idea of how to talk to women there. He could handle the ones who approached during class or at the library, but in social settings where he already felt uncomfortable, his niceties filter was completely shut off. While his friends were used to his abrupt talk and overly honest commentary, they had informed him that what he usually said off the top of his head could come off as rude, or in this case, insensitive. "N-Nothing. Dumb thing to say."

"I'll say."

Zach looked back up at the woman who had a saccharine grin on her face. "Maybe the heat's getting to your head, you should probably do yourself a favor and take off that sweater vest."

Zach narrowed his eyes at her. "I like my sweater vest, thank you very much."

She smiled at him. "And I like my wagon, so why don't you just say sorry and we both move on with our days."

Zach bit down hard on his lips; apologies didn't come easy to him, but he just wanted to go home, so through gritted teeth, he said, "Sorry. Didn't mean to be rude."

"Apology accepted," she chirped with a very smug smirk before giving him another once-over. "Now, you need help getting up?"

It was then that Zach fully felt the gravel underneath his palms and realized he was still lying on the pavement. He quickly scrambled to his feet. "I'm fine."

"Good," she nodded, giving him another toothy grin before wrapping her dog's leash around her hand. "Then have a nice day. Come on, Appa." And with that, the girl and her dog went back to walking down the street, her wagon squeaking behind her.

Zach scoffed at the sight before wiping the excess rocks off his hands. He looked down at his sweater vest and grimaced at the dregs of dog drool and fur left on it.

Without another thought, he shoved it off and balled it up, cringing as he felt a wet substance squish against his hand. He turned back toward the parking lot and made haste back to his car. Now, he couldn't get home fast enough; his shower was calling him.

After passing through the town square, the older brick buildings faded into true suburbia. Houses and cars lined the streets, leaving barely enough room to drive down them, but Zach managed to get to his childhood home without having to pull to the side to allow someone else to pass him.

They lived at the end of the street at the end of the final street of their neighborhood, which always made Zach feel they were boxed into a corner. The idea of walking to town from there was preposterous; it would take over an hour to walk through the neighborhood to the main road, and another half hour to get anywhere fun. He was fortunate though that their home wasn't cramped enough to make him feel like he was stepping on anybody's toes in a house of five. It was a house with white sideboards and gray windows that barely looked like it was two stories, perfectly nested at the end of the cul-de-sac.

After pulling into the driveway that was barely big enough for two cars, he sighed. It immediately felt like the last four years hadn't happened. He had spent summers and most of his winter breaks here, but now he was moving back as a college graduate for an undetermined amount of time. *So much for holiday and birthday visits.*

He took a deep breath to push those thoughts away. He needed to focus. His siblings were still in school, and his dad and grandmother were at work; he needed to take advantage of an empty house while he had it.

He grabbed his bags and aloe plant out of the car and walked up to the front door. Once he unlocked it, he quickly moved to turn off the house alarm and put down his things. He took stock of the living room to his right, and the kitchen to his left, both unchanged except for a few of his younger brother's toys hanging around. The stairs in front of him hid the way to his father's and grandmother's bedrooms, and the laundry room. Upstairs were his and his siblings' rooms. He should count himself lucky that he didn't have any random roommates to deal with after graduating; his first roommate in college had been a pain in the ass, and while Beau wasn't bad to live with, it had been hard for him to take a gamble on asking to bunk with someone he only talked to when they were in class. He knew what he was coming back to for the most part: a rambunctious six-year-old, a moody teenager, a gruff father, and a sweet old lady. He could handle that.

He took off his shoes, lugged his things up the stairs, and went to his room. He immediately smiled at his bookshelves once he opened the door. They were filled with all of his favorites that he'd bought from The Book Haven over the years. The whole thing was one of his prized possessions that he had been devastated to leave behind for college. His bed still sported the quilts that his Mimi made him as a Sweet Sixteen present. The mahogany desk that was his father's growing up was empty, but it would soon be filled with his notebooks, pens, and laptop again.

He put his aloe plant on his window sill, before dropping everything else at the foot of his bed and going into his bathroom. He groaned when he saw the mess that his little sister, Amaya, had made of it in his absence. She invaded it every time he went back to school. He had no desire to deal with the cleanup, though, so he just shoved all her stuff to the side, stripped off his soiled clothes, and took a quick shower, rinsing off the dog drool, gravel bits, and hopefully most of his stress.

After getting out, he changed into a t-shirt and some sweatpants he found in his dresser, before going out into the hallway housing the variety of family photos that they had taken throughout the years, and which charted the progression of their family growth. There were some early shots of just him, then plenty of shots from after Amaya was born before their little brother, Corey, was added to complete their family six years ago. Zach's high school diploma sat proudly under a group photo of him and his friends from graduation, and he knew his college one would be added soon enough next to his father's.

Right where his mother's used to be.

He took off his glasses and was starting to rub out the wetness welling in his eyes when he heard the door unlocking downstairs. He went downstairs just as the first shipment of Roberts came through the door. The smallest of them spotted him first.

"Zach!" Corey squealed at the top of his lungs as he ran over to his older brother, who immediately stooped down to hug him.

"Hey, bud," Zach chuckled as he held his mini-self closer. The kid was already growing up far too fast for his liking. "Mimi pick you and Maya up from school today?" he said, pulling back.

"Yeah, can you pick us up tomorrow? I want to show you my

school. You can meet Mrs. Jones."

Zach didn't have the heart to remind Corey that he'd gone to his school and had had Mrs. Jones, previously Ms. Thatcher, as his teacher long before he was born, so he just nodded. "Sure, bud."

"Yay!" Corey screeched as he held onto his brother tighter.

"'Sup, loser?"

Zach glanced up to the door to see Amaya standing there, as well as her perpetual shadow of a boyfriend, Owen Miller. She had grown up far too fast for his liking as well while he was at school. Before he went to college, she was a somewhat sweet, and slightly nerdy twelve-year-old. Now she was a full-blown pain in the ass. She had started modeling herself after MJ from the newest Spider-Man franchise, and it took up far too much of her personality for his liking, but given that MJ looked pretty similar to her (except for Amaya's umber brown skin and hair), it wasn't a surprise. Still, he didn't like that her *Marvel* fascination just enhanced the amount of snark that she'd been developing over the past few years.

"Go away, nerd," Zach said as he let go of Corey, who promptly ran up to his room. He then turned his attention to Owen, who was already staring at him nervously. Owen had been one of Amaya's best friends in middle school, so he wasn't unfamiliar with him, but Zach had been shocked to get the news that they had started dating when he came back during winter break. So, like any good big brother, he went into overprotective mode whenever Owen was around, which was a lot. "Miller," he said, looking him up and down.

"Hey, Zach."

Zach just kept staring at him blankly, making the boy shrink in on himself. At least, shrink as much as a Black, broad-shouldered, beefy lacrosse player could.

Amaya rolled her eyes, grabbing Owen's hand in hers before

dragging him up the stairs.

Zach groaned as they walked through the house without taking their shoes off, but didn't get a chance to yell at them before Mimi came through the door, immediately unwrapping the scarf around her graying locs. She hugged him with a wide grin across her face. "It's good to see you, baby."

Zach rolled his eyes. "You saw me two days ago."

"Doesn't mean I'm not happy to see you."

Mimi was one of the sweetest people you would ever meet. If he ever needed somebody to lean on for support, he knew that he could count on her. Also, she was the only one who could order his dad around, so having her in his corner meant everything to him.

Zach pulled back from her before looking at the keys he put in the dish earlier and plucking them out. "Thanks for letting me use your car," he said, trying to take it off his keychain.

"Keep 'em."

Zach looked up at her. "What?"

"You probably have more use for it than I do anyway," she said with a smile. Zach tried to contain how giddy he felt, but it probably showed on his face anyway.

"Seriously?"

"Consider it a graduation present," she said while using her bright red nails to pinch his cheek, which he didn't mind at all. This was one of the reasons why Mimi was the greatest. He had a car. It was probably only going to be for the summer, but he now had a way to leave the house whenever he wanted.

Finally.

Zach smiled before putting the keys back into the dish. "You are the best, Mimi."

"Anything for you, baby," she said after releasing his cheek.

"And I swear, I'll drive you anywhere you need to be this

summer," Zach promised, making her smile wider.

"I know you will."

As she went to go to her room, Zach was ready to go hole up in his own when Corey attached himself to Zach's legs.

"Zach, can we go to the park later so I can go down the big slide?" he asked, looking up at his older brother.

Zach shook his head. "Not today, buddy." He knew how their dad would feel if they went without his permission.

Corey looked like he wanted to hop up and down and hold onto him until he said yes, but then the door opened again. Zach felt his spine stiffen as his father walked through the door, already shucking off his suit jacket.

Corey just ran up to him and hugged his legs. "Daddy!"

"Hey, Corey," Jedidiah smiled as he rubbed a hand over his youngest's head, then looked up at his oldest. "Zach."

Jedidiah Roberts was already intimidating as hell with his large stature on a good day for Zach, but today, when he felt like he'd already had enough, he was feeling like a new kid coming in halfway through the school year and being met by the captain of the football team, which Jed was back in his day. Just one of the many differences between Zach and his father.

Zach was an academic through and through, but his father had always wanted him to get into sports growing up. It felt odd because he was now one of the town librarians, but he was still a huge football fan, yelling at the screen during every Ravens game and coaching the little tag football team in town. He tried to have Zach join it when he was younger, but Zach lacked hand-eye coordination, hated running, and the idea of tackling or getting tackled scared him out of his mind. Eventually, his father accepted it, but it took a long time, and Zach still felt like it was hard to talk to his dad about things he wanted. Talking to him in general was hard.

"Hey," Zach said quietly.

Jed raised an eyebrow. "Excuse me. Just 'hey.' Try that again."

"Hi, Dad."

Jed nodded. "That's better. Did you unpack already?"

Zach shook his head. "Not yet."

"Well, get on it, then you can come help with dinner."

"Oh, Daddy, can I help?" Corey said as he bounced on his toes while pulling on the sleeve of his father's dress shirt. "Please, please, please!"

"Corey—"

"Please," Corey said as he practically climbed up their father like he was a tree. There was a time when Zach was like that with him too. That moment had long since passed, though.

"I could take him off your hands. He wanted to go to the park," Zach suggested, but his father immediately scooped the little one into his arms.

"No, that's fine. Let's go cook, little man."

Corey cheered as they walked into the kitchen, allowing Zach the chance to scurry back up the stairs. Once he was up, he peeked into Amaya's room and saw her and Owen cuddling on the bed, her head on his chest. If it was anybody but his sister, he would've thought it was cute, but since it *was* his sister, he knocked on the doorframe. The sound made Owen fall off the bed into the nest of pillows Amaya kept next to it.

Amaya turned to the door and glared at him. "Hey!"

"Don't 'hey' me. Dad's home, and I'm pretty sure he wouldn't want to see y'all in a bed together, so you should be thanking me. Keep to your separate corners. And I expect you to take your stuff out of my bathroom after dinner." He left with a chuckle, but the smile slid off his face as soon as he closed his bedroom door behind him.

He needed a new plan.

If he got lucky, whoever was working full-time at The Book

Haven would give up the job, and Zach would have an easy way back into his retreat, but he couldn't rely on that.

He took a deep breath and sat down on the edge of his bed.

He just needed to focus.

As long as he didn't get distracted, he could make this work.

Other Job Types to Consider

1. Tutor (School's Almost Out, not worth starting up)

2. Server at Papa Porter's (Far too many people go there and I'll have to talk to a ton of them)

3. Mowing Grass (Taken, everybody uses the same guy)

4. Freelance...reader

5. Fuck my life

Chapter 3

Waking up back in his childhood bedroom felt like being stuck in a bad dream.

In a good dream, he'd be in New York, woken up by an upstairs neighbor's footsteps or honking horns. Today, he was woken up by somebody jumping on his bed. After dinner, he'd spent most of the night scrolling through old job posts on the town website. He was beyond tired and had hoped he could sleep in, but moving back in with a six-year-old meant that that probably was not going to happen for a while.

"Wake up! Wake up! Wake up!" Corey's little voice screamed next to his head.

While it wasn't a nightmare to wake up like this, it wasn't pleasant either. Zach and Amaya had never been morning kids, very much night owls, but Corey was the complete opposite.

Zach groaned as he dug himself deeper into the bed. "No, thank you."

"You have to get up. We need to eat breakfast," Corey said as he tried to pull Zach's quilt off his head.

"Well, why don't you go wake up Maya then, bud? You're the ones who have to go to school today," he mumbled as he kept his hold on the blanket.

"Maya's mean in the morning."

While Zach was tempted to be the same way to Corey, he was more interested in being mean to Amaya. "Well, let's wake her up anyway," he said as he scooped Corey up in his arms, walked around the bins from his apartment that he had yet to unpack, and walked over to Amaya's room, lightly lit by her LED lights, computer, and bits of sunshine coming from behind her blackout curtains.

"Delivery," he announced before dropping Corey on top of Amaya's sleeping form.

Corey laughed as he crawled over Amaya and started bouncing on her bed. She just groaned loudly. "Are you serious?" she said under her covers.

"Hey, you guys have school, not me, and you have to go earlier than him, so get up," Zach smirked. "See you later."

"I hate you."

"Love you too," he teased as he strolled out of her room, smiling when he heard Corey laughing and asking Amaya to stop tickling him. He looked at the analog clock above his desk when he got back into his room.

6:46 A.M.

It was far too early for anyone in Lillet to be up who didn't deal with school or going to work, but there would be one place in town open that Zach wouldn't mind staying in for a couple of hours. After shoving on some clothes, he rushed down the stairs with his messenger bag in hand, ready to run out the door when he heard, "Where do you think you're going?"

Zach turned around slowly to see his father looking at him from where he was preparing breakfast in the kitchen. "Out."

"You don't need to be going out anywhere, probably spending money you don't have."

Maybe I just want to get out of this damn house, ever think of that? Zach reminded himself not to say that out loud and was about to give an excuse but he stopped and noticed the look on his father's face. It was amazing how one look could make you feel like a no-nothing teenager again. He put his bag down next to the door and sat down at the counter after grabbing an orange from the fridge.

Jedidiah went back to scrambling eggs on the stovetop. "So, how have you been?"

"Fine," Zach shrugged as he started to peel the fruit in his hand.

"Fine, that's it?"

"Not much has changed since you saw me ten hours ago." When Zach looked up from his peeling, the look on his dad's face said he was toeing a thin line. He changed course. "I've just been eating, sleeping, and filling out job applications."

"Well, I hope you keep sending them in even when you start at the store," he said as he scooped the cooked eggs onto a plate on top of the white counter. "You have a degree now, you should be shooting for jobs higher than that."

Zach bit his lip as he tossed the full peel in the trash. He had managed to avoid the subject last night, as Corey had done most of the talking throughout dinner, but he had just been delaying the inevitable. "Actually, I'm only going to be working at the bookstore part-time. On the weekends."

"Really? I thought we talked about you working on the weekends. That's family time."

"I know, but like you said, I need the money." *Especially to move out of this house.* The joy of rent-free living and no grocery shopping would only last so long. "And if I get back to it, maybe I can get the full-time position back."

Jed's eyebrow raised. "The position that you had when you were seventeen? Zach, be serious."

Zach looked down at the orange and started playing with the white bits of rind wrapped around it. He knew his father probably meant well. Growing up, his father always said that he hoped that his children would do better than him career and education-wise. So, yes, he should be aiming higher than the position he got in high school, but there were worse places to work. Besides, at least Des got back to him with an answer within a couple of seconds. Companies that he sent applications to months ago still hadn't even replied to say that they hired someone else.

"Good morning," Mimi greeted as she came into the kitchen, looking like a marshmallow in her thick robe.

"Morning Mimi," Zach mumbled before stuffing a piece of orange in his mouth.

"What are you still doing here, baby? You should be getting out of the house and getting familiar with the town," she said as she grabbed a mug out of the cabinet for her morning tea.

Jed looked up from where he was cutting up fruit. "Mom, he doesn't need to—"

"Nonsense! He needs to go out and be around people, especially after being cooped up in his apartment for those finals." She turned to Zach. "Go on now," she said, giving him a private wink that made him smile. Even though he wasn't a people person, he was not going to waste the out Mimi just gave him.

"Yes, ma'am."

With a kiss placed on Mimi's cheek, he ran out the door, got into the car, and headed towards Main Street.

Zach arrived at the strip a while later but skipped The Book Haven in favor of one of the other spots in town where he spent most of his time: Toe Beans.

While the name wasn't the most intriguing to the everyman, those who took a moment to think about it would realize that they were being invited into a cat-themed coffee shop. Black outlines of cartoon cats doing various activities, like climbing trees or lying in the sun lined the light blue walls as patrons came in. Along the tiled floors, little paw prints leading to the counter not too far away from the door where a plethora of feline-themed treats sat behind the plexiglass: cookies frosted to look like cats sitting and stretching; little round cakes that had kawaii cat faces on them; plain cookies made of multiple colored doughs to look like calico cats; even sandwiches made with cat-shaped bread. There were also a bunch of plain-look-ing treats as well, but those were usually left at the end of the day while the cat-themed ones were always sold out.

Most people came for the cats, but many stayed for the owners, the Park family. Sora Park, the matriarch of the fam-ily, known affectionately as Oma, moved to Maryland from South Korea long before Zach was even a concept, and she always made sure that customers felt welcome in her store. That trait had been passed down to most of her children and grandchildren who worked in the cafe with her, along with their signature raven black hair and walnut brown eyes. The middle child of her oldest son's clan, Sunny, was currently at the counter checking out a customer. He caught a glimpse of her older sister, Umi, as she came out from the back with a tray of sandwiches, flour staining her usual black ensemble, before going through the swinging door back into the kitchen. Zach had briefly contemplated asking the Parks if they needed help for the summer last night, but he wasn't the best when it came to baking.

When Sunny was finished with the other customer, she

hadn't looked up yet as Zach approached the counter. "Welcome to Toe Beans, how can I..." Her eyes widened once she saw him. "Zach?"

"Hey, Sunny."

"Oh my God, Zach! How are you?" she asked with her usual cheery smile. "Joon said that you were headed to New York. I didn't expect to see you back here so soon."

"Didn't expect to be back so soon," he said with a shrug as he tightened his grip on his messenger bag strap. "Just hanging out in town for the moment."

Sunny smiled wider as she tapped the register screen in front of her. "Well, let me welcome you back with a proper cup of coffee. Whatcha want?"

"Um, one black coffee with two sugars."

Sunny nodded as she typed it in. "You got it. Anything else?"

"Nah, I'm good," Zach said as he dug his wallet out to pay.

"You know Oma doesn't make family pay."

Zach bit his lip before taking out his card and tapping the reader anyway. "It's fine."

Sunny frowned but shrugged as she pulled out his receipt. "For here or to go?"

"Here," he said as he took it and put it in the designated paper pocket of his bag.

Sunny nodded and told him to find a seat as she made his order. The cafe wasn't nearly that busy yet. Only two other people were in the cafe, both standing up and primed to leave after they got their orders. Zach migrated to the back of the shop next to the kitchen door and set his bag down on the seat when the door opened again.

"All I'm saying is that you should have told me that you weren't seeing Yousef anymore," someone said as they walked in, someone Zach definitely knew the voice of.

"It's not a big deal," someone with a deeper voice said, another one that Zach was deeply familiar with.

"Um, it is a big deal because I'm not going to be hanging out with your ex."

"Don't you still talk to Avery?"

"Yeah, but Avery has the best recommendations for places to go, though. I wouldn't have found half of my favorite places without her, and besides, you're friends with her new boyfriend, anyway."

"True but..."

Zach tuned out the rest of their conversation as he turned around. He felt like he was watching the exchange through a window as he took a good look at the two of them.

Kit Akiyama and Joon Park.

The last time he had seen them was last summer and he hadn't messaged them much since then unless they initiated it.

He could try to blame it on finals, or his job hunt, but the truth was that he wasn't the best at keeping in touch with the two of them. He always felt like he was annoying them if he reached out for no reason, and when he had a reason, he felt like he should wait to make sure that he wasn't interrupting their daily lives, and then he ended up not messaging them at all. It was hard for him to know if they actually wanted him around sometimes.

Kit and Joon always had some sort of weird telepathy thing going on where they could always tell what the other was thinking, like twins separated at birth. When Joon told Zach that he had wanted to add blue streaks to his black hair when they started high school, Kit came over with a box of hair dye an hour later. Neither boy had sent her a text. When Kit told Zach that she wanted to try and make a fusion dish to celebrate her Norwegian and Japanese heritage, Joon called to ask her if she wanted something since he was already at the grocery store.

In both cases, Zach had helped them clean up the messes—neither had turned out the way they planned—but it felt like he was only there in case something went wrong.

That's what he brought to the group. He was the rational mind that could always tell how something could go wrong and came up with the plan to try and make sure that it didn't. Kit was the energetic fireball who drove them to actually do things, and Joon was the calm one who usually kept it together when something went awry. That's how they had worked for so many years, and Zach didn't know if their dynamic would stay the same.

"Zach?"

Zach looked up sharply to see Kit and Joon staring at him with huge smiles on their faces. He awkwardly waved at them. "Um, hey?"

Kit squealed before she ran over and practically tackled him in a hug, her chocolate brown hair brushing against his neck as she did, "OMG, you're back!"

Zach grimaced as he returned the gesture. She was deceptively strong for her size, but at least there was no question that she missed him.

She pulled back, keeping her hands on his arms as she looked up at him, "How are you? What have you been up to? Did you get that care package that I sent to you?" Kit turned to Sunny and waved. "Hey! Surprise me." Kit sat down at his table. "Why didn't you tell us you were back in town? We could've had a little welcome-back party, like at that new ice cream parlor before the turn because it looks so cute, and it's the perfect season for it. Did I tell you about the ice cream that I had in Japan because it was—"

"Kit," Zach interrupted, smiling down at her.

"What?"

"Hi."

"Hi," she said leaning onto the table with her head in her hands.

Zach snorted and shook his head. Kit was just as energetic as the last time he saw her. Growing up, she was always running around and finding new things for the three of them to do. Whether it was helping her turn her backyard into a faux drive-in movie theater, or making ice cream in a vintage machine she found online, Kit was always down for an adventure. As such, she, her father, and her grandmother had taken a trip to Japan during winter break for a camping expedition, so he'd missed her the last time he was in town, but he was glad to see her now.

Zach looked over at Joon, who just stood there, looking at them with a small smile on his face, rocking back and forth on his feet. Zach rolled his eyes—he knew both of his friends were huggers—and held his arms open. "Come on and get it over with."

Joon smiled wider and bolted over to wrap his arms around Zach, though it was mostly around his shoulders. Joon stood out in the shop with his broad shoulders and tall figure. Zach rolled his eyes and held his arms open. He knew both of his friends were huggers. "Come on and get it over with."

Joon smiled wider and bolted over to wrap his arms around Zach, though it was mostly around his shoulders. Joon stood out in the shop with his broad shoulders and tall figure. Zach had to look up at him slightly when they talked. "It's good to see you."

Zach smiled a bit. "You too."

He wasn't lying. Kit and Joon truly did make living in Lillet bearable for him, not to mention that if there was one thing that Zach missed while living in the dorms, it was Joon's cooking. Joon was always trying out new recipes, and Zach was always first in line to be a taste tester. As he was such a good cook, Joon had ended up on catering duty for the cafe last winter, so Zach hadn't been able to see him either.

Joon pulled back. "But seriously, can you get better at texting? I know you're not great at tech, but a writer like you should not leave someone on read for weeks at a time."

"I don't do that…as much anymore."

Joon and Kit shared a knowing glance at his blatant lie before looking back at Zach. "Sure."

"Hey," Sunny said as she walked over to the table with a mug and plate in hand. "Joon, you're already late and we need you in the back kneading the dough for the bread."

Joon glared at his sister. "Don't we have a mixer for that now?"

Sunny stuck her lip out in a pout. "Why use that when you've been getting so buff recently? Now scoot."

Joon rolled his eyes, before patting Zach on the shoulder and heading into the kitchen.

"One coffee and an orange scone for you," Sunny said as she placed them down on the table.

"I didn't order—"

"It's on the house," Sunny said before scurrying back through the employee door.

Zach sighed. Sunny was prone to giving out freebies to customers, so he shouldn't have expected anything less. He always felt weird taking them, but the smell of his favorite treat from the store made him a bit more comfortable accepting it. He took his seat before pushing the pastry towards Kit, but not until after he'd pinched off a piece for himself.

Kit just smiled and broke off a piece as well before looking back at him. "So?"

Zach rolled his eyes but smiled and said, "I'm doing okay, been studying like crazy. Now I'm applying for jobs like crazy. I did get the care package; thank you for providing the sweets that got me through finals."

"You are very welcome," she smiled before popping the piece of scone in her mouth. "I can't believe we're all done with college and officially in the real world."

"We all still live with our parents," Zach mumbled as he grabbed another piece of scone and dipped it into his coffee.

"I don't."

Zach's eyes widened. "What? You moved out."

Kit started to nod but then shrugged. "Kind of. You remember that separate addition that my dad made for Oba?"

"Yeah. You moved in there? Where's Oba?"

"Living with Oma."

Zach felt the scone piece dissolve in his fingers and into the coffee. "Seriously?"

"Yeah, apparently she wanted to spend more time with her friends than her family, so I got her space. I'll show you around sometime. I have a hotplate, microwave, and rice cooker in the little kitchenette, so I'm living the dream. Which reminds me, you should join us for movie nights now that you're back in town."

For a second, Zach thought about declining, but he knew that wasn't a request. It was a directive. The one time that Zach and Joon had tried to skip without a good excuse, she'd had them watch *Howl's Moving Castle* for the first time the next time they came over, but it was the Japanese version without subtitles. She sat there happy while the boys had to get by with context clues.

"Can one of us pick the movie this time?" Joon asked as he walked over to the table, depositing a take-out cup and a white gabled take-out box in front of Kit.

"As long as it isn't depressing this time."

"Hey, *Never Let Me Go* is a great movie."

"It's sad as fuck. Never again."

Joon rolled his eyes before walking back to the kitchen, just as the front door of the cafe opened.

Zach glanced and did a double-take.

It was the woman who'd tackled him with her dog yesterday.

She had the biggest smile on her face when she noticed Sunny behind the counter, and Sunny reciprocated it.

"Hey, can I get—"

"One frozen vanilla latte with toffee and a croissant," Sunny said while putting a take-out cup and bagged treat on the counter.

The woman giggled. "Am I getting that predictable now?"

"I'd say consistent."

"Thanks, Sunny." She tried to pull out money to pay, but Sunny insisted it was on the house like she did for all her favorite customers, and she went on her merry way out the door. Zach found himself staring after her as the rising sun shined against her hair as she walked by the front window until Kit snapped her fingers in his face.

"What?" He turned back to her and immediately frowned at the smirk on her face.

"See something you like?"

Zach really hoped his brown skin hid the heat rushing up his face. He picked up his cup and swirled it around. "Who was that?"

"That's Belle. She's new in town."

"I gathered that," Zach said with narrowed eyes. The last person around their age Zach remembered moving to Lillet was their classmate, Gem, back in middle school. Parents with little kids moved to Lillet. Older people who were ready to retire moved to Lillet. Not a single twenty-something-year-old. If she was single, but that didn't matter to Zach.

"She's renting Linley Cottage. She's really sweet, and she has the cutest dog."

"A behemoth you mean?" Zach said as he lifted the mug and took a sip of coffee. He kept himself from moaning with pleasure as the coffee immediately warmed his body. After drinking commercial coffee on campus for months, drinking the Park Family blend felt like sipping pure gold.

Kit sat back in her seat with a raised brow. "You've met?"

"Her 'dog' ran me over yesterday."

Zach did not like the wide grin growing on her face as she leaned forward. "Oh my God, you had a meet-cute."

"A meet-cu..." Suddenly years of all the terms he learned from being forced to sit and rewatch Kit's favorite rom-com movies for her birthday flooded his brain. "No, no, this is not one of your rom-coms, Katrina."

"You never know, Zachary. I happen to know that she moved here by herself," she said with a nonchalant shrug as she took another piece of scone.

"That doesn't matter," Zach said, cringing as his voice cracked a bit. He took another sip of his coffee and put down the mug. "I'm only here until I find a full-time gig in New York. I don't have time to date."

That wiped the smile off Kit's face. "You're planning on leaving?"

"If I had a job, I'd already be gone. I mean, who wants to be stuck in Lillet all their life?"

Kit shrugged. "Sure. I guess," she said as she picked her goodies off the table. "Well, I'm gonna head out. I just got a job at Town Hall."

"Really?" Zach asked. Kit had done a degree in public relations, but she never said anything about wanting to work at Town Hall. That had been her mother and grandmother's thing, as town historian and mayor, respectively.

"Yeah, Grandma's gonna put me to work. See you guys later." Kit waved at Joon who was coming out the back before pointing at Zach. "Get better at answering your texts."

As she left, Joon came to stand by him with a floury apron on, and a mug in hand. "So, what are you going to be doing for the rest of the day?" he asked as he took a sip of his drink.

"The same thing that I've been doing for the last few weeks," he said as he pulled out his laptop out of his bag and opened it up. "Looking for a job."

Joon gave him a coy smile. "Good luck."

"Thanks." Joon went back to his post as Zach stared back at his screen. "I'm gonna need it."

zachslibrary 2h
Thank you all for the congratulatory comments on my last post!
Happy to finally have my degree and, if you need the help of somebody with an English degree, I'm your man.

Chapter 4

Zach liked routines.

They helped him focus when things got overwhelming, which he definitely needed at the moment, so he let himself fall back into one for the rest of the week: wake up, go to Toe Beans for coffee, chat with Joon a bit between sending in applications, pick up Corey and Amaya from school, have family dinner, pretend to read before going to bed, repeat. It occupied him from the fact that he still hadn't heard anything back from any of the companies that he applied to. He had continued to apply for mostly New York publishing-based jobs, but he also threw in a few local jobs as well so he could find somewhere else that he might be able to go during the week. There wasn't much available in Lillet itself—most businesses were family-run and they had enough family members to run their stores—but he found opportunities just outside of town. None of them had gotten back to him either though.

The weekend came just in time to give him some hope. When Zach walked into The Book Haven on Saturday morning, he could feel the familiarity of his old work routine calming his anxious brain. He went back into Des's office space behind the counter, where a little cubby was waiting for him to put his things. Des had texted him that he would meet the other employee as well since they also had an early shift on Saturdays.

It wasn't long after he put his bag down that somebody with swoopy black hair, star stickers under their eyes, and a non-binary flag pin attached to their Spongebob t-shirt came walking into the office. They took a step back when they noticed someone else was in there, but quickly collected themselves and grinned at him. "Oh hey, you must be Zach. Des told me that you would be starting today. I'm Jaime, nice to meet you," they said, holding out a hand to shake.

Zach shook their hand. "Likewise. Where's Des?"

"Getting items to restock the impulse buy area," Jaime said as they opened up one of the wooden cabinets. "And I get the pleasure of cleaning up the bathroom."

Zach winced. Even though he wanted the full-time shift again, he did not miss bathroom cleanup duty. "Good luck."

Jaime said a quick thanks before heading back out, saying a quick hi to Des as he came into the room, his hands occupied with a large cardboard box.

"Hey, Z. Ready to get to work?" Des asked as he put the box on his desk.

"Of course."

Des chuckled before picking up a name tag off the desk and handing it over. Zach grinned when he noticed it was the same one that he'd had from the beginning, the glasses sticker barely holding on at the tail end of his name. "You still have this?"

"Call me sentimental." Des smiled as he sat down at his desk.

Zach knew for a fact that Des was more than sentimental. Des was a true proprietor of the idea that if it ain't broke, don't fix it. He still had the old computer set up from when he was in high school. He only replaced his old tennis shoes after the soles came off three times. He still had a flip phone, for Pete's sake, which made Zach wonder sometimes if he was a super spy just trying to stay off the grid.

But he could crack that mystery another day. Zach quickly clipped his nametag on and asked, "What's first?"

"I need you to put these," Des said, tapping the box he brought in, "next to the register, and then man it for a while."

"Yes, sir," he said as he took it and went back out to the main area.

The muscle memory of rearranging the counter came back to him in an instant. He put the free bookmarks with the shop's logo in a mug, while the others went on the turning display on the counter. After placing candles on the shelves attached in front, he put some stickers on their display. He moved some of his favorites to the back so he could save them for himself to buy later like he used to do when he first started working there.

Zach moved around to the front of the counter to look at his work when the bell rang. While the store did have designated hours, Des didn't mind letting people come in early or stay late to shop. Zach took a deep breath, ready with his customer service voice and smile, but it immediately turned into a frown when Zach saw who it was coming in.

"Well, would you look here?" The man smirked, making Zach's stomach curdle.

Baxter Tonlin was, for a lack of words, a douche in high school. There was always this misconception that people mature after high school, and start to act like adults once they hit twenty-one, but given the stupid smirk on his face while he ran his hands through his fiery red hair, Zach would guess that Baxter hadn't changed one bit since he saw him last. He couldn't believe they had been friends at one point in their lives.

Zach took a breath. "Whatcha doing here, Baxter?" he asked through a tight smile, his heart rate picking up as he moved the now empty box onto the floor.

"Looking for a book. Duh," he said, looking at Zach the same way a shark looks at prey. "Man, I didn't think I'd see you back here any time soon. What gives?"

Zach half shrugged. "I'm just here for the summer."

"Really." Baxter got closer and put his pasty arm around Zach. Zach had to bite his tongue to resist the urge to push him away. "I'm in town visiting the folks too, and my dad made me come here to get something for my cousin."

Zach gritted his teeth as he said, "Need help finding anything in particular?"

"My dad says she's into mermaids. Should be up your alley, right? You know all about water, don't ya?"

Zach could feel his lungs tightening in his chest as he broke himself out of Baxter's grasp. His eyes searched frantically before seeing a book with illustrated mermaids on the cover. He quickly walked over to grab it and held it out to the redhead. "This one should work."

Baxter took it and turned it over in his hand. He shrugged. "I'm not sure."

"Need help finding something?" Jaime said as they came over and placed the cleaning supplies in the empty box.

"Nah," Baxter said, giving them the once-over before looking back at Zach with his toothy grin. "Zach can help me, can't you?"

"Actually, I need him to add these books to the Pride table, but I can help you," Jaime said as they picked up a stack of books and plopped them into Zach's arms, pointing him away from the front. "Here, it's over there."

Zach nodded before walking away with the books, taking deep breaths to bring down his heart rate. He'd expected to see Baxter around town at some point, but not this soon. He was one of the many reasons why Zach had wanted to hightail it out of town after graduation, and if he was going to be around for a while, Zach didn't need another reason to leave.

He smiled a little when he reached the area Des had set aside to share some Pride month recommendations. The table even featured a doodle of Wyatt holding up a Pride flag. Zach felt himself relax as he took a moment to rearrange everything to include the new books, before taking a picture with his phone. He texted it to Beau and Mateo in their group chat, and to Joon, giving him a bit more time to breathe before walking back over to the counter and, luckily, Baxter was gone.

Zach walked over to Jaime, who was booting up the cash register, and said, "Thanks for that."

Jaime smiled at him and shrugged as they closed the till. "No problem. Guy seemed like a real douche."

Zach nodded, picking up the empty box from before. "He is."

"Well, feel free to let me deal with him if he comes back," Jaime said, smirking with a twinkle in their eye. "I love getting under an asshole's skin."

Zach guffawed as he adjusted his hold on the box. "Noted."

Before he knew it, the afternoon had come with a little rush of people during the lunch hour. Jaime helped most of them, leaving Zach time to wander through the shelves, looking through the titles to make sure that everything was in alphabetical order by author. He was asked the occasional question about where to find a certain book, but he mostly spent his time reacquainting himself with what was on the shelves. He saw many of the books that were popular on Bookstagram in the stacks and was sad to notice that a few of his favorites weren't on the shelves. He would have to ask Des about that.

He made it halfway through his inspection in one aisle, when he noticed one book that was in the wrong section completely. *Who leaves a fantasy book in the non-fiction section?* He went to pick it up when another hand brushed over his to grab the same book. He turned and felt his heart flutter when he saw Belle staring right back at him.

"Hey," he greeted.

"Hi," she replied.

Zach glanced at her hand on top of his before looking back at her. "Are you interested in this book?"

"That's kind of why I was reaching for it."

"Right." Zach quickly slid his hand from underneath hers and let her take it off the shelf. She immediately turned it to see the back cover.

Zach stood there for a moment, shifting back and forth on his toes, waiting to see if she put it back or not. The seconds she took to read the description felt like hours, so he broke the silence. "Um, you're Belle, right?"

She looked up at him with wide eyes, and immediately took a step back. "How did you—"

"Um, you came into Toe Beans the other day. I saw Sunny take your order. Her younger brother, Joon, is my best friend. I think you also know Kit?" He questioned.

She slowly nodded. "Yeah. I know them. And you are?"

"Zach," he said, lifting his name tag.

She nodded again before putting the book back on the shelf, but Zach snatched it off again. Before she could say anything, he interjected, "It was in the wrong spot."

"Ah," she said with a nod, standing there for a second just looking at him.

He bit his lip before quickly turning away, and walking over to the fantasy section. It was only when he got to the book's proper spot that he noticed Belle had come over to the same area. She walked over to one display of fantasy romance books and started gazing at them.

It would have been easy to walk away and continue his organizing, but he couldn't help but take note of how she was struggling to hold in her hands. "You need a little help?"

She turned to him, and let out a small laugh as she readjusted her hold on the books. "A little."

He spotted one of their little shopping baskets and picked it up. "You planning on reading all of those soon?" He asked as he handed her the basket.

She giggled as she accepted the basket and put her books in it. "A few. Some of them I already read on my tablet, but I wanted a physical copy. I plan on at least reading two of these this week."

Zach felt his eyebrows go up and nodded. "I wish I could read anything right now. I haven't had a slump this bad since I finished reading through the *Grishaverse*."

"You should try a graphic novel. They usually help me get back in the act when I haven't read for a while."

He shook his head as his father's words coursed through his head. *Those don't count as reading. It's all pictures.* "No thanks. They're not really my thing."

"Then what is your thing?"

Zach's mind went blank. He couldn't think of a single book he'd ever liked or even his most-read genre. All he could think of was, "Just something that's not pictures."

Belle scoffed, "What's wrong with pictures? They only enhance the storytelling process."

"What they do is give people a chance to skip over the words that the author spent so long trying to string together."

"What if the words are a mere distraction from the hard work of the visual artists?" She shrugged.

Zach's eyes widened. "You cannot...you have got to be messing with me right now."

She just smiled at him, her brown eyes twinkling with mischief. "Now, whyever would I do that?"

"Because it seems like you love messing up my day."

"When have I ever messed up your day? We just met."

"Do you not remember when your dog attacked me?"

She scoffed a laugh. "He did not attack you. He just wanted to say hi."

"Tell that to my sweater vest."

"Honestly, he did you a favor so you wouldn't boil to death in that ugly thing."

He narrowed his eyes at her as he felt his face heating up. His sweater vests were not ugly. "Well, let me do you a favor and suggest that you never take that janky wagon of yours in public again."

"Okay, first, leave my wagon out of this. Second, you might want to take a minute to relax a bit. I think it would do wonders to calm down that vein popping out of your forehead." She shot him a toothy grin. "Trust me, you'll thank me later."

Zach seriously doubted that. He looked the woman up and down, and said with all the conviction he had, "I hope all your bookmarks fall out."

Her eyes widened. He leaned forward and added, "And I hope you never forget that you will never finish all the books you want to read."

Perhaps that was a bit too far, but Zach couldn't help but

smile when a glare overtook her face.

"I hope you realize how unpleasant you are," she quipped.

"Likewise," he argued. With any luck, they would be like passing ships in the night, and not have to see each other for the rest of Zach's time in Lillet.

"Hey, Zach, I need you to—" Des said, coming through the aisles before seeing the scene before him. "Oh, I see you've met Belle. She's one of our newest best customers. She's in here almost every weekend."

Zach looked between her and Des before letting his eyes land back on his boss. "Really?"

"Yeah. You'll probably be seeing a lot more of her."

Zach looked back at Belle and he could tell that she was just as thrilled about this news as he was.

"Great."

When Zach came back home, he was more than ready to take a nosedive into bed. After his conversation with Belle, a group of daycare kids came in and practically blew up the children's section, continuing his unlucky streak of the day. He and Jaime spent the afternoon reorganizing shelves, removing books with torn pages, and looking online for a replacement caboose for the toy train on the activity table. Luckily, Jaime was a very competent coworker and knew what they were supposed to do, which meant that Zach's work days wouldn't be horrible.

After taking off his shoes and dumping his bag, he looked up and saw Owen and Amaya sitting on the couch, getting up to who knows what on their phones, while Corey was lying on the floor with coloring books sprawled around him. The two teens looked up at him, and Owen immediately looked nervous, reinvigorating Zach with power.

"Do you spend any time at your own house?" Zach said, looking down at him.

Amaya glared at him. "Why don't you go to one of your friend's houses? If you still have any, that is."

Zach narrowed his gaze at her. "I'll pass. I have a standing appointment with my bed. She really missed me."

Before he could leave the entryway though, he heard his father call him from the kitchen.

"Ugh," he groaned as Amaya smirked at him.

"Tough luck." She glanced over at Corey before turning back. "B-I-T-C-H."

Corey looked up from his coloring book. "What's a B-I-T-C-H?" he asked, making all three of the older ones look down at the first grader in terror.

"Coming, Dad," he said, taking his retreat in stride.

The kitchen was filled with the smell of Italian food simmering. Jedidiah stood next to the stove stirring a pot of sauce, while Mimi worked on cutting up salad vegetables. Zach plucked a piece of bell pepper off the cutting board before asking what was up.

Jed turned down the heat on the burner before turning to his son. "We have a position at the library that you can fill."

"I don't need it. I'm doing fine on my own," Zach said immediately.

Jed raised a brow at him, "You've been looking for a job for how many weeks now?"

Zach bit his lip. "A couple."

"So why are you turning down a job offer right now?"

"Well, it's not really a job offer, because I didn't do anything to earn it. You're just trying to slot me into place somewhere."

"You have the necessary skills."

"How do you know that? I haven't taken any classes in library sciences, so how could I possibly be good at that job? The last thing I want to do is take a position from someone who actually knows what to do."

"You can learn it."

While Zach knew that that was probably true, he did not want to take a job where he was most likely going to spend his entire day dealing with his father telling him what to do. "Dad, I don't need you to get a job for me. I can find something on my own."

Just as Jed went to say something else, Mimi looked up from her chopping. "Jedidiah, let him be." Jedidiah went to talk again but Mimi held up a hand. "Zach just wants to work hard and get a position on his own. I remember when you was young, I let you walk around to neighbors to see if they needed their grass cut during the summer. He trying to be grown, just like you were."

"Well, he's not grown yet," Jed said before looking at his eldest. "I'm serious Zachary, if you don't find something by the end of Monday, I expect you to take this offer."

"Why Monday?" he asked softly, his heart clenching in his chest as he talked.

"The sooner you have something stable, the sooner I can sleep at night. You don't need to be sitting around this house slacking off all summer when I can put you to work."

"Well, why don't you have me babysit Corey then?"

"Corey's going to summer camp at his school."

"What about Amaya?"

"She's already volunteering as a children's room monitor at the library. You should follow her example."

Zach's eye twitched at those words and he bit his lip harder. "But, what about what I wan—"

"End of discussion."

Zach felt a bit of blood come out from where he bit down. He ignored it. "Yes, sir," he nodded before glancing at Mimi's sympathetic gaze. "I'll be in my room if you need me." He turned to leave but immediately turned back. "By the way, Amaya's teaching Corey how to spell cuss words, just thought you should know."

Zach took a little bit of joy from his father calling for Amaya to come into the kitchen as he went up the stairs, but the feeling quickly faded once he realized what was at stake.

The idea of working for his father shouldn't have been so terrifying, but it was. It felt as if the walls were closing in around him as he all but ran over to his desk and opened up his laptop, going straight to his emails.

A bunch of spam emails were littered through what he was looking for, making him scroll that much more frantically, but nothing in the subject lines eased his worry.

Your application has been sent.

Your application has been sent.

Your application has been viewed.

Your application has been sent.

Not a single interview request, message, or rejection in the bunch.

Zach's fingernails dug into his skull as he leaned back in his chair.

What the hell was he gonna do?

Snippet from "Project Void" by Zach Roberts (2nd Draft)

Floating in deep space with no destination was terrifying. There was no safety to be found with nothing solid beneath the ship and shooting towards the ground was only a recipe for disaster.

"Why won't you just tell the captain the truth?" Nova said to Ty. "He'll listen to you."

Ty closed his eyes and sighed. "The captain only cares about two things: taking down the Armada and getting home. And he doesn't care how we do it, either."

"But if we don't try to save those data towers, then everything we went on this mission for will be gone! We didn't work this hard just to have nothing to show for it. That information—"

"Is the perfect bait to take down the Armada." Ty opened his eyes and stared out the porthole before them. "We can target them at their weakest. It's a solid plan."

"Is it worth it though? Sacrificing all our work to come home without completing our mission."

"We'll be home." Ty glanced over at Nova and tried hard to ignore the tears welling in her eyes. "And for him, that's enough."

"But what about us? What about what we want?"

"I don't think that matters to him anymore," Ty said, looking back out into the deep space that surrounded them, the darkness encapsulating everything in sight.

Months ago, he hadn't known what lied out there. He hadn't explored it for himself. He hadn't met the crew that shared his curiosities. They wanted to know what lied beyond the darkness, but there were those, like the Captain, who only wanted to stay in the light.

The thing was that by constantly staring into the light, eventually he lost sight of what more could be out there.

Chapter 5

Zach had never been much of a coffee drinker until he got his first major paper in college.

After struggling with writing a single word for weeks, two days before the essay was due, Zach found himself camped out in the corner of the library cafe with nothing but three bottles of pre-made coffee, his laptop, charger, headphones, and the sheer will to write. It turned out that Zach did his best writing under pressure and fueled by caffeine, as he got an A on that paper.

He prayed that this method would help him find any sort of job.

The Monday after his father's ultimatum, he had made camp at the table nobody wanted in Toe Beans. It was next to the bathroom, but for Zach, it was a necessity to keep any breaks he needed during that time to a minimum, and he kept his headphones on to filter out any distractions. He had already spent the entirety of Sunday barely keeping it together during his Book Haven shift and spent the night working on different versions of his resume so he could send them out with ease when he came to the cafe the next day. He had already finished four cups of the cafe's cold brew, along with two orange scones, as he scoured any website that had ever offered a job. He went through a handful of freelance websites to see if anyone would pay him for reading, and he nearly took a book reviewer job, only to lie and say he already found something after realizing that he would be paid to give five-star reviews to books he wasn't expected to read. He knew he couldn't afford to be picky at that moment, but he refused to compromise his reader morals for a quick buck.

He was in the midst of writing a proposal for a beta reader position when Joon came over to his table with another cup. Zach glanced up and noticed that the liquid was decidedly not dark brown.

"What is that?" he asked, pulling his headphones onto his neck.

"Lemongrass tea."

Zach pushed it back towards his friend. "No thanks. More coffee, please," he said as he put his attention back on his keyboard, trying to figure out his next sentence. *How do you say you're the best reader to read somebody else's book?*

"Not a chance. I'm cutting you off."

Zach sharply looked up at Joon, who nearly jumped back at the sight of his bloodshot eyes and gritted teeth. On any other day, Zach would have been delighted at the idea of poking fun at his friend, but today was not that day. "You can't do that."

"Oh, but I can," Joon said, looking Zach up and down with concern in his eyes. "You need to chill."

"No time to chill," Zach said as he went back to typing. "I

have to find a job before I end up being my dad's coworker."

"I can't be that bad. I work with my parents."

"Yeah, but your parents aren't control freaks who want to be in charge of every bit of their kids' lives. He already has my home life. He can't take my work life too."

Joon nodded and shrugged. "Fair enough, but I'm still cutting you off."

Zach covered his mouth to muffle his screams as Kit walked into the cafe. She came over, brows raised and lips pursed. "Looks like I got here just in time."

"What are you doing here?" Zach muttered as he looked at her through narrowed eyes.

"Joon texted me and said he was concerned about your well-being," Kit explained as she took in his ragged appearance. "And I can see why." She turned to Joon. "I'll take it from here."

Joon nodded as he picked up the empty mugs and plates from Zach's table, and went back into the kitchen. Kit sat down in the other seat at the table, giving him a disappointed look once she saw how many cups Joon was taking away.

"Leave me alone. Not all of us can run on apple juice and fanfiction."

"Don't knock it till you try it," she shrugged.

"Kit..." Zach buried his head in his hands. His sleep-deprived state was starting to catch up with him. "I'm serious. If you don't have a job for me to apply to, I want to be left alone."

"I have a job for you to apply to."

Zach uncovered his face and looked up. "What?"

"Belle came into Town Hall today asking if she could post a

job listing on the town website."

Zach ignored the part about Belle and asked, "For what?"

"Some sort of assistant for her online shop. She said she was going to send me the full listing later, and as of right now—" She pulled out her phone and tapped on the screen. "—I do not have anything from her in my inbox."

Zach looked back at the blinking cursor on his proposal. Next to it, an information box saying that over 50 people had applied for this position that had been posted two weeks ago and no one had been hired yet. If he was being realistic, he knew that this job was going to be another dead end, and he was running out of time. Another shop job was not going to add any publishing experience to his resume, but it would give him something to do in the meantime if he got it. His qualifications could potentially convince Belle to give him a chance. Besides, it would be temporary anyway.

He looked up at Kit. "Where does she live again?"

Zach drove up the hill towards Linley Cottage with a pit in his stomach. For the first time in a while, his mind went blank when it came to all of the interview prep he'd done. His brain was only buzzing about how he needed this to go well.

Once he reached the top of the hill, he stepped out to take in the view. Linley Cottage was isolated on its hill, looking down into the valley below where the rest of Lillet laid. A hint of the harbor could be seen, along with the tip of the Lillet Lighthouse peeking over one of the hills in the distance. It was only a sixteen minute drive from his house but it felt so foreign to him. He walked over to the front door of the chamomile brown brick house. The front door had one of those old knockers on it, and Zach's inner child couldn't help but use it.

As soon as he knocked twice, he heard barking start behind the door.

He groaned.

He'd forgotten about her dog.

A chain on the door rattled as it opened to reveal Belle, and she, once she saw who was there, glared at him. "What are you doing here?"

Zach shifted his stance as he tried to find the right words. "Kit said you were looking for a shop assistant?"

He saw a bit of her shoulder shrug through the crack in the door. "Yeah, she texted me that she was sending over a potential... She was talking about you?"

"Yeah, I'd like to apply."

He could see her raise a brow at him. "Really?"

"Yes."

Belle's eyes trailed his body before closing the door. Zach's stomach nearly dropped to the ground until he heard the chain moving again. Belle opened the door wider, her leggings and oversized t-shirt coming into view, and gestured for him to come inside as she walked deeper into the house.

As soon as he stepped in, Zach felt his heart lift a little when he noticed the shoe-free home sign next to a shoe rack at the door. He quickly slid off his shoes before walking further into the front room. It wasn't very spacious, which he'd expected from the small features outside, but it didn't feel too cramped, either: a kitchen to his right and a living area to the left, all of it filled with frilly little items that one might see in vintage farmhouses, with a bunch of greens, pinks, and white spread throughout the space in blankets, baskets, and such.

When he heard Belle clear her throat, his attention was brought back to her. "So Kit told me that you run an online shop," Zach said as he stepped further into the house.

Belle crossed her arms over her chest. "Yeah, I do."

Zach shifted again under her piercing gaze and asked, "What exactly do you sell in your shop?"

"You didn't ask about that before you came here?"

Zach sucked in his teeth. "Uh, no." It was then that Zach realized that he had never done an interview before. Des had just given him the job at The Book Haven soon after he applied (benefits of having known him for so long). Sadly, he didn't know Belle at all, except for the fact that she liked pictures, pulled a wagon around, and had a huge furry dog that was currently trying to sniff around his ankles. He tried to shuffle away from the shepherd, but he followed.

"Appa, go lie down," Belle commanded. The multicolored dog immediately walked over to the living room, and lied down on the edge of the woven rug. "You're not off to a great start here," she said as she walked over to her coffee table and picked up a flower-covered notebook from it. "Have you ever heard of cottagecore?"

"Vaguely."

She turned back to him. "Think daisies and baby's breath. Woodland creatures having tea parties and growing gardens. My merchandise has that sort of thing going on," she said handing over the book.

Zach turned over the notebook in his hand to see her logo at the bottom of the book: LB with a bunny sitting between the letters. "Cool."

"Maybe not for you. It's all pictures."

Zach's face sucked in like he licked a lemon. His sarcastic wit was definitely coming back to bite him in the ass now. "I know I'm most likely not your top candidate for this position."

"Definitely not," she said with a saccharine grin on her face, which made him feel a bit uneasy, but he persisted.

"But I really need a job right now."

"I thought you worked at Book Haven?"

"Only part-time, and while I might not be as into pictures as you, I'm a hard worker, and I've got a ton of experience in shops. Ask Des if you don't believe me. Not to mention, I've been told that I'm really good at customer service." He could see a scoff building up in her body when he said that. "Shocking, I know."

"Very," Belle said with a nod. "Is this really what you want to be spending your time doing? Packing stickers and sweatshirts."

"What I want to be doing is writing my book and finding a job in publishing, but that really hasn't been working for me at this point."

Belle snorted a laugh. "I appreciate the honesty."

Zach let out what he hoped was a friendly smile at the statement, before taking a deep breath and saying, "Look. I just need a chance to prove to my dad that I can get a job without his help and that I don't need him to try and have everything done for me." He shrugged. "I just wanna live my own life."

As Belle stood there processing his words, he was shocked at the fact that he actually bore all of that to her, yet also relieved. Maybe it was because she didn't know him, or that he was desperate for the job, but for once, he didn't feel like the ground was going to swallow him up for saying all of that out loud.

"I get it."

Zach felt the tightness in his shoulders release a bit at her words. "You do?"

She nodded. "Yeah. That's why I moved here. I wanted to live my own life for once."

"You had an overbearing parent too?"

"Something like that." Belle adjusted her glasses. "What are you doing tomorrow?"

Zach could feel the hope rising in his chest but he squashed it down for a moment. "If this doesn't work out, heading to work at the library under my dad's supervision."

Belle took a deep breath before uncrossing her arms. "I'll give you a shot."

"Really?" Zach tried to keep relief out of his voice, but the soft smile on his face would give it away anyway.

"It's only a trial run to see how well we could work together. Even though this might be temporary, I'm not gonna sit in a room all day with someone whose presence is gonna annoy me. If you can help get things done, I think we can come to an agreement."

"Got it."

"One condition though."

"Name it."

Zach was immediately scared by the smirk that rose onto her face. "You have to apologize to Appa."

Zach's jaw almost dropped to the ground. "You can't be serious!"

Belle looked over at Appa, who trotted over at the sound of his name. "He's waiting."

Zach looked between the two before groaning and getting

down to the dog's level. "I'm sorry."

Appa decided to lick his face with such gusto that he knocked off Zach's glasses as a response. "Oh, come on!"

"I think that's an acceptance." Belle giggled as she pulled Appa back, leaving Zach to try and wipe off the slobber from his glasses and face with his shirt. "Tomorrow then."

Zach looked between her and her dog and prayed that he hadn't made the biggest mistake of his life.

Belle's To-Do List

- ☑ Finalize the Barry, Carry, and Terry Summer Collections
- ☑ Call Local Vet about setting up a check-up for Appa
- ☐ Call Printer about Barry Stickers
- ☐ Edit Current Vlog Clips
- ☑ Hire Assistant

(Potential Hire Found, We'll See How This Goes)

Chapter 6

When Zach first started working at The Book Haven, it didn't take long for him to figure out the flow of how things worked there. It felt like a natural transition to go from frequent patron to paid employee, but he had spent so much time working there that he never really thought about what it would be like to work somewhere else.

Zach came back to Linley Cottage the next day with determination in one hand and a bagged lunch that his grandmother had forced into in the other. She'd made it alongside Corey's, so he was expecting to pull out a PB&J and pretzels around lunchtime, but that didn't matter. If he did well today, he could finally rest easier at night. After he told his dad he found something that might pan out, Jed had given Zach a one-day extension to see it through, so his sanity was riding on him not screwing this up.

No pressure though.

Zach walked up to the front door and used the knocker, the

sound of barks quickly following before the door swung open to reveal Belle with her phone pressed to her ear. "Yes, I understand that it takes four to five weeks for shipping but it's been six and there's been no movement and I just wanted to check to make sure that—" she rolled her eyes as the person on the phone spoke, and gestured for Zach to come inside.

Zach said nothing as he took off his shoes and put his bag down. He had seen Des in a similar state when they didn't get deliveries of new releases in on time, and in those moments, he just let Des fight it out with whoever was on the phone. Luckily, Zach didn't have to stand by the door for too long before Belle hung up. She turned back to him with frustration riddled across her face. "Sorry about that. I've been waiting for a shipment of stickers to come in, and the tracking number hasn't been updated in weeks, and"—she brushed fallen strands of her hair back behind her ear—"it's already been a long day." She looked down at his hands. "Nice lunch box."

Zach looked down and his cheeks felt a bit warmer. He'd forgotten that Mimi put the lunch in one of Corey's old *Paw Patrol* lunch bags. At least, it wasn't one of Amaya's *Doc McStuffins* ones. "My grandmother was making one for my younger brother, and she decided to make one for me too."

Belle smiled a bit before pointing at her fridge. "Well, you can leave it in there. Let's get to work."

She went further into the house, and Zach quickly shoved his lunch in the fridge to run behind her. Belle guided him up an old wooden staircase near the back of the house that led to a lofted attic space, and it immediately felt like he stepped into a warehouse: metal racks of boxed-up inventory and clear containers filled with stickers of flowers and little cartoon animals; wooden shelves brimming with thick sweatshirts in pastel colors; two big desks were shoved in between them on each side of the room, each piled high with envelopes and tissue paper that were just as floral as everything else in the space. Zach had taken the initiative to look over the shop website to familiarize himself with what Belle sold, and there was more listed on there than what he could see at the moment.

Belle pointed to the desk farthest away from the staircase. "You can work over here."

He nodded and took a seat, digging his phone out of his pocket, and putting it to the side.

"So, I'm doing a restock of the shop soon, and I try to have everything packaged and inventoried before I list it on the site," she explained as she dug out one of the boxes from the stacks around them. "I've already done quality checks so I just need you to pack and count these."

She placed the box in front of him, and he peeked in to see white circular patches with daisy bundles in the middle of them. Belle then demonstrated the packing process for him, sealing the plastic bag before putting a label sticker on as a final touch. It was easy enough to catch onto, and Belle was quickly satisfied that he could do it himself; she went over to her desk to do some tasks on her own. She turned on her computer and brought up files with different designs of woodland creatures and flowers before turning on her printer. As the machine came to life, she got up from her seat, looking toward the staircase before glancing back at him. "You want some coffee?"

Zach was mid-yes when he remembered the fragile nature of the merchandise before him. "I'd rather not risk spilling something on your stock."

Belle nodded and went back down the stairs. For a brief moment, Zach wondered if that was a test of whether he would be careful around her inventory, but he decided to not think too much about it. He let the repetitiveness of the task settle in, and by the time Belle came back up the stairs, he was already done with a stack.

He turned in time to see her set down a box on the other table and take out clear glass cups. They were similar to the ones that were already on the shelves, but there were no designs on them. She took the stack of papers she'd printed out before and started wrapping them around the cups and taping them in place.

Zach turned back to his task and actually took a look at the design. It wasn't anything grand or genre-breaking, but it was a cute little thing. If he brought one of them home to Amaya, he could see her immediately trying to attach it to her book bag and probably try to make some of her own with the embroidery kits that she built with Mimi. Maybe after he proved to Belle that he was a good employee, he could talk to her about buying inventory before she listed it online.

When Belle moved to the area next to him, he looked over to see that she was putting one of the wrapped cups into a machine that looked like it came out of a sci-fi writer's imagination. It looked like it belonged in a factory, not in a cottage attic. "What's that?" he asked.

"A heat press," Belle said as she closed up the device. "I use this to get these designs"—she pressed down some buttons—"on these cups. I have one for the sweatshirts too."

"Anyone can just buy one of these things online?"

"Yup."

She went back downstairs before he could ask more. He took a look at some of her other machines and they all looked like heavy-duty machines that cost a pretty penny. He turned back to his task but jumped in his seat when he felt something brush against his leg. He looked down and saw it was just Appa sitting next to his table, making him roll his eyes. "Shouldn't you be following Belle around?"

"He usually does," Belle said as she came back up with another cumbersome cardboard box in her arms. "But he seems to like you. Probably wants to interact with someone besides me, since we're pretty much here all the time," she huffed as she put the new box down next to one of the wooden shelves.

"You need help bringing those up?"

She shook her head as she used a box cutter to make quick work of the tape seal. "Nah, I'm used to doing it on my own," she said before she started pulling out some more glass cups.

He nodded. Silence filled up the space as both of them continued working on their individual tasks. The smell of hot paper filled the air, but he didn't mind it as he finished up another stack.

As Belle put on some gloves and removed the cup from the press, Zach decided to ask "So. where are you originally from?"

"New York."

Zach's ears perked up at that. "Really? Worked there too?"

"Yeah, I did content marketing for an advertising firm."

"Which is?"

"Convincing people to buy stuff on social media."

He held back a scoff. "So you made TikToks?"

She turned to face him, eyebrow raised. "Is that judgment I'm hearing?"

Zach shook his head. "No, no. Just curiosity." *Stop saying dumb things around her dammit!*

"Mhm." She turned back to put the cup to the side before putting another in. "I made a lot of different types of content, not just short form. It depended on what audience companies wanted to connect to, along with what would engage them the most, and showing how reliable the brand was in making products that people would actually like. Video content was my specialty, though."

"Do you still do that?"

Belle shrugged as she started to peel off the paper on the cup, revealing the floral design underneath. "In a way, but I've been able to make the shop my full-time job. I'll do consultant work if asked, but most of my days are spent designing and making the products that I can here."

"That sounds like a lot," Zach said as he put the last packaged patch in a small basket with the others. He was used to doing a lot of stocking and other bits of manual labor at the bookstore, but it would have been another thing entirely if they'd had to bind the book themselves.

Belle shrugged. "It can be. That's why I need an assistant. But it's been better since I started outsourcing my stickers to another printer." She went over, grabbed one of the stickers, and smiled. "They've been coming out pretty good," she cooed as she gave Zach a glimpse of the design: a bear reading a book.

Zach smiled; he could definitely relate to the bear.

They worked in silence for the next hour. Zach easily packed up all the patches before moving on to another design with a bear reading in the middle, "The Cozy Club" written around the edge of the patch. Belle worked behind him making cups with daisy designs running along the bottom of them.

It was easy work, but Zach found it quite calming. He was tempted to go get his headphones out of his bag to listen to music while he worked, but given that this was a trial day, he didn't want to tune out Belle and miss something. So, he kept himself in the zone by thinking about plot lines and fixes for his current work-in-progress. He could already imagine plot filler moments where some people on the ship could be working on maintenance down in the boiler room and be forced to have a heart-to-heart. He was in the middle of daydreaming about the dialogue when Appa started pawing at his leg. He glanced down at him. "What do you want?"

Belle turned around and winced. "Appa, no. He's not here for that."

"Here for what?"

"That's his way of saying he needs to go out."

"Oh." Zach glanced at Appa, who was looking up at him, tongue hanging out of his mouth. "Yeah, I..." He looked up at Belle. "No."

Belle chuckled, shaking her head as she petted Appa. "It's okay. Dog-sitting will not be one of your responsibilities." She beckoned Appa to come with her, leaving Zach to finish the current stack of patches in front of him. He looked at the final design. It had the same bear, but the text around the edge read "No Hugs Please." Zach snorted a laugh before he started packing again.

A while later, Belle came back up with Appa trailing behind her. He laid down on a small bed next to her desk while she started typing on her desktop. When Zach was reaching the end of the inventory in front of him, he noticed Belle starting to gather items from different shelves in the room out of the corner of his eye. She made little stacks of stuff on her table, getting out different-sized boxes and rolls of craft paper. When she sat down and started to bundle up all the items she had gathered, she did it without missing a beat, while labels printed off on the machine beside her.

Not even the Parks worked that cohesively in the cafe. The siblings in particular had to stay in their separate corners if they were all working together, or risk getting angry when they started bumping elbows.

By the time he finished counting the last stack, Belle had finished packing everything she had gathered before. She turned to him, and he saw her glance back and forth between him and the orders, before she finally asked, "Hey, do you think that you could drive these over to the post office for me? Otherwise, I'll have to walk them there myself with the wagon."

Zach's eyes widened as he took a look at the folded-up wagon in the corner. *She had been taking packages filled with cups, mugs, and other fragile items down the steep hill and into town in that thing?* He really shouldn't have said anything about the wagon before. He put the last patch in the box with the others. "Sure, but if you need to you can just take my car and I can—"

"No," Belle snapped. She took a step back. "I mean, thanks but I'd rather just hand it off to you to drive down while I finish these cups."

Zach didn't understand her hesitation but didn't dwell on it as they began to gather everything on the desk and bring it down to the car. Appa tried to get into the car with the packages, but Belle managed to wrangle him back into the house with the promise of a treat. She explained that all Zach had to do was drop them off at the front desk.

Easy enough.

But not really because when he walked into the post office, he felt like he'd walked into BWI airport the day before Thanksgiving.

The post office wasn't anything special, just a small building next to the town hall with a wall of PO Boxes and a stand of different mailers and stamps next to the main counter, but it always tended to be a hub of activity in town. At one point,

Zach had started to sell some of his old books to make some money before Des started buying used books from people to put in little libraries around town. When he'd come in to mail them off, there'd always been a line. Today was no different as he stood with many others who had large packages in hand, and Zach knew that, most likely, they weren't already labeled and ready to go like his.

So, he not so patiently stood there, swaying side to side until he heard someone come up behind him and say, "Zachary?"

He went stiff; there was only one person who called him by his full name when he wasn't in trouble besides Kit. He turned around slowly with a tepid grin on his face. "Hey, Gigi."

The older lady shifted the package in her hand before smacking his shoulder. He had to shift his weight again to keep the mailers from falling. "Why haven't you been over since you've been back?"

"Gigi, I saw you last week at graduation."

"And?"

Zach kept his mouth shut. He knew better than to argue with her. While Mimi was a soft-spoken type of grandmother, Gigi was a force of nature that should never be reckoned with, at home or in court. Even retired, she still had the presence of a lawyer riddled throughout her body.

Gigi glanced at the baby pink mailers in his hand. "What you got there?"

"I'm just shipping off some orders for someone."

Gigi grabbed the top one of his stack and looked at the label. "Love, Belle?"

Zach nodded. "She's a stationery shop owner. I'm just helping her out," Zach said, grateful to see that the line was finally moving, but when he took a step forward, Gigi was right behind him.

"I thought you were gonna be working full-time at the bookstore."

"Who told you that?"

"Marian."

Zach sighed. He'd forgotten how close his grandmothers were. Even though his parents were divorced, their bond remained strong. "I'm only going to be working part-time at the store right now."

"Oh," Gigi said, leaning back a bit with open eyes before she shook it off. "Well if you need something to do, I have some consultant work that I need organized, and—"

"I'm good, Gigi," Zach said swiftly. "Promise."

She raised a brow, looking him up and down, but luckily didn't fight him on it. "Alright. But you let me know if you need help with anything. And tell your father to bring yourself and your siblings over Sunday dinner soon, or I'm coming over there to get y'all myself."

"Yes, ma'am."

"Next!"

Zach looked up to see that the rest of the people in front of him had finished already. He scurried up to the counter and dropped off the orders before turning back and saying a quick goodbye, wishing he had fewer relatives in town as he left.

When Zach got back to the cottage, Belle was stationed out front with a camera in hand, and Appa sitting before her.

"Stay, Appa," she commanded as Zach opened his car door. "Stay."

Zach walked around and got a good view of Belle taking pictures of Appa, his tongue hanging out of his mouth as he looked at the lens. "Good boy," she cheered before taking a treat out of her pocket and giving it to Appa, who happily gobbled it up.

"Is dog photography one of your specialties?" Zach asked as

he came closer.

"Actually yes," she said with a smile as she put down her camera and pet Appa. "I used to work at an animal shelter back in the city, and I took a lot of pictures of the shelter dogs when we were trying to get them adopted."

"That where you got Appa?"

"Yeah. I took a break from volunteering for a while, and he was there waiting for me when I got back." She scratched the fur on his neck and she pressed her nose against his. "He's been my buddy ever since. Haven't you?"

Appa responded by licking her face, which made her laugh. Zach couldn't help but smile a bit at the interaction. He never had a pet growing up, and as long as he lived in his father's house, his aloe plant was going to be the closest thing he would have to one, but he hoped that one day he could have a special bond with someone once he got to New York. He knew that the city would have what he needed.

He took a breath before stepping closer to Belle. "So, what's next?"

Belle stood up, brushing the dirt from the back of her jean shorts, before looking up at him. "Um, nothing. I've only got some admin stuff left to do today." Zach nodded as a small smile came up Belle's face. "But I'll have more for you to do tomorrow."

Zach leaned forward a bit, and he smiled wider. "Really?"

"You're hired."

"Really?"

"Yeah, if you're still interested, that is."

"Very much still interested."

Belle held out her hand. "Welcome to Love, Belle, Zach."

He happily shook her hand and felt nothing more than relief. It might not be the high-time publishing job he was looking for, but it was a job, and a step in the right direction. He would gladly take it.

Belle smirked at him. "But I hope you don't mind being a package jockey, 'cause once I set up the restock online, we're going to be sending out a lot of packages."

"Won't be the worst thing I've done for work."

She smiled at him more, and Zach felt his heart skip a beat. Her smile really was beautiful.

Appa barked, and Zach was suddenly aware of the fact that they had not let go of each other's hand yet. They both dropped them before Belle opened the door to let Appa inside.

Zach went in to collect his things upstairs feeling as light as a feather. He had a job. It wasn't working for his dad, and he'd got it on his own.

He could finally breathe a bit easier.

Zach's New Summer Goals

1. Get a Great Recommendation from Des

2. Ask Belle more about what it's like to live in New York

3. Set up Alerts for NYC Publishing Jobs

4. Buy a New Lunch Bag

Chapter 7

Zach didn't make friends easily.

Throughout his childhood, he usually had temporary friendships that lasted until the end of the school year and faded away during the summer. Maybe they would reignite during the next year, but if they weren't in the same class, it wasn't likely. When he got to college, friends usually only lasted for the semester at best. Kit, Joon, Beau, and Mateo had been the exceptions to this rule, and Zach didn't really feel like he needed more than that. Along with that, his family kept him entertained enough with their own antics.

The morning after he officially got the job with Belle, he came downstairs and chuckled when he saw Amaya in the kitchen sneaking some Lucky Charms from the box.

"You know that's a weekend-only food," he teased as he walked into the kitchen.

"Sue me," she challenged, popping another marshmallow in her mouth as she thumbed through her phone. "I have three finals to take today."

"I thought you were getting some of your finals waived since you took the AP exams for them," he said as he took the box from her and ate some.

"Only in AP English and Environmental Science. Physics is still on, and I have Calculus and Health on top of that."

"Sucks to be smart."

"I'm not that smart," she said with a shrug.

He looked at her with a raised brow. "I mean, you're not Shuri or Riri smart, but you can hold your own." He leaned over and got himself in her eye line, which got her attention off her phone. "And you shouldn't think otherwise when you've taken six AP classes already."

Amaya smiled a bit, right before Zach smirked at her. "Trying to be the second Roberts valedictorian in a row?"

She scoffed a laugh. "No way. You can keep that title all to yourself."

He threw a charm in the air to catch in his mouth, successfully might he add, before coming over to stand behind her. "Whatcha looking at?"

She tilted the screen towards him slightly where he saw one of the many job sites that he had been visiting for the last few months. "Why are you looking for a job?" he asked.

"You're not the only one in this family who wants to make some extra cash and not work at the library. I only told Dad I would do it so he wouldn't make me do it. Besides, gaming equipment costs money and there are these really cute Kuromi controllers that I want to buy for my Switch and I'm not waiting for Christmas to get them."

He scoffed. "Yeah well, good luck with that." He'd sent

another resume out last night and checked his inbox to see no responses from any company. If Amaya had any better luck than that, there was something truly wrong with the universe.

She snickered with a grin on her face as she grabbed another handful of cereal out of the box. "Wouldn't it be funny if I found a full-time job before you?"

Zach grimaced through the wheat bits of cereal. "Don't joke about that."

"You don't need a job that bad, you know? It's not like Dad or Mimi are going to kick you out if you're not employed."

"I know that, but I need a job so that I can actually get a place of my own, and I'm not gonna get the money for that with just selling books and packing stickers," he reminded her.

"You could just stay here, it's not that bad..."

Zach gave her a look and she nodded. "Okay, maybe it is, sometimes. But promise me that if you do move somewhere far away that you won't completely forget about us here."

"Don't worry, I'll be back for your graduation at minimum." A smirk crawled up his face. "Someone needs to yell things up at the stage like you did for me."

His sister's eyes widened. "No."

"Oh yeah, karma's a bitch. I'm bringing a bullhorn and everything."

"That won't get in the building."

"We'll see." He put the box down and started to make his way to the front door, but turned back. "But hey, if you need something to do, I need a gift made and I'll pay you to make it. We can talk about it when you get back home."

She smiled. "Sweet, thanks," she said while she put the box back in the pantry. "I'm gonna go cram some more." She took one step closer to the stairs before skipping over towards him and giving him a big hug. Zach stiffened for a second before lightly returning it. He and Amaya weren't the most affectionate sort of siblings. Their love language between each other was more along the lines of insults and taking each other's food. "What's this for?"

"Nothing. I just missed you," she said before releasing him and running up the stairs.

A small smile creeped up his face because he had missed her too.

But he would never tell her that to her face.

When Zach got to the cottage, he could immediately feel the stiff energy in the air as Belle opened the door. The few times he had seen her before, her hair was pulled back into ponytails or buns by scrunchies or scarves. Now she stood in the doorway with her hair loose and curls flailed about like she'd been pulling at them to the point of almost tearing them out.

"Is everything okay?" he asked as he slowly approached her.

She scoffed with a smile on her face. "Oh, things couldn't be more wrong at this moment," she said as she started to pace about the room.

"What happened?"

"That shipment of stickers I was waiting for came in. But they were printed completely wrong," she explained, pointing at the box. "I can't sell these."

Zach took a look inside the box and pulled out one of them. It was of the bear that he'd seen in some of her other work. Here he was flying a kite, the words "Fly with Me" beneath the image, except everything was cut small. The bottom of the words and the tip of the kite were cut off. You could tell what it was supposed to be, but from a consumer standpoint, you wouldn't pay full price for it.

"This was gonna be one of the big item drops to go with the rest of the collection and now—" She stomped over to her couch, next to Appa, and threw her face in her hands. "Ugh." She took a deep breath before trying to compose herself. "Sorry. I just... sorry."

"No, it's fine. If I entrusted someone with this sort of thing, and I got this, I'd be pissed too."

"Well, me being pissed isn't gonna fix this. The bundle is ruined."

Zach took a second and thought for a moment, looking at the stickers before looking back at her. "Your bundle, what does it entail exactly?"

Belle sat back on the couch, her hand brushing over Appa's fur, "It's a collection of themed items around some of the different characters I made for the shop. I offer a cup, sweatshirt, notebook, bookmark, patch, and sticker with the same design on it. It's a staple in my shop every season and I have ones for my two other mascots, but Barry is usually the best seller, and now I can't launch his collection when I said I would."

Zach took another look at the stickers. "Do you ever offer messed up stuff for free on your site? We give out free misprinted stickers of Wyatt all the time at Book Haven."

Belle looked up at him. "I've thought about it, but I hate the idea of giving people a product that isn't up to my standards."

Zach could a hundred percent understand that. The perfectionist in him never wanted anybody to see any of his work before it was perfect. "Well, it's one thing if you purposely sell someone a crappy thing, but if they knew right off the bat that this is an item that wasn't done the best, then they might be more understanding. You don't have to sell it with the bundle, just lower the price of the bundle and send a freebie of the sticker to people who buy it."

Belle sat with the idea for a moment before pulling out her phone and going over to the box. She took a photo and typed something before turning back to Zach. "I'm asking the shop's Instagram followers what they think about it, but it's not a bad idea."

"Thanks."

Belle shook herself out and took a deep breath. "Okay, enough of that." She plastered a smile on her face as she walked over to her tiny kitchen. "You want any tea or coffee? I bought some of the Toe Beans blend if you—"

"Say less."

After the two of them got their respective drinks, they made their way up to the attic. Now that Belle had officially taken him on as an assistant, they discussed the full extent of his responsibilities. It was simple things, like packing inventory and orders at first, but Belle was open to training him on using the machines to make some of the products later on. He sat and watched as she filled out a calendar of things that would be happening for the shop during the summer season. Besides the release of her collections based around her characters, she was also restocking some of her best-selling stickers and cups, not to mention some crocheted goods that she hadn't had time to make when she first moved and settled into the cottage.

Belle walked him through the process of packing orders; it took a lot more thought than he believed it would.

Choosing the right container to send everything in on the first try.

Making sure there was enough padding to keep the more fragile items safe.

Bundling things into the same packaging to reduce waste.

When he'd seen Belle do that yesterday, it seemed like second nature for her to eyeball everything, but he wasn't there yet. It was easy for him to choose packages for the flat items like the stickers, notepads, and notebooks, but when orders contained the cups, mugs, bowls, or sweatshirts, it took him ten minutes to pack the items, while Belle could do three orders in the same amount of time.

Eventually, she just put him to work with inventorying the rest of the bundle items so she could focus on order packing. He went over to his station and looked at his headphones hanging off his bag. He looked over at Belle, who was furiously typing on her computer, and asked, "Do you mind if I wear my headphones?"

She turned to him and shrugged. "No, go ahead." She looked back at her screen. "Usually I have music on but I didn't want to distract you yesterday," she said as she clicked around her desktop before turning back to him with her hand out. "Oh, by the way, let me put my number in your phone."

His eyebrows scrunched as he slowly dug the device out of his pocket. "Why?"

"So I can text you if I need you for something instead of trying to yell at you over your music?"

He hadn't thought of that, but realistically, he should have her number anyway since she was his boss, so he just unlocked it. "Efficient."

"Work smarter, not harder," she said with a smile. Zach chuckled as he handed over his phone with a page for a new contact already open.

She quickly typed in her number and texted it from his phone before handing it back. "Now, if you'll excuse me. I have to politely tell this company off after they assured me that they could do this job right." She turned back to her screen where he could see an email box open.

He decided to leave her to it and get back to work.

Once Zach slipped on his headphones, he completely zoned out from everything around him.

His hands were constantly moving between grabbing and putting items in their containers and ticking off inventory counts. He was so focused that he almost didn't notice when his phone buzzed on the table next to him. He only glanced at the screen when it lit up with a notification of a text.

Belle

Lunch Break!

Zach

Still working on counting. I don't have time for a break.

He almost put it down to get back to work, but Belle's response was swift.

Belle

You'll make the time before I send Appa up there.

Zach groaned as he took off his headphones and made his way down the stairs. When he got to the front room, Belle was sitting on the couch in the living area, her feet propped on the coffee table and a book lying on her lap as she munched on some celery. Appa had taken refuge underneath her legs and momentarily lifted his head at the noise of Zach coming in, but he just laid back down for once and fell asleep.

"That's playing dirty and you know it," Zach snipped as he went over to the fridge and pulled out his brand new generic black lunch bag.

"Got you down here, didn't it?" she said with a shrug, not taking her eyes off her book as she turned the page, completely entranced by the words before her.

Zach could relate to the feeling of not wanting to be disturbed while reading, so he just plopped himself down at her small circular dining room table for two. He opened up the bag and took out the sandwich Mimi made him, along with his daily orange and a bag of Turtle Chips. One of the good things about being back in town was that he had access to Joon's snack stash again.

Joon had a closet in his apartment with Sunny above the cafe dedicated to housing a large variety of snacks to satisfy everyone's cravings. Zach had taken up Joon's offer to try them once and instantly got hooked, so Joon was always willing to give him a few bags.

After finishing his sandwich and chips, he started to peel his orange when he took a moment to look at Belle's bookshelf. It took up the wall with a bay window in the middle of it, opposite the kitchen. The bookshelves wrapped around the window, including above and below it. Belle had also put a cushion on the window ledge along with a couple of pillows, making it a cozy little reading nook.

When he glanced at some of the titles of books on the shelves, he was happy to see that a few of his favorites were on the shelves.

The *Grishaverse* Books.

Eliza and Her Monsters.

The *Sea Guardians* Series.

Sure, dozens of romance books took up most of the shelves, but even though they weren't his preferred genre, he could understand the love for them.

A book with a guaranteed happy ending was always welcome.

Especially when life had enough sad endings anyway.

"I like how you have your library set up," he commented as he finished peeling his orange.

Belle looked up at him and smiled. "Thanks."

He smiled back. "Mine is just a shelf that I found at the town farmer's market a couple of years ago," he said as he pulled off a piece of orange and threw it in his mouth.

Belle straightened up in her seat. "A farmer's market? This town has a farmer's market?"

Zach nodded as he swallowed. "Oh yeah. It's near town hall on Wednesdays throughout the summer going into the fall a bit. Kit convinced me and Joon to go with her one year while her aunt went shopping for the thrift store, and we ended up being her pack mules to bring back this huge record player that she found." Belle laughed at that, of course, but he continued. "But they have everything there: produce, baked goods, homemade soap, old clothes. It's pretty nice actually, you should check it out."

Belle nodded before grabbing a highlighter in her hands and twirling it around. "So, Kit and Joon are your best friends?"

He nodded again. "Ever since elementary school. It's always been the three of us for pretty much everything: sleepovers, movie nights, birthdays. Growing up, we didn't have big parties 'cause all we needed to do was invite each other, and everything was fine."

Besides Joon's sisters and Amaya tagging along sometimes, it was mostly them being able to do their own thing. Because they were such a small group, they usually got to do bigger things for each other's birthdays; for Zach's tenth birthday, they went to a two-day-long fair down in D.C. modeled after the *Sea Guardians* books, and they all got to meet the author. For Joon's thirteenth birthday, they went to an expensive Korean barbecue restaurant and got to go wild with the menu as Oma helped them order a variety of food to eat. For Kit's sweet sixteen, they ended up taking a week-long trip to the beach and exploring the coastline and fairgrounds nearby.

"They sound like really good friends," Belle said.

Zach nodded. They'd had many adventures together, and Zach hadn't believed that he could find friends that he would ever be closer to. Beau came very close and Mateo, by extension, but Kit and Joon would always hold a special place in his heart.

"They're the best friends a person could ever have," he said fondly.

Belle smiled before looking down at her current activity, and Zach's eyes widened once he noticed that she was highlighting a book that she had bought from Book Haven the other day. "What are you..." Zach quickly clamped his mouth shut as she looked up, eyebrows already raised for a fight.

She glanced between him and the book. "Let me guess, you're not a fan of annotating books?"

He sucked his teeth, eyebrows furrowed. "As a librarian's son, I just can't get behind that."

She smirked at him as she deliberately ran her highlighter slowly over a passage, making him wince. "Well, one, it's my book so I can do what I want with it. And, two, I'm not asking you to get behind it, so why don't we just agree to disagree?" she said, head on her hands with a saccharine grin on her face.

"Fine," he grumbled.

It was then that Appa woke up from his nap, and noticed his current obsession sitting in front of him. Appa immediately trotted over and put his head on Zach's lap. Zach flinched, but eventually patted the dog's head to appease his obvious need for touch.

Belle giggled as Appa sat down next to Zach's feet. "Do you really just not like dogs?"

"I'm not particularly fond of them," he said, staring back down at the mutt gazing up at him.

"Why not?"

"Because they're messy, they shed, and they have no sense of personal space," he said, pointing down to Appa rubbing against his leg once more before going back to sit next to Belle.

Belle sucked her teeth as she grabbed a new highlighter to work with. "You're worse than the Grinch."

"How?"

"He liked dogs."

Zach took a deep breath as he glared at the woman, which made her giggle. Zach ignored the way his heart skipped as he picked up his trash and threw it into her waste bin, except for the orange peel that he would drop off at the Akiyama's compost pile later. "Can I please go back to work now?"

She shrugged as she highlighted another passage. "I won't stop you, but first can you bring all those sticker boxes upstairs?"

"Sure," he said as he moved towards the stairs, only for Belle to call out to him again.

"And then you can bring up the new order of cups," she said with a smirk. "And the sweatshirts."

He turned around slowly. "Is that it?"

She looked up thoughtfully as she scratched Appa's head. "Yes," she chirped. "For now."

He glared at her. "You're enjoying this, aren't you?"

She held up her fingers with a minuscule amount of space between them. "Just a little bit."

"Oh of course," he teased. "Only a little bit." He nodded condescendingly as he walked over to her boxes of unmade products.

She giggled again, and he ignored another heart skip.

lovebelle 6h

Hey Lovelies!

Thank you all for the
feedback on the Barry
Sticker Snafu!

I have officially decided to offer
the bundle with the sticker
added on as an oopsie freebie.

Everybody who buys one
though will get a coupon code
for their next order.

If you put it in, I'll add one of
the newly printed Barry stickers
once I have them.

The shop restocks this
Friday so be ready!

Love, Belle

Chapter 8

Zach used to enjoy the days when he would go to work with his dad because he got to spend his day reading.

When he was younger, he believed that if he read enough, he would gain telekinetic powers like Matilda Wormwood, but even when that didn't happen, he enjoyed reading all the same. He knew that one day he wanted to be one of the people who wrote books like the ones he'd devoured during his childhood.

But the thing about being an aspiring author is that they have to articulate the fully-fledged stories in their head to others, and that was where Zach struggled. An English degree had given him great editing prowess, but it didn't help him write out his thoughts any better. At least not at this moment in time. He had spent over an hour after he got home from Belle's struggling to write the feelings that Ty was dealing with while meeting the villain face-to-face for the first time. He opted to skip that and focus on the dialogue of the scene, and that was when he finally started making progress.

He decided to work in the living room before his siblings got home from school. Amaya had insisted on walking Corey home from the elementary school at the edge of their neighborhood as a treat for their last day of school before summer break. Zach let them so he could enjoy the last bit of quiet in the house.

With a nearly-empty cup of coffee in hand and his pen in the other, he felt perfectly calm. It almost made him want to spend more time at home.

Almost.

"Freedom!" Amaya shouted as she ran through the front door, making Zach scratch his pen over the page.

"Freedom!" Corey yelled as ran behind her up to their rooms.

"And that's the end of that," Zach mumbled as he put down the pen to assess the damaged paper.

Corey ran back down the stairs with a stuffed school folder in his hands. "Zach, look. Look at all my drawings," Corey said as he put the folder down over Zach's notebook.

Zach chuckled as he opened it. The first drawing inside was the common family portrait with all their family. Corey had drawn himself, Amaya, their father, and Mimi standing in front of the house. Gigi stood off to the side. Zach frowned when he saw a tiny figure that looked like him.

"Why did you draw me so small, bud?" he asked.

"Because you were away at college," Corey explained as he pulled out another drawing. "But you're back now, so I drew this one today." He pulled out a drawing of himself, Amaya, and Zach in his room, with what looked like cards in their hands. It must have been a depiction of last night when Zach and Amaya taught Corey how to play Go Fish. He smiled, quickly flipped through the rest, and saw flashes of dogs, rainbows, and trucks.

"These are really good, bud."

Corey's smile got even wider if that was possible. "And look," he said, grabbing his older brother's hand and dragging him over to the front door. "Mrs. Jones gave us all these kites."

Zach looked over the red kite and grinned at Corey. "Very cool." He handed Corey the folder. "Now, go put this folder in your room so Dad can look through it later."

Corey ran off again without another thought. Zach turned back to his seat to see that Amaya was standing there now, holding his notebook in her hands.

His eyes widened. "Maya, put that down."

She flicked him away with her hand, "Shush, I'm reading my favorite part." She said in a teasing tone, which made Zach all the madder.

"Amaya!"

Zach was not proud to admit that he started to chase his little sister around the room, like when she took his toys when they were kids, but he really didn't give a fuck at this point. His little sister was annoying as shit.

"'Why would you waste this power? You have everything in your hands, and you squander it for mere praise and adoration,'" she read aloud in a raspy voice as she ran around the couch and the coffee table.

"Amaya Evelyn Roberts!"

"'You could be great. Dare I say, immortal, if you used it correctly...'"

Zach snatched the book out of her hand before noticing the thoughtful look on her face. "That's actually pretty good."

"Don't patronize me. I'm not in the mood."

"No seriously, I'm impressed. And a little bit scared. These aren't your plans for world domination, are they?"

"I'll never tell," he smirked as he plopped down on the couch, Amaya flopping down next to him.

"Well, if they are, please cancel them. The last thing we need is bookworms taking over the world."

Zach scoffed a laugh. "That is incorrect. If bookworms took over the world, it would be a much better place: areas to lie down everywhere, free education, and great quality books provided for all, not to mention, mandatory breaks for reading that could be used for anything you wanted, honestly."

Amaya stayed quiet for a moment, letting the ideas wash over her before saying, "I don't... hate that."

"See?"

They sat for a moment, the ticking of the hallway clock filling the room with a comfortable silence, as Amaya leaned her head on Zach's shoulder.

"So, how's the embroidery going?" he asked.

"Good. I should have it ready for you to send by next week."

"Cool," he said right before Corey came racing back down the stairs and beelined over to his older siblings, grabbing their hands in his tiny ones.

"Can we go to the park, so I can fly my kite?" he asked in a chirpy tone.

Amaya lifted her head, and the two older siblings looked at each other with skeptical eyes; they both knew what their father would say if he were there. He never liked them going out without him or one of their grandmothers present. Corey really didn't understand that yet, and it made Zach miss the days when he was that innocent too.

Zach sighed as he got off the couch and bent down to his brother's level. "Not today, bud."

The bottom of Corey's lip stuck out in a pout. "Why not?"

"Well, it's getting late and we need to make dinner..."

"It's only three. We still have plenty of time before we have dinner to play."

Zach glanced over at the clock, and it was indeed only five minutes after 3. He looked over at Amaya. She shrugged. He was the oldest—it was up to him—but being the oldest sibling in the Roberts' house didn't mean much when their father was home.

But he wasn't home at the moment.

He looked at Corey with a small smile on his face. "I guess we could go for a while."

The way that Corey's face lit up made any lecture Zach would get later worth it. "Yay!" Corey ran to the front door, shoved on his shoes, grabbed his kite, and was out the door like a flash of lightning.

"I'll get him," Amaya said while shooting up out of her seat. "You get some snacks. We'll meet you in the car."

Zach nodded and quickly went up to his room to put his notebook away before coming back down with his messenger bag. Luckily their grandmother liked to have a lot of prepped snacks in the house to encourage the children—and their father—to eat healthier, so Zach took some of the containers and shoved them in a tote from the closet.

He took a step towards the door but paused. He backtracked into the kitchen and grabbed a notepad and pen off the counter.

Amaya and I took Corey to go play in the park. We'll be back before sundown.

~ Zach

Zach quickly stuck it to the fridge with a magnet before taking a picture, texting it to his father, and finally heading out the door.

When they arrived at the park, they could see that many people were deciding to celebrate the last day of school the same way. Parents were chatting amongst themselves as they sat on the hardware benches around the playground. Children were running around the park with large bubble wands and baseball bats, ready to enjoy all that summer had to offer. Zach could hear Corey bouncing up and down in his car seat, waiting in anticipation to join them.

Zach parked the car and turned back to Corey with a serious look on his face. "Now what are the rules, bud?"

"Always stay where one of you can see me, and be on my best behavior."

Zach nodded. "Good job. Let's go."

"Yay!" Corey started to make quick work of his seatbelt, which prompted Zach and Amaya to get out of their seats so they could move around back and get Corey and the rest of the things they brought. As soon as Corey's feet touched the ground, he grabbed his kite from Amaya and ran straight towards the middle of the field, Zach and Amaya chasing after him. He had already unspooled half of the kite string by the time they caught up with him, looking up at them with anticipation in his eyes.

The next ten minutes were spent teaching Corey how to run with his new kite, and what to do once he got it in the air. It took them a couple of attempts, but eventually, the red kite was soaring.

"I did it! I did it!" Corey cheered as he held on to his toy.

Zach rubbed his little brother's head. "Yeah, you did, bud." He looked over at Amaya, and they shared a smile at the sight of their sibling's pure joy. They knew this would not be the only time they came kite flying that summer.

"Appa! Yip Yip!"

Zach turned from where he heard the call to see Belle sitting on a bench near a fountain a few feet away, her iPad in one hand and a ball that she threw away for Appa to chase in the other. She had changed out of the t-shirt and shorts that Zach had seen her in earlier and into a light blue floral dress and cardigan. He must have missed her when they came in, as all their attention was on Corey. After throwing the ball, she went back to doodling on her iPad.

Even though he had just spent the day preparing for the restock with her, it couldn't hurt to say hi.

Zach leaned closer to Amaya. "Watch Corey for a minute, okay?"

"Sure," she said before following the flight path of the kite further into the park.

Zach slowly approached Belle and noticed that she had a camera pointed toward her that she manipulated a bit before drawing a bit more.

He unconsciously felt himself adjusting the collar of his button-down shirt, and smoothing out nonexistent wrinkles. "Hey," Zach greeted once he was close enough to Belle, making her look up in shock.

"Hi," she said as she pressed a button on her camera and folded in the video screen. "What are you doing here?"

"Teaching my little brother to fly a kite. You?"

"Tossing around a ball with Appa to get out some of his energy. He's been getting a bit restless." Appa came back with a ball that he dropped in front of Belle and sat down with his tail wagging wildly behind him. Belle smiled before putting down her iPad. "Ready boy? Appa! Yip Yip!" She yelled before throwing the ball as far as she could across the park. Appa immediately bolted after it, giving Belle a chance to glance down and add another line to her drawing.

Zach sat down on the bench, their legs nearly touching, and watched her work. He had seen her finished products every day throughout this past week, but to see her actually making the designs themselves was something else entirely different. She added to her work line by line until it came together as a scene of the mascots Terry, Barry, and Carry coming together for a tea party in the middle of a golden forest.

Zach wasn't someone who gravitated towards cuddly content, but he could appreciate how comforting it must be to Belle's audience. One day, when he'd gone to drop off some packages at the post office, Belle had also asked him to pick up some things from her P.O. Box. It turned out to be filled with a bunch of fan mail that Belle shared with him when he returned. All of them said that they appreciated her making a brand that made people feel welcome.

It was one of the things that he admired about Belle.

He was about to ask her about what inspired her to make the design when he heard someone coming up to them.

He looked and saw Amaya holding Corey's hand, tears running down his face.

Zach frowned. "What happened?" he asked.

Corey pointed to Amaya's hand. "My kite."

Amaya handed it over, and Zach winced at the damage. The fabric was torn through the middle, with the ribbons attached to the end in tatters.

Corey sniffled. "It got stuck in a tree and I tried to pull it down and it got ripped."

Zach put it down next to his feet. "Hey, it's okay, bud."

Corey shook his head. "I'm bad."

Zach knelt to his level and quickly wiped the tears from his face. "You are not bad, it was just an accident. A mistake."

"Mistakes are bad. I'm bad." Corey said as more tears rolled down his face.

Zach quickly wiped them away. "It's not bad to make mistakes, bud. It means you're growing up 'cause you're gonna learn something from this, right? No kite flying near trees anymore."

Corey nodded as Amaya bent down and used her sleeve to wipe away the last of his tears. "And we can ask Mimi for some of her fabric scraps so we can fix the tear. It'll be good as new, and we can fly it again, okay?"

"'Kay." It was then that Corey noticed it wasn't just the three of them, and cowered behind Zach at the sight of Belle.

Zach chuckled. He had forgotten that Corey was usually shy around new people before he got to know them. Luckily, Belle didn't seem to mind. She just smiled at them as Zach stood up and brought Corey forward. "Don't worry. This is my friend, Belle. Belle, these are my siblings, Corey and Amaya."

"Hi," she said with a wave as Appa trotted back over to her and dropped his toy at her feet. "This is Appa. Do you want to say hi?"

Corey looked at Appa with wide eyes as his grip on Zach's pants tightened. Corey loved dogs. All Zach ever saw him watching on his tablet was *Paw Patrol*, *Bluey*, and *Clifford the*

Big Red Dog, but he'd never really met one before.

Unless he met one while Zach was on campus which was highly unlikely because their father was very anti-pet. Not even a goldfish made it into their home when he was growing up. But he knew that Corey had always wanted a dog, and even though there was one in front of him ready to meet, he still clung to Zach, as if he would be in trouble for acting on his puppy fever.

When his little brother glanced up at him, Zach gave him an encouraging smile and pushed him forward. Corey let go and slowly inched forward, holding out his hand for Appa to sniff. The shepherd licked it, making Corey giggle. He took another step closer and tentatively petted Appa's head. The Australian shepherd snuggled into it.

Belle picked up the ball before looking back at the little guy. "You know, I think Appa would really like to run around some more. Do you want to play with him?"

Corey jumped up and down with the biggest grin on his face. After getting the yes from Zach, he took the ball and started running around the field in front of him while Appa chased him. Hearing him laugh just made Zach feel that much lighter than he had before.

Amaya saw one of her friends in the distance and went to talk to her, while Zach sat back down on the bench to watch Corey and Appa play. "He's going to be insufferable about getting a dog once we get home," he remarked. "He's always wanted one."

Belle laughed. "Oh, I can relate. I remember the day when I finally got Appa, I couldn't stop staring at him because it was so hard to believe that he was actually mine. One of my childhood dreams fulfilled."

Zach chuckled as he settled back against the bench. "I've been meaning to ask you something."

"What?"

"Why did you name him Appa?"

She scoffed. "Because I love the character."

"From what?"

Her brow quirked up. "*Avatar: The Last Airbender*."

He shrugged. "Never seen it."

She turned to him with wide eyes. "You've never seen *Avatar: The Last Airbender*?"

"I was more of a book kid than a TV kid. The only time I watched TV was when I went over to Kit's house."

Before Belle could share her displeasure more, his phone buzzed. When he took it out, he did his best not to groan when he saw his father's name on the screen.

"Hey, Dad," he greeted as he shifted on the bench.

"Where are you?" Jedidiah asked in a gruff tone.

"At the park with Corey and Amaya, we—"

"Without my permission?"

"I sent you a text. We just wanted to hang out at the park, so they could celebrate the last day of school. That's it."

The silence over the phone was so loud that it made Zach's heartbeat pound hard enough to feel against his ear before his father decided to talk again. "We'll talk about this later. I want y'all back home now."

"But we—"

"Now!"

Zach bit his lip so hard that he drew blood. He quickly licked it off. "Yes, sir."

His father hung up without another word, and Zach resisted the urge to throw his phone across the field. Instead, he clutched it tight, then put it back in his pocket. He turned and was taken aback when he saw the worried look on Belle's face.

Zach just coughed and stood up. "We gotta go." He said softly, glancing at Corey. The smile across his brother's face made him relax a bit before he turned back to Belle. "Thank you for this. He'll be talking about this for a while."

She smiled again, and he felt himself relax just a bit more. "I hope so. If you ever want to set up a playdate for him just let me know."

"I will." He turned and yelled, "Corey! Amaya! Time to go!"

Corey ran back over with Appa's ball in hand. "But we just got here."

"Dad says we have to go home," he said as Amaya came back over, making her roll her eyes.

"Seriously?" she said.

"Yup." Amaya rolled her eyes again before saying bye to Belle and stomping over to the car. "Say goodbye to Belle and Appa, bud," Zach said as he picked up Corey's kite.

"Bye, Appa," Corey pouted before depositing the dog toy back in Belle's hand and hugging her. "Thank you for letting me play with your dog, Miss Belle."

"You're very welcome." She looked up at Zach and smiled. "See you later."

"Bye." Zach grabbed Corey's hand and brought him back to the car, where Amaya was waiting for them with a smirk on her face. Once he had Corey buckled in, he looked back and saw that Amaya was still looking at him over the top of the Mustang.

"What?" he finally asked.

"Belle's pretty. She your girlfriend?" she asked in a sickly sweet tone.

He quickly shook his head. "No, she's my boss," he sighed as he opened his door. "Leave it alone, Amaya, so we can prepare to get yelled at on the way home."

Amaya groaned and face-planted against the roof. She looked back up at him with her chin still on the car. "Is it too late to try and live by your bookish rules?"

He pursed his lips. "I'm afraid that's not gonna happen anytime soon, Maya," he said, hating how much had to admit it, but it was the truth.

As long as he stayed in Lillet, he couldn't live by his own rules.

So when he got home and made it past his father's cold shoulder, he filled out another New York-based job application.

Requirements for Zach's Future NYC Apartment

1. Bathroom in the Apartment

2. Nearby Laundromat and Grocery Store

3. Relatively Easy Commuting Distance from Job

4. Enough Space to put up at least Two Bookshelves

Chapter 9

In a perfect world, Zach would be able to sit in Book Haven all day, and just read to his heart's content, without worrying about having to interact with any other human being. Ever.

But today was one of the few days when people actually knew that The Book Haven existed, so customers had been coming through the door all day like it was a merry-go-round. Zach had been relegated to cashier duty, while Des met with the delivery man at the back of the store, and Jaime helped out some people wandering around. Zach didn't mind though; this was the best position for him to be able to write down some of his story ideas in his notebook...when he wasn't attending to customers that is.

Des didn't care what his employees did when people weren't around, as long as they got the job done, so when Zach heard the bell ring for someone coming inside, he put his pen down and closed his notebook.

"Hey, Zach." He looked up and grinned.

"Hey, Gem," he greeted.

Gemini Dixon was one of the few people that his trio of friends would talk to a lot. She wasn't too close of a friend to them, but they did enjoy having her around. When she first moved to Lillet during middle school, she made it a point to give Sweet Tart-flavored candy canes to people she considered friends the day before they left for winter break. When Baxter tried to ask for one, she made a big deal of telling him that he was not her friend. Zach, Kit, and Joon accepted theirs with smiles, as well as all the party invites she sent them over the years because that girl knew how to throw a party.

"Heard you were back in town," she said as she stood in front of the counter. Her smile slipped a bit when she said, "I haven't really seen you since..."

"Your graduation party. Yeah." Zach didn't see much of anybody in their class after that party besides Kit and Joon, who were either over at his house or dragging him out of it at least twice a week that summer.

"It's nice to see you."

"You too." They both stood there awkwardly for a moment before Zach finally said, "did you need help finding something?"

"Um, yeah. There's this new romance book—"

"*Infinite Ways to Love* by Sherry Marshall?"

Gem laughed, taken aback. "Yeah. You've read it?"

"Try devoured it. It's not usually my type of book, but it came highly recommended, and it did not disappoint. I just put a few copies on the Love in Lillet shelf," he said, pointing to the wall of romance books. "We've got some of her other books there if you're interested."

She smiled. "Oh, thanks." She popped over to the shelves and soon found the book she was looking for. But she stood there a bit longer, browsing through the author's other titles before picking up two more and coming back to the counter. After Zach checked them out for her, she put them in her oversized handbag but didn't leave immediately. "Um, Zach...about what happened at the party..."

"Don't sweat it," he said quickly. "It wasn't your fault. I've moved on," he shrugged, straightening up the counter.

"Okay, I just—"

"Gem, I promise it's fine," he insisted, making her nod reluctantly. "I hope you enjoy your book."

"Thanks, Zach."

"No problem. See you, Gem."

She smiled at him, her long braids whipping behind her as she went to leave before Kit came into the store.

Gem smiled at her. "Hey Kit, you going to the town hall meeting tomorrow night?"

"Can't miss it," Kit shrugged as she adjusted the beret on her head.

"Thank God. I'll have someone to talk to. See you then."

"See ya," Kit said cheerfully before turning her gaze to Zach. "Hello!" she greeted as she skipped up to the counter.

He raised a brow. "Aren't you supposed to be organizing food trucks for the Fourth of July?"

"Oh, so you do read the texts? You just don't answer them."

"I didn't think it needed a response. Now, what do you want?"

She put her hand on her hip, looking him up and down. "Is that any way to speak to a lady?"

"I'm not talking to a lady, I'm talking to you." As far as Zach was concerned, Kit was in the same tier as Amaya when it came to how he would treat her.

"Rude," she said with an eye roll before straightening up. "So, you read the text about the food trucks, but not about the books? That sounds very much unlike you."

Zach's eyes widened. "You sent me a text about books?" How could he have missed that?

"Yes. I asked if you could find me some books about starting a podcast so I could pick them up during lunchtime today."

"Podcasts? You wanna start a podcast?"

"I don't know, maybe." She shrugged. "I've been watching these documentaries on YouTube about the old radio shows with the cheesy sound effects, and I got curious about bringing it into a modern setting. You know I love everything 1940s. The clothes and furniture I mean, definitely wouldn't want to live during that time because you know..." She gave him the look and he nodded. "So I was thinking about gushing about romance movies with the masses 'cause I need someone to rant to that isn't you or Joon. I'm thinking of old-timey sounds and dramatic readings of stuff. I just had this idea last night, so I'm not sure about all of this, but it's a start."

Zach smiled. This was usually Kit's process of all the big things she did. She got an idea in the middle of the night and, by the end of the week, she would bring it halfway to fruition. "Why don't you just do some research online?"

"Because I want to support local businesses, duh?"

Zach rolled his eyes as he started to move from behind the counter. Luckily, the other people that Jaime had been working with left, so Zach asked them to switch for a moment while he took Kit over to the tech section. Surprisingly, they did have a few books on the history of radio, so he left Kit there to rummage through them as he went back to the front, just in time to see Belle walking through the door, her arms fully covered in the straps of tote bags filled to the brim with a rainbow of plush yarn.

He chuckled as she walked up to him. "Do you think you bought enough?"

She looked down at her bags before looking up at him. "Honestly, probably not."

He snorted. "Where did you even get that?"

"That store, Sew Crafty, I found out that they were having a sale on yarn and I had to stock up."

"And then you came here to find a book on how to do some special sort of crochet pattern?"

She nodded cheerfully. "You know me so well."

He chuckled. "You need help?"

"I know the way," she said brushing past him, letting him get a whiff of her intoxicating vanilla perfume. His head trailed a bit after her before he shook it off and walked back over to the counter where Jaime was already doing transactions, so he took over placing new stock on the Juneteenth table display. One of the books happened to be *River Misfortune*, a book he had read a couple of months ago and loved. It was his goal to make as many people read it as possible, so he put it front and center.

Apparently, he spent too much time trying to make it stand out because he heard giggling behind him as he adjusted its position for a third time.

"You like that book?" Belle said as she came over to stand beside him.

"A little."

She grinned and came over to pluck it out of his hands. "What's it about?"

Zach smiled as he went on a full ramble about the main characters leaving their riverside village to go on a quest to learn about their magic abilities over water and defeat a warlord intent on taking over their land. The whole story had been a rollercoaster ride of emotions, and he believed everyone should experience that ride at least once.

It was only when he realized that Belle was just staring at him and not nodding along that he realized he had been talking for a long time. "Sorry," he coughed as he turned back to the table, feeling the heat rush up his face.

"Don't be. It sounds good, but if you like this book so much, I don't understand how you've never watched *Avatar*. It's a pretty similar story."

"It is?"

"Yeah. The four nations live together in harmony until the Fire Nation attacks and the Avatar has to master all four elements in order to defeat the Fire Lord. It sounds right up your alley."

"Huh?" he said thoughtfully, looking between the book and her. "Well, I guess I could give it a try, but I don't know where to watch it."

Belle's eyes widened as she started bouncing up on her toes. "I have the whole series on DVD. We could watch them together."

"You don't have to—" he started to say but she didn't listen.

"In fact, we could have a watch party and I could make some treats for each season as we watch. Book One is water so I could make some Water Tribe-themed food." She pulled out her phone and started tapping on the screen. "You don't have any food allergies, do you?"

"No."

"Great! We're gonna be pretty busy with packing in the early part of the week with the restock, so how about Thursday?"

"Um...sure. I guess."

"Great! I need to plan out menus," she squealed as she shoved her phone into her bag and bounced up and down on her toes. "This is going to be so much fun! See you later."

With that, Belle ran out of the shop. It would be later in the day that Zach realized that this was the first time since he'd known her that Belle had left the bookstore without buying a single book.

He slowly made his way back to the counter and felt a nervousness bubble in his stomach when he saw Kit standing there, obviously waiting for him to take over from Jaime.

He relieved Jaime and glared at the smirk on Kit's face. "You were eavesdropping, weren't you?"

She nodded frantically before frowning. "First of all, how have I never forced you to watch *Avatar: The Last Airbender*? It's only one of the best shows in cinematic history. Second,"— she pointed between him and the door—"what was that?"

"What was what?"

"You and Belle."

Zach's eyes widened. "What? No, Katrina. I've already told you that this is not a rom-com, so take off those rose-colored glasses right now!"

"Ugh," she scoffed with an eye roll. "Fine, Zachary. On one condition though."

"What is it?"

"The farmer's market starts up again next week, and you have to go with me and Joon," she said, putting her pile of books on the counter.

Zach shrugged as he started to scan them. "I don't know. I don't want to intrude."

"On what?"

"You know, you and Joon," he said, pointedly looking at her.

Kit's jaw dropped before she started laughing. "What! We are not nor will we ever be a couple! That's like dating my brother. Ew! What would even give you that idea?"

Zach shook his head as he took her reusable bag from her. "Come on, you two have always been closer. I'm just a third wheel."

She frowned. "Since when have you felt like that?"

"I don't know, always." He shrugged as he packed her bag.

When they'd initially met in elementary school, things were simple. All of them had sat in the corner of the playground during recess after the other kids made fun of them for being smart when they won the first three spots in their fourth-grade spelling bee. While everyone else played, they quizzed each other on words the other kids missed. They stuck together like glue after that. As they got older though, their parents weren't always eager to spend the day chauffeuring them between hous-es. Even when they were old enough to drive, none of them had cars. Kit and Joon lived one street away from each other, and not that far from the town square. It was easy for them to hang out on a whim, but when they wanted to include Zach, it had to be planned out.

When it came down to it, Kit and Joon were more similar than Zach was to either of them.

They were both Asian (while he was also a minority it wasn't the same).

They were both pretty close with their parents (he definitely couldn't relate to that).

Not to mention, they both went to college close to home (he didn't consider any college within a 20-mile radius of Lillet).

Zach had seen multiple posts of theirs on Instagram of them linking up on the weekends to hang out, and it was hard not to feel left out. He'd felt the same when he saw pictures of Beau and Mateo moving into their new apartment in New York. He'd once heard that there is always a duo in a trio, and when it came to Kit, Joon, and Zach, it felt more like Kit and Joon, sometimes with Zach. But it was his own fault that he chose to go to school away from them and that he didn't stay in touch more.

Kit's brow was quirked up when she leaned into his eyeline, getting his attention again. "You know, some people do actually want you around. Even if it's only to stop us from making impulse purchases."

He scoffed with a small smile. "Like I could ever do that."

"Then that's how you know that we actually want you around."

He rolled his eyes but smiled more regardless. Perhaps it was time for him to start reintegrating himself into the trio again. "Fine. But seriously, you and Joon..."

"Are just friends. I might love a friends-to-lovers arc in my movies, but I just enjoy having my boys who have had my back since day one," she said as Zach pushed her books across the counter.

Zach smiled at that. They might not be the perfect trio, but Zach had to admit that he was happy that they'd all decided to stick together that day.

"Alright," Zach nodded. "I just want you to remember these moments of teasing, because I will be just as vicious when your love story finally starts to evolve."

A blush crept up Kit's cheeks. "I doubt that's in my future anytime soon." She smirked. "but I'm happy you're admitting that there is something there between you and Belle." She snatched her bag from the table. "Bye!" She yelled as she ran out the door before Zach could respond.

He sat back in his seat with a groan. He couldn't believe he'd fallen into her trap, but honestly, he had nothing to worry about. He and Belle got along, they liked a lot of the same things, but they were probably going to be like Kit and Joon: friends, but not a couple.

There was nothing that could possibly change that.

Liked by **beaupeep** and **41 others**

zachslibrary Book Review for "River Misfortune" by Dorian Moses

To everyone who kept yelling at me to read this book, thank you. It's hard to find a standalone fantasy book that hits hard and this one does that and more. This book has a great mix of epic magic, found family, and character growth. Watching Lotus and Hildy evolve from orphaned fishers to powerful warriors was a fucking delight. Moses does an great job of creating such an immersive world and telling an inspiring story of two people finding their purpose in life.

If you like badass female characters, unique natural magic systems, and underdog stories, then I highly recommend this book!

[Image ID: A Book with the title "River Misfortune" written in gold calligraphy, and blue wavy lines that mimic water that goes from the top to the bottom of the book in the background sits on a dark hardwood surface]

Chapter 10

When Zach went back to work at Belle's the next Monday, she couldn't stop smiling. He could see her eyes light up every-time she started thinking about all the plans she had for their *Avatar* watch party. Every once and a while when they worked, she would do random things that he could only assume were related to her ultimate scheme.

On Monday, she asked if he knew how to use chopsticks (his best friends were Japanese and Korean; of course, he knew how to fucking use chopsticks so they wouldn't laugh at him while he struggled to pick up a piece of chicken and resorted to stabbing it).

On Tuesday, she inquired about whether he preferred cup-cakes or cookies (he was more of a cupcake guy).

On Wednesday, she turned on a lo-fi playlist video on her tablet with a graphic of a buffalo-looking thing floating in the air, and smiled the whole day (he didn't put on his headphones so he wouldn't appear anti-whatever it was, but he didn't mind the music in the end).

By Thursday, he could feel her practically vibrating with excitement throughout the day as they finished packing up the last of the major restock orders. When they brought down the packages at the end of the day, Zach saw some pots simmering on the stove in the kitchen, but she wouldn't let him get close enough to see what it was. She practically shoved him out the door with instructions to pick up some treats she'd asked Joon to make after he went to the post office.

He came back to the cottage an hour later with blue and white cupcakes, but strict instructions to stay in the car until she permitted him to come back in. He felt a bit apprehensive about what could be waiting for him behind the door, so he took the time to scroll through Instagram, gathering new book recommendations and polishing off the small coffee he picked up while he was at the cafe to keep his mind off of it.

His phone dinged with another text message notification, which he went to swipe away when he read a bit of what was there.

Amaya

Me and Corey have been kidnapped.

Zach immediately opened his messages to read the rest.

Amaya

Me and Corey have been kidnapped.

By Gigi.

For a Sleepover.

He chuckled as he texted her back.

> **Zach**
>
> What did Dad think of that?

Amaya

> Oh, he wasn't happy.
>
> But Gigi didn't let him get in a word edge-wise.
>
> Corey is excited to spend the night watching the game show network.

Zach smiled at the memories of his own sleepovers with Gigi where he did the same thing. It was at Gigi's house where he'd truly started to understand his love for words and facts while playing along with Wheel of Fortune and Jeopardy!. Gigi had also introduced him to the world of crosswords, which had become one of his favorite activities to do when he got stressed.

> **Zach**
>
> Course he is. I'm gonna be at Belle's so save me some sweet potatoes.

Amaya

> Sure. Have fun with your girlfriend.

Zach

She's not my girlfriend!

After sending the last text, he was about to go back to scrolling when a knock on his window almost made him jump out of his seat. He turned to see Belle standing outside his driver-side door with the goofiest smile on her face, bouncing up and down like a maniac and frantically pointing at the front door before running back inside. He scoffed a laugh as he grabbed the cupcakes.

When Zach walked back in, the living room had been completely transformed.

The couch was now covered in a woven blanket made of blue and white yarn. Two black and white koi fish candles occupied the coffee table on either side of a full moon-shaped serving dish. The wall behind the couch and her bookshelves were lit up by fairy lights that emitted a golden hue, making the space all the warmer.

Belle made grabby hands at the takeout container in his hands and he slowly gave it over as he took a look over to the kitchen. Two ceramic bowls filled with soup had steam rising from the top and the smell of green onions and chicken broth filled the air.

He looked back at Belle, who was now transferring the cup-cakes onto the moon serving dish. She had changed out of the flowy two-piece that she had worn earlier into a pair of leggings and a light blue hoodie that sported the words "Water Tribe" and a wavy symbol on it. She turned around with a wide grin on her face.

He'd thought that Kit was extra when it came to her themed movie nights, but this put hers to shame.

"Was this really necessary?" he asked as he toed off his shoes.

She raised a brow at him. "It's called ambiance," she quipped as she sauntered over to the kitchenette. "And if we are going to indoctrinate you into the fandom, we need to do it right. Book 1 is Water so I have some Water Tribe-themed snacks." She looked back and nodded at the couch. "Sit."

He slowly did so as Belle came over with the tray of goodies.

"'Kay," she said as she placed it down on the narrow space that was left on the coffee table. "So I have chicken udon soup, dumplings and rice, sesame sticks, and mint tea."

Zach nodded. None of the food was new to him; it was nearly identical to some of the meals that he ate when he was at Kit or Joon's house. He took the soup spoon that Belle gave him as she set up a bowl of treats for Appa to munch on. The warm broth went down his throat as he ladled some of it in his mouth, and the taste was downright homey. "Not bad," he said before picking up the chopsticks to grab some of the noodles.

"Such high praise," Belle smirked as she sat down on the couch and snatched up the remote, turning her TV on, and epic instrumental music started playing.

"Seriously, you didn't have to do all this," he said before he took a bite of noodles and slurped them down.

"It's no problem. I like doing stuff for my friends."

"Oh, we're friends now?" he said jokingly.

She looked over at him with a small frown on her face. "Aren't we?" she asked quietly.

Zach smiled at her, hoping to relieve her worry. "Yeah. We are."

"Good," she chirped as she grabbed some sesame sticks and wrapped the blanket around her shoulders. "Now, as your friend, let me introduce you to greatness."

He scoffed, but sat back and let himself settle into the couch. While the show played and the characters began their adventure, he felt himself calm even more. He honestly hadn't felt this relaxed since freshman year of college, when everything felt easier and the ensuing pain of joining the workforce wasn't lingering over his head like a storm cloud.

But when the giant six-legged Bison came up on the screen, he was thrown for a bit of a loop. He looked back and forth between the dog and the mythical beast, before looking at Belle. "You named him after that?"

"Of course. Appa is one of the greatest animal companions of all time. Next to Momo."

"Who's Momo?"

"All in good time."

It didn't take long for him to get sucked into the fantastical world of *Avatar*, and, he had to admit, he couldn't believe that this was his first time experiencing this world. For once, he was kind of sad that he was more of a book nerd than a TV kid growing up. He understood why Belle thought he would be intrigued by this show after all he said about *River Misfortune* because it seemed this show had everything he loved about the book and more.

When they arrived in Kyoshi, Zach had finished with the soup and his share of dumplings and rice and had started in on the cupcakes, when his phone buzzed.

He saw a message from his dad asking where he was. His father had an event at the library and was probably just checking to make sure that all of his children were where they said they were.

Zach quickly texted him back to remind him that he was

at Belle's and wouldn't be home until later that night before he turned off his notifications, so he wouldn't get distracted anymore. He leaned forward in his seat as Aang went out to ride the elephant koi, but his attention was drawn away when he noticed something moving out of the corner of his eye. He turned slightly and saw Belle moving her yarn-wrapped hands around each other, her eyes not leaving the screen as she did so. "What are you doing?" he asked.

"Crocheting a blanket for Appa."

He raised a brow. "Seriously?"

"My son deserves to be warm at night."

"He's a dog."

She finally ripped her eyes away from the screen to glare at him. "He's my son!" Appa ran over to her and put his head in her lap. "You're my goodest boy, aren't you?" she cooed as she petted his head and nuzzled his nose.

He snorted. "You are not a real person."

She frowned a bit as she looked back up at him. "What do you mean?"

His eyes widened and he quickly said, "I didn't mean it as a bad thing. I just mean, you're very much you. It's a good thing. You kind of seem like you have it all figured out."

She scoffed as she paused the show. "Please."

"No, I'm serious," he said, turning towards her. "I mean, you're living your dream life, aren't you? You're living on your own in a cottage, you own a successful business where you get to make money from things that you're passionate about, and you got the dog you've always wanted." He sighed as he took off the cupcake liner to his treat. "I wish I could achieve half of what you have."

Belle stayed silent for a minute as he bit into the cupcake before saying, "You said you just graduated right?"

He nodded.

"Well, there you go. I've been doing this for a long time, and it took me way more than a month to get here. I started drawing when I was fifteen, and I didn't even covet the idea of making my own products until I was already out of college with a corporate job. You still have plenty of time to achieve the things you want to achieve."

Zach leaned his head back on the couch. "I don't know what I want anymore. Besides writing books, everything else just seems murky."

"Hey." She reached out and squeezed his hand, making him turn back to her. "I know for a fact that you're way more than a pretty face, and when the time comes, you'll figure it out."

Zach smiled. It was nice to hear someone say that. Especially someone who wasn't his family or close friends, who hadn't liked him much when they first met. But now, "You think I'm pretty?" he said with a smug look on his face.

"Shut up!" she said as she shoved his face away. Zach could've sworn he saw a bit of red on her neck, but he ignored it as she picked up the remote again. "Now pay attention so you don't miss the Unagi."

He chuckled, but did so regardless, letting himself lean back into the seat even more. The show was actually quite relaxing.

Well, as relaxing as a show about war could be.

But he could let his mind drift and forget about his current worries and really believe that everything would work out while he watched it. The last thing he remembered before he felt himself drifting off even more was Aang realizing who the King of Omashu was.

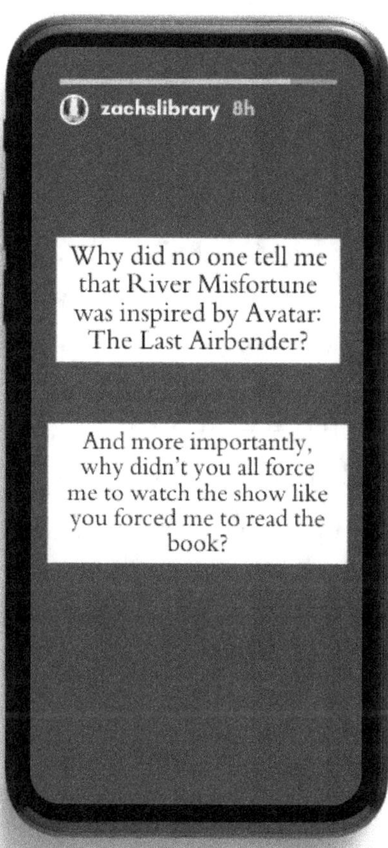
zachslibrary 8h
Why did no one tell me that River Misfortune was inspired by Avatar: The Last Airbender?
And more importantly, why didn't you all force me to watch the show like you forced me to read the book?

Chapter 11

Something wet woke Zach up from his deep sleep.

Actually, something wet was licking his face.

When he finally opened his eyes and rubbed away the sleep, he found himself looking up at Appa, who was staring back at him with his tongue hanging out of his mouth. Zach winced as he felt the dog drool on his beard.

He definitely wasn't at home.

He looked down to his feet to see that he had been covered in a plush blanket, similar to the one that Belle had been making before, but this one was sage green, and his glasses had been neatly put on the coffee table, where the plates of food were removed and replaced with a glass of water.

As he sat up, his brain started to feel less foggy as he inhaled the scent of something sweet. Rays of sun shined through the window and, last time he'd checked, it was supposed to be close to 10 o'clock at night.

He looked over to see that Belle was hard at work in the kitchen, humming as she worked because of course she would be so fucking happy in the morning. He groaned as he moved his feet off the couch, the furniture creaking as he did so.

The noise drew Belle's attention to him. "Hey," she said with her usual smile.

"Hi," he said groggily.

"Sleep well?"

"I think so." He put on his glasses and stood up slowly, letting his bones crack as he did. No matter how comfy Belle's sofa was, he doubted that it was meant to be slept on. "What time is it?" he asked while picking up his phone.

8:30 A.M.

Zach looked back over at Belle, who was currently chopping stuff up on her cutting board. "You're up this early willingly?"

"Yes," she chirped. "The sun is awake, so I'm awake." For a moment, he thought she was gonna twirl around in her bow-covered pajama set, but she restrained herself to keep cooking. He couldn't help but scoff though. That made her turn back to him with a laugh on her lips. "Well, aren't you a ray of sunshine in the morning?"

"No, that would be you."

"I try," she chirped again.

Zach just shook his head. "It's far too early for me to snark at you, so you win." He picked up the glass and took a drink of the water, strongly wishing that it was—

"Coffee?"

He turned his head, and his eyes widened when he saw a mug in her hands. He quickly went over to retrieve it. "You're an angel," he said before taking the mug, blowing on, and then sipping the liquid gold. He moaned with his eyes closed when he realized it was the Park family blend. "This is truly heaven."

"Glad to see that's all it takes to make you happy in the morning," Belle chuckled as she went back to her cooking.

Zach sat down in what was becoming his chair at the table and said, "Sorry for crashing here."

"No need. I don't mind the company. Plus, I've had worse sleepover guests," she said as she flipped something in her pan. "I hope you like crêpes. Strawberries okay?"

"Yeah." He took another sip of coffee. "You make crêpes often?"

She shrugged. "Only when I'm feeling up to it. They can be easy to mess up." She turned off the burner and put the last crêpe on a pile before bringing them over to the table. "But they are one of my comfort meals, and I felt like making them today. And I don't mind making extras." She brought over a bowl of cut-up strawberries, a small bowl of what looked like melted chocolate, and a shaker with a white substance in it.

He nodded at it. "What's that?"

"Powdered sugar."

He scoffed as he looked at the display before him. "You have this much sugar for breakfast?"

"Occasionally. Don't worry, I have an extra toothbrush ready if you're scared of cavities."

He chuckled as he picked up a few of the crêpes using his fork, just as Belle placed an already peeled orange in front of him. He glanced between her and the orange, but she had already started working on filling up Appa's food bowls. He grabbed the orange off the plate and started breaking it up as she sat down. She filled her crepes with strawberries and chocolate before dusting them in powdered sugar, while Zach put some strawberries on the side with his orange and added a bit of sugar to the top. They ate for a bit, letting silence fill the room but it didn't feel awkward.

Zach felt quite calm actually.

After spending so much time in Linley Cottage, he was beginning to think of it as another safe zone: a place where he could just relax and be at peace. He was actually looking forward to spending some time working there.

"So, do you need any help with anything today?" he asked as he started cutting up his crêpe.

Belle shook her head. "You're free to go whenever," she said before taking a bite.

He frowned a bit. "You sure?"

"Yeah." She looked between him and her food. "We handled the packing and I only have a few admin and production things to do. I can handle it on my own."

"But, you hired me to help you. You really used to do this all on your own when you were in New York?"

Belle frowned before quickly scooping and dumping more of the chocolate on her plate. "Well no, my friend, Kailey, helped me out when I first started." She poked at the strawberries, before grabbing her knife to cut them up even smaller than they already were. "It's hard getting used to having help again."

He wasn't one for asking for help either. His friends always said that was one of his biggest flaws. That, and the fact that he always felt a need to correct their grammar in text messages. In his defense, they always went back on that dig when it came time for them to write essays for school.

He nodded and grabbed up more of his orange. "So, is Kailey still up in New York? 'Cause my friend Beau just moved up there with his boyfriend and—"

"Kailey's dead."

Zach nearly dropped his fork as he looked back up at the solemn look on her face. "She died last year in a car accident."

His heart broke a bit, and he couldn't help but say, "Sorry."

Belle shook her head, knocking her glasses loose, but she quickly pushed them back up her nose. "It's not your fault." She shrugged and put down her fork. "Seriously, we've worked for four days straight on packing orders, and we've managed to get them all out. We could use the rest. You want another orange?"

"Sure."

Belle got up and went digging through her fridge again, and Zach started eating again, watching her and ignoring the sour feeling in his stomach at the thought of leaving. When she sat back down, he thought it would be best to change the subject. "So you were right."

"About what?"

"The show. It's actually really good."

"I told you."

"Yeah, you did." He glanced between her and the TV. "Do you think we can watch some more while we eat?"

Belle smirked. "Absolutely."

When Zach got back home an hour later, he was already prepared to plop down on his bed and nap until lunch when he walked through the door.

"Where the hell have you been?"

Zach jumped around to see his angry father standing there in the front hall. He could already tell that his plans were about to be derailed.

"I was at Belle's," he said slowly while placing his bag down and taking off his shoes.

"All night?"

"Yeah, we were watching her favorite show and I fell asleep."

"So, that's why you weren't answering my calls?"

Zach's eyes widened as he quickly took out his phone, turned his notifications back on, and a stream of text messages came in from his dad, all from that morning.

"Do you know how worried I was?"

"I can imagine," Zach admitted, putting it back in his pocket, his stomach twisting in knots. "I'm sorry, I didn't expect to fall asleep there."

"Right," Jedidiah scoffed. "I never thought you would be so irresponsible."

"I'm sorry. You know I'm bad at keeping up with my phone and—"

"Then why the hell am I paying for it then?"

Because if I didn't have one at all, you wouldn't let me out of your sight.

Zach bit back the words because that wouldn't help his situation at all. Talks like this were expected with his dad. He had already been protective before the divorce, but he'd become the worst kind of helicopter parent when their mom left. Even when Zach was away at school, he'd had phone calls every night to ask about what he was doing and where or he would have campus security looking for him. He was just happy that his father wasn't tech-savvy enough to know about the Find My Friends feature on their phones, otherwise, he would have to deal with his father calling about why he was off-campus at a golf emporium with Mateo or a bar with Beau.

After years of dealing with this, Zach knew that the best course of action was to apologize and try to avoid similar situations in the future. "It won't happen again," he said with a grim smile on his face, but his father did not return it, just stared at him with furrowed brows and pursed lips.

"Yeah, because you're not working there anymore."

Zach's eyes widened. "What? Why? Belle really needs the help."

"Cause I need to know where you are."

"You did know. I told you where I was. I sent you text messages and left a note on the fridge—"

"Was I supposed to really believe that you were there the whole night? You could have left. You could've ended up somewhere, like a biker bar or..."

Zach scoffed a laugh. "A biker bar? Me? Dad, come on. You'd sooner find me at an underground rave or a fight club than a biker bar."

"How am I supposed to know that if you don't call?"

Zach could vaguely hear the door open but didn't turn his gaze from his father. "Because you know me. I'm only ever in three places besides this house. I don't go anywhere special, or do anything special, and even when I get the invitation to do so, you always make me tell you first, and then I have to pretty much get your permission to go, even though I'm an adult. Why do I, as a grown man, have to tell my father where I am twenty-four-seven? Don't you trust me?"

"Why should I, especially after last night?"

"Oh come on, last night was a first-time offense, if that."

"And that's all it takes for you to end up dead on the side of the road!"

"Hey!"

Zach turned to the front door to see his siblings and Gigi standing there, all their hands filled with bags, but all Zach focused on was the fact that Corey's eyes were filled with tears threatening to fall.

"Is Zach gonna die?" Corey asked quietly. Zach could see his father take a step back.

Zach went over and squatted down in front of his brother, quickly wiping the tears from his eyes. "Hey, no bud. That's not gonna happen anytime soon. I promise."

"Corey, Amaya, go upstairs," Gigi ordered in her lawyer tone, leaving no room for an argument. Corey bolted up the stairs without another word, but when Zach glanced at Amaya, he saw the pointed look on her face before she ran up after Corey. They were going to be talking about this later.

Gigi placed two paper bags, probably filled with food, down on the floor before crossing her arms and glaring at her former son-in-law. "I was trying to let you two talk this out, but you have no right scaring that little boy like that, Jedidiah. Now, what is going on?"

Jed just glared back before glancing at Zach. "Your grandson has decided that he can ignore my phone calls."

"I didn't," Zach said in a voice that was too akin to a whine for his liking.

Jed held up his hand. "The adults are talking."

As his father kept on telling his side of the story, Zach felt like he was in a parent-teacher conference, caught in the middle of a tense tennis match, like it always was when his father and Gigi were in the same room. Ever since Gigi's daughter skipped out on them, his father was not keen on her being in his house, but Gigi was never one to be pushed aside even when their mother was there, so she always made her presence known and refused to be pushed out of her grandchildren's lives, and Zach was honestly grateful for that, for he could not imagine dealing with his father without her. Even though Mimi kept Jed from having all the control in the house, Gigi always tried to make things clear from an outsider's perspective, which was always useful. She always made him feel like an adult, while his father was keen to make him feel like a child.

After Jed finally finished his version of the events, Gigi said, "Now, we both know that Zachary has never been a problem." She paced about the room like she was delivering a statement to the jury. "He has always been respectful, responsible, and, above all else, truthful. Jedidiah, I don't know if you've noticed but your son is a grown man now."

"Not while he lives under my roof."

"He's not gonna be if you don't quit babying him," she said with a raised brow.

Jed huffed as he rubbed his hand over his tired eyes. "I am trying to keep him safe."

"I am perfectly safe at Belle's," Zach interrupted as he moved to stand in his father's eyeline. "All we do there is pack up her products, listen to music, and watch TV," he said with a scoff. "Her place is pretty much the calmest place in the universe, and there is no reason for you to worry about me when I'm there because Belle is just about the sweetest person in town." He took a step closer to his father, noting the lack of his words relaxing him even a tiny bit. "You have to let me live in the world at some point."

Jed just glanced between his son and his former mother-in-law before moving to grab his bag. "I have to get to work. We'll talk later." He left with the door slamming behind and Zach felt his jaw clench as the familiarity of the situation washed over him.

"Zachary."

"I'm fine, Gigi," he said, turning to face her with a false smile on his face. "I have some work to do, so I'll just..."

He quickly made his way up the stairs and into his room and started clearing some space on his desk, almost throwing everything on his bed when Amaya came in with a quizzical look on her face. "What was all that about?" She asked.

"Nothing. Quite literally nothing, but as long as I live under Dad's roof, I have to report back my whereabouts to him every hour."

She leaned against his desk. "That sucks," she murmured.

"That's an understatement," he grumbled, plopping down into his chair and opening his laptop. "How's Corey?"

"He's okay. I gave him my tablet so he could watch *Bluey*."

"Good." He glanced up at his sister. "Was he like this when I was at school?"

Amaya shrugged. "A little. I spent most of my time here or with Owen or Sheila, so he didn't have much to complain about, but when I got invited to parties and other things... yeah, he wasn't too excited to let me go."

Zach scoffed. "Figures." He turned back to his laptop and started opening his job hunt windows. "Can't wait to get out of this hell hole."

Amaya said nothing before walking back out of his room, closing the door behind her for once. He took a deep breath before going to his email and pulling up the section where he kept all of his job posting information. His eyes widened when he read the title line of one of the emails.

Hiring: Editor Assistant for Juvenile Fiction at Retna Publishing

A new job listing for one of his top publishing houses was just what he needed to see. He wasted no time opening up the listing.

Cover Letter for Retna Publishing

To Whom It May Concern,

My name is Zach Roberts and I am interested in joining your editorial team at Retna Publishing. I have been an avid reader for years, and my passion lies in sharing stories where young people can see powerful characters that look like them. I would like to help your team with your goal of creating great fiction for a younger audience.

I earned a Bachelor's Degree in English at Walker University, where I took classes in editing and children's literature…

Chapter 12

No one as obsessed with books as Zach should ever have felt as sad and angry as he was while being in a bookstore.

He was surrounded by one of his favorite things in the world, but all he could think about was the fight he'd had with his father. When Jed came back home from work that day, they hadn't talked about the fight or anything really, but Zach shouldn't have expected anything less at this point. His father was never one to talk about how he felt. Zach would just have to continue walking on eggshells and try not to do something else that would piss his father off.

Luckily, he had his writing to keep him from tearing his hair out while he made rounds in the aisles.

It was a slow day at The Book Haven. Rain was falling outside, making it a prime day for people to stay at home. A few people walked past with Toe Beans cups in hand, but only a handful entered their store as well. Most just browsed and left but one person had asked for help finding an obscure book that they happened to have on the shelves. It surprised him just how much variety they could hold in such a small space, but Zach felt that it made the store that much more special.

That could probably be the base for an analogy for the data banks in Project Void.

The customer had agreed, saying the store was a treasure trove, and that they wanted to tag them on social media. Sadly, Zach had to tell them that the shop didn't have any, not for lack of effort from him and Jaime trying to convince Des otherwise. Apparently, both of the adult figures in Zach's life were stubborn as hell.

"Zach?"

He turned to see Jaime standing in front of him with a quizzical look on their face, hands filled with books. "What?"

"You okay?" they asked.

"Yeah, just thinking and possibly drifting off," Zach said as he took his lens cloth out of his pocket and wiped the dust off his glasses.

"Same. Rain always makes me sleepy," Jaime said as they put some books back on the shelf. "Anything you want to talk about?"

Zach scoffed as he put his glasses back on. "I doubt you want to hear about my problems."

Jaime shrugged. "Well, I'd rather hear about your problems than think about how I'm gonna make rent next month."

Zach's spine stiffened up. "You okay?"

"Oh, yeah for now," Jaime sighed. "I guess. Just tired. After my shifts here, I moonlight as a rideshare driver, and it's getting to me." Jaime looked over at him, the bags under their eyes quite apparent now that Zach was looking for them.

"You mind taking the counter for a minute while I hide in the aisles?"

Zach wanted to remind them that barely anyone else was there, just a mother and her kid reading in the children's area, but he just nodded and went to the front. He plopped down onto the stool behind the counter and pulled out his notebook from his hiding spot, taking the time to write down his data bank idea.

"Hey."

Zach slammed his notebook shut and looked up to see Belle standing there with a pile of books in her hand. "Hi. When did you get here?"

"Six minutes ago. I tried to say hi to you when I passed you in the fantasy section."

"Oh." He must have been more out of it than he'd thought. "Sorry." He put his notebook underneath the counter and started scanning her books.

"It's fine. Are you okay?" she asked, shifting her bag to pull out another tote that Zach got used to seeing as Belle's bag for books.

"As fine as I can be," he said before pausing to look at one of the books she was buying. He knew he'd seen it before, specifically on her shelf at the cottage. "Don't you already have this book?"

"Yeah, but I don't have one with this cover and *The Limits of Love* is one of my favorite books of all time, so I pretty much collect every edition of it that I can find."

Zach felt his brow furrow as he put it down to scan the next book. "Seems excessive." While he loved books, he only had a prescribed amount of room on his shelves, so getting multiple copies of the same book felt like a waste of space to him.

Belle shrugged. "My shelves, my rules," she said as she put down her book bag. "Appa's not here, so what are you really annoyed about? Someone use the wrong version of 'there' in a text?"

"Don't even joke about that. Cash or card?"

Belle giggled as she pulled out her card, and Zach could swear that his heart skipped a beat as the sound hit his ears. He quickly swatted the feeling away.

"Seriously? What's wrong?" she asked again after swiping.

He let out a breath. "My dad. I came home late after we did that watch party, and he lost his shit on me even though he knew where I was."

Belle frowned and Zach hated how that looked on her. "Oh, I'm sorry, I—"

"It's not your fault. I mean, I didn't answer his calls. But I was asleep so I..." He sighed. "It's just annoying to go from living on your terms on campus to having to go back home and answer for every little thing you do. And it's not like I can move out because I don't have enough money to pay for any sort of housing anywhere and..." He looked up and saw the sympathetic look on her face. "Sorry. I shouldn't be dumping all of this on you." He quickly bagged up the rest of Belle's books in her tote and slid them over to her. "Enjoy your books."

"Thanks." Belle took the bag into her hands, swaying back and forth on her tiptoes before she said, "I'm sure your dad is only trying to look out for you."

Zach tried hard not to scoff, but she wasn't completely wrong. "I know but"— Zach took his glasses off his face to rub his eyes before looking at Belle again—"he always just makes me feel like the world is constantly out to get me, or that something is always gonna go wrong when I leave the house. I just hate when he tries to make safe spaces feel like danger zones."

Zach bit his lip once he realized that he actually said that out loud. He usually never felt comfortable enough to admit that to anyone, afraid they would just pity him.

Belle didn't wince or cringe though, she just looked at him with kind eyes, or what looked like kind eyes through his blurry vision. "I get it." She smiled. "But I'm glad that you feel safe at the cottage."

Zach put his glasses back on and looked at her newest bag of books. "How do you read so many books?"

"What?" she chuckled.

"You literally come in here every week and buy a new batch of books. How the hell can you read that fast?"

"Most of the books I buy I've already read on my e-reader, or I listened to as audiobooks while designing. I just buy the ones that I really love so I can annotate them," she said, smirking as Zach cringed at her mention of defiling books. "Which I know you hate but..."

"They're your books, so you can do what you want with them."

Her smile widened. "You're learning. Good."

He rolled his eyes but still smiled as she shifted her bags onto her shoulder.

"I also read a lot of graphic novels." She leaned forward with a smirk. "I like the pictures."

Zach snorted a laugh and sucked his teeth before looking up at Belle. "You got any recommendations for a graphic novel newbie?" he shrugged.

Belle shifted on her feet like she was trying to contain her excitement. Zach could understand the feeling. It was rare when people came to him for book recommendations. Well, in real life; his online followers were always trying to stump him for very specific book recommendations, and he'd been able to fulfill them all. "You like fantasy, right?"

He nodded.

"Then I would start with the *Tea Dragon Society* series. It's this really cute series about raising these mini dragons that grow tea leaves, and the characters are amazing. I think it'll be right up your alley."

"I'll take a look at it," he said with a nod.

Belle went to walk away.

"Hey, Belle?"

She turned back. "Yeah?"

"Thanks."

"For what?"

"For being you."

That made her smile even wider before she left the store, just as the mother and child came to the counter. The mom lifted the little girl, who smiled at Zach.

"I would like to buy this pwease," she said in a squeaky tone that made Zach laugh.

"Of course," he said, taking the book with a smile. He didn't know if he was smiling because the kid was adorable, or because Belle was just that good at brightening up his day.

Hours later, when they were ready to close, Zach went

through his duties of cleaning up the children's area and organizing books back into alphabetical order. He was halfway through the graphic novels when he saw the word "Tea Dragon" on a larger book. He pulled it out, and saw a beautifully illustrated cover of two human-like characters having a picnic with mini dragons. He smiled a bit and put it under his arm as he finished up his tasks.

He quickly got his bag, and went up to the counter where Des was closing down the register for the night, and had Des check out the book for him with his employee discount. Des took the book and chuckled at the cover.

"What?" Zach queried, shifting on his feet.

"I saw Belle rearranging the shelves to put that book forward a couple of weeks ago," Des said as he handed the book back to Zach.

Zach glared at him before snatching the book away and shoving it in his bag. "Bye Des."

He made his way out of the store and started to turn towards the parking lot when he heard, "Zachary, there you are."

He turned back towards the rest of the shops and saw his grandmothers slowly making their way toward him from a table outside of Toe Beans. "What are you doing here?" he asked as he took a step back. His grandmothers didn't frequent the strip often, which meant only one thing.

It was an ambush.

"We're heading to Solomon's," Mimi explained once they got close to him. "Could you give us a ride over?" she said while looping her arm around his.

"Aren't you gonna wait for Oma?"

"Umi is driving her over after she prepares the treats for tomorrow," Gigi said, taking his other arm and dragging him to the back parking lot.

He reluctantly helped both of the older women into his car before quickly getting in the driver seat, and heading to Solomon's in the restaurant strip.

The silence that he usually enjoyed after his shift was broken when Mimi said, "So Gigi told me that you had a fight with your father."

Zach gripped the wheel a bit tighter. Definitely an ambush. "Dad didn't tell you about it?"

She scoffed. "Have you met my son?"

"Unfortunately," he mumbled. "Mimi, it's nothing to worry about."

Mimi sighed. "You know how Jeremy—"

"Yes, I know how Uncle Jeremy died but...it doesn't mean I have to spend my life confined to that house. None of us should."

They didn't say anything for a while, the sound of the blinker filling the car when Zach pulled up to an intersection. Zach knew they meant well, but he was honestly very tired of people constantly trying to defend his father to him. He knew it was a father's job to keep his children safe, but everyone has their limit, and Zach had reached his years ago. It was the main reason why he chose to go to a college that was three hours away from home; low chances of his family dropping by, not to mention the fact that Corey had still been very much a helpless toddler, meaning his father had to focus on the baby of the family, not him, and he had relished being able to just walk around campus and go nowhere.

But that time had passed.

"Well, I've heard you've been hanging out a lot with that new girl in town, Belle. What is she like?" Gigi asked, breaking the silence.

Zach shrugged. "She's nice. Keeps to herself a lot, but she has a huge dog to keep her company."

"She pretty?"

He hummed a yes before realizing what she asked. "Gigi!"

"What? You can't blame an old woman for wondering when she's going to get grandchildren."

"I'm your grandchild."

"But being a great-grandmother would be nice," she hummed. Zach could see Mimi gleefully nodding in the rear-view mirror.

He shook his head. "Oh no. I am not having children any-time soon, and I think Belle is busy enough right now with the store. Besides, nothing is going on between us."

"If you say so. So what does she sell?"

"Home goods. Mugs, cups, notebooks, sweatshirts, stickers. That kind of stuff. She draws all of the characters herself."

"Oh isn't that nice? I'll need you to send me the shop link."

"Will do," he said, turning the car into the complex that housed Solomon's Tea House. The white-paneled building's parking lot was pretty empty; more people would be at Papa Porter's at this time of night, but that's how his grandmother and their friends liked it.

He helped them both out of the car and guided them up to the front door. Gigi went right in, but Mimi paused and turned back to him, cupping his cheek in her hand. "You are an amazing man, Zachary Roberts. Don't forget that."

He let a small smile slip onto his face. "Yes ma'am. You need me to pick you up later?"

"No, Beth is driving us back. You go home." Mimi patted his cheek and went in, leaving Zach just enough time to be home for dinner before his dad sent out a search party.

It had been a while since Zach had taken out his reading light for a bit of late-night reading, but that night he pinned it to the top of the *Tea Dragon Society* book as he flipped through it page by page, drawn in by the beautiful illustrations and the entrancing story. He was a sucker for soft storylines and fantastical settings.

Since it was a graphic novel, he was done quite quickly and he regretted not picking up the other books that matched from the shelves but he would get them tomorrow.

He traded the book for his phone and opened his chat with Belle. His thumbs hovered over the keyboard for a second when he saw the time, but he pushed onward, hoping she wouldn't get annoyed at the message.

Zach

I hate to admit it but you were right about these tea dragons

He went to close it immediately, but a pending message bubble popped up on the screen before he could.

Belle

I told you

Zach

But I do maintain the fact this is a very easy read

Belle

What's wrong with that?

Not every book has to be life-changing or genre-breaking to be good.

A good story is a good story

Zach

True

Have any other recommendations?

Belle

How much time do you have?

He chuckled as he typed a response.

Zach

Well it depends on how late my boss doesn't mind me being in the morning

Belle

I think she'll cut you some slack ;)

Provided you bring her a vanilla latte as a bribe

He laughed out loud, but quickly covered his mouth. Biting his lip, he looked under his door; luckily there weren't any lights turning on out in the hall. He relaxed back into his pillows and texted Belle back.

Zach

I think I can do that ;)

zachslibrary 3h

If someone has any
recommendations for
books with dragons,
please leave them here! I
have a new obsession
that's been unlocked and
I need to fulfill it.

Chapter 13

The Lillet Farmer's Market was a special event.

The only area in town big enough to host all of the incoming vendors and visitors was in front of Town Hall, and blocking it off caused traffic problems for those trying to easily get through town, so they couldn't afford to do these types of things often during the school year. It was the reason the market was cherished by many and, despite him whingeing about going, Zach was one of them.

Zach yawned as he pulled into the makeshift parking lot on the other side of the post office. He had been up late texting Belle, a new habit for the past few nights, and he'd forgotten that he'd promised to go shopping with Kit and Joon until he got a notice in the middle of him and Belle talking about doing a buddy read of *River Misfortune*. He'd cut the conversation short to get some sleep before rising at dawn for the market.

He got lucky with his spot; he was early enough to find somewhere close to the entrance, so he wouldn't be complaining about having to lug bags back to his car. He grabbed a few of Mimi's totes and the list she shoved in his hand last night before getting out.

When he got to the huge banner that signified the start of the market maze, he saw Joon standing there with a few cups of iced coffee in hand. When Joon noticed Zach coming his way, he held one out to him.

"God bless you," Zach said, taking the cup and sipping the iced drink. Milky coffee and cinnamon coated his throat, and he could not be more pleased. Though it was only 8 am, the temperature was already creeping towards the forecasted mid-80s.

Joon nodded as he took a sip of his own milky blue drink—probably the blueberry latte that he'd been raving about trying to make—before looking around. "Where's Kit?"

"I don't know. I'm not her keeper."

"If she's gonna make me get up at six A.M., she should be here."

"Don't you have to get up at six most days?"

"Not by choice. On my non-work days I want to sleep in. The only reason I should be out this early is to sneak out of someone's house."

"You haven't brought anyone to your place yet?"

Joon's brow quirked up. "And risk them walking down to the kitchen with my sisters there?"

Zach sucked his teeth. "Never mind. You still talking to Lana?"

"Definitely not. Turns out she was very against the idea of dating someone bi."

Zach gagged. "Ew," he said before taking another sip of a

drink to get the sour taste of that statement out of his mouth.

Joon shrugged. "Yeah, I think I'm just gonna cool it for the rest of the summer. People are exhausting."

"Agreed." Zach nodded, noticing the solemn look on Joon's face. He never understood why somebody would reject Joon because he liked guys and girls. Kit and Zach were there for him when he'd figured it out and had been with him through several instances where someone refused him because of that. One was so bad that Zach had taken a train down from university during midterms to be there for Joon, while also trying to keep Kit from going after the guy with a baseball bat and pepper spray.

Luckily, there was an easy way to cheer Joon up.

"Want to look at cat videos until Kit gets here?"

Joon smiled as he pulled out his phone. "Do you even have to ask?"

They had just got through their third compilation of scared cats running from something when the sound of a sputtering motor heading their way made them both look up in time to see Kit riding towards them on her cream-colored scooter. She pulled into the designated bike spot and smiled at them. "Hey, sorry I'm late," she said, pulling off her helmet. "I sat with my dad a little bit longer than I thought this morning."

That made Zach snuff all of the snarky remarks he'd had ready for her. Joon shifted on his feet beside him. Kit had lost her mother last year, and her father had had a really hard time with it. The two of them had been high school sweethearts turned long-time lovers; you could feel the love radiate off them when they walked anywhere in town. Seeing Mr. Hiroko walking around town by himself was a sad sight for anyone to see, which was why Kit made a lot of effort to spend extra time with him. They couldn't fault her for that.

Joon nodded and passed Kit a cup with caramel drizzled around the edge. She took a cheery sip of it before looking at them. "Well, what are we waiting for?" she said after Joon tossed the cup holder. She hooked her arms around both of theirs and smiled up at them. "Let's go."

The boys rolled their eyes, but began making their way into the market anyway. They were immediately greeted by the sight of thrifting stands, freshly baked bread, and other homemade goodies. Joon tried to lead them towards the cheese stand, but they pulled him back.

"Aren't you lactose intolerant?" Zach asked.

Joon blinked at him. "So?"

Zach and Kit shared a look before letting their friend make terrible decisions. They instead headed over to a stand full of vintage items for sale. Kit flicked her way through the clothes, while Zach looked at the books. Nothing caught his eye until he saw a vintage black typewriter, something he'd always wanted in his room, but a look at the price tag on it reminded him why he hadn't fulfilled that dream yet.

He went back over to Kit, and let her fill his arms full of different cardigans and collared dresses quite similar to the ones she was already wearing. He didn't understand why girls needed so many variations of the same outfit, and he said so to Kit.

Her brow quirked up. "How many polo shirts and button-ups do you have?"

Zach pursed his lips. "Fair point."

She smirked before throwing another cardigan on the pile. They stayed there for a moment, Zach taking note of a few of Kit's favorites that she didn't buy so he could get one for her birthday in August. By the time Joon came over with a bag of cheese, Kit had narrowed down her haul to three cardigans and one rust-colored dress.

This pattern of stopping and shopping continued for the next hour where they wandered through the market row by row. Kit had found many vintage knick-knacks to spruce up her little apartment, while Zach and Joon grocery shopped for their families. By 8 A.M., they each had about three bags full of food and home goods.

They had just stopped at a fruit stand where Kit and Joon were sampling everything, when Zach noticed a very familiar wagging tail in the distance.

He walked away from his friends and, sure enough, it was "Appa?"

The Australian shepherd burst up at the sound of his voice and immediately ran over to circle Zach and ask for pets.

Zach smirked as he scratched the fur around the dog's neck. "Where's your momma, boy?"

After he was sufficiently satisfied with attention, Appa trotted off to the other side of the aisle where Belle was standing behind a table in a flowy white top, jean shorts, and ballet flats with her hair pulled into a ponytail with a ribbon.

Appa nudged her until she looked up at Zach and grinned. He ignored the skip of his heart and said, "Hey."

"Hi. Didn't expect to see you here."

"Got dragged into shopping with those two," he said, pointing over to Joon and Kit, who were currently throwing grapes into each other's mouths. "How about you?"

"Got dragged into setting up a stand."

"By who?"

"Mayor Hadlow. She heard about my business and apparently, it's 'just the thing that could bring some new flair to the market'."

Zach winced. "That's probably my fault. I mentioned your shop to my grandmothers when they were on the way to an OWWA meeting. They probably told her about it."

"OWWA?"

"Old Women with Attitude."

Belle burst out laughing before quickly covering her mouth. "Seriously?"

"Seriously."

"And I thought my grandma had 'tude."

"Every town has its group of sassy grandmothers. The OWWA is ours and it's literally all of our grandmothers."

"As in?"

"My Mimi and Gigi, Kit's Nana and Oba, and Joon's Oma. They met at one of our birthday parties when we were little, and the rest was history."

"How does Mayor Hadlow..."

"She's Kit's Nana. Town pride literally runs through her veins."

"It sure does," Kit agreed as she bumped into Zach when she and Joon came over. "Hey, Belle. Whatcha selling?"

Belle smiled and was just about to say something when she paused. "Actually, do you all mind if I practice my pitch with you all? I've been freaking out about it since last night."

"You don't need a pitch here. People naturally browse the stalls and buy anyway," Joon said before popping another grape in his mouth.

"I wanted to challenge myself to try and entice people

over"—Belle swayed on her feet—"but I'm not good at randomly talking to people about stuff. Especially when it's my own products."

"Why not? These are so cute!" Kit cooed while picking up the Terry the Terrier plushie. "This reminds me of the stuff I used to get for my American Girl Doll."

Belle's eyes widened. "You had one too?"

"Oh my God yes! That's literally all I wanted for my tenth birthday. I was like, forgo the party and any other presents, I just wanted one of the dolls."

"Let me guess...Kit Kittredge."

Kit's eyes widened so much that they almost popped out of her face. "Oh my God, yes! No one gets that. It took me forever to explain to these guys why I wanted to be called Kit instead of Kat."

"Please tell me you watched the movies growing up."

"Growing up? Still do. Samantha's movie is one of my go-to holiday movies."

"December, you and I are having a Samantha Holiday-themed tea party."

Kit squealed before going around the table to hug Belle tightly. She turned back to Zach and glared at him. "Zach, why have you been keeping this gem to yourself?"

"What do you mean?" Gem asked as she came over.

"Oh no, not you, Gem. I'm talking about Belle and her adorable creations, look at these."

The three women started to gush about everything Belle had set out on the table, and Zach smiled.

Belle was gonna do great.

Joon leaned over to Zach and whispered, "Would they even notice if we left?"

"Probably not."

"Good. I'm going to get some bread. Coming?"

"In a sec."

As Joon crept away, Zach looked over everything else that Belle had on the table before picking up one of her business cards. Even though he packed them into almost every order they sent out, he never really took a chance to look at them.

Love, Belle

Finding Magic in the Little Things

Instagram | TikTok | YouTube

Zach's eyes widened as he glanced over to the YouTube link next to the QR code on the card. How could he not have known that she had a YouTube channel? She always had a small camera when she was doing stuff around the house, or she was quickly putting it away when he came into the room. He glanced between her and the card before stuffing the card in his bag and turning away.

"Are you going?"

Zach looked back at Belle, trying hard not to focus on her biting her lip as he said, "Um...yeah."

"I can't talk you into manning the table with me today." She gestured over to where Kit and Gem were trying to decide between two sets of her character collections.

Zach winced. "Sorry, after I wrap up here I gotta go back and deliver this stuff to Mimi," he said, lifting his bags.

"Oh." She started picking at her nails, something Zach had noticed her doing at the cottage when she got anxious. "Okay."

"Hey," Zach said as he walked back to her and moved her hands apart slightly. "You got this. Your products are amazing." He looked her directly in the eye. "And so are you."

Belle smiled, and he felt her squeeze his hand. He smiled back as he reluctantly let her go. "Just be yourself and you'll be fine."

She nodded, and Zach took his leave, flexing his hand to shake away the tingling sensation in them as he went.

Later that night, Zach found himself binge-watching videos on her channel.

Her videos mostly consisted of daily vlogs of her life as a small business owner living in a cottage. It felt a bit weird to see Belle in that context when he had been in the kitchen where she was making all these whimsical dishes, and up in the attic where she makes all of her sweatshirts and bookmarks, but the videos felt very much like Belle.

Calm. Reassuring. Bright. Happy.

He scrolled through her video history and noticed that there was a jump between the video upload dates that went from one year ago to four months ago.

He looked at the title of the last video before the break.

For Kailey

Kailey...Kailey, as in the best friend Belle said she lost last year.

The thumbnail of the video was a young woman around Belle's age smiling at the camera. She seemed so different from Belle, from her light freckled skin to the tight and neat style of her black hair, to the bright orange eyeliner and butterflies surrounding her green eyes and a nose ring to top it all off. The more he looked at it, the more it felt like looking at Belle, but maybe in a more expressive font.

He went to click on the video when his eyes flickered to the time.

11:59 P.M.

He dropped his laptop on his bed before snatching up his phone and opening his FaceTime app. The moment it turned to midnight, he called Beau, who answered after two rings.

"Hello?" Beau greeted as his face came up on the screen. Zach could see a bit of his kitchen in the background.

"Happy Birthday!" Zach screamed at him quietly, glancing at the bottom of his door to make sure it was still dark before glancing back at the screen with a smirk. "Did I beat him?"

"Happy..." Mateo shouted as he ran into the room on the screen, from where Zach assumed their bedroom was. He hadn't taken the time to let either of them give him a proper tour of the apartment, but neither had they offered, probably not to rub where they were in Zach's face.

Mateo glared when he saw Zach on Beau's screen. "Bastard."

"I don't think Happy Bastard works in any context," Beau smirked.

Mateo ignored his boyfriend as he came closer, glaring at Zach through the phone, but Zach could see that Mateo was holding in a laugh. "You couldn't let me have this, could you?"

"You already live and work with him. How much more of his

attention do you need?"

Mateo looked ready to argue, but Beau lightly shoved his face away. "Hey, let me enjoy the fact that he actually called me without me having to send him five thousand texts." Beau smiled and kissed Mateo's cheek before looking back at Zach. "So, have you found anyone to take your attention since you've been back in Lillet?"

Zach groaned as he plopped back down on his bed. "Must you keep trying to involve yourself in my love life from afar?"

Beau raised a brow. "Is there a love life to get involved in?"

"No," Zach hissed. This man was almost as bad as Kit. "Who would I meet here? I already know everyone."

"Fine, any old flames rekindled then?"

"No. My life has been perfectly dull, thank you very much."

"Of course it has, I'm not there."

Zach rolled his eyes as he hefted himself from his bed to move about his room, putting some of his writing craft books back on the shelves they came from.

"Any luck on jobs?" Beau asked as Mateo puttered about the kitchen.

"Don't let me depress you on your birthday. I'm fine. I'm still part-time at the bookstore and I've got a job assisting a friend with her store."

"Her?"

"Stop it. It's not like that with Belle."

"Belle, huh? That's a new name." Beau smirked as he snatched a bag of jellybeans out of Mateo's hands.

"Well, she is new. She moved here from New York, actually."

"Is she pretty?" Mateo asked as he took a jelly bean out of the bag behind Beau's back.

Zach bit his lip as he looked at a thumbnail of Belle in one of her videos on his open laptop screen. "Yeah, she's pretty." He looked back at his phone. "But I'm just working with her temporarily before I move, and dating her would not be the best idea."

"But you've thought about dating her?" Beau asked, which was answered with a glare from Zach, making Beau hold his hands up in surrender. "Fine. Happy to see that being at home hasn't made you lose your sparkling personality."

Zach rolled his eyes. "Did you get your present?"

"I got something from you. You didn't have to get me anything." Beau said as he picked up a wrapped box off the counter in front of him.

"Well, my sister is practicing embroidering with my Mimi, and I thought she could practice by making something for you."

Mateo took the phone and filmed Beau as he opened up the package, and pulled out a shoe box. Zach waited with bated breath as Beau opened it up to reveal some black Converse chucks, one of Beau's favorite things, with a pen and paper embroidered on them, Beau's name written out in orange cursive by the pen.

Beau gasped at the craftsmanship. "I love them." He looked up at the camera. "Tell her thank you for me."

Zach grinned a bit. "I will. There's also a card in there but..."

Beau quickly pulled out a yellow envelope and revealed a happy birthday card with a lizard wearing a cowboy hat on the front. Beau read it silently and teared up a bit at the content before looking at the camera again. "You do have a heart."

"Shut up. I got work tomorrow, so good night and happy birthday."

"'Night. Say 'night babe."

The phone beeped after Mateo's finger went over the screen, making Zach snicker. He missed his fellow grump.

Zach put his phone on the charger before going back over to the laptop and looking at Belle's picture once more. He found himself staring at the screen a lot longer than he should, but God, Belle was pretty. Maybe he didn't really pay attention when they were in the workshop together because they were pretty much back-to-back the entire day, but her cinnamon eyes on the screen drew him in, and the smile on her lips was blinding.

Her lips probably tasted like strawberries.

Zach took a step back before slamming the laptop shut and practically throwing it onto his desk.

He could not have those types of thoughts about Belle.

She was his friend.

Nothing more, nothing less.

Summer days in my cottage: crafting bookish things, farmer's markets and doggy cuddles

Hi, My Lovelies,

Happy to say that I finally feel like it's summer now and I can post all of the Summer collections that I was working on at the beginning of the year. You guys have already been sending me pictures of you sticking them on your phones and using the bookmarks and I am just so grateful that you all love them so much. Also, thank you so much for being so understanding with the Barry misprint. I freaked out so much when I opened that box, but luckily someone made me realize that you guys are some of the kindest and sweetest people and that you wouldn't be as mad as I thought you all would be, so thank you again and I hope this video makes you smile.

Love, Belle

@TiaDoll · 40 min ago

Ugh, I wish there were farmer's markets near me so I could buy stuff like what you're selling locally. Also, of course, we were going to be understanding we know it's not your fault.

@lovebelle · 15 min ago

I know, I still get nervous about it at times though. It's the Virgo in me! :'D

@TiaDoll · 1 min ago

Oh so relatable! XD

@luvbug1236 · 2h ago

Appa is the cutest! Please give him all the kisses for me

    @lovebelle · 17 min ago

    Kisses given! :)

@PokeyDokey · 2h ago

I love that bandana! Are they coming to the shop soon?

    @lovebelle · 16 min ago

    ;) Stay tuned!

July

Chapter 14

Zach did not like being in busy spaces.

He tended to get distracted when other people were around. It happened to him a lot in the bookstore when he tried to focus on his work. He always had the feeling in the back of his mind that he needed to be alert. What would happen if someone came up to him mid-task to ask him a question? Would he have to drop the task he was doing to help them? Would he remember what he was doing, or would he have to start over completely? People, in general, just made him nervous because they came with so many unknown variables to dissect. Would they be in a good mood when you saw them, or would they take their bad mood out on you? It wasn't an uncommon occurrence for someone to come in and call him incompetent because they didn't have the latest book by a popular author that hadn't even been released yet. That in particular he'd dealt with far too much, and since "the customer is always right," he had to take their crap instead of saying how he really felt.

One of the reasons why he enjoyed working with Belle at

the cottage so much was that it was just easy to be around her. Whether it was just the two of them up in her attic organizing products where they could either zone out to their own music or sitting in her living room watching episodes of *Avatar* while packing up new inventory in bags, it felt nice to have developed a rhythm with her, to be able to talk to her about nothing or to not have to say anything at all.

At the moment, they were in their usual corners, working on their own tasks. They didn't say anything, but Zach didn't find himself trying to start conversations anymore. They could just be in the same space and work. Zach had been promoted to product maker and was now allowed to use the embroidery machine and heat press. He was currently using the embroidery machine to add little daisies on t-shirts while Belle was sketching out new ideas for her future launches.

Or trying to at least.

"Ugh!" She yelled, startling Zach out of his machine-like stupor of loading and unloading shirts from the machine.

"What happened?" Zach asked as he took his overhead earphones off.

Belle swiveled around in her chair and sighed while taking off her glasses. "Oh sorry, I'm used to being alone when I work." She held out her hand. "Can I use your lens cloth?"

He scoffed a laugh as he pulled his out of his pocket. "With how much you keep losing yours, you should add one to your product lineup."

"Ha ha," she said as she snatched it out of his hand.

"But seriously, it's no problem," he said with a shrug. "That's like me with writing. Sometimes I just want to throw my notebook across the room."

Belle nodded sharply as she handed the cloth back. "Sadly,

this tablet is far too expensive to do that with." She looked up at him. "You write your stuff longhand?"

"Is that judgment I hear?" he teased, scrunching his brow as he went back to his station.

"No. Just curiosity."

He looked over at her, saw the smirk on her face, and laughed. "At the beginning, yeah, I did." He turned a bit more in his seat to face her. "I'm just better at remembering things when I write them down."

"Same." She swiveled back to look at her desk while adjusting her drawing glove. "But all the long hand is doing for me today is giving me a hand cramp and stressing me out."

Zach nodded, before loading up another shirt and heading downstairs. At this point, Zach had full access to Belle's kitchen as well. He'd tried to get her to let him bring in some stuff for her to eat too but she insisted that he save the money, especially since the only things he tended to get in the kitchen were orange juice, coffee, and crackers. Nothing she couldn't easily replace, but he still didn't like the idea of somebody providing everything for him.

While he was in the cabinet getting a cup for his juice, he also caught a glimpse of one of the daisy mugs that Belle had manufactured.

Before he knew it, he was adding water to her tea kettle, and grabbing a tea bag from her drink cabinet. He came up the stairs slowly with a cup of juice in one hand and a mug of fruity and floral-smelling tea in the other, which he slowly placed down on Belle's coaster once he got next to her desk.

Belle glanced up from her drawing to look at it. "What's that?"

"Passion Tea with Honey."

She looked between him and the mug of hot liquid. "You made me tea?"

"Yeah, why not?" He shrugged before walking away. He took a sip of juice, put down his glass, and got back to the embroidery machine. He looked over his shoulder to see Belle smiling into her mug before blowing on the tea to sip it. Her smile got wider.

After finishing the last shirt, he started to fold them all up when he heard the clickity clack of claws coming up the stairs.

Appa went over to Belle and sat down at her side, looking up at her with his brown puppy dog eyes. She smiled as she rubbed her boy's head. "What's up, buddy? You gonna try and help me with these stupid designs?"

Zach bit his lip as he slowly walked up and snatched the tablet from her desk to see these frustrating designs for himself.

Belle immediately stood up and tried to grab it. "Hey, give that back."

He just held it high up as he looked at the doodles of hearts all over her digital canvas. "Cute, but isn't it a bit too early for Valentine's designs?"

"Give it!" She yelled at him, and for a second, he thought he saw a bit of blush on her neck, but he ignored it as he moved the tablet out of her reach again.

"Come on, surely you can reach higher than that, Sunshine?" he chuckled. "Never knew you were so short."

"You're like two inches taller than me," she said, her eyebrows scrunched up and lip out in an adorable pout. She actually looked very cute at that moment.

"Well, two inches can make all the difference," he joked.

Belle stopped jumping up as she looked at him with a smirk

on her face, one eyebrow raised, "Can it?"

Zach's eyes widened as his arms dropped to his side. "Um…I…"

She snatched back the tablet while he was distracted. His eyes narrowed at her. "Well played."

Belle smiled as she put the tablet back on her desk before turning to him with her arms crossed, "So, Sunshine?"

Zach's eyes widened and he could feel the heat traveling up the back of his neck, "Oh, yeah. That kind of slipped out. You know, the inner voice becomes an outer voice." He cringed at himself.

"You call me Sunshine in your head."

"No, I don't but…you are like sunshine to me."

"How?" she snorted.

"You brighten up my day."

The fact that he was freely admitting that to her was starting to freak Zack out. He really hoped that Belle wasn't freaked out by it, but thankfully the look on her face was not one of shock and disgust. More so of wonder, and…was that admiration? He couldn't tell.

She bit her lip, and all Zach wanted to know then was if it really did taste like strawberries, and what was keeping him from finding that out for himself. He started to lean down, and he swore he heard the floor creak under Belle's feet as if she were leaning forward, but the sound of ceramic on wood pulled them back as they looked to see that Appa had knocked Belle's desk, and sloshed tea onto her workspace.

"Appa!" She yelled in a scolding tone as she quickly moved to grab a towel. "You know better than that, buddy." She looked down at her pet as he laid down on his stomach, nearly looking guilty. "What time is it?" She glanced at the clock on her desktop and Zach did the same.

4:15 P.M.

Belle's eyes widened. "Oh, it's getting late. I haven't taken him on a walk yet today, no wonder he's restless."

She looked up at Zach awkwardly. "I..."

He waved her off. "No worries. I'm pretty much finished with the shirts, and I promised Kit I would come over and watch a movie with her and Joon so..."

"Oh okay. So I'll see you later then."

"Yeah, later."

He quickly folded up the last two shirts and put them in their designated area, but when he turned back around, he bumped into Belle and nearly knocked her over. He quickly pulled her close, wrapping his arm around her waist. He could feel their chests press against each other.

For a moment, it felt like nothing else besides this attic and them existed.

But Appa's barking reminded them that wasn't the truth.

Zach quickly dropped his arm and said goodbye, before rushing down the stairs and into his car.

Once he slammed the car door shut, he took a deep breath and sat back in his seat.

"Get a grip, Zach."

He didn't really remember driving over to Kit's house, but

ended up there anyway by muscle memory.

Kit lived two neighborhoods over from him, and was a ten-minute walk away from the town square. The Akiyama house was a modest old school two-story like his own home, but it had a more modern extension off to the side, which had once housed Kit's Oma. He walked over to the front door of it and knocked.

"Hello!" Kit greeted in a sing-song voice as she opened the door.

"Hey," he said before pushing in.

Zach could feel her glare on the back of his head as she closed the door. "What's up with you?"

"Nothing," Zach said as he glanced around Kit's space. She had turned it into her little vintage hideaway, complete with a record player, popcorn machine, and old furniture that she found at thrift stores and online markets. Zach and Joon had spent many Saturdays growing up helping her refurbish every goodie she found, and it was impressive to walk into a tiny space that felt so homely, but it did nothing to calm Zach's nerves at the moment.

Kit came around, and could blatantly read them off his face. "Your attitude isn't saying it's nothing, right Joon?"

"She's right," Joon said as he cut vegetables in the kitchenette.

Zach hated how easily they could see through him at times, but he ignored them, and he sat down on the circular barstool next to the counter. "What are you making?"

"Beef Bulgogi, now"—he pointed the knife at Zach—"answer the question."

"It's nothing."

Before the other two could argue more, Zach's phone buzzed in his pocket. He answered quicker than he'd ever answered a phone call before, but when Beau's face popped up on the screen, he just groaned. "What do you want?"

Beau's appalled face quickly turned into a glare. "Well, hello to you too, babe. Yes, I'm doing well today."

"What do you want?" Zach repeated.

"Why are you assuming that I want something? Can't a guy just call to make conversation with his best friend?"

"Best friend? Wait, who's trying to take our spot?" Kit questioned as she came over to the phone. Zach pivoted. It wasn't that he didn't want his friends to meet, but he'd pretty much kept them separate while he was in college, and old habits were hard to break.

"Wait, Zach, did you leave the house?"

Zach rolled his eyes, pointing the phone at the rest of the room. "Kit and Joon, this is Beau, old roommate. Beau, this is Kit and Joon, childhood friends." He turned the phone back to his face. "Are we good now?"

"What's up with you?" Beau asked.

"Nothing. Now, why are you calling?"

Beau didn't say anything for a moment, but eventually sighed and said, "Fine. What do you put in your collards?"

"What?"

"Mateo and I are grocery shopping—say hi, Mateo," Beau said, pointing his phone at his boyfriend.

"Hi Mateo," Mateo said, barely glancing at the screen as he looked over the produce in front of him.

Beau hit the back of his head before saying, "I want to make some collards for meal prep, and I hate to say this and boost your ego, but yours are the best. So, what goes in them?"

"Can't tell you," Zach said with a shrug.

Beau pouted. "Why not?"

"Roberts' family recipe. Mimi would kill me, yours are... okay."

Beau's eyes narrowed at him through the screen. "I heard that judgment. Have you not found something to help you relax yet?"

"I am relaxed."

"Sure. So nothing's happened with that Belle girl?"

Kit came around to stand in front of him with too wide of a grin on her face. "You told him about Belle?"

"So, something is going on with Belle," Beau said with a smirk.

"Oh, if he can tell there's something between you on the phone, there is definitely something there."

"Nothing is going on between me and Belle," Zach insisted, but he refused to look straight at Kit when he said it.

Kit stepped closer to Zach to get in his view, narrowing her eyes and saying, "Zachary. Look me deadass in the eye and say that again."

A grin grew on Beau's face as he threw his head back in a laugh, making Mateo look over at him. "Ooh, I like this girl. Zach, give me her number."

"No." The last thing he needed was those two in free contact. He could only take sass from one or the other, and he did not want them double-teaming him.

"Say it," Kit insisted.

Zach would not give in, mainly because there was nothing to say. Nothing was going on with him and Belle, and there was nothing that any of his friends needed to know.

"I almost kissed Belle," he blurted out.

"What?" the boys yelled

Kit squealed, "I knew it, I knew it, I knew it!" before she hugged Zach tightly. "The Rom-Com Gods are smiling down on you.”

Zach shoved her away. “There are no such things, and it didn’t mean anything.”

Everyone in the room—and on the phone—was silent as they stared at him with blank expressions pasted on their faces.

“Can someone smack him for me?” Beau asked.

Joon came around the counter and took the initiative, making Zach yelp in pain.

“Thank you. Zach, give me his number too.”

“What?” Zach asked as he rubbed the back of his head. “I said we almost kissed, but that doesn’t mean Belle actually likes me.”

“But you like her,” Mateo stated, his face leaning in to take up most of the phone screen. “Like, you like her like her?”

Zach scoffed. “What are we, in middle school?”

Joon rolled his eyes. “Stop changing the subject. Do you like Belle or not? Because I ship Zelle.”

“Ze—” Zach looked over at Joon, jaw dropped. “Tell me that you did not make a couple name for us?”

He shrugged. “What? It just works.”

“He’s right,” Beau said with a nod. “It works far too perfectly for it to not be a thing. So, is it a thing, ’cause I can get some shirts made.”

Kit raised her hand as she leaned over to get her face on the screen. “Oh, I’ll take a medium.”

“Guys,” Zach interjected, bringing all their attention back to him. “Just because I think Belle is funny, and pretty, and smart, not to mention easy and great to be around, it doesn’t mean that I...” Zach leaned back against the counter. “Oh, fuck.”

“Finally he gets it,” Joon praised, raising his hands to the sky.

“He really struggles when it comes to matters of the heart,”

Beau said before glaring at something on the screen. "Mateo, put the candy back."

"But it's a great value."

Beau swiveled back to glare at him. "Now." He looked back at the screen with a Cheshire Cat grin. "So, what are you going to do about it?"

"I don't know." Zach had only figured this out two seconds ago, and it felt like they were already expecting him to plan a wedding.

Beau groaned, "This isn't right. Zach finally has a potential girlfriend, and I'm a three-hour train ride away. Life isn't fair," he pouted.

Zach sighed. "Seasoned Salt and Pepper."

"What?"

"Get some Lawry's Seasoned Salt and Pepper for the collards and you're halfway there, okay?"

Beau smiled. "You hear that, babe?" Beau looked, and Mateo was already gone. "Oh shit, I gotta find him before he makes a break for the checkout counter with a cart of candy. Talk later. Kit, Joon, you find me on Instagram at BeauPeep. We've got a lot to talk about. 'Night."

Zach flopped down on the couch. Kit sat next to him with a shit-eating grin on her face, while Joon went back into the kitchen. "Don't worry. I'll help you through this."

That was just what Zach was worried about.

Reasons Not to Ask Out Belle

1. I work for her (It could make things awkward and I like having her as a friend)
2. She's so snarky (Does she always have to have a comeback?)
3. She comes with a dog (A Big Fur Shedding Dog)
4. She's so fucking optimistic that it burns like sunlight (Seriously, who is that smiley?)

Reasons those Reasons Don't Matter

1. I won't work with her forever (Hopefully done before the end of summer)
2. I like our back and forth (She's fucking smart and it's really hot)
3. Appa is not the worst dog ever (He can be cute, sometimes. But he still sheds too much)
4. I like that she's warm and cheery like sunshine (It's one of the best things about her)

Chapter 15

Zach rarely called out sick.

When he was younger, his parents would make him and Amaya march their asses to school with a running fountain for a nose and a pack of tissues. It was instilled in him to keep working, even when he didn't feel his best. It was only when Beau found him slumped over on his desk with a high fever during their first year of being roommates that Zach first missed a class. Beau had dragged him over to the on-campus health center, made him get a check-up, then made Zach take his medicine, and brought him food every couple of hours. Zach was able to repay him when Beau ended up with food poisoning after an excursion to a new pizza place near campus, but it was still hard for Zach to take a rest.

The day after he almost kissed Belle though, all he wanted to do was feign illness. He texted Belle that he had come down with a stomach bug after he went to Kit's, and wasn't going to be able to come to work, which wasn't a complete lie; he did feel sick to his stomach with all the nerves. It was a coward's move, but he did not want to figure out what he was going to do about his feelings for Belle. He wanted to rewatch the entirety of *Bones* for the third time and relate to early Temperance Brennan far too much.

What did it mean when your comfort character was someone who struggled with accepting love and friendship and took six seasons to admit they were in love with their partner?

A knock on his door caused him to pause the current episode where Temperance confessed her feelings only to be rejected. "Come in."

The door opened to reveal Corey standing there with a near-ly full cup of juice between his hands.

"Bud, what are you doing?"

Corey slowly walked over. "I'm bringing you some orange juice so you can feel better," he said with a grin, showing off the gap of his second missing tooth that Zach had helped his father exchange for a five-dollar bill the other night.

Zach chuckled as he took the glass from him. "Aw thank you, buddy." He took a sip.

"Do you feel better yet?" Corey asked immediately after.

Zach struggled not to laugh out loud as he swallowed. "Not yet, bud." He put the glass on the coaster on his bedside table. "But you could bring me some apples to help out with that."

"Okay." Corey ran out of the room, nearly bumping into Amaya as she walked into the room.

She stood by his bedside and glanced at his screen. "You sure you're sick?" she queried with a raised brow.

"I know for a fact that I'm sick of you," he said with a Chesire grin.

She glared down at him. "Ha ha," she teased before messing

with the fidget cube he had on his nightstand. "Seriously, if you're gonna sell this to Dad, you're gonna have to be more convincing."

"Already done." He shrugged before settling back in his bed. "I asked Mimi if she could make me some of her chicken soup 'cause I wasn't feeling well. Dad couldn't get a word in edge-wise."

Amaya's eyes widened. "Wow," she said with awe. "I've never thought of that."

"You have much to learn, young Jedi."

Corey ran back into the room with one of Mimi's pre-made snack bags filled with Honeycrisp apples. "Here's your apple, Zach."

"Thank you, buddy," he said with a smile as he took the bag. "Now go get ready for summer camp. Mimi's gonna drop you off."

Corey ran off without question, but Amaya stayed, flicking the button on the cube in her hand.

"You can feel free to leave too," Zach prompted.

"Nah." Amaya shrugged. "I might just stay here today. Take a chance to borrow a book, or use your laptop, or lie down right here..." She attempted to fall back on the bed but Zach quickly shoved her off.

"Get out!" He snapped, making her throw the cube at him, laughing her ass off before running out of his room.

Zach groaned and flopped back down in his bed, rubbing his hand over his face and knocking his glasses askew. He took them off and tossed them on his nightstand, trying to stave off the oncoming migraine, when his phone dinged.

Afraid it was Belle asking for something, he opened his

phone but sighed in relief when he saw that it was only a message from Joon. The content of the message, however, made his
heart beat a bit faster.

Joon

Did you tell Belle that you got sick after eating
my cooking?

Zach bit his lip. Joon took his cooking very seriously and always felt some type of way when it was critiqued for no reason.
He quickly typed a reply.

Zach

Maybe?

Zach winced as he waited for the response to come through.

Joon

You bitch! I cooked good shit for you and you
fucking blame your inability to make Zelle a
thing on me

Zach

I'm sorry

Joon

Oh you will be

I'm not gonna be your turtle chip dealer any-more

And I told Belle you had a weak stomach

So you were probably gonna be stuck on the toilet all-day

Zach's jaw dropped. Not only was he losing his turtle chips, but also his dignity.

Zach

What the fuck, J?!?

Beau

Damn

Kit

Nice one, Joonbug

Joon

Thank you :)

Mateo

Sucks to be you Zach

Zach was about to type out a plea but did a double take when he saw Beau and Mateo's names in the conversation.

Zach

Wait a minute

When did you two get in this chat?

Beau

This is a new chat that we made last night

Zach

Why?

Beau

Because we knew that we would need to coach you through this situation

So you don't drag this out and do something stupid

[Beau has changed the group chat's name to "Zach's Love Gurus"]

Zach glared at the screen; Beau's audacity in saying that to him.

Zach

You can't fucking say anything Mr. I'm gonna order Hazelnut lattes for weeks

To impress a barista even though

I'M FUCKING ALLERGIC TO HAZELNUT!

Beau

Uh...

Mateo

crying laugh emoji

Oh yeah, I forgot about that

Good job babe

Beau

Shut up

Joon

Wait, you really did that?

Beau

I mean it worked

Zach

rolling eyes emoji

After I slapped it away from your mouth and
asked him out for you

Kit

Why don't you do that to Belle?

Zach

Slap her drink out of her mouth?

Mateo

Ask her out you idiot

Zach felt his jaw clench as he replied.

Zach

I'm not an idiot

Joon

We know you're not

Kit

But we also know that you don't have any good reason not to ask her out

Zach

What about the fact that I'm not gonna be in town forever

Why start something when you know it's gonna end

That doesn't make sense

The chat stayed quiet for a moment before another typing bubble popped up.

Kit

Well, how do you know it's gonna end?

Zach

I don't know okay

Can you all just go back to work and let me have my sick day, please

They all sent different variations of "okay" before Zach put down his phone with a sigh.

After finishing another three episodes of *Bones*, Zach was starting to feel the itch to do something productive again. He opened up his Project Void file and started to add filler descriptions to a few of the unfinished chapters. He was trying to find a word for something to describe the emptiness of the Captain's memory deck when he noticed Mimi standing in his doorway in one of her Sunday dresses.

"Where are you going?" he asked.

"Tea with the ladies," she said as she buttoned up her purse.

"Didn't you all just have tea?"

"There is no limit to how many times you can feel fancy," Mimi reminded him as she straightened up the big church hat on her head, making Zach chuckle. "I just wanted to check on you before I left. How you feeling now?" she asked as she put her hand on his forehead.

"Better." It was true. He no longer felt sick to his stomach, but he was still nervous at the idea of seeing Belle again.

"Good." She looked over his shoulder. "What are you working on?"

"Nothing," Zach said as he slowly shut his laptop before she could look at it, making her suck her teeth.

"You know," Mimi said as she took a seat on the edge of his bed, setting her purse down. "If you are going to actually publish something of yours one day, you have to let people look at it."

Zach shrugged as he twirled his pen in his hand. "It's not ready for anybody to read yet."

"When will it be?"

Zach stayed silent, making Mimi suck her teeth again. "You always say that you want to be an author. You've been saying that since you were three, but I don't know if you could handle it."

"Mimi—"

"I don't think authors who want to publish their work have the luxury of keeping things to themselves."

Zach snapped his mouth shut.

"If that's what you really want, baby boy, you have to be willing to put yourself out there."

"I do put myself out there."

She raised a brow at him, but he just coughed as he looked down at his laptop. "Besides, there's no point in trying to do that right now when I'm leaving soon. I'll save that for New York."

"If you say so." Mimi got up and cupped his cheek in her hand, making him turn towards her. "But I don't want you to spend your life waiting for bigger things. Sometimes you need to live in the moment." She smiled before kissing Zach's cheek, quickly wiping away the lipstick mark after she did. "Love you."

"Love you, Mimi," Zach responded.

Mimi left, closing the door behind her, and Zach let himself sit with her words.

Live in the moment.

It seemed easy enough to do, but he was more focused on the repercussions for the future.

To live in the moment meant to live carefree and not worry about what happened next.

But all Zach did was worry at times.

He hadn't figured out how not to yet.

If he was more like Belle, then he would just spend his days writing like there was no tomorrow, not caring if anyone else liked it, and talking about his passions to everyone without a care in the world.

But he wasn't like Belle. She was the complete opposite of him.

She was filled with cheer and optimism, and he couldn't remember the last time he didn't try to anticipate things going to shit.

In what world do two people like them ever work out?

The water flows through the land, overcoming all obstacles and changing its surroundings as it goes. To be one with the water, you have to be willing to adapt. Willing to let yourself change and blossom into something different. Perhaps what you were always meant to be.

Lake from *River Misfortune* by Dorian Moses

Chapter 16

Simple logic dictated that ignoring something would not make it go away, but Zach did his best to ignore the nagging feeling in his chest when he thought about Belle.

Belle was special, there was no denying that, but it didn't mean that she thought about him the same way. If he asked her out, he wasn't sure she was going to say yes, and that would mess up the whole friendship dynamic that they had built over the past few weeks.

Besides, Zach was sure that most romantic relationships wouldn't end well for him. It just wasn't a Roberts family trait. His grandfather had left Gigi when his father and uncle were young. His mom left his dad when Corey was barely one. Who's to say that Zach wasn't destined to have the same thing happen to him?

He'd once read that the true definition of insanity was doing the same thing over and over again and expecting a different result. So, why let history repeat itself? But Zach could figure that out later. Right now, he was focusing on Spades.

No Roberts family gathering was complete without a game of Spades. Especially on the Fourth of July, which was essentially their family Spades tournament.

Zach remembered when his father had first taught him how to play the sacred game when he got to middle school. Jed had caught him playing one of the many card games that had been circulating in his school. At that point, Zach knew how to play Slapjack, Spit, Garbage, and more but his father had been appalled when he'd realized that he hadn't taught his eldest how to play Spades yet.

Soon, Zach was indoctrinated into the game, and if he didn't walk away from an event without winning a round, he felt like a failure. He refused to let that be the case today. He and Gigi were teamed up against his father and Amaya, who was just as into the game as he was. Corey was off to the side coloring with Mimi, who was laughing at the trash talk that the pairs threw at each other. It was one of the only times when he could tell his dad off, and Zach relished moments like that.

"Ready to give up, old man?" he chuckled as he picked up his cards for the round. They were forged in black, and the abundance of spades and face cards made him nearly giddy.

Jed scoffed as he picked up his deck. "Not even your Blind 6 can save you and Gigi now. We're a hundred up, all we need is forty points to win, and I have those forty in my hand right now."

Zach glanced over at Gigi; the look she gave him just proved how much his father was bluffing. She threw out the Big Joker, and he smirked at the little one in his hand, before throwing out the two. Before they knew it, his father and Amaya were bled dry of their few Spades and Zach started throwing out his face cards, getting him the six books he needed to get double points for his final count.

Jed looked down at his one book as Gigi swiped the last few cards from the table to add to her growing stack. "What the heck?" he yelped.

"And like that, Gigi and I are up 150 points, bringing us to 520, and that will be game, ladies and gentlemen," Zach said with a smirk.

"No!" Amaya cried as she fell back in her seat.

"Yes," he boasted, leaning over the table and holding his hand out for Gigi to shake. "Pleasure doing business with you, ma'am."

"Same to you, Zachary," Gigi said with a victorious smile across her face.

"And with that, I'm out," Zach said, getting out of his chair.

"Same," Amaya said as she pushed back from the table.

"What do you mean out?" Jed questioned, looking between his two oldest. "We should play another round."

"Dad, I promised Owen that I would go to the town barbecue with him," Amaya explained as she got one of her Iron Man water bottles out of the fridge.

"And I was supposed to meet Kit and Joon there an hour ago," Zach said as he stretched from his time sitting. Kit was having none of him avoiding the world any longer and told him that if he didn't go to the barbecue with her and Joon, she would send pictures of his goth phase to Belle. Zach had no choice but to get Jaime to take his shift for the day.

His father went to say more, but Mimi hissed at him, "Jed, we've already taken their morning, so let them go do their thing." She nodded toward the door. "Go have fun, you two."

"Thanks, Mimi." Amaya pecked a kiss on Mimi's cheek

before turning to her older brother. "Can I get a ride?"

He rolled his eyes and let out a faux sigh. "If I have to," he said before waving at the group.

The two were in the car and out of the driveway soon after. Sadly, this turned out to be the common time that everybody was leaving the neighborhood, so Zach constantly had to pull over to the side to let other cars pass them on the narrow road, and once they got to the main road, the stoplight kept them from moving forward. Zach groaned, his foot bouncing up and down as he waited for the light to change. He let his mind wander to what Belle could be doing right then. They hadn't texted since the morning he'd called in sick, and it was the longest time that they'd gone without messaging since they'd started.

The fact that they weren't talking made Zach even more nervous; *what the hell were you supposed to do when it came to talking to a girl that you kind of wanted to date but you were afraid to date?* He hated to admit how useless he was when it came to dating. Setting Beau up with Mateo had just been a matter of asking Mateo out for his roommate before Beau got himself put in the emergency room, but he had no clue what to do when his heart was on the line.

The sound of harsh guitar riffs brought him back to reality just as the light turned green. He moved the car and turned off the Olivia Rodrigo song playing over the radio, making Amaya scold him.

"Who said you could touch the radio?" Zach asked as he put both hands back on the wheels.

Amaya's back bounced against the seat. "Come on, we need something going on in here."

"Some of us like driving in silence."

Amaya let the silence sit for less than a minute before she queried, "Why do you want to go to New York then?"

"What?" If he didn't know any better, he would say that he caught a glimpse of her eyes tearing up.

"New York is loud as fuck, isn't it? If you like the quiet so much, why are you moving there?"

"It's where I need to be," he said with a shrug.

"Why?"

"All the good publishing houses are in New York, so that's where I need to be for work."

"I thought you wanted to be an author, not a publisher."

"Well yeah, but I can get some insights into the publishing industry for when I query if I'm already working there. Not to mention help some great books get published. I told you this a long time ago."

"Sure, but..."

Zach glanced over at her as he stopped at the red light going out of their neighborhood. "What?"

She glanced at him before turning to look out the window. "I don't want you to go."

Zach's eyes widened. He'd never imagined that those words would come out of Amaya's mouth. When he left for college move-in, she was the first one to wake him up in the morning, so he could get out as soon as possible. What had changed between now and then? He tried to play it off by saying, "But, if I go, you get your own bathroom."

Amaya scoffed. "I don't want that." She pushed her curly brown hair over her ear as she looked back at him. "I want you to be here. With us."

Zach sighed as the light turned green, and focused on driving once more. "You know I can't stay in that house forever," he reminded her after a minute.

He could see her slump out of the corner of his eye. "I know."

"Hey," he said, poking her ribs slightly as he did. "But that doesn't mean I'm gonna forget about you or Corey." His grip tightened on the steering wheel. "I'm not gonna be like her. Okay?"

"'Kay."

When they stopped at another light, he looked over and felt a nagging sadness as he looked at his little sister. But she wasn't so little anymore. She was sixteen and turning into a young woman. She was already prepping for college applications herself and insisting that she didn't need Zach's help with it. But, regardless of what she thought, he would always be there for her when she needed him.

He turned the radio back on but changed the channels until he heard some Stevie Wonder go through the speakers. Amaya turned to him with a smile on her face before singing along with all her heart.

Zach chuckled as he turned his attention fully back on the road, happy about the fact that his sister wasn't tone-deaf.

Amaya stayed fully occupied with her one-woman cover band until they arrived at the park.

He could already see groups of people making camp throughout the green space between barbecues and games as they got out of the car. Amaya let him know that she would be getting a ride back with Owen before she left. He quickly lost her in the crowd. He started to search for his friends as he walked in himself.

The Fourth of July Barbecue was an unofficial tradition in Lillet and one of the major times when the small town actually came alive. People were already getting ready for the fireworks display by saving their spots with lawn chairs across the park. Food trucks were parked around the curb selling ice cream, vegetarian vittles, and more. Families were scattered about getting food together, playing yard games, and talking amongst themselves.

He saw Kit and Joon in the distance and went to get their attention, but when he got closer, he nearly tripped over his feet.

Belle was with them.

What was she doing here? Last he heard, she was going to be spending the day at home, and he was not prepared to have any conversation with her yet. Sadly before he could run back to his car, Joon spotted him, waving at him to come over. "Hey, where have you been?"

Zach gulped hard before taking the first step. "Beating my family's asses at Spades. It's tradition," he said as nonchalantly as he could before turning to face Belle with as much confidence as he could muster. "Hey."

"Hi," Belle greeted with her usual smile plastered across her face, making his confidence waiver even more than it already was.

"I didn't know you'd be here."

She shrugged. "Kit forced me to come when she heard that I planned to stay home and sketch for the day. Besides, it gives me a chance to get Appa looking festive," she said, tugging at her dog's American flag neckerchief that matched the one that was hanging out of the center pocket of her overalls. Her off-the-shoulder white top and the red bow she wore in her hair made her look so fucking pretty that he couldn't stand it; he distracted himself by leaning down to pet Appa's head before Kit guided them all toward a seating area she had scouted out near the makeshift stage in the park. Mayor Hadlow took the stage to give a speech about unity in their diverse community that was surprisingly really sweet and left some in tears. Afterward, the four of them played catch with a frisbee that Belle bought for Appa. Zach was happy that he opted for a plain white t-shirt and jeans instead of his more academic look for once.

After Appa ran away with the frisbee for the third time, Kit declared that they needed snacks, so she dragged Zach over to a truck selling the most generic fair food available while Joon and Belle tried to get the toy back.

He noticed Des in line at another truck and waved at him as Kit skipped up to the window when it was their turn. "Can I get two corn dogs, two cheesesteaks, four pretzels, two cherry cola slushies, an orange slushie, and a blue raspberry slushie?"

"And a cup of ice," Zach interjected. The vendor nodded as Zach felt an elbow to his ribs. He turned to see Kit's raised brows. "For Appa."

"Ah."

Zach glanced over at Belle and Joon, who were now returning to their chairs, and turned back at Kit. "Why did you invite Belle?" he whispered.

"Well one, I didn't want Belle to be alone." Kit shrugged as she moved them out of the way of the next customer. "Nobody should be alone on a holiday. And two, I knew that if I didn't do anything you wouldn't even attempt to ask her out any time soon."

"That is not true," Zach insisted.

"Oh, so you have a plan?"

Zach bit his lip, and Kit nodded in victory. "That's what I thought."

Zach groaned. "We don't even know if she likes me like that."

"Come on, why wouldn't she?"

Zach could list several reasons, but the best one he could articulate was, "Because she's her and I'm me."

Kit looked him up and down with a touch of panic in her eyes. "I think that's the worst grammar I've ever heard you use," she gasped out.

Zach pressed his palms against his fizzing head. "God, I feel like I'm back in middle school."

"You say that like any of us dated in middle school," she reminded him as she paid for their treats. "Look, you're a great guy. Sometimes a know-it-all, but, objectively, you're a hot nerd. The boys agree with me, even though none of us would ever date you."

He blinked at her before grabbing the tray of slushies. "Thank you for that vote of confidence."

"Hey, she's here, it's done, so take the opportunity and shoot your shot." She gathered her change and put it in the tip jar. "What's the worst that could happen?"

"What do you want, Donna?"

Zach turned to see Des standing next to one of the other trucks across from a Black woman with straightened black hair cut into a bob, her hands on her hips as she stared down at Des with a determined look on her face.

Donna Quinn.

Des's ex-wife, who Zach hadn't seen in over a year, and for good reason.

"I'm trying to talk to you, like an adult," she snipped at him, "unless you forgot that's what we are."

Des scoffed before noticing all the people who had turned their heads to watch the scene unfold. "I think that you've said all that needs to be said." Des walked away from the line he was in, only to have Donna strutting after him.

"Don't walk away from me, you bastard!" She called after him.

"Didn't think we would see her around here again," Zach heard someone mumble in the crowd.

"Looks like we're getting more of that drama. Poor Des," someone else said.

Zach wanted to say something to shut them up, but the thing about a small town where everyone knew everyone was that gossip was the norm. Everyone knew about Des and Donna's story.

They were one of the *it* couples that came out of Lillet. The homecoming King and Queen of their year who got into their dream university together before settling back down in Lillet, where they'd both been middle school teachers before Des opened The Book Haven. Zach had heard how many people wondered why they were together though when the fights had started.

It had started as simple bickering, before it exploded into fights at the store and school. Mayor Hadlow almost had to ban them from public events because every time they went somewhere they kept fighting, and everyone had no choice but to stand by until everything was resolved. That was, until last year's Christmas fair, when laid-back Des finally got sick of Donna's scathing insults, and finally shouted that if she was so unhappy, then she should just leave.

And that's just what she did.

Another couple that Zach looked up to shattered into a million pieces.

"Ending up like them," he said to Kit. "That's the worst thing that could happen."

By the time the group finished indulging in their lunch, a local cover band that Kit had procured started playing some summer songs.

When a Taylor Swift song started playing, Kit and Belle were up dancing as soon as they recognized it, singing the chorus at the top of their lungs as if no one else was around. Zach and Joon sat on the blanket that Belle brought, sipping their slushies and laughing at the girls' impromptu concert.

Zach didn't realize how much he was watching Belle in particular until she looked his way and winked. He felt a blush rush up his cheeks and turned his attention to downing the rest of his slushy until a shadow blocked out the light from the setting sun.

He looked up to see Belle standing above him with her hand out to him. "Come on," she chirped.

Zach's lips pursed and shook his head. "Nah, I don't dance."

Belle frowned a bit before Kit called her back over after one of the more popular Swift songs started playing. As soon as she started dancing again, he felt a sting on the back of his neck. "Ow!" He turned to look at Joon, who was glaring at him. "What?"

"Dude, she wanted to dance with you," he hissed.

"...Oh."

"Yeah, oh. You need to let loose a bit if you're gonna win over Belle."

Zach scoffed. "Have you met me?"

"Yes, which is why I say you need to let loose."

He rolled his eyes before taking another empty sip of ice. When Joon took one of his own, both of them made their way over to the trash can. On their way, Zach glanced over to the food trucks again, and his eyes widened when they landed on a head of ginger hair.

"What's Baxter still doing here?" he groaned. "Wasn't he trying to make it big in Hollywood or something?"

"He did. He tried to come in the other day and flirt with Sunny," he guffawed, and Zach scoffed. As if, Sunny would ever go out with Baxter. "Said he booked a commercial."

"For what?"

"Life insurance or something. I don't know." Joon shrugged. "Didn't care enough to remember."

Zach didn't care enough to want to know anymore, and he was more than ready to ignore him, except that Baxter chose that moment to turn toward them. Zach felt his heart drop. Baxter smirked, and nodded in his direction.

"Zach?" Joon said, probably. Everything was muffled in Zach's head, like the missing signal sound of a television. He felt the slushie cup drop from his hand.

He had to get out of there.

He didn't know where his legs were taking him, but he didn't care. He passed the games, the food trucks, and row of cars before he finally stopped. He stumbled in between two cars and slid against one of them to the ground, his body trembling. He dug his head between his legs to try and drown out the intrusive thoughts spiraling in his head.

It was stupid.

He felt so stupid.

The fact that a stupid look could transport him back to that moment and make him feel so... helpless again.

Why couldn't he get over it?

Another shiver trailed up his body when he felt the shadow of a tall body blocking out the warmth of the sun. "You okay?"

Zach let out a deep breath and leaned back against the car before glancing at Joon. "I'm fine."

"Zach—"

He turned to Joon sharply. "I said I'm fine," he hissed through gritted teeth, but he immediately regretted it when he saw the worried look on Joon's face. He sighed and leaned forward on his legs again. "Sorry."

"It's okay," Joon said as he sat down with him.

Zach heard something ruffle, and the next thing he knew, something was being shoved into his hands. He lifted his head and saw a bag of his favorite turtle chips from Joon's snack collection. He let out a soft smile as he looked up at Joon. "What happened to cutting me off from the turtle chips supply?"

Joon shrugged. "I can make exceptions, you know," he said as he pulled out his phone. "Did I show you this new video yet?"

Zach smiled a bit more and opened the bag while Joon moved the phone in front of him. The great thing about being friends with Joon was that he never forced anyone to talk about things if they didn't want to. He would just sit with them until the feeling passed, and treat them like a normal person when it was over. The exact type of person Zach needed at that moment.

"Did you ever think of a new name for our pop-up book and coffee truck?" Zach asked after they finished their third video and the bag of chips.

"I'm still partial to Jay and Z's."

"No."

"What are you two doing?"

The boys looked up to see Kit and Belle standing there, their picnic things and Appa in hand. Kit looked down at them, more so Zach, with a pointed look on her face, hands on her hips. "Well?"

Zach bit his lip as he looked at the crumbs at the bottom of his chip bag. Eventually, Joon spoke up and said, "Baxter's here."

Zach looked up in time to see Kit's face soften. "Oh."

Belle looked between the three of them. "Who's Baxter?"

Kit shifted on her feet. "Um..." She looked at Zach again.

Zach pursed his lips but accepted the inevitable. She was going to find out about everything one way or another. "It's okay," he said as he sat up taller against the car. "He's someone we went to school with, but he and I were friends when we were younger. Sadly, he became a jerk the older we got, and the three of us were his favorites to mess with at school."

Kit nodded. "So Zach took a stab at him during his valedictorian speech. Said that only small-minded people think it's fun to disrespect others and that maybe they're trying to compensate for something."

Belle snorted a laugh. "Damn."

Zach smiled a bit but the memory of how he felt then didn't erase how he felt after. "Yeah. A lot of people found it funny, but he didn't." He sighed, trying not to let the memories overtake him. "One of our classmates held a pool party to celebrate graduation. I had no intentions of swimming, but Baxter *insisted* I get in on the fun so he and some of his friends pushed me into the deep end."

Belle looked at him with wide eyes. "Wow, that... sucks."

"Yeah," he scoffed. "What sucks more is that I couldn't

swim."

Belle dropped the bag in her hand. "What?"

Zach nodded. "Yeah. I was supposed to learn at summer camp with him when we were little, but the idea of lake water in my ears freaked me out, so I opted for more reading time. Lot of good that did me." Zach could still remember the feeling of sinking in the pool. He felt the memory start to suck him in until he saw Belle sitting in front of him. He glanced up at her and saw the stunned look on her face.

"So he knew you couldn't swim and he still did that?"

"Yup," he said with a pop. He glanced over at his best friend before saying, "Luckily, Joon's a strong swimmer, so he dove in to get me out and eventually taught me how to swim." He slapped a hand on Joon's shoulder. "Forever grateful for that."

Joon smiled at him. "You'd do it for me too."

"Yeah—" he looked up at Kit "—and Kit punched Baxter in the face before we left the party. He had a black eye for weeks." Zach suspected that the reason that no videos ever surfaced of the incident was because Baxter didn't want video of him being punched by a girl circulating either.

Kit smirked. "What can I say, my two years of karate class paid off," she said, flipping her hair over her shoulder. "And it was a great pleasure to be the one to finally sock him." She sighed as she gathered up her things in her hands more. "But if we don't want a repeat of that, we should just head to our usual spot for the fireworks."

Again, Belle was left confused. "What's your usual spot?"

"Wow, and I thought I had a good view," Belle said as all of them got out of Zach's car.

It was true; no view in town could compare to the Lillet Lighthouse, the monument that actually made it stick out from other sights on the freeway.

On the hill opposite the cottage, the white brick building stood proud near a cliff. While most people wanted the view close to the fireworks, the trio had grown accustomed to sitting in the "back row," not having to worry about disturbing anyone behind them or having people get in their way. They enjoyed coming there to escape the town below, and hearing the waves crashing against the bottom of the cliff, seeing the soft glow of the light bounce against the water.

Everything at the lighthouse always made them feel at peace in some way.

Zach came up with Project Void there after the three of them played flashlight tag up there once. Zach and Kit listened to Joon gush about his first girlfriend there. Joon and Zach sat with Kit there as she grieved the loss of her mother.

It was their special place, and he was happy to share it with Belle.

"Is it still active?" Belle asked as she took a step closer to the railing that blocked off the edge of the cliff.

"Yeah, but it's automated now. The last lighthouse keeper retired long before we were born, and by that point, we became one of the lesser-used harbors in the state," Kit explained as she walked towards the visitors' area. "My mom used to tell me a story about the lighthouse keeper's daughter and a sailor who was lost at sea. The keeper got sick one night and..." She looked back at the rest of them with pursed lips. "Sorry, you all are probably tired of this story by now."

Joon shrugged. "Go ahead, Belle hasn't heard it yet."

Belle quickly grabbed Kit's hand and dragged her over to a nearby bench, before sitting across from her, ready to hear it all. Kit launched into an animated retelling of Oliver, the sailor lost at sea finding love with the lighthouse keeper's daughter, Amelia, and how she always ended up guiding him home as the sun went down and the lighthouse came to life.

Kit had always had a knack for pulling out all the obscure town lore. When your mother was the town historian, it was hard for anyone not to absorb all that knowledge over time. Most people in school had made fun of it growing up, but Joon and Zach truly appreciated the stories, and—luckily—so did Belle.

"And you know what the funny thing is?" Kit said with a scoff as she finished the story. "She was known as the Belle of Linley Cottage."

Belle guffawed. "Wow," she said as she turned to give Appa some belly rubs. "Is that why you all let me rent the cottage?"

"No. But I think it was fate. Maybe it means that you'll be able to guide someone home too."

"If I could only be so lucky."

Kit's phone pinged, and she announced that the fireworks were starting soon. They all sat on the bench as they watched the sparkles begin to fly high from the valley, lighting up the sky. Appa tucked his head into Belle's lap as she covered his ears with some headphones that had crocheted ears on them.

After a couple of minutes, Zach glanced over at Belle, who was sitting between him and Kit, with Joon on the other end. She kept her gaze on the sky, and the flashes of red, white, and blue light shined on her face, lighting up her smile even more.

His heart rate picked up as he let his hand fall on the bench next to Belle's, their pinkies brushing against each other.

It felt like an eternity until he felt Belle's hand brush over his, gripping it slightly and making his heart skip a beat, before racing again.

The silence was getting to him.

After the fireworks, Zach offered to drive everyone home. He had already dropped off Kit and Joon at their respective places and was now driving Belle back up to Linley Cottage, glancing at her figure in the rear-view mirror constantly. They still hadn't managed to talk about the almost-kiss yet, but without the barrier of Kit and Joon, he knew it was inevitable, though he doubted that was on the forefront of Belle's mind at the moment. It had been surprisingly hard to get her in the car to go to the lighthouse, and she tried to insist that she could walk to the cottage from there, but none of the trio were having that. She spent the drive just looking out the window, her hand constantly brushing over Appa's fur as they moved through the town. He didn't know if it was being in the car, or being in the car with *him* that was really making her nervous, but he didn't want things to be awkward between them, so he took a deep breath and asked, "So, what did you think?"

She looked at him in the mirror. "About?"

"You know, the barbecue? The fireworks? Must seem a bit tame compared to how y'all celebrated up in New York."

She smiled as she brushed her hand over Appa's sleepy head. All the play they had done had pretty much worn him out. "Yeah. I kinda like that actually though."

"Seriously?"

"Yeah, everything up there was a bit too loud for me. I would much rather spend holidays indoors most days."

"What about New Year's in Times Square?"

"Overrated. You're basically in a sardine can, and if you don't start saving a good spot in the morning, you'll be out of luck by noon. I only let Kailey drag me there once, and then I vowed never again. Sometimes bigger isn't always better."

He nodded as he turned up the hill to the cottage. He had to agree with her. He did enjoy the intimacy that Lillet-sized events made. You knew everyone, and you could just enjoy the day (unless your childhood bully who was still an asshole showed up, but that didn't happen often.)

He had just barely pulled up to the cottage and turned off the car when Belle asked, "So are we not gonna talk about it?"

Zach's hands on the steering wheel tightened as he glanced up at the mirror, finding Belle's eyes staring back at him. "About what?"

She raised her brow at him, calling his bluff without saying a word.

He sighed. "What's there to talk about?"

She sucked her teeth and unlocked the car door. "See you later."

As Belle woke Appa up and ushered him out of the car, his mind was buzzing with questions about what he should do.

Should he just leave it and go home?

What would it be like between them when he came back to work?

Would she still want him to come back to work since he didn't address their almost-kiss?

Belle didn't seem like the type to cut someone off for something like that, but was that a risk he was willing to take?

Was he willing to let Belle walk away?

Zach scrambled to open his door, leapt out of the car, and around to the other side where Belle was still standing as she waited for Appa to do his business. "Hey, um..." He tugged at the belt loops of his jeans, trying to keep his mind focused on what he wanted to say. "Hypothetically, if I were to... ask you out…"

Belle's eyes widened, but he persisted.

"What do you think you would say?"

She bit her lip as she leaned against the car and turned to him. "Is this a hypothetical or is this you asking?"

Zach groaned. She was not going to let him off easy, but his grandmother's words kept ringing in his head, so he said fuck it. "I'm asking you out."

Belle immediately smiled. "Yes."

Zach's eyes widened as she strutted to the front door and unlocked it, calling Appa over. When she turned back to close it, she gave him a little wink.

Zach scoffed at her cheekiness, but his smile grew regardless. "Yes!" He shouted out in a jump before realizing that Belle was not that far away. He quickly got back into his car and started to make his way home.

He had a date with Belle.

He didn't know how it was going to go, but, at the end of the day, it was summer. Everyone indulged in romance during the summer, and then by the time fall comes, the feelings fade away like leaves falling to the ground.

Maybe he could indulge just for now, and then the feelings would fade.

[Zach's Love Gurus Group Chat]

Zach

Guys, I did it

I asked Belle out

And she said yes

Mateo

What

Kit

EEEEEEEEEPPPPPPPP!!!!!!!

Joon

YAS! Operation Zelle is a GO!

Beau

THERE WE GO BABE!

Zach

Yes thank you

Thank you so much

WHAT THE FUCK DO I DO NOW!?!?

Chapter 17

Zach's first date hadn't gone to plan.

He hadn't even known it was a date at that time.

When he got asked by a girl in one of his English classes to meet at the student union for dinner, he thought they were just studying. He came with a charged laptop and ideas for the project they had just been assigned, but halfway through his idea list, she interrupted and said that she didn't want to talk about class. It led to a very confusing night for Zach, as they spent their time talking about their majors, favorite movies and coffee orders over Panda Express, before the night ended with them sleeping together in Emily's dorm room. He and Emily didn't end up talking much after their project was submitted.

This ended up being Zach's general dating pattern throughout most of college. He would work with a girl, they would show interest and invite him out on a date, and sometimes he got lucky. He even agreed to a date with Beau at one point when he'd briefly questioned his sexuality, though he had known that was a date. They realized they would be much better off as friends halfway through it, and they acted as each other's wingman for the rest of the evening.

Even with all of that, Zach still lacked actual dating experience. He was twenty-one years old and had never planned a date, which made him feel inadequate when it came to romance. Kit always gushed about the male leads in rom-com movies being suave, debonair, and confident when it came to women, and he was none of those things. He actually preferred it when the girls asked him out because it took the pressure off.

He'd had a few crushes throughout school, but he'd tended to flub on asking them out; the fact that he followed through with Belle was astonishing, but that didn't mean the date was planned for him yet. After texting Belle when he got back home, they decided to go out after Zach finished his shift at The Book Haven the next day, which gave him less than twenty-four hours to plan something. His friends came up with a few ideas in the group chat, but nothing they suggested felt right for him and Belle. He spent the night frantically looking for ideas online before he finally settled on something, and texted Kit and Joon for help at 3 A.M. As he suspected, Kit was still up, and had her part done by the time he arrived at work. He was still antsy throughout his shift as the minutes ticked away until the time Belle would show up. He leaned on the counter, looking at the clock every two seconds, desperately trying to think about something else. Luckily, Des walked by just in time.

"Hey Des," Zach prodded. "Did you pre-order copies of the newest *Future Awakening* book yet, because it releases next week so—"

Des rolled his eyes before looking at him pointedly. "Yes, you asked me that ten minutes ago."

"Oh."

Des turned to him fully, crossing his arms as he did. "You good?"

Zach straightened up. "Yeah, I'm fine. You good?"

Des shrugged. "Yeah, why?"

Zach sucked his teeth, not knowing how to bring up what he saw. "At the barbecue…"

Des uncrossed his arms, waving Zach off. "Nothing happened. Forget about it. I have." Des walked back into his office without another word.

Zach wanted to call out again, but the bell above the door rang, snapping his attention over to the front. He relaxed when he saw it was just Joon. "Hey."

"Hey." Joon put a gabled takeout box and a tray of drinks on the counter, along with a lanyard filled with keys. "Here's your order and here are the keys. Kit says you gotta drop them off at Town Hall tomorrow morning."

"Okay," he said as he took stock of all the items before him. "Okay."

"Hey." Zach looked up at Joon. "You got this, dude."

"You don't think it's a dumb idea?"

"I actually think it's very sweet," Joon said with a puppy dog pout. "Didn't know you had it in you," he said before punching his shoulder. "Where'd you come up with this idea anyway?"

"Pinterest," Zach muttered, his brain filling with thoughts about how dumb this idea could be when executed, but Belle loved Pinterest. She spent hours scrolling it while she was designing. Combining that and the popular moments from the books that they shared on their individual shelves, he had an idea of what kind of dates she would potentially like the most.

What he planned should impress her.

Probably.

Hopefully.

The bell rang again, interrupting his thoughts and, finally, announcing Belle entering the store. She smiled at Zach as soon as her eyes found him. "Hey."

"Hi."

Joon looked between them with a smirk. "Well, have fun." Joon patted Zach's shoulder one more time before walking out of the store as Belle walked up to the counter.

"Where's Appa?" Zach asked as he moved the things Joon brought to the side.

"He's outside."

Zach looked out and saw Appa sitting next to the bench outside the store. "You could bring him in."

Her face scrunched up in the cutest way before she said, "Eh, he's not a service animal, so I don't want to give people the wrong idea." She shifted on her feet, looking at him through her eyelashes, because, of course, his heart wasn't already beating fast enough. "So..."

He nodded. "So..." They broke at the same time, both laughing at how awkward they were being. Zach had to remember that this was Belle. He'd never had to play a character when he was around her before, so there was no reason to start now. He took a breath and said, "So I thought since we both love books so much—"

Belle raised a brow at him. "Understatement."

He chuckled. "I thought we could get each other three books, which I'll pay for, by the way, and we could go read at the lighthouse with a little picnic." He looked up at her and saw no reaction on her face. "Is that a dumb idea?"

Slowly, a smile trailed up her face, and Zach felt his heart unclench from his previous nerves. "I love it."

"You do?"

"You should know that the way to a bookish girl's heart is buying her books." She glanced around the store, probably trying to think of books to pick before looking back at him. "Besides, I can't date someone who doesn't have good taste in books. This would never work out otherwise."

Zach chuckled and came out from behind the counter to switch with Jaime, who smirked at him as they passed him. Since Belle was also quite familiar with the shop, it didn't take long for both of them to find where they wanted to browse. They spent a good ten minutes walking down the aisles to find something else for the other to read. It took Zach a while to find something that wasn't already on Belle's shelves, especially since she only kept books she read and liked on her shelves, so he didn't want to give her something that she might want to return. He knew that she liked romances and a bit of fantasy, so he picked out a fantasy romance that he'd enjoyed before and added it to the pile before meeting Belle at the counter to check out. She forced him to look away when she put her choices on the counter while Jaime scanned them. Zach rolled his eyes, but obliged her, having her do the same when it was his turn.

After Zach paid and got his things from the office, they got Appa and made their way to the Mustang. Zach put the food and books in the backseat with Appa before quickly moving to open the passenger door for Belle. She grinned and slowly slid into the car. By the time he got over to the driver's side of the car, he had calmed down significantly and was feeling far more confident in his plans. He glanced over at Belle, who was gripping the armrest with one hand and flicking her nails on the other.

He reached out and placed his hand on hers. "You good?"

She looked over at him and nodded. "Yeah." She smiled. "It's just...you and me on a date? Could not have imagined this when we first met."

Zach scoffed a laugh before turning his attention back to the road. "Neither could I."

"Are we going to sit out here?" Belle giggled when they stopped in the parking area of the lighthouse.

"No." Zach unbuckled his seatbelt and got out of the car. When Belle didn't get out as well, he looked back in and saw the apprehensive look on her face. "Come on."

Belle slowly got out of the car and got Appa out as Zach took out the treats he got from Joon. He looked over at Belle, who had walked toward the bench near the edge of the cliff to look at the setting sun. The last bits of sunshine bounced off her curly black hair that she let hang free that day, and Zach found himself smiling just because he was looking at her.

He called her over and guided them to the small house attached to the lighthouse. He took out the keys that Kit had secured for him and searched for the right one.

"Are we allowed to be in there?" Belle asked.

Zach nodded after he found the right one. "Yeah, Kit got the all-clear from her Nana. All we have to do is stay out of the control room. Easy enough." He pushed the stuck door open with his shoulder, letting the bit of the dust at the top of the door fall before he walked in. He could hear Belle's footsteps following behind him. He flicked the switch that turned on the lantern lights around the house, bringing the front room to life.

Nobody went inside the house much after the lighthouse went automatic, aside from the occasional maintenance person, but it was still in pretty good shape. The white bricks of the walls were dingy with dust, and the muslin curtains were a bit tattered from age, but they had their own rustic charms. The beechwood furniture strewn around the room set the scene of a life well lived from when the keepers would stay there to keep the light going. The more delicate paperwork and photos were moved to town hall long ago to preserve the history, but one sepia-toned family photo still hung above the mantle of the fireplace: a father holding his young daughter in his arms, both smiling at the photographer.

Belle walked around the space, admiring every little detail. He could already see the cogs turning in her head for ideas of things she could sketch later. After putting their books and food down on the dining table, he beckoned for Belle to follow him up the stairs. They went up the spiral staircase, Appa making the climb as well until they were nearly at the top. He stopped them near a window that pointed out to the water beyond the cliff.

"Alright it should be coming on..." he started as Appa stood on his hind legs. "Right about... now."

The whirling sound of the old mechanics of the lighthouse turned on, and out of the top of the hole that led to the room where the light was held, they could see the warm beams start to circle before they made their way outside.

"Oh wow," Belle gasped as her eyes followed the light. Zach smiled as he petted the top of Appa's head, understanding the feeling entirely. It hadn't been on during the Fourth of July, so this was her first time experiencing the lighthouse up close. Zach could recall the first time that he'd seen it with Kit and Joon; they were at a sleepover at Kit's house when her mother said that she wanted to take Kit and the boys somewhere special. She packed them up in the car with a few blankets and bottles of apple cider and drove up to the lighthouse. She sent out a small picnic for them, and they made it in time to see it come on for the night.

Zach had never seen something so magical.

Until he saw Belle smile.

They watched for a moment longer before they slowly made their way down the stairs. "So this is where Amelia's father stayed?" Belle questioned once they made it down to the ground floor.

"Yeah." Zach went over to the food, quickly cleaning off the table with a towel he brought before unpacking the treats Joon gave them. "The town allows private events here and since I know somebody in town hall…"

She smiled and looked out the window once more. "It really is pretty."

Zach followed her gaze in time to see the light bounce off the waves beneath them. "Yeah, it is." He continued to unpack their snacks.

Joon had given them two small drinks of milk tea, a few of their calico cat cookies, and cat-shaped mini sandwiches, along with some treats for Appa. They presented each other with their books, and Zach was not surprised to see that Belle had selected a mixture of fantasy and romance books for him, but a glance at the synopses of the books read very much like the books he'd been enjoying lately. He had chosen for her a cozier sci-fi that he'd read a few months ago for the found family vibes, a contemporary story about a young artist, and a fantasy that dealt with the magic of art and star-crossed lovers communicating through letters.

They sat there in silence, reading their books and munching on the snacks as they got swept up in the narratives of the stories. Zach was caught deep in the graphic novel story of two shoemakers when he heard Belle struggling to hold in her laughter. He looked over at the giddy look on her face as she read through the most romantic of the books he'd chosen for her. "What?" he asked with a chuckle.

She shook her head. "Nothing. It's just I would never think that this is one of the types of book that you were drawn to."

"What did you expect me to read?"

She shrugged. "A book with more dark academia vibes, I guess."

"Dark academia?"

She turned to him with raised brows. "Oh come on, you've had to have heard of dark academia, it's like your whole aesthetic."

"What?"

"You know, brick-and-mortar universities with dark secrets and academia prowess to be the best. Sweater-vests and loafers. Writing in leather-bound notebooks. The need to be right all the time. I mean that's you to a T."

He scoffed a laugh. "Now that you mention it, I think I have heard of those types of books on Bookstagram."

She sat up with a huge grin. "You know about Bookstagram?"

Zach bit his lip, turning away a bit, making Belle lean over to look at him. "Zach, do you have a Bookstagram? Oh my God, you have got to let me see it."

"Oh, that would be a horrible idea."

"Please?"

He looked into her eyes, and realized that was a mistake; he couldn't deny her anything at that moment. He hoped that this wouldn't be a constant thing. He took out his phone, unlocked it, and slowly handed it over to her.

If it was even possible, the smile on her face widened even more as she scrolled through his feed. "Oh, this is cute."

"It's something." Zach took his phone back as she pulled out her own, and the next thing he knew, he had a notification saying that he had a new follower. He smiled as he opened up her account and took stock of the various pictures of the cottage, Appa, and food she had posted before following her back.

"So what do you think of my book recommendation?" she asked before taking a sip of her milk tea.

He pondered as he flicked through the pages he'd already read. "It's very you."

"And what do you mean by that?"

"It seems very happy and sweet."

"Is there something wrong with that?"

"No, it's a nice change of pace actually," he said as he pulled out the receipt to use as a bookmark while getting a cookie. "So, I will admit I was wrong about graphic novels."

"Well, maybe now you'll believe that I know a thing or two when it comes to books."

"I'll say you know a little bit more than that," he scoffed, noticing the smirk on her face now. "You're not going to let this go, are you?"

"Oh absolutely not," she giggled.

He found himself laughing with her and, for a moment, he felt like everything was right with the world. Once they stopped laughing, they looked at each other, and Zach hoped that she was thinking the same thing as him.

"Can I kiss you?" he asked, his voice riddled with hesitation.

She smiled and leaned forward without a word, letting her

lips brush against his.

He was right; her lips tasted like sweet strawberries with a hint of vanilla.

"Ugh," she said, suddenly pulling back.

"What?" Zach didn't think he was that bad of a kisser.

Then he looked down at where her gaze was and saw that the book in her hand was completely closed. "You made me lose my page."

He scoffed a laugh while bringing his hand up to her cheek. "I'll make it up to you." He pulled her lips back to his, and he felt her smile against his lips. Her hand came up to grab the back of his neck and, for a second, Zach wondered how much earlier they could have been doing this if he hadn't hesitated. But when Belle nibbled at his lip, he decided to focus on the present and licked more of the strawberry gloss off her lips.

But he wasn't able to stay in the moment for long as Appa started to paw at his leg. He sighed, momentarily regretting that he'd allowed Belle to bring him along. He broke from the kiss and let Appa out. They went outside with him and made their way over to the railing, watching the light shine over the water from there.

"The water looks like it goes on forever," Belle sighed as she leaned forward on the steel railing.

"Yeah, it does," Zach mused as the light came around again. "It's what inspired me to write my novel."

"Really?"

Zach turned and saw Belle's raised eyes and a giddy smile on the lips that he'd just spent too short a time kissing. "Yeah, it's..." His voice trailed off.

"What?"

He messed with his glasses. "I've never really talked to anybody about my novel before," he admitted.

Belle's jaw dropped a tiny bit before she shook her head. "Well, you don't have to—"

"No, I want to though," he insisted. "I mean, you share your art with me every day." He shrugged. "Why don't I share some of mine with you?"

Belle smiled again, and he felt more at ease. "Well, go on. Dazzle me."

Zach chuckled and thought about where to start, but honestly, what better place than the beginning? "Well, it follows this spaceship crew who have been on this expedition to gather data about what's left of the universe..."

For the rest of the night, they talked about his writing, her art, and their books, and by the end of the night, when he was driving her back to the cottage, her hand in his, he truly believed that the night couldn't have turned out any better.

 Liked by **lovebelle** and **87 others**

zachslibrary Book Review of "Laces Between Spaces" by Annalise Dale

I'll admit this book is not my usual type of read. I usually prefer an SFF book because I don't like reading stuff that can mimic reality too much. But this book exceeded my expectations and is probably going to be one of my favorites of the year. And it's about two shoe designers. While this story doesn't focus on an epic quest, the journey the characters go on is no less memorizing. Watching Crissy and Larry learn to love and grow as individuals over the years and designers was so fucking satisfying to read about.

If you like books about witty banter and fun characters, you're going to love this.

[Image ID: A Book with the title "Laces Between Spaces" written in bold white letters mimicking the laces of teal blue shoes with a pink background on the cover sat on a dark hardwood surface]

Chapter 18

"You good?"

Zach turned to look at Jaime, who stared at him with wide eyes, and shrugged as he handed over another *Future Awakening* book to put on the shelf. "Yeah, why do you ask?"

They slowly took the book from him, eying him up and down as they did. "You just look more *relaxed* than usual," they said with a shrug.

Zach chuckled. He was not the most smiley individual, so it had been a surprise for everyone when he'd started walking around with a Cheshire grin on his face. The day after his date with Belle, he started to smile a lot more. So much so that Kit, Joon, and Amaya, in particular, had wondered if he had been replaced by an alien, because they all said he looked slightly deranged. Mateo had straight-up asked if Zach was on drugs when they FaceTimed a couple of days ago, but he was just drunk on Belle.

He cringed at his own train of thought.

"Is that a bad thing?" Zach queried.

"No, just weird. You're usually so consistent with your dower mood, but hey, I like to see the change." Jaime sighed as they put up another book. "At least someone does around here," they mumbled.

Zach raised a brow before he realized what Jaime was pouting about. "Let me guess, Des turned down the Instagram account again?"

"Yes," they grumbled. "I don't understand why he doesn't want to get with the times."

Zach could see where Jaime was coming from. In the age of social media, being a part of a business that didn't have any whatsoever felt weird. While social media was not the only thing that could lead to sales, it definitely helped, and on days when they weren't stocking a new release, it felt like they should be doing something else to bring in daily traffic. But Des was not for it. "He thinks word of mouth is enough," Zach said with a shrug.

"Social media is word of mouth," Jaime pointed out. "Everybody has social media. Even you."

Zach groaned. "I knew I shouldn't have told you about my Bookstagram."

"Hey, your recs are fire. And if Des would just let us make an account we could...doesn't matter."

Zach believed there was more to it, but decided to change the subject regardless. "How are the double shifts going?" he asked as he unpacked the last book.

"Fine. But they might be ending soon." Jaime said with a smirk before they picked up the ladder.

Before Zach could ask about that, the doorbell rang. He smiled when he saw the round glasses and traditional Akiyama hair with a few streaks of gray splattered throughout it. He turned to Jaime. "I got this one." He walked over to the counter. "Hey, Mr. Hiroko." Zach greeted once he was in front of the older man, who chuckled and reached out for a hug.

"What happened to Mr. A? Have I lost all my cool teacher cred?" Kit's father said once they pulled back.

"You're not my teacher anymore," Zach reminded him as he went to stand behind the counter. Hiroko Akiyama was one of the coolest teachers that he'd had in high school. He had originally only taken his AP Environmental Science class because he knew him already, but two weeks into the class, he had become truly interested in the content. Mr. Hiroko made the class fun with demonstrations, outdoor excursions, and assignments that challenged them to think outside the box. Students could always see the extra effort that he put into his curriculum, and it always left them excited to do the work.

Zach looked under the counter at the books on hold. "I assume you're here for," he started as he picked up the title, "*Precious Spaces: A Guide to Protecting Planet Earth*?"

"That would be the one. Just prepping for next year's lessons," Mr. Hiroko said as he pulled out his wallet, giving Zach a glimpse of the Akiyamas' wedding photo. Annie Akiyama's smile was a mirror of Kit's, one of the main things that Kit got from her mother; the rest of her was her father through and through.

"How are you?" Zach tentatively asked as he took the man's card.

Mr. Hiroko took a deep breath, fingers gliding over the cover of his book. "I'm doing okay," he said with a nod before looking up at Zach. "Gotta go. I'm having lunch with my mother."

"Okay. Well, tell Oba I said hi."

"Will do," Mr. Hiroko said as he took his things and left the store.

Zach sighed as he sat down on the stool behind the counter, trying not to think of the tragedy of losing Mrs. Annie. Since his mom left years ago, Kit's mom had slotted in to fill the void, whether by inviting him and Amaya to go to a theme park with her and Kit or giving him extra of his favorites to take home when he visited their house.

He was never close to his mother, so her absence didn't hurt him that much.

Or that's what he told himself.

The bell rang again, and Zach turned to see a gaggle of young women come into the store and walk straight back to where the *Future Awakening* books were held.

Zach sighed as he stretched out his wrists to prepare for all the scanning he was about to do.

The spring in his step had calmed down significantly by the end of the day when Zach was cleaning up the day's aftermath, but the excitement of his next day with Belle still had him pepped up. They had moved on to the next season of *Avatar: The Last Airbender* and Belle had said the next episode contained an immense library. He was excited to see it, along with their continuing audiobook read of *River Misfortune* while they packed orders. He had just grabbed his bag in the office when Des came back into the room.

"Hey Zach," Des said as he threw a few papers on his desk. "Need to talk to you before you go." He gestured to the chair in front of his desk.

Zach slowly sat down as he looked at the serious look on Des's face. He felt his heartbeat speed up.

Des took his own seat, folded hands on the desk as he sighed, "Jaime is going to be leaving us soon."

Zach's eyes widened. "What?"

"Yeah, they're gonna be taking a job at Storybound."

Zach scoffed. "What does Storybound have that we don't have?"

"Better pay."

Zach's mouth snapped shut. Admittedly, Zach couldn't argue with that. While he loved The Book Haven and would love to sell books for free, the main draw of any job was pay, and you'd be dumb to not take a job that paid you more to do the same thing. His Mimi once said that the biggest factor next to that was a good work family; that could keep anyone in a position until they retired. Des was one of the reasons that he always liked coming back to work at the store, and one of the few reasons why he didn't want to leave town.

Des's chair squeaked as he shifted a bit in his seat, regaining Zach's attention. "So, I was wondering if you want the full-time position again. I understand if you're not interested anymore but I…"

"Of course I'm interested," Zach interrupted, scooting forward in his chair before he calmed himself down. "But…I need to talk to Belle."

Des leaned back in his chair with a smirk on his face. "Really?"

Zach felt the blush rushing up his cheeks but he continued, "Yeah, well, I've been working with her on her shop, so I don't want to leave her out to dry."

Des nodded. "Alright well, let me know."

Zach nodded, before he got his things and headed out of the shop, the worry about what he should do next flooding his brain.

The full-time job at The Book Haven was the job that he'd really wanted when he'd come back for the summer, and now it was within his reach again. At the same time, he didn't want to leave Belle to do all that work by herself. She had just told him the other day while they were packing the new set of the Barry Summer Collection orders that he had helped her make her process so much more efficient. She'd even thanked him with a long makeout session after they'd finished.

Rewards like that aside, he enjoyed spending time with Belle, and if he just gave up their working relationship, he didn't know if that was going to strain their other budding relationship, the one he cared about more.

When Zach got home, he had gone through a million different ways of how to break the news to Belle, but that didn't take away the impending guilt of abandoning her to work alone. As soon as he got inside, he glimpsed over at the living room and saw Corey playing with a toy car on the carpet, while their father sat reading a book that shined with the library-mandated plastic cover on it. His little brother was revving up two of the cars to race each other while Zach started toeing off his shoes. By the time they were off, Corey practically threw the cars into the coffee table's legs.

"Corey," Jedidiah's voice boomed. "I've told you about running your toys into the furniture."

"Sorry," Corey said with a pout as Jed took the cars from him.

Zach looked between the two before digging into his bag to

pull out a book. "Hey," he said, walking over. "Corey, I got you a new book. Can you read the title?"

Corey slowly took it from his brother's hand. "*The Boy, The Mole, The Fox and The Horse.*" The little smile that lit up his face calmed Zach down significantly. "Thank you! Can we read this tonight?"

"Of course," Zach said with a nod. "Go put it on your nightstand."

"Where did you find that?" Jedidiah asked as Corey ran up the stairs.

Zach shrugged. "I was just hanging out in the children's section at work and found it. Thought Corey would like it."

"Why are you still hanging out in the children's section? Thought you were grown now."

Zach pursed his lips. "I don't think you can ever get too old for children's books."

"I beg to differ," Jed said with a definitive turn of his page.

Zach chose to bite his tongue and went upstairs. When he neared the top, he noticed that Amaya's door was open, the glow of her purple LED lights shining into the halls as she played a game on her Switch. He was about to go into his room when the answer to his conundrum struck him like lightning. Zach quickly walked over and knocked on her door frame. "Hey."

She glanced up as the sound of Mario Kart victory music played before looking back down at the Switch. "What's up?"

"You still looking for a summer job?"

lovebelle 30m

Hey Lovelies!

I am happy to announce that the new shipment of stickers for the Barry summer collection is in and printed correctly!

The Barry, Carry, and Terry Summer Collections will restock tomorrow!

Don't forget, if you order one that was previously messed up you can use your coupon code to get a new one.

Love, Belle

Chapter 19

Zach tended to separate people in his life into different categories: family, friends, and work colleagues. He rarely let them overlap.

Kit and Joon knew his family but they didn't come to his house often; his family rarely stopped by his place of work to shop; he rarely had co-workers that he could eventually call friends. It was easier for him to keep them all in their own corners, but after Belle breached the line between "coworker and friend" to "whatever they were now," it was getting harder to keep all his worlds separate from each other.

The next time that Zach went to Linley Cottage, Amaya was in the car, singing along to the radio all the way there. Normally, he would be more annoyed by her presence, but given the big favor that she was doing for him, he held his tongue as they got out of the car and got to the front door. "Hey," he greeted once Belle opened it.

"Hi," she said before looking over his shoulder at his sister.

"You remember Amaya, right?"

"Yeah," she said with a little nod before gesturing for them to come inside.

Appa immediately padded over to him for pets once they were in, but Zach ignored him. "Des offered me a full-time job at the store."

"Oh." Belle's smile turned to a frown, which she quickly tried to salvage. "Congrats."

"Yeah, thanks," he said before glancing between her and Amaya. "But I didn't want to leave you without help and Amaya's been looking for a job this summer, so I thought maybe she could take over for me." He bit his lip. "If you don't mind? I promise she's not as annoying as she looks."

"Hey!" Amaya challenged, but Belle just smirked in response.

"Well, no one could be as annoying as you were," she said, making Amaya laugh out loud. She looked at Amaya. "Thanks for offering to help. We can use today as a trial day."

"Great. I can't wait to get started. But first, can I use your bathroom?"

"First door on the right."

Amaya quickly left, leaving the other two in pitted silence. "I hope this is okay," Zach said as he took another step toward her, finally giving Appa the pets he was begging for.

Belle smiled again, standing on her toes to kiss his cheek. "It's fine. We already established that this was gonna be temporary for you anyway."

"I know, but I didn't want to just up and leave without talking to you about it first."

"Zach, it's fine," Belle insisted, putting a hand on his shoulder. "You don't need to spend your whole summer here doing something you're not even interested in."

Zach let out a small laugh. "But I like spending time here," he admitted.

Her eyes widened. "Really?"

He scoffed a laugh, a smile creeping up his face. "Yeah, it means that I get to spend time with you, doesn't it?"

Belle bit her lip. "Who knew that you could be so sweet?" she cooed as she took another step before them.

He shrugged as he wrapped his arms around her waist. "Just because we're not working together on the shop doesn't mean that we have to stop hanging out."

She chuckled. "Well, I would hope not. I like spending time with you too." She stood on her toes a bit to place a kiss on his cheek. "But, can you still drop off orders for me at the post office? Otherwise, I have to pull my wagon out again."

He laughed before leaning down to kiss her. "I can do that."

"Good," she said before leaning up to kiss him again, this time on the lips, which he quickly returned.

"Hey, stop kissing my boss!" Amaya yelled, making the two break apart. Zach glared at his sister, but she just gave him a cheeky smile in return before she looked at Belle. "So what do I do?"

They spent the morning teaching Amaya about doing inventory and walking her through organizing stuff for orders. After the restock orders started coming in, they were back on the grind of getting stuff together to ship out, but this time in much larger volumes. People would make orders that ranged from three stickers to one Carry the Rabbit Summer collection, to all three summer collections, five sweatshirts, and four water bottles. It was a lot for even two people to handle, so having Amaya help on this particular day was quite useful.

Amaya enjoyed looking through the stock and squealed when Belle said that she would be able to take some "defects" home with her. She bopped to the rhythm of Belle's playlist as she moved between her station at Zach's desk to the shelves like she hadn't a care in the world, and Zach and Belle couldn't help but be amused by the sight.

"Are you sure you two are siblings?" Belle questioned with a smile on her face.

Zach laughed softly as he loaded another cup into the heat press. "I ask myself that all the time. But given how much I remember of our mom's pregnancy, I can't deny that she came from the same place."

Belle nodded, wrapping another cup. "So I assume Amaya's more like your mo—"

Zach's eyes widened and he sharply turned to Amaya who was busy unloading more sweatshirts. "Hey Amaya," he called. "Can you get my bag from downstairs?"

Amaya shrugged. "Whatever." She twirled to the other side of the attic before running down the stairs.

As soon as she was out of sight, Belle turned to him with a single eyebrow raised. "What was that?"

Zach waited until the cup was done and took it out of the machine to cool before looking back at Belle and sighing. "Our mom left about five years ago."

Belle's furrowed brow dropped immediately. "Oh."

"Yeah." That was pretty much the response he always got when he said that. "One day, we came home from school and she was gone. All she left was a note for Amaya, and she can barely stand hearing people talk about her, so I'm assuming nothing good was in it. She really hates being compared to her."

Amaya came back up, and the conversation dropped as they continued packing the first round of orders before they took a lunch break.

Amaya pulled her Doc McStuffins lunch box out of the fridge, along with Zach's, while Belle puttered around the kitchen cabinets.

"Do you guys want some chocolate chip cookies?" Belle asked as she dug out some bagels from her bread box.

"Sure," Amaya chirped after popping a grape in her mouth. Belle smiled and brought over a tray of huge cookies that were almost the size of Zach's hand.

Zach grabbed one, took a bite, and immediately was blown away by the warm feelings that washed over him. "Oh my God," he moaned. "These are amazing."

Belle smiled as she picked up a cookie for herself. "The secret is brown butter."

"I've heard of browning butter," Amaya said through a full mouth. "I'm so afraid to try it out 'cause I'm afraid of ruining our pans."

Belle nodded and waited until she swallowed to say, "Oh, I ruined at least two before I got it right. I wasn't much of a cook or baker before I got out of school, so it took a lot of trial and error, but it was worth it."

"Totally," Amaya nodded as she broke her cookie into smaller pieces. "Do you actually have a YouTube channel?"

Belle smiled and helped Amaya find the channel on her phone; they both started gushing about social media while Belle made lunch for herself and Appa. Zach sat in his chair, looking between the two of them in wonder. Watching the two of them interact was both satisfying and terrifying. Amaya was by far the most important girl in his life, and he knew that she struggled to connect with other girls, given that not many of the others at her school were as into Marvel and gaming as she was. Outside of Owen, the only other friend that he knew of hers was a girl named Sheila who she'd met at summer camp one year and she went to school outside of Lillet, so Amaya rarely got to see her during the school year. Seeing her connect with Belle was great because he knew that she needed more people like Belle in her life, especially since their mom wasn't there.

But Amaya also knew a lot of embarrassing stuff that Zach did not want Belle to know.

Luckily, the conversation never turned to him, as Amaya asked Belle questions about what it was like to live in New York, which he eagerly listened to as well. Her descriptions of the cars, sights, and people were vivid enough to imagine you were there yourself, and Zach couldn't wait to see it for himself one day soon.

"Moving all this stuff here must have been hard," Amaya commented after finishing her second cookie.

Belle nodded solemnly. "It was, but it was worth it," she mused before taking a sip of her strawberry milk. "My Grammy used to always say that home will be with you as long as you're surrounded by things you love." She shrugged. "I'm just lucky that I can do my work wherever I want to, so I can be in the places that I really want to be."

Amaya nodded. "Can you show me how that embroidery machine works?" she inquired after putting away her lunchbox. "I usually do all of mine by hand."

Belle sucked her teeth after she closed the fridge. "Well, I really need to go get some more craft supplies for the cozies."

Zach looked up from where he was cleaning the table. "Well,

I can show her if you want to drive over there in my car."

Belle's eyes widened. "Oh no, um," she stammered. "I don't drive."

"You don't? I thought you said that New York was a bitch to drive through."

She bit her lip. "Well, I have a license—" she tucked a loose hair behind her ear "—but I just don't drive that much anymore. I prefer walking."

Zach had noticed how nervous she was in cars at times, but he'd never commented on it, and he wasn't about to start now. He softly smiled at her, ignoring how much he wanted to bite that lip himself before saying, "Don't worry, Sunshine. I'll take you anywhere you want to go."

She smiled, brightening up the room. "Thank you."

"Sunshine?"

Zach's eyes furrowed. "Shut up, Amaya."

Zach just wanted to smack the mocking look off her face as she looked at him with puppy dog eyes and said, "Oh well, aren't you so—"

He covered her mouth with his hand and just looked at Belle. "You're an only child, right?"

She nodded.

"Be grateful." He felt slobber against his hand and immediately jumped back. "Ew! Maya!"

"Oh my bad," she apologized without a hint of sorrow in her voice.

"Oh my bad," he said in a mocking tone before lunging at her and tickling her sides.

"Stop! Stop!" Amaya screeched as she tried to push Zach away. Zach didn't relent as he pulled her in close and wrapped his arms around her stomach to hold her in place. "I surrender!" She eventually yelped.

"Good," he said as he released his hold on her.

But the moment his back was turned, Amaya yelled, "Never mind!" and she jumped on his back with a force he had not seen before from her. She tackled him down to the ground before tickling right under his ear. His true weakness.

"Stop!" He wheezed as he tried to push her off, but her attacks had him at half his normal strength. "Maya!" He looked up at Belle with a begging look in his eyes. "Help!"

And she did.

She helped hold him still so Amaya could continue her tickle attack.

Zach's Plans for the Week

1. Accept Full-Time at Book Haven

2. Deliver Love, Belle Packages to the Post Office

3. Work on getting Kit's Birthday present

4. Pause Alerts on Job Hunting Websites… For Now

Chapter 20

When Zach had a day off, all he would usually do was write.

After having ideas rolling around in his head for days, he was always happy to have a chance to get them down on paper before he transferred them over to the story document on his laptop. He was taking advantage of his last chill day before he started full-time at The Book Haven again, and since he and Amaya had helped complete all the orders Belle needed to do before she ran out of stock, she'd given them the day off. He planned on spending it at home writing in his designated chair in the living room while Amaya went out with her friends.

"Corey, come put your shoes on," Jed called up the stairs as he came into the living room. He glanced over at Zach as he grabbed the reusable bags from the hall closet for the weekly grocery shopping trip after his shift. "Where's Amaya?"

"At the arcade with Sheila and Owen," Zach answered as he twirled his pen around in his hand.

"So, you gonna be hanging out here for the rest of the day?"

Zach almost confirmed such when he saw a notification from Belle come up on the screen with a request to meet at her house. "I might be doing something with Belle actually," he said, already opening the message thread.

"Well, when I call you to ask where you are..."

Zach looked up. "Answer."

Jed nodded. "Glad we have an understanding."

An understanding or an order? Zach didn't dare comment as he looked back down at his notebook, trying to figure out how much more he wanted to finish before he left.

"Corey!" Jed called once more.

Loud footsteps came running down the hall from upstairs. "Ready, Daddy!" Corey smiled as he ran down the stairs, before going over to hug Zach. "Bye, Zach."

"Bye, buddy." Zach smiled as he let go. The little one ran out the front door with their father following right behind him.

Zach bit his lip as he looked at the scene between Ty and Captain Wan that he was writing. The Captain kept dismissing all of Ty's ideas as "utter malarkey." The desire to keep on with this scene had left, so he shut his book and grabbed up his writing gear to take it to his room before he left.

When Zach pulled up to the cottage, he could see Belle in the distance, standing in the floral meadow that stretched out behind the house. Kit had told him once that Linley Cottage was named so for the flax meadow that surrounded the property. The reception wasn't the best in the area so what the cottage lacked in modern jumps, it made up for in beauty. That was abundant in spades at the moment as Belle walked through the field with her camera glued to her eyes. He slowly made his way to her, and his hands hovered over her waist once he was close enough.

Until she elbowed him in the stomach.

"Ow!" he yelped, taking several steps back as he cradled his midsection.

Belle swiftly turned to face him and her eyes widened in fear. "Oh fuck, I am so sorry."

"Ow," he repeated as he leaned on his knees.

"Sorry." Belle put down her camera and grabbed something. "Sorry," she repeated, pressing something cold into his stomach, before narrowing her eyes at him, "God, you should know better than to sneak up on a girl from the city."

"Oh, believe me, I've learned," he choked out.

"Sorry."

"It's okay," he said as he removed her hands from his stomach. "Let's start again." He stood up to his full height. "Hey."

She smiled up at him and kissed his cheek. "Hi."

"So, you were very cryptic with what exactly we're going to be doing."

"Well before someone decided to sneak up on me, I was setting it up." She grabbed his hand and dragged him over to a clearer area of the field. In the space laid a tan gingham blanket with a wicker basket with plates and silverware strapped to the lid on top of it. He could see small containers of food stacked on the inside, and Belle had made a few platings of fruit and sandwiches on the blanket already, probably for whatever video she was making.

"A picnic?"

She shrugged. "I've always wanted to go on a picnic date."

"Didn't I technically take you on a picnic date?"

"Yes, but this is a fancy one," she said as she picked her camera back up to get more footage of the setup. "Besides, I made all of this for a food video anyway and I didn't want it to go to waste."

He chuckled. "Oh, so I'm here for content."

"No, you're here for cleanup."

Zach wanted to continue their banter, but honestly, he was too hungry and the sandwiches she had plated looked pretty good to him. He sat down on the blanket as she explained her entire setup, from the sparkling pink lemonade that she'd put in a pitcher she bought at the thrift store, to the mini strawberry shortcakes in their own little dishes. She asked him to take a few photos and videos of her with the picnic, capturing angles of her eating and putting down plates before he was finally allowed to dig in. After the first bite of the sandwich, chased by a bit of lemonade, he was more than happy to be there. They fell into their easy rhythm of enjoying each other's company like usual. Even with the constant buzz of bugs in his ear, he enjoyed talking to Belle about the books that they had both read this week, catching up on how Amaya was doing at the shop and how Zach's writing was going.

Sometimes, it scared Zach with how easy it actually was. To talk to someone about everything he was doing without filtering certain things out. When he was with his other friends, he was pretty straight forward, but he never brought up things like his writing or his reading. Not because he thought they would make fun of his interests, but because he thought they would get bored with hearing about it. On his Bookstagram, he found other people who were just as excited about books as he was, but he hadn't had someone who he could talk to about them with in real life. His father would just question his book choices, and Des was more of a nonfiction guy.

With Belle, he could talk about the amazing way that Dorian Moses had described the magic system in *River Misfortune*. They could both get worked up about how great the character relationships were done in *Avatar*. She could gush about a scene in a romance book where the two main characters got lost in an infinite bookstore, and he would hang on her every word. He liked listening to her talk so passionately about things that she loved, even when it was things as ridiculous as fairies hiding in the grassy meadow around them.

"Fairies don't exist, Belle," Zach protested for the third time with a smile on his face.

"How do you know they don't exist?" Belle questioned as they laid on the blanket, their bellies filled with treats as Appa rolled around next to them.

"They've never been seen before."

"That's because they hide. Humans freak them out," Belle said with such confidence that Zach almost didn't want to argue with her.

"I can relate to that," Zach admitted, "but I'm not gonna believe in them until I see them with my own eyes."

"You don't have to see things to believe in them."

"Uh-huh." Zach closed his eyes as the sun came out from behind a cloud. The mix of clouds in the sky made him a bit apprehensive about how much longer they would be out there, but he didn't want to suggest packing up just yet.

"Seriously." Belle poked his shoulder, making him turn more toward her. "Like you don't see love, but you believe in it, right?"

"Yeah," he admitted with a shrug.

"So I will continue to believe in fairies," she asserted before leaning back on the blanket. "Even if I can't see them."

Zach chuckled; he already knew that there was no chance he was going to change her mind, so he just leaned over and kissed her cheek. "Whatever you say, Sunshine."

Appa chose that moment to trot over and press his nose into Zach's forehead. "Hey, Appa," Zach said as he reached up and scratched Appa's neck, prompting the dog to drop his toy and lean into the touch. When Zach stopped, Appa kept staring at him like he wanted something.

"He wants you to play with him," Belle finally explained.

Zach made a big show of rolling his eyes as he rolled over. "If I have to." He stood up, picking up the ball as he did. He threw it as far as he could, and Appa took off. Zach chuckled as the shepherd slipped around the field in his enthusiasm to get the ball. When Appa came back with the ball, Zach bent down and rubbed his head before throwing it again. As much as he hated to admit it, Appa was becoming one of the other reasons why he liked coming to Linley Cottage so much.

After he threw the ball as hard as he could one last time, he noticed Belle looking off in the distance with a somber look on her face.

"What?" he asked as he sat back down.

"It's just…" She shrugged. "I never thought I could have this."

"A picnic in the middle of a bug-infested field?"

She shoved him, making him laugh at how little he moved. "No. I mean, growing up, I would watch shows and movies with things like this—picnics, garden parties, dancing at fancy balls—and would always say 'I want to do that when I get older,' but…"

"What?"

"The characters in those things never looked like me."

A familiar pain stirred in Zach as she continued, "I mean, come on, when's the last time you saw a fairy-filled, cutesy, whimsical, drama-free show starring a Black girl?" Belle started playing with the edge of her white and pink floral dress. "I remember when I was younger, I always related more to the shy characters in the show, but they never looked like me. I would try to say that because they had a dark hair color they were just like me but...I was just desperate to find something in those shows because those were the stories I wanted to be in. Whenever I did see Black girls in shows, they were wild, fiery, and not afraid to speak their mind, and that wasn't like me at all."

Zach sat back a bit. "You have no problem speaking your mind to me."

She scoffed. "Well, when you have a shitty year of loss, you stop caring when people get in the way of things you enjoy."

Zach cringed as the memories of their first few meetings ran back through his head. He grabbed her hand in his. "I'm sorry if I made you feel bad about being happy about those things."

She gave him a grim smile as she laid back on the blanket. "You've long been forgiven."

"You shouldn't forgive me that easily," he said lying back with her.

"Oh, I didn't. I was very much still convinced of your arrogance and snobbery until I saw you with your siblings. The way you are with them, I think that's more likely the real you."

"I like to think so." He shrugged. "Or I try to be that me, especially when Corey's around. I just want the best for him. Like, Amaya will be fine, she's a force of nature, but Corey...he can be really sensitive sometimes and life is gonna be stressful for him when he gets older. I want him to have as many years as he can of just being carefree and not thinking the world is out to get him."

Belle squeezed his hand hard, making him turn to her. Her brows were fraught with worry when she asked, "Do you think the world is out to get you?"

Zach quickly shook his head. "No," he sighed, "but...it doesn't feel like it's helping me either." He shrugged. "I just thought stuff would be easier once I got out of college."

She scoffed. "Who told you that?"

He chuckled. "I think I just believed it. I mean, most people just roll from college into a career. Everything gets laid out from there. Thought it would be simple."

"Life isn't simple," Belle lamented, "but it can be fun." Zach turned in time to see a mischievous smile blooming on her face. She stood up and straightened the wrinkled skirt of her dress before holding out her hand to him. "Come on."

He raised a brow at her, but still grabbed it to stand up. "What are we doing?"

She turned towards the field where Appa was now rolling around in the grass. "We're going to run through the field with fairies."

He took his hand back as he rolled his eyes. "Belle," he protested.

"Come on. Maybe if we run fast enough, we can see them before they turn invisible," she said, bouncing on her toes.

"And risk getting covered in ticks, no thank you," he said, shoving his hands in his pockets.

Belle poked his ribs.

"Hey," he scolded, flinching away

She moved her assault to his neck.

"Belle, stop—" She tickled his stomach, and no matter how much he doubled over, she didn't stop for a good minute before she slowly backed away from him. He glared at her with a smile on his face. "Oh, you're gonna pay for that."

She squealed before running away into the field. He chased after her. Both laughed as they ran through the grass, kicking up dandelion fluff as they went. Belle was quick, able to dodge him as soon as he got close to her, but he was persistent. Appa decided he wanted to join in the fun, and proceeded to run after Belle as well, making it much harder for her to avoid her pursuers.

Eventually, she had to stumble back into Zach to get away from Appa, and Zach wrapped his arms around her and swung her feet off the ground to keep her from escaping. "Gotcha, Sunshine."

Belle giggled. Once he put her feet back on the ground, she turned around in his arms. "Yeah you did," she said with a smile, before leaning over and kissing him lightly on the lips.

That wasn't enough for him. He pulled her closer, making her yelp, but the moan that came out once he kept their lips locked was soon followed by her hand coming to rest on his cheek. It was a pretty perfect moment until he felt something wet splash against the back of his neck.

He looked up and saw the gray clouds hovering over them as more drops fell from the sky.

Belle giggled as the water started to fall faster, but Zach was not a fan of being caught in the rain without an umbrella. Zach grabbed her hand and started pulling her back to their picnic. Belle called for Appa to follow them to the blanket where they shoved everything into the basket before running back to the cottage. Belle went to open the door but the door wouldn't budge.

"Of all the times I remember to lock the door," she groaned as she tried to dig through her dress pockets, thunder rumbling above them. "Ugh, it's in the basket." She glanced at the basket in Zach's hand before shaking her head and picking up a small rock from next to the door. She took out a key, unlocked the door and they both burst inside. Belle called for Appa to come in; the dog was wet to the bone when he did.

"Appa, don't—" Belle tried to command, but it was too late. Appa shook his fur out, thoroughly splashing the two of them and the front area with water and dog fur. "Ugh, buddy," she chided as she went and grabbed his collar. "Come on, let's dry you off."

As Belle took care of him, Zach started unpacking what was left of the picnic, putting containers in the fridge and dishes in the sink. Once he finished, he took note of how soaked his button-up shirt was, and how it clung to his body.

"I could dry that for you," Belle said as she came back into the room with a dry Appa, walking right over to him. Her fingers brushed over the top button.

Zach felt his throat drying up as her hand brushed over the bare part of his chest showing. "Sure," he coughed.

Belle started slowly unbuttoning his shirt, her nails dragging along his skin to get the next one. She glanced up at him through her lashes, her glasses hanging on the edge of her nose. It felt like torture as she slowly guided her hands up his chest before finally pushing it off his shoulders. While he didn't have the washboard abs and the physique of a harlequin male model, he had inherited his dad's broad shoulders and straight build. He could see Belle's eyes tracing him before she looked down at her own soiled dress. "I should probably take this off too," she murmured.

"Probably."

He moved a bit, giving her enough space to peel off her dress, revealing the pink bra and gray shorts she wore underneath it. His eyes started tracing the curves of her stomach and breasts before they met her eyes, which were filled with the same things that his were: desire.

He didn't know who moved first, but the next thing he knew they were clinging to each other, lips locked as she pulled him back towards her bedroom. He paused as they crossed the threshold.

"What?" she asked.

"You know this is actually the first time I've been in your room."

The room seemed quite like the rest of the house: old, worn, muted, gray wood furniture with touches of laces and flowers on them; a couple of plush items in the corner that resembled Carry, Barry, and Terry; a white quilt with pink roses dotted across it covered satin-looking pink sheets that laid on the bed. It felt like Belle had easily put her touch in this space of the house as well.

"Is that what you're really focusing on right now?" she questioned as she walked back toward the bed. She didn't sit down on it; her eyes were hinting that she wanted him to lie on it with her.

"Yeah, no." He walked over to her and cupped her face in his hands before attaching their lips again. He had seen a glimpse of the pink tube of strawberry lip gloss that she kept on her bedside table as he licked it off her lips. He knew he was going to have to buy her more of it.

As she placed her hands on his chest, his trailed down her stomach until he reached the top of her shorts. He glanced up at her. "Can I..."

She nodded. "Yes, please."

His hand dipped into her shorts. She was already wet, but he didn't know if it was from the rain or if she was just as turned on as he was. The moan she let out when he rubbed his fingers over her entrance probably meant that it was the latter. He took his other hand and pulled down her shorts and underwear, revealing the tufts of black hair covering the top of her pussy. He wasted no time pushing her to sit on the bed and kneeling at the edge, pushing her legs open for himself. He glanced up at her again, asking for permission.

She nodded immediately.

He opened her legs just a bit wider before he tentatively licked her pussy, making her gasp out. Zach smiled. She was just as sweet down there too.

He licked again, this time with more vigor, burying his tongue between her folds, enjoying the moaning as she squirmed in his hands. He held down her hips to keep them in place as he ate her out. "You like that?" he questioned, pulling back for a moment.

"Yes," she moaned before pushing his head down again.

He went back in, alternating between sucking her folds in between his teeth and flicking his tongue between them, before he started fingering her.

"Oh my God," she breathed, affirming that he was in the right spot.

He chuckled as he went faster, pausing every so often to adjust his position, savoring every moan she let out. The taste of her was more addicting than any drug he could consume.

"Z-Zach," she stuttered. "Zach! Yes!"

"That's right," he said with a smirk, smacking his lips as he pulled back from her. "Scream my name, Sunshine," Zach ordered as he pushed in one more time, and sent her over the edge.

"Zach! Oh, God!" She plopped back on the bed, breathless for a moment, before looking down at Zach with narrowed eyes. "I hate that you're good at that," she gasped out.

He smirked as he climbed up the bed and leaned over her. "Why? You benefit from it."

She raised a brow. "Because you're gonna be so fucking smug about it," she sighed as she ran her fingers over his arms.

"Not really." He pecked a kiss on her lips. "Maybe a bit."

She giggled as she pulled him in for another kiss, but he couldn't enjoy it for too long; his phone buzzed against his hip.

He pulled back with a groan. "You have got to be..." Zach reached into his pocket, pulled out his phone, and rolled his eyes when he saw Amaya's face on the screen. "What?" he snapped when he put the phone up to his ear.

"Can you come pick us up?" Her voice was muffled, and he could only attribute it to arcade sounds of whirling machines and bells.

"Are you fucking serious?" he groaned as Belle's hand trailed down his stomach toward his pants. Zach quickly grabbed her hand before he added, "Why you calling me? Call Dad."

"Dad's still at work and Mimi is at Gigi's for their monthly lunch. Please."

He groaned, his head falling between Belle's breasts. "Fine. But you owe me." He hung up the phone, picked up his head, and looked down at Belle, trying not to get distracted by how pretty she looked laid out like that. "I gotta go."

She pouted. "Oh okay."

He leaned down and pressed a kiss to her soft lips, enjoying one last taste of strawberries, before he got off the bed and headed into the hall. He looked at his soiled shirt on the floor and dreaded putting it back on.

"Here—" he turned to see Belle holding out a sweatshirt "—wear this."

He smiled when he saw it was one of the larger Barry ones

that said "No Hugs Please." "Thanks." He pulled it over his head. The cottony feel of the shirt felt nice against his skin. He leaned down and kissed her lips again. "See you later, Sunshine."

She bounced on her toes to peck another kiss on his lips. "I'm counting on it," she said just as one of her bra straps slipped off her shoulders.

He groaned and put it back in place before he gave in to his desire to see what was underneath it. He said one last goodbye before rushing outside to his car, blasting an old-school playlist that reminded him of his grandmothers to calm himself down before he got to the arcade.

"small business vlog: designing for fall already? Packing orders, picnics, and frolicking in fields searching for fairies"

56,823 views · 4h ago

Hi, My Lovelies,

I thought this week I would show you a week in my life as a small business owner. I have the privilege of being able to work from home and do something I love because of all of you and I wanted to show you how the process works, along with some other snippets of my week, like my picnic date. Hope you enjoy it!

Love, Belle

P.S. The recipes for the picnic food you see are on my blog if you're curious. ;)

@AlwaysAlthea · 3h ago

You always remind me that life can be magical. You're such an inspiration! How did you figure out how to decorate your space?

@lovebelle · 10 min ago

Oh, thank you so much! That really means a lot to me. Also, 75% of my screen time is Pinterest so I get all of my inspiration from there.

@wejft · 2h ago

I started drawing again because of you and that tutorial you posted a while back!

> @lovebelle · 8 min ago
>
> Amazing! Message me on Insta, I'd love to see your work if you shared it.

@luvbug1236 · 4h ago

Does anyone else want to go on a picnic date with Belle?

> @TiaDoll · 4h ago
>
> If only we could be so lucky :(

Chapter 21

When Zach showed up to the office for his first full day at The Book Haven again, he was excited to fall back into his usual routine when he stepped into the office.

"Hey," Des said, barely looking up from the page in front of him.

"Hey," Zach chirped as he put down his things. "So where do you need me? Bringing in stock? Reorganizing the children's section?"

"Cleaning the toilets," Des answered, pointing to the cleaning cabinet.

Zach pursed his lips. "I really should have seen that coming."

Luckily the toilets weren't at their worst, but they definitely weren't at their best. He ended up needing to get a refill of wipes halfway through the job, but the relief of finishing was just what he needed to put a small smile back on his face. When he went back into the main office, Des was still looking at paperwork.

"Hey, sit down for a moment," Des requested after Zach put the supplies back in the closet.

"What's up?" Zach asked as he plopped down in the chair.

"I'm just doing a mid-year meeting," Des shrugged. "See how you're doing with your position."

"I've only been back in this position for half an hour."

Des's eyes narrowed at him with a chuckle. "Okay, smart ass, reel it back."

Zach scoffed a laugh. "What's going on you? You're never this serious."

"I'm just trying to get an idea of what we can do better when it comes to the store." Des shoved some papers aside as he picked up a notepad and pen. "Increase sales, get more people in the door, and as one of our best employees..."

"I'm gonna be your only employee."

"And our best customers," Des continued as if Zach hadn't interrupted. "I thought you might have some good ideas."

Zach pondered; he had many ideas for the store. Most of them were on his bucket list of non-realistic dreams, right between having the space fight in Project Void turned into an amusement park ride and getting married to his bookish soulmate. He actually had a list of ideas in his notebook in his bag, but he resisted the urge to bring that out for fear of scaring Des with being overly dedicated. Instead, he mentally scrolled through his list. "Well, we could try to get a website up, or make some social media accounts, too—"

"We don't need that."

"Why not?"

"Because some things are better done in person than through a screen," Des said with a raised brow. "Like reading. What else you got?"

"Well, we could try stocking up on a larger variety of romance and children's books, since those are our best sellers at the moment. Also, have you got the summer reading list from the local schools, 'cause we can stock up on those for when all the parents come in near the end of summer to buy up the stock."

Des nodded as he scribbled on his notepad. "Good idea. Anything else?"

"We can get customer recommendations. Ask what their favorite books are and have a display for them now that the major summer holidays are over."

"Not bad."

"And we could even do some of these trends that I've seen on Bookstagram where we stock books based on favorite authors and storylines."

Des stopped writing to look up at him, "What's a Bookstagram?"

Zach sighed. "And I thought I was bad with tech."

A chime on Des's phone went off; his eyes widened when the clock came up. "We gotta move. These are some great ideas," Des smiled as he unclicked the pen. "When you have some time, see if you can work on a customer survey for their recommendations."

Zach's face would hurt later from how big his grin grew at the suggestion.

For the next few hours, the store was about as busy as an ice cream shop during winter.

Since the rush of the newest big release had died down significantly, very few people came in, and most just browsed for a bit before leaving. Zach manned the counter, writing in his notebook as the minutes ticked by without another soul entering until Jaime came in to clock in for their shift. "Hey Zach," they said as they walked over to the counter.

"Hey," Zach nodded as he closed his notebook. "So, this is your last day with us?"

"Yeah."

Zach softly smiled at them. "It's been fun working with you."

"Yeah, I'll miss your dry humor."

Zach rolled his eyes but laughed regardless.

"But Storybound has way more to it than this place, right?"

That stopped Zach short. He had to keep himself from yelling at Jaime, instead shrugging before countering, "I don't think so. I like the small feel of it. Especially since they made that store seem more like a warehouse than a place to relax."

Jaime shrugged as they adjusted the fallen strap of their overalls. "Well, to each their own."

Zach slowly opened his notebook again as they walked into the back, not knowing what to say. Sure, The Book Haven wasn't a flashy store with every single book out there on their shelves, but Storybound was just about as generic as you could get. They might have more shelves and a built-in cafe, but The Book Haven had character and Toe Beans down the street. Not to mention, Storybound was notorious for only carrying the first book in a series, or having completed series on their shelves in a mix of paperback and hardback. No bookworm wanted to deal with mixed editions and covers if they didn't have to. Sadly, Storybound did have a great marketing team behind them that was always doing promotions and themed events at their store, which was why they were always busy. Zach wished he could convince Des to do the same. That might really help the business, or at least give them more fun things to do during slow hours.

"Hi."

Zach slammed his book shut, but relaxed when he saw it was just Belle. "Hey, what's up?"

She shrugged as she put a small takeout box from Toe Beans on the counter. "I thought I would just bring you something to eat on your break."

Zach scoffed a laugh as he pulled the container close and opened it, revealing a small orange cake with a tiger on top of it. "Thanks."

She smiled as she put a huge pile of books on the counter, making Zach chuckle. After he checked out her latest haul, he noticed the pink bag on her arm. "Is that the new tote bag design?" he asked.

"Yeah, I just got the sample in," she said, turning to show it off. The side read "Sweet Thief" with a doodle of Carry the Rabbit with frosting all over her face, and a half-eaten strawberry cake.

"Cute. It's a little story in one frame."

Belle nodded. "I enjoy making up all these little scenarios about what the characters are doing and drawing it out. It makes the design process easier."

Zach looked at her thoughtfully as she packed up her book bag. "Have you ever thought about making a children's book?"

"What?"

"I mean, you already have all the illustrations that you would need for one so..." he said, putting her card back in its spot in her wallet.

Belle licked her lips. "I mean, I'm good at drawing, but I don't think that the words would come as easily to me."

"I could help," Zach shrugged. "Maybe we could write a book together one day."

"Hm...you doing the words, me doing the pictures. It could work." Belle smiled and leaned forward on the counter. "We already know we work well together."

Zach took the hint and pressed a kiss against her lips.

"Hey!" Des called from the side. "No canoodling with the customers."

Zach chuckled as they pulled apart. "I thought you wanted us to like each other."

"Like each other when you're off the clock."

"It's okay," Belle giggled as she hefted her bag on her shoulder. "I have to go anyway. Text me later."

"Will do," Zach said as he moved his cake off the counter, watching the door close behind her as she wandered back down the street. When he brought his attention back to the counter, he saw Des staring at him with a smug grin on his face. "What?"

"Nothing." He nodded at the door just as the bell rang again.

Zach sat up in his seat and smiled when he recognized the mother and daughter who had come in a couple of weeks ago to buy a book. When Jaime started to walk over to help them, Zach called out, "Don't worry, I got this."

He ended up spending twenty minutes with the two of them, helping them choose books that the daughter, Laila, would enjoy. He also helped the mother, Trina, find some books that she wanted. On his break, he sat in Des's office, eating his cake and feeling proud of what he did, thinking about how Laila said she wanted to read more magical books with animals. His mind started to wander away from Project Void as he began thinking of scenarios for books that she might like, starring the characters that Belle created. Excited, he put down his cake and picked up his notebook, opening to a blank page.

Barry, Carry, and Terry
<u>B</u>ook <u>I</u>deas

- Having a Picnic
- Playing in the Park
- Making Dinner
- Playing Catch
- Looking for Fairies

Chapter 22

Maryland weather tended to fluctuate frequently throughout the day.

When Zach woke up on his day off, he could hear the pounding rain against his bedroom window. When he went downstairs not twenty minutes later, the rain had quieted down to a misty drizzle that brushed his face as he left the house. When he arrived at Toe Beans, the skies were completely clear, and if it weren't for the patches of dry road underneath some of the parked cars in front of the cafe, he would have thought he'd imagined the earlier storm. It was strange how things could ebb and flow like that.

When he walked in, Joon was sitting behind the counter with a look on his face that said he was holding something in.

"You good?" Zach asked, knocking Joon back into reality.

"I'm fine," Joon replied as he straightened up.

"You sure? 'Cause that's usually the look I have when I want to stab a pen in someone's eye."

Joon shifted on his feet. Zach's eyes widened. "Oh God, are you actually contemplating doing that? I'm telling you now, I'm not gonna be much help with burying the body."

Joon waved him off. "Don't worry. That's why we have Kit. Seriously, it's nothing." Joon started tapping on the register screen. "The usual."

"Yeah, and one of those orange tiger cakes that Belle brought me the other day."

"Coming right up." Joon puttered around the espresso machine behind him. "Hey, is Belle okay?"

Zach felt his heart drop at the question. "What do you mean?"

"She didn't come in to get her usual today," Joon said as he held up one of their little take-out containers with Belle's name written on it.

That really made Zach start to panic. Belle was consistent, just like him. She had an unofficial schedule that she followed to the letter, and it rarely deviated from the usual; Mondays were for website maintenance and customer service catch-up; Tuesdays for designs and doodles; and so on. He could tell what day it was based on what Belle told him she was doing for the day. For her to change her routine meant something was off.

"You know what," he said, staring at the box like it was a bomb. "I'll just bring it to her."

"Okay," Joon nodded as he put the container and Zach's order on the counter.

Zach pulled out his wallet as Oma came out of the back with a tray of cupcakes and glared at him. "Put that wallet away, Zach," she said in a firm voice. "You know the rule, family—"

"Doesn't pay. I know." He snatched the treats off the counter.

"See you later," he said, leaving the store without waiting for either of them to say goodbye. Any other day he would try to fight back against the rule, but at that moment, Belle was the only thing on his mind.

He managed to get up to the cottage in record time without breaking any speed limits.

He got out of the car with the Toe Beans food in hand and power walked to the front door, knocking as soon as he was close enough; there was no answer.

"Hello," he said with a knock again.

He finally heard some noise from inside the cottage: Appa's barking. No other sounds accompanied it.

"Belle?" he called out.

He got impatient, picked up the hide-a-key rock from the pathway and unlocked the door. Immediately, Appa barreled past him into the yard. Zach looked down at his watch.

It was noon, and Belle had not taken out Appa.

If he had not been worried before, now he was downright terrified.

"Belle?" he called again as Appa came back into the house. The dog ran toward the bedroom, and Zach threw the food containers on the counter after closing the door behind him. He slowly approached the open door to the room. His eyes immediately focused on the lump of quilt on the bed that Appa was staring at. He looked closer at Belle's head peeking out of the top of the quilt. Her bonnet was still on her head, her eyes red and glazed over.

"Belle," he said softly as he scooted onto the bed, finally gain-ing her attention. "Are you okay?"

Her lips wobbled as her breath stuttered out. "No." Tears started rolling down her cheeks as a sob rang from her mouth.

Zach gathered up her body in the blanket and pulled her against his chest. "I got you, Sunshine," he whispered before kissing her forehead. "I got you."

Zach didn't know how long he laid there, but by the time he re-opened his eyes, his watch had turned far past 2 P.M. He looked around to see that Appa was staring up at him as his own stomach growled. If he was hungry, he could only imagine how Appa felt.

He quickly made work of following the steps that he had seen Belle do a hundred times to make up Appa's food bowl and gave him some water that he quickly gobbled up. He took a sip of his Toe Beans coffee but cringed at the coldness of it. He puttered around the kitchen trying to figure out a way to turn it into a sort of iced drink with milk and sugar that he found lying around. He gave it another sip; it wasn't horrible. He grabbed his phone off the table and saw that he had a new string of messages from his group chat with Kit and Joon.

Kit

Are we still on for movie night later?

Cuz I need to do my yearly rewatch of Legally Blonde

Joon

I'm down but Zach might be busy

Kit

Boooo

Zach pull yourself away from your girl so we can see you too

Answer your phone!

Joon

Might be a minute

He went to check on Belle after he stopped by here

I haven't heard from him since

Kit

WHAT?!?

What happened to Belle?!

ZACH!

ZACHARY!!!

ZACHARY NICOLAS ROBERTS!!

Answer me before I march up there!

Zach immediately started typing a response.

Zach

Don't worry she's okay.

She just seems sad.

I don't know why.

Kit

nearly crying emoji

Oh, my sweet bean!

Is there anything we can do?

Zach

I don't think so.

I haven't been able to talk to her yet.

I'll let you know

He sent a quick message to his father saying that Belle wasn't feeling well and was staying to take care of her for a while, then turned off his phone, and went back into the kitchen to make a plate of food for her. When he came back into her bedroom, she was just waking up.

"Hey," he said as he walked over to her side of the bed. "Here, you need to eat."

Belle glanced between him and the plate before finally taking it in her hands. "Thank you." She teared up again, distressing him.

"Hey, what's wrong?"

"I haven't taken Appa out all day."

Zach looked over at the door to see Appa standing there, now done with his food. "Hey, don't worry. I let him out, fed him lunch, and he's fine." He came back around to the other side of the bed and crawled over to sit next to her. "Are you okay though?"

Belle took a small bite of one of the cheese crackers he bought her. "It's just been a really bad brain day."

"Bad brain day?"

She nodded as she switched to a blueberry. "That's what me and my therapist call it when...it's just a really bad day." She traced the floral vines on the plate. "I haven't had one in a while, but then I remembered what today was and..." She shrugged. "It all just hit me."

"What's today?"

"Kailey's birthday," she said softly as she leaned against the headboard. "She would have been twenty-five today." She scoffed, before moving the plate to the wooden nightstand, bringing her knees up against her chest. "It's her golden birthday. We were supposed to go to Disney World and spend the day eating our way through Epcot and go see their Cirque du Soleil show. She always wanted to go see it. It was her biggest dream, and she never got to do it." A tear fell down her face. "And it's all my fault."

Zach quickly wiped the tear track off her face. "It's not your fault."

"Yes, it is, I was driving the car."

Zach let his hand fall from her face. "What do you mean?"

"I was going to visit my Grammy last year. She was in the hospital after we found out that she had a mass in her stomach." She brought her hands into her lap and picked at her nails. "We didn't even know she was sick. It was like one day she was fine and crocheting scarves with me, and then she was lying in a bed unresponsive. The nurse called me a few days after she was admitted and said that she might not have a lot of time left, so I went to go see her, and Kailey insisted on going with me because that's the type of friend she was. I was driving and next thing I knew, I just felt this crushing pain and then nothing." She shook her head, as though trying to keep the full memory at bay. "When I woke up, I was in the hospital, and someone told me that a driver hit my car on the passenger side and...and that Kailey was dead." She let out a shaky breath. "And then to top it off, when I was finally able to contact my grandmother's nurse, she told me that she had passed away while I was out." She sniffled. "I lost the two most important people in my life in a split second and I couldn't tell either of them goodbye."

Zach couldn't even begin to imagine losing everyone you loved in one fell swoop.

"What about your parents?" he asked.

She scoffed. "What about them? They divorced when I was in elementary school, my father took off, my mother dropped me off at my grandparents' house, and I haven't heard from either of them since. My mom didn't even show up to Poppy or Grammy's funeral, so I could really care less about what either of them are doing," she sneered before looking at him again. Her face softened as the clicking of her nails filled the room. "I'm sorry."

Zach reached over and grabbed her hand, pulling it away from the other before placing a kiss on the back of it. "It's fine."

A small smile grew up on her face. She laid her head on his shoulder. "Growing up, it was just Poppy, Grammy, and me. When I moved schools, I met Kailey, and she basically took me under her wing. I would just follow them around cause I didn't know what else to do. Poppy died a couple of years ago, so Grammy and Kailey were my everything. I mostly did things because they told me to. Grammy told me to go get a degree and a real job, so I did. Kailey told me I should make an art business, so I did. They told me to start a YouTube channel, so I did. They both helped me with everything, but for a while, I didn't feel like I was doing anything because I wanted to. I just did it because they told me I should and it was easier to not have to think for myself.

"And when I lost them—" she let her legs stretch out and stared at the brick wall across from them "—I couldn't function. I quit my job. Closed the shop. I basically shuttered myself in my grandparents' house for months. It was the worst time of my life."

Zach let all the information wash over him; he just felt heartbroken for her. His mom had left too, so he could empathize with that part of her story, but being alone like that was something he had never faced before. As much as he complained about his father's overprotective nature, Zach knew that it also meant he would never be left behind and he was eternally grateful that he hadn't. No one deserved to deal with something like that, especially not someone like Belle. Not someone who tried to bring so much light into the world with all she did.

Then again, maybe it was because she went through so much darkness that she wanted to bring back some light.

"What changed?" he asked, his thumb brushing her hand.

She squeezed his hand tighter as she shrugged. "I randomly got a DM from one of my followers," she said with a little laugh. "She wanted to check on me and ask if I was doing okay, and it had been a while since I had anyone ask me that. Then I opened up my messages and saw just how many people were worried about me. It made me feel like I wasn't completely alone for the first time in a long time, in some way." She smiled a bit as she sat up and took her bonnet off, letting her hair fall down. He pulled her closer as she continued. "It gave me the boost to do something to feel normal again, or find a new normal, I guess."

"What did you do?"

"I got a therapist, and after a few sessions, she suggested I get an emotional support pet so I have a reason to leave the house more, and when I went back to the shelter to volunteer again and I saw Appa, I said fuck it and adopted him the same day. We started going on walks and going to the park, and I found myself drawing him, and then I realized how much I missed drawing and the shop and making videos, so I just picked them up again, and it felt really good." She smiled with a dazed look in her eyes. "Then I saw this ad to rent a cottage in Maryland."

Zach's heart skipped a beat.

"I'd always wanted to live in a cottage, and the opportunity was staring me in the face so... I did it. When I got here and started decorating and making more stuff, it felt like a weight had been lifted off my shoulders." She sighed. "I thought everything was going to be okay after that but..." She shook her head. "It's stupid. I'm stupid."

"You're not stupid," Zach insisted, cupping her chin to make her turn back to him. "You're one of the smartest people I know." His thumb caressed the side of her face. "You did all of that by yourself. You did that. You're so fucking brave, Belle," he chuckled, probably sounding like a madman as he did, but it made her smile. He kept going. "That's a lot for anyone to deal with, so if you have a really bad day every once and a while, it's fine. You already know you can get through it," he said, squeezing her hand again. "Give yourself some grace, Sunshine."

She nodded as she let her head fall into his chest again. "I'll try."

He smiled and placed a kiss on her cheek before pulling her

closer to him. "That's all I ask."

As Belle set up an emergency appointment with her therapist, Zach took Appa out on a long walk. If anyone had told him the day he came back to Lillet that he would be volunteering to spend time with the furry behemoth that ran him over, he'd call them nuts. But Appa wasn't a bad dog, just very enthusiastic, like when he saw that there was an unfamiliar car on the path that led to the cottage, he immediately started barking at it. Zach, however, recognized it, and went up to the driver's door to knock on the window. "What are you two doing here?" he asked as Kit and Joon got out of the car.

"We were worried about Belle," Joon said after grabbing a tray of drinks from the floor of the backseat.

"Yeah, you said she wasn't feeling well, so we wanted to come cheer her up. We made some food and brought some treats," Kit said in her usual cheery tone. She balanced a box of stuff on her knees, while hip bumping the door closed. "And I made her a little care package."

Zach had never been more happy to have such good friends. "You guys did all that for her?"

Kit shrugged. "What, like it's hard?"

Zach guffawed before moving towards the front door. Appa immediately ran over to Belle once the door was unlocked, leash and all. He jumped up on the couch and snuggled into her, making her smile as she pet his head. "Hey, buddy. Did you have a nice walk? Find any squirrels to chase?" she cooed at him.

"No squirrels," Zach said as he came over to unclip Appa's

leash. "But I did find these two outside."

Belle's eyes widened as she found the two newcomers. "Hey."

"Hi sweetie," Kit greeted as she plopped herself down on Belle's other side and hugged her. "Heard you weren't feeling well, so we wanted to bring you some things to cheer you up." She directed Belle's attention to the box. "I brought some curry and rice, and Joon had some leftover cakes and tea from Toe Beans. I also brought you a pair of fuzzy socks, a coloring book, some markers, and a candle. I hope you like brown sugar."

"Thanks," Belle said, her lips trembling as she did.

Joon must have seen it as a bad thing; he shifted on his feet and said, "Oh, did you just want to be alone 'cause we can leave if you—"

"No, I...I would really like the company actually," Belle said, wiping a tear that fell. "I was just gonna spend the rest of the day watching *Avatar* with Zach. You two want to join us?"

Kit sat up straight with a grin. "We'd be honored."

While Kit and Joon started to pull out everything they brought, Zach walked over to Belle and sat with her on the couch. "Are you feeling better?"

She sighed. "A little bit. I know this is not gonna last forever." She looked at him. "Thank you. For being here."

Zach smiled and kissed her forehead. "Anytime, Sunshine."

He hugged her close as Kit and Joon managed to get everything together and bring it over to the living area, both of them opting to sit in Belle's lesser-used plushy armchairs.

"So what episode are you up to?" Kit asked after she set up her station.

"*The Tales of Ba Sing Se*," Belle replied.

Kit's eyes widened; she immediately stood up and started pacing around the room, making Zach's brow scrunch up in confusion. "What are you doing?"

"Prepping myself for 'Leaves from the Vine'."

"For what?"

She turned back to him with a disgusted look on her face. "Seriously, how did we not make you watch this show?"

"Because your priority was rom-coms and Joon's was K-Dramas."

"Oh right," she said as she plopped back down in her chair. "By the way, Belle, what's your nation? Joon is an Air Nomad and I'm Fire Nation."

"Oh, Water Tribe for sure." She looked over at Zach. "What about Zach?"

Joon and Kit shared a look before they said, "Earth Kingdom."

"Is that meant to be a compliment or an insult?"

They said nothing as they picked up their dishes while Belle cued up the next episode.

Once they got to the Tale of Iroh, Zach found himself the tiniest bit emotional, but he just blamed that on the fact that he had such good friends who would come help someone so important to him. He was a lucky guy to have such great people in his life.

"Remembering Kailey: Dealing with grief and trying to move forward"

67,904 views · 6h ago

Hi, My Lovelies,

I know this is different from most of my videos lately but sometimes life just takes a sharp turn and I want to sit down and acknowledge it. Moving might have helped my mental health but that doesn't mean that everything is perfect now. It's been a while since I've talked about Kailey on this channel and I know you all loved her too. A lot of you sent me messages on her birthday and I thought we should take a moment to remember our favorite Kailey moments. I hope this video made you smile.

Love, Belle

@luvbug1236 · 5h ago

Thank you for being so vulnerable with us. I'm happy that you're in a better place physically and mentally now. I rewatch the video of you and Kailey going ice skating for the first time often and it made me fall in love with skating again.

@TiaDoll · 3h ago

Not me crying two minutes into the video. I lost my sister two years ago and I know what it's like to struggle with the grief of it all. It doesn't really go away but life will go on and you find ways to keep your head up. I'm glad that this is one of the things that helps you.

@AngelainRoseGold · 4h ago

Sending you hugs from Rio, querida. You make the world a much brighter place, just like Kailey. She'd be so proud of all you've accomplished.

Chapter 23

Zach was never keen on having siblings.

When his parents had announced they were pregnant with his first sibling, four-year-old Zach had felt entirely indifferent about the situation. After his mother came home with a tiny human being and a flatter belly, he took it as it was: a new house guest who took his parents' attention off of him. When they'd announced a new addition ten years after the first, Zach was much more invested this time around; a brother he could teach so many new things to, and who might actually look up to him instead of down like Amaya had started once she'd learned how to sass people like Bugs Bunny. But such a large age gap between them meant that by the time Corey was old enough to do fun things, Zach was headed off to college. Sometimes, he'd been afraid that Corey wouldn't recognize him when he came home during breaks and would cry the moment he was put in his older brother's arms.

Lucky for him, that wasn't the case; all Corey wanted was to be Zach's mini. He wanted to read books with Zach before he went to bed and play mini-golf with him at the park. He wanted to tag along and do "big-boy" stuff with Zach. At that moment, they were both getting their hair done at the local barber like Zach and their dad had done when he was little, and Zach cherished these moments. He didn't know how many of them they would have after he moved.

If he moved.

His phone pinged as he sat on the bench after getting his hair trimmed to its normal height. Corey was getting his blow-dried. Zach smiled when he saw Belle's name on the screen.

Belle

> I think that I might have a book-buying problem

Zach chuckled as an image of piles of books in front of Belle's bookshelf came through before he moved to type his own message.

Zach

> Not true

> But you do have a bookshelf problem

> Don't worry, I'll buy you a new one

Belle

> I knew that I liked you for a reason

> Are we still going to Papa Porter's tomorrow

Zach

Of course, it's a crime that you haven't been there yet

Belle

I've been busy

Which reminds me, I have to email that new sticker printer

TTYL

kiss emoji

Zach

* smiling emoji with hearts around it*

Before putting his phone away, he looked through more open jobs in one of his employment apps. He had pretty much exhausted most of the New York-based ones that were interesting, and had started looking for more in Maryland. He'd applied to a few during the last few weeks, but he found himself feeling less and less inclined to send out resumes as the days went by. He was honestly pretty content with everything, so why apply to a job that he didn't need?

He glanced up from his phone in time to see his barber, Mr. Elliot, put down the hairdryer.

"Alright little man," The older man said as he swiveled the chair around so Corey could face the mirror. "What do you want your hair to look like?"

Corey said nothing, just stared at himself in the mirror,

which worried Zach. Corey was the talker in their family; Amaya would ramble on about subjects she was excited about occasionally, but Cory could talk your ears off at any given moment. Just like the Energizer Bunny, he had relentless energy that seemed to go on forever. It was rare when he said or did nothing.

Zach glanced over at the other waiting customers, before pulling up Pinterest on his phone as he walked up to Corey's other side. "Hey, why don't we look through some pictures and tell Mr. Elliot what you want?"

Corey nodded. Zach started scrolling through a range of hairstyles for young Black boys until he pointed to a style very similar to Zach's but quite mundane for Corey. His little brother usually enjoyed having his patterns in his fade to show off some personality.

"You sure?" Zach asked once more, letting Corey answer with a nod before he showed the style to Elliot.

"Good choice."

Zach sat back down, but instead of letting himself get absorbed in the phone he just kept looking at the neutral expression on his brother's face.

As Zach drove himself and Corey over to Gigi's house for a mandated lunch, he couldn't help but glance into the backseat every so often. Corey still didn't seem as bubbly as he usually was. "Hey, bud," Zach said, prompting Corey to finally look up from his lap. "Do you want to stop at Toe Beans before we go to Gigi's to get a little treat?"

Corey shook his head. "No, thank you."

That made Zach raise a brow. He nearly put on his turn signal as he pulled up to a stop sign. "Why you being so quiet? I thought we were gonna have a long discussion about the newest *Paw Patrol*," he asked outright.

Corey just shrugged.

"What's wrong, bud?"

Corey's eyes flickered between his hands and his brother. "I talk too much."

"No, you don't."

"My teacher told Dad that I talk too much and that I need to work on that."

"When did she say that?"

"When we went grocery shopping. She said I distract the other kids at camp too much."

Zach sighed as he continued driving. "Well, when you're with me, you can talk all you want. Okay, bud? How else am I supposed to stay up to date on the best new shows?"

Corey snorted.

"I'm serious, you turned me onto *Bluey*. Top-tier content right there." He poked Corey's leg, making him giggle. "Right?"

Corey smiled a bit, and that was good enough for him. "Okay. Zach?"

"Hmm?"

"Can we see Miss Belle's dog again?"

Zach let out a deep chuckle. "You know what? I'll ask if we can stay for a visit after we go to Gigi's."

"Yay!" Corey squealed as he bounced up and down in his car seat, making Zach relax again.

"There are my boys," Gigi greeted as she opened the door, hugging both of them to her. "Where's my girl?"

"She's at work," Zach said as he toed off his shoes. "You need help with anything?"

She waved him off. "No, lunch is almost ready, just wait a moment."

Corey immediately ran over to the bin of toys that Gigi had for her grandchildren. Over the years, the toys had rotated many times from train sets to Barbie dolls to building blocks. The rest of Gigi's house had stayed pretty consistent since their Pop passed away a few years back. The same Alpha Kappa Alpha blanket laid on the couch, alongside the quilted pillow Mimi made for Gigi when Zach's parents got married. The photo gallery had grown a bit, though. More pictures of the OWWA were hung proudly, alongside his newest graduation photo, but one stood out to him for all the wrong reasons: his mother sitting on the front porch of their house, Zach and Amaya standing behind her, and Corey in her arms.

He remembered that day. It was a month before she'd left. She had dressed them up for Easter and said she wanted one nice photo with all her kids. They didn't know that would be the last photo of all of them together.

He picked up the photo, and scoured the similarities be-tween her and Amaya (their face shape, skin tone, and hair), but touches of him and Corey were in there too (particularly their eyebrows).

"I'll never forgive that girl for what she did to y'all."

Zach quickly put down the frame and looked to see Gigi standing behind him with a bowl of fruit, which he moved to grab from her. "It's not your fault she left, Gigi."

"Can't help but feel like it is at times. How did I go so wrong for my daughter to abandon her children like that?"

Zach placed the bowl on the table. "I don't think it was anything you did." He sat down in his seat. "I just don't think she wanted to be here anymore," he confessed.

As much as he wanted to be mad at his dad and say that the divorce was completely his fault, he couldn't say his mom was guilt-free. He wished he could say that his mom was perfect, that she never did anything wrong, but there were times when he felt she didn't want to be there.

Like she didn't want kids at all.

Gigi clearing her throat got Zach's attention again. "Well, I want you kids to know that I will always be here for you," she said firmly, cupping his chin in her hand and placing a kiss on his forehead.

He let out a small smile. "Thanks Gigi."

"I'm not lying. If you need anything, let me know."

"I will."

"Alright. Corey! Time to eat."

As Zach sat down at the table, another text came through from Belle.

Belle

Of course, Corey can come over. Appa loves new playmates

Zach

Which is why he couldn't stop tackling me when we met

Belle

What can I say he's a lover

Zach

Like his mother

Belle

Exactly

"Zach, no phones at the table," Gigi said with a snap.

"Yes, ma'am," Zach said as he shoved it back in his pocket.

Just then, the house phone rang. Gigi picked it up. "Hello?"

"Gigi, no phones at the table."

The older woman glared at her grandson before turning towards the phone, "I'll call you later Sora. I'm having lunch with my grandbabies. Yes, talk to you then." Zach snickered as she hung up the phone. "Hush up and bow your heads for prayer, you two."

Zach and Corey did as she said. Zach enjoyed spending lunch talking to her about what it was like working with Belle, and how much he was enjoying being back full-time at The Book Haven, while Corey cut in every once and a while with a summer camp story.

By the time they went up to the cottage to pick up Amaya, Corey had regained his energy and immediately started playing with Appa. Belle gave him Appa's favorite tug-o-war toy to play with. The three of them watched the two play together, enjoying a new playlist Amaya had made to work to. It honestly felt like they were on a side quest in some of the fantasy games that Zach had played growing up; no danger to worry about or a task to complete at the moment. They could just rest and be present in the moment.

He didn't want to let that feeling go anytime soon.

He didn't want to leave the cottage anytime soon.

He didn't want to leave at all.

zachslibrary 7h

I need the links to some of your favorite bookshelves. It's time to expand the library.

Also, I've gotten a few inquiries about my new Avatar-themed bookmarks and they were a gift from @lovebelle! She says she might have them as a free download soon on her website so go check it out!

I promise you'll thank me later!

Chapter 24

Zach liked to think that every small town had that one thing that kept it going.

For some, it was that once-a-year festival that brought in all the tourists to see how great their town was. For others, it was that place in the city where everyone works, regardless of their skill set. For Lillet, that thing was Papa Porter's. Papa Porter's was the place where you go in town to celebrate.

When report cards came out and their kid got all As, parents would take their kids to Papa's.

When there was an engagement announcement to be made, couples took their families to Papa's.

When people who moved out of Lillet came back for a visit, the number one request was dinner at Papa's.

Everybody in town loved being at Papa's, and Belle had never been. When Zach learned of this, he immediately booked them a table for Thirsty Thursday, so Belle could get the full experience of Papa's. They ended up having to walk a bit down the road since parking closely was not an option as the Thirsty Thursday discounts drew in the crowds of summer students from the nearby college. When they went into the restaurant, it was as lively as any club he had walked past in college.

As soon as they walked inside, the smell of Old Bay and butter wafted past them, as R&B music hit Zach's ears. The old wooden floors shined with lacquer and old scuff marks while fishing nets hung across the ceiling. Glass jars covering the light bulbs gave off a warm glow that made Zach feel right at home as they were escorted to their reserved table.

"You know, you see places like this in brochures, but I don't think I've ever been in one," Belle giggled after they sat down and were handed their menus.

"Well, I'm happy to bring you to your first," he said with a smirk.

"Is that my boy, Zach?" a deep voice said behind them.

Zach grinned as he turned to see none other than Papa Porter himself approaching the table. He quickly got up to hug the man. "Hey, Papa!"

The old man chuckled as he held him tight. "Man, you got old on me."

"Not as old as you're getting," he joked, pointing to the man's completely gray head.

Papa just ran his hand over the fuzz with a chuckle. "God willing I'll live to a hundred. Has Gigi given me an answer yet?"

Zach shifted on his feet. "She told me to tell you...that it's not gonna happen."

"Oh come on," he guffawed loudly, but a coughing fit quickly cut him off.

"You okay?" Zach asked, placing his hand on the man's shoulders.

"Little cough been hanging on, I'll be fine," he said, waving him off before turning to Belle, "So who is this young lady right here?"

"This is Belle," he said. Papa made a point of shaking Belle's hand. "She moved to town a few months ago, and she still hasn't experienced true seafood before."

Belle scoffed. "I've had crab cakes in New York."

Papa and Zach immediately shook their heads. "Nuh-uh, a Maryland-style crab cake is nothing like an actual crab cake from Maryland," Zach advised.

"Don't worry about ordering, I'll take care of you tonight. Gotta make a proper introduction, don't we?" Papa said with a wink, before making his way back into the kitchen.

"You Marylanders act like you invented crabs," Belle said with an eye roll as Zach sat back down.

"And don't you forget it," he affirmed. She just laughed more as she put down her purse.

"So you come here a lot then?"

He nodded. "I had my eleventh birthday, sixteenth birthday, and high school graduation party here."

"Wow, you were able to get a space for you and all your friends here?"

"Well, it was mainly just Kit, Joon, and family so yeah," he said as he shucked off his blazer. It had been a while since he put on his preferred garb of a suit, and a dinner date with Belle felt like the perfect occasion to dawn the outfit again. He'd dug out the first real pair of suspenders his Pops gave him before he passed. While he did like Papa Porter, he doubted Gigi would ever love a man like she loved Pops. They were one of the only couples that he could point to and say he would be fortunate to have a love like theirs.

Belle cleared her throat and he caught sight of the flush of red on the side of her face. "You alright?"

"Yeah," she said, licking her lips. "Just a bit thirsty."

Luckily, Papa came back to their table with his entourage of family members bringing drinks, along with a plate of crab cakes and a skillet of sizzling crab mac and cheese, the house special, that left Zach salivating. This was definitely not something that he could've found on campus or in New York. Once Belle took a bite of it, he could tell that she was over her sentiment of New York crab cakes being acceptable.

"Oh my God." Belle covered her mouth as she moaned around the food.

Zach had to shake away the dirty thoughts that entered his mind at that sound. "Told you. Nothing can compare." He filled his fork with a good bite of mac and cheese, smiling around it in his mouth.

"So, is this where we finally ask all those awkward first-date questions that we've been avoiding?" she asked as she grabbed some of the mac and cheese for herself, moaning again at the taste.

Zach chuckled. "We are far past the first date questions at this point, don't you think?"

She shrugged. "I don't know. Have we gone through the basics?"

"What basics?"

"Like..." She paused as she picked up her glass of half-and-half that Papa brought over. "When's your birthday?"

"November first. When's yours?"

"August thirty-first," she answered before taking a sip.

Zach's eyes widened. "Wait, that's close."

She shook her head. "It's a month away."

"Still close enough that you should've told me." Zach sat back in his seat. "I need at least two months' notice for birthdays."

"Why?"

"Because I don't like giving sucky last-minute gifts."

Belle giggled. "Don't worry, I'm not hard to please."

"You say that now, but if I showed up with a generic-ass gift card, you'd feel some type of way." She grimaced, telling him all he needed to see. "See?"

"Okay, but seriously don't worry. I've kept my birthdays lowkey for years. Twenty-five isn't going to be anything special to me."

Zach sat up in his seat. "Wait, you're twenty-five?"

"Twenty-four turning Twenty-five. Pay attention, babe."

"I am," he chuckled, crossing his arms over his chest and smirking. "I'm dating an older woman."

"Shut up," she said, putting down her glass.

"No seriously, how has this never come up before?"

"Because it is not a big deal," she insisted before taking another bite of crab cake. "Next question."

He chuckled as a bucket of shrimp, crab legs, potatoes, and corn—all covered in Old Bay—was sat on their table. Zach spent the rest of their dinner teaching Belle how to properly crack open a crab leg to get the most meat out of it in one go.

The look of glee on her face when she did so just filled his heart with the same feeling.

Zach drove them home an hour later, and Appa came running out the door as soon as it was opened. He made a big show of running around the two before going into the field to do his business.

Zach took a moment to drink in Belle. She'd always dressed cute, and he'd always known she was beautiful—that was the only thing he'd thought when he first saw her—but seeing her in a short floral dress that showed off a bit of her leg as her jean jacket fell off her shoulder, exposing the tiny straps holding up her dress, reminded him of something else.

She was really fucking gorgeous as well.

Not to mention, alluring.

"What?"

Zach stopped his gawking as he noticed the confused look on Belle's face. "Nothing." When she kept staring at him, he chuckled. "I just really can't believe I'm dating an older woman."

Belle scoffed, "Oh come on, I'm only like 3 years older than you, it's not much."

"But it's hot," he blurted out, eyes widening the second he realized what he'd said.

Where the fuck did that come from?

Zach took a step back, trying to look anywhere but Belle's face. "Sorry, I shouldn't have..."

Belle turned his face back toward her; she didn't look offended in the least. She looked flattered and maybe a bit... intrigued. "You think that's hot?" Belle said as she took a step closer.

"Um..."

Belle bit her lip.All Zach wanted to do was bite it himself. "Do you want to come in?"

"Sure," he sputtered out.

Belle unlocked her door and went inside, looking over her shoulder with tempting eyes as she did.

"Fuck." Zach caught Appa as he went to trail after her. "Hey. Look at me. Look at me." Appa sat there with his face in Zach's hands, tongue hanging out of his mouth. "If you let me have my way with your mom tonight, I will bring you the biggest bone and a new chew toy. Got it?"

Appa barked.

"Good boy."

zachslibrary 3m
(Hidden from @lovebelle)
Any suggestions for book lover birthday gifts?
Particularly for someone who loves romances, crochet, and pink lemonade.

Chapter 25

Zach wasn't a virgin by any means.

He had accidentally gotten a reputation on campus for being a good partner in bed actually. His first time, he'd just asked Emily what she wanted, then done it (much to her surprise it seemed). Apparently, she had relayed the news to friends who'd wanted to see if he would do it for them as well, which was how he'd ended up with as many hookups as he did, and one girl who'd given him a hundred bucks before she left, leaving Zach dumbstruck in the hall of his apartment until Beau had come home and snapped him out of it When Zach had explained that he may have accidentally become a prostitute, Beau had just shrugged it off and said they could use the money to fuel their mutual caffeine addiction. Zach did eventually get things under control and closed the revolving door to his bedroom, but the fact still stood. He knew what to do.

He went inside the cottage, locking the door behind him. He toed off his dress shoes before laying them next to the heeled sandals that Belle had on and telling Appa to go lie down, which he did without question. His heart began to race when he walked into Belle's bedroom. Belle shucked off her jacket as Zach closed the door before throwing it on her dresser. She smiled as she turned to face him. Her eyes screamed, *come hither.*

He didn't need more than that to walk toward her. "Hey," he murmured as he stepped into her space. She didn't move back.

"Hi," she whispered, her voice barely reaching his ears.

He slowly moved his hands to rest on her waist, giving her time to say no. If she didn't want it, he wouldn't force it, no way in hell. But, instead of backing away, she wrapped her arms around his neck and got on her toes to brush her lips against his. He felt his cock start to tent against his pants.

It had been months since his last time. Job hunting and finals didn't leave him any time to desire such things. Belle's fingers caressing the back of his neck and her lips brushing against his cheek made all his desires come rushing back in.

"Do you want this?" Belle whispered against his earlobe.

"Do you?" he inquired through a shuddering breath.

"I asked you first."

"Well, I'm certainly not opposed to it," he chuckled before Belle pulled back from him, scoffing a laugh as one of her hands started to trail down his chest. His heart skipped his chest. "Yes, I'm very sure I want this." He let his hands roam the small of her back before they tentatively glided down the skirt of her dress and over her ass. "How about you?"

"God, you have no idea how much I want this."

"I think I have a pretty good idea," he said before moving one of his hands to grasp her chin and pull her lips to his. The faint taste of her strawberry gloss and a bit of the chocolate cake they'd had for dessert met his tongue as he licked her lips. Belle moaned.

She pulled away and shoved his blazer off his shoulders. "How do you make suspenders so damn sexy?" she quipped as she pulled him closer by them before making quick work of the buttons of his shirt.

"The same way you look so fuckable in these little bow-covered shorts," he countered as he pushed up her dress. He pushed her shorts down, revealing her white lace underwear with a little pink bow in the middle of it. He smirked. "You wear this for me, Sunshine?" He played with the lace detailing on the edge of them. "You want me to unwrap you?"

"You'd love that, wouldn't you?" she giggled, shoving the suspenders and his shirt off his shoulders. "Me dressing up in lace and satin just for you."

He turned her around and pushed her on the bed, her ass up as he shoved the skirt of her dress onto her back. "I won't say the thought hasn't entered my mind," he murmured, placing a soft kiss on her ass, making her moan and giggle at the same time.

She pushed him back and kneeled on the bed, pulling off her dress to reveal a strapless bra that matched her underwear.

"Damn, Sunshine," he said in awe as she threw her dress to the side.

She pushed on his bare chest after a minute of him gawking. "Hey. What's the hold-up? I thought you wanted to unwrap me," she teased.

"Damn right I do," he said, his hands tracing the curves of her stomach.

"Then get to it," she said with a smirk.

Zach shook his head, moving his hands around her back. "You've got a mouth on you, woman." He enjoyed seeing her shiver from his touch. He moved his hands around her back, unclipping her bra and letting her breasts hang free. He immediately leaned forward and kissed the top of each one, enjoying the feel of his mustache and beard rubbing against them. The moan Belle let out as he started to play with her nipples between his fingers probably meant that she was appreciative of it as well.

She grabbed his hands and pulled them away from her breasts. "Then maybe I should put my mouth to good use."

Before he could blink, she grabbed his shoulders and shoved him down on the bed, straddling his legs with hers. He groaned as she rubbed her pussy over his dick, making it clear how little clothing they had between them as the spot got damp. She crawled backward on the bed to unbutton his pants and shoved her hand in his boxers, smiling as he scoffed out a sharp breath. "Oh wow," she gasped as she pulled out his cock. She glanced up at him through her eyelashes. "Good to know you can back up that big talk of yours."

"You got that right, Sunshine," he breathed out as she stroked him. He did have a bit of a reason to be a bit cocky at times. He didn't have the biggest cock in the locker room, but length wasn't everything. He helped her pull down his pants and underwear, shoving off his socks as well before lying back against her pink satin pillows, completely at her mercy as she pumped his cock even more. Before he lost all his intelligence to his small brain, he had to use his big brain. "Wait. Damn." He looked at his pants on the floor. "I need to get a condom."

"No need." She reached over into her bedside drawer and pulled one out.

Zach scoffed when he saw the writing and picture on it. "Of course, you got fucking strawberry-flavored condoms."

"Why not?" she said with a shrug. "Now, shut up or you're

just gonna be jacking off."

"Yes, ma'am."

She straddled his lap again, slowly tore open the wrapper, and took out the condom.

"Are you sure you want to do this though?" he questioned through tight lips as she slowly rolled it on his cock, positioning her mouth above it. "I don't need it to—" She took his cock in her mouth and started sucking on it. "Oh fuck," Zach gasped as his head slammed back against the pillow. "Belle," he hissed as she went down again, his cock nearly touching the back of her throat as she did. "Damn."

She giggled as she pulled out his dick and kissed the tip of it. "I'm sure. I like you like this," she teased as she stroked him once more before placing more kisses down along the side of it. "Completely beholden to my will." She pulled back and dragged one finger up along his cock, the light glinting of her glasses as she smirked down at him.

"I'm always beholden to you, Sunshine," he gasped out. She smiled wider and leaned back down, slowly wrapping her mouth around the top of his dick. "That's right," he moaned before leaning up on his elbows to watch her work. She pulled back and took in his cock just a bit more every time she went down. "Suck that cock, Belle." He bit down on his lip as she sucked harder. "Take it in that pretty little mouth of yours." Belle took him in as far as she could, spit covering her mouth as she held it there. "Fuck yeah."

When he couldn't take it anymore, he took his cock out of her mouth and brought her lips to his, licking the artificial strawberry flavor off of them. He pulled back from the kiss with a smack and snapped the band of her underwear. "Take those off."

She smirked as she rolled onto her back, bringing up her legs and pulling off her panties with a pop. She slowly brought them up her legs and lifted them off. She tossed her underwear to the side and opened her legs, exposing the glistening lips of her pussy to him. She smirked as she began moving her fingers over them slightly, teasing him like the damn vixen she was.

He needed his cock in her pussy. "Come here," he commanded.

She didn't move an inch.

"Now," he hissed through his teeth.

She slowly got on her hands and knees, taking her sweet time crawling toward him, but he couldn't take the wait. He grabbed her waist and yanked her up the rest of the way. She gasped as her chest slammed against his, her pussy brushed against his dick. He snaked his hands around her body until they went under her arms and anchored on her shoulders. He pulled her back slightly and took one of her nipples into his mouth. Her head fell back as he moved his attention to the other, rubbing herself against him. He needed to get inside her, but after that jacking off comment, he didn't want to squander the opportunity of having her at his mercy a bit.

He moved one of his hands down her stomach to in between her legs, and ran his fingers over her folds. "Damn, Belle," he chuckled. "You're fucking drenched." He reached up his free hand and pushed back her loose hair. "You liked my cock that much?"

"Mhm," she moaned as he rubbed against her more. He pushed one finger into her and she gasped, grabbing his shoulders. She almost seemed desperate for more as she started grinding against his hand, which made him smirk.

"What?" he asked as he teased her with another finger. "You want my cock in this tight little pussy of yours instead?"

"Mhm..." She nodded, but he wouldn't give in for that.

He pushed the second finger in, making her shudder above him. "I need you to use your words, Belle," he insisted. "I'm not gonna do it unless you tell me to do it."

Belle breathed hard as she leaned her forehead against his. "I want your cock inside me."

"Please?" he mumbled, his lips brushing against hers. "Say please."

Her lips brushed past his again. "Please," she whispered.

"What was that?" he asked, hooking his fingers inside her.

"Fuck me, Zach," she whimpered. "Please fuck me!"

"There we go," he smirked before swiftly removing his fingers and caressing her cheek again. "All you had to do was ask," he said before kissing her lightly.

He wasted no time lining up his cock with her entrance and slowly guiding her down it. "Fuck!" She gasped out as she stretched around him. She tried to move back up, but he held her hips in place.

"No, not yet," he asserted. "Take it all in," he ordered, slowly pushing her down as he did to give her time to adjust. "Be fucking greedy with it."

"Oh my God," she moaned, halfway down.

"Yes," he hissed out. "That's it." When she bottomed out, he let her sit there for a moment to adjust. His fingers rubbed the top of her pussy just slightly, making her whimper and moan again. He smirked before he pinched her chin between his fingers and pecked a kiss on her pouty lips. "Now bounce on that cock, Belle."

She nodded as she slightly moved up before slamming herself back down. He let her set the pace, and held her hips to keep her steady as she went up and down again and again. She wrapped her arms around his neck, head hooked on his shoulder as she rode him, digging her nails into his shoulders.

He moaned as he pressed kisses on her shoulders, before he tightened his hold on her hips and brought her down hard, using his hips to match her movements.

"Oh!" she cried out as he changed his angle. "Please don't stop."

"Don't have to tell me twice." He slammed her down again, making them both gasp before Belle brought him close again to attach her lips to his.

She pulled back with a gasp. "Ah!"

Zach knew by the look on her face that she had to be close. He took his thumb and moved it over her clit again. "You wanna fucking come?" he asked as he quicked his finger's pace. "You wanna come, Sunshine?"

She quickly nodded. "Yes. Yes, please let me come, Zach. Please."

He smirked and kissed her again, licking the last of the strawberries off her lips. "Go ahead, pretty girl."

"Fuck!" She cried as she came, Zach not too far behind her. Belle slumped against him, and he wrapped his arms around her to keep her steady.

He removed himself from her, making her whimper. He placed a kiss on her forehead as he laid her down on the bed before he dealt with the condom.

He quickly put on his boxers and walked over to her bathroom, soaking one of her washcloths in warm water, and going back into her bedroom. He took the cloth and cleaned her off, placing the lightest of kisses on her inner thighs as he did.

"That was fucking incredible," Zach chuckled after he threw the cloth on the ground with the rest of their clothes, and leaned over her.

"Agreed," she said softly before pinching his chin in between her fingers and bringing him down to kiss her. He happily obliged.

"God, I hope you realize how amazing you are," he said between kisses.

"Likewise."

Sadly, they only had a moment to breathe before his phone buzzed on the floor. He groaned as he reached down to grab it out of his pants, and saw a message from his dad.

"Do you have to go?"

Zach turned to Belle and took note of her furrowed brow. "Do you want me to go?" he asked.

"No," she admitted, shaking her head.

He smiled and placed a kiss between her brows, making them relax. "Then I'm not going anywhere."

He sent a quick text to his father saying that he was spending the night at Belle's, before tossing the phone on the nightstand and crawling back into bed. He pulled Belle against him, spooning her from behind and kissing her neck. Her head turned; she had a tired smile across her face, but she leaned in for another kiss regardless, before reaching over to take off his glasses and placing them next to hers on the nightstand.

She took his arms and wrapped them around her before she settled into his embrace.

It took him a while to drift off—it had been a while since he went to bed anywhere besides his childhood room—but with Belle in his arms, he felt at peace.

When he woke up two hours later, he felt content and eager to share the feeling with Belle, so he woke her up as well.

With his tongue.

On her clit.

Luckily, she had a drawer full of those condoms; he was not leaving her side anytime soon.

zachslibrary 5m
(Hidden from elovebelle)
They also like
strawberries if that helps.

August

Chapter 26

It took a while for Zach to be comfortable in new places.

When he first got to Walker U, it had felt like walking into a different country with a culture he didn't understand but over time, as he went to classes and student events, he got used to his new environment and flourished. He joined the English department's tutoring program, helped people revise essays, and even did a small stint of working at the library. When his college career ended, it felt like he was closing a chapter of his life that he wasn't ready to finish. He supposed that was part of life, it kept moving forward whether you wanted it to or not.

After dropping off Amaya at Belle's a few days later—and giving Appa a big bone from the pet store,—Zach drove down to the bookstore in blinding rain. He ran into the store after parking and welcomed the warm air that surrounded him. He removed the random jacket he found in the house and went toward the back to put his stuff away when he heard voices coming through the office door.

"I don't know why you're acting like I owe you anything," Des said.

"I was your wife, wasn't I?"

Zach bit his lip to keep himself from freaking out.

"Yes, you were. As in, past tense," Des argued. "You made it quite clear what you thought about that marriage when you rolled out of here without even a goodbye, so why do I owe a reason as to why—"

"Because you're still doing the same damn thing. Settling for something good, when you could have something great."

"This place is great, and your name isn't on the deed, so you ain't got nothing to do with this decision. Your momma shouldn't have said nothing, and when it comes to this matter, there is nothing more that I need to say to you."

"Can't believe the time I wasted with you."

"Likewise."

Zach scooted behind the counter as Donna stomped out of the store, her heels clicking behind her as she went. Zach stood there awkwardly, not knowing where to look as Des came out of the back.

Des clocked it right away, "How much of that did you hear?"

"Enough. Is everything okay?"

"It's fine. Nothing you need to worry about."

"But—"

"Just worry about dealing with that kid's section. We got a shipment of some of those recommendations you had coming in, so you need to make room for them."

"Okay."

Zach would have loved to argue and say that something

needed to be said, but he decided he didn't know enough to comment, so he went ahead and started doing his job, hoping the day would get better.

Four hours later, Zach was praying that business would pick up eventually but at this point in the day it was unlikely that it would. The rain had deterred pretty much any customers that would have come in that day.

At least, he hoped it was because of the rain. The last three days didn't have many people come in either, and Zach spent most of his shifts wandering through the aisles or rereading passages from books he already owned on the shelves. At the beginning of the summer, he had wished for days like this, but now, they just gave his mind too much time to wander between the multitude of thoughts that were getting more irrational by the minute.

What if his book got torn apart by people because it didn't accurately depict interdimensional space travel? Would he have to go into hiding and change his name to hide from the embarrassment and harassment?

Did Belle really mean that he was good at oral or was she just trying to keep up his male ego? (He would later scoff at this thought; Belle had never been afraid to take shots at his ego before. She still made fun of the vein on his forehead when he got frustrated with certain characters in books.)

What if Baxter came back to corner him again, and Zach couldn't get away? Jaime wasn't there to act as a buffer anymore.

What were Des and Donna fighting about before? What was Des just settling for? Was that what caused their relationship to break up in the first place? Was Zach settling for—

"Zach."

Zach looked up sharply to see Des staring down at him. He looked around, and noticed that he had wandered over to the children's section and sat down in one of the beanbags. He blinked, trying to bring everything back into focus. "I'm sorry, what?"

"Are you okay?" Des questioned, his brows furrowing even more.

Zach felt the water settling in his lungs: not getting higher, but not lower either. "Um... yeah." He looked up at Des again. "Do you mind if I take a break?"

"Yeah. Take all the time you need."

Zach gave his boss what he hoped was a reassuring smile before he got up and walked back to the office on shaky legs. When he finally plopped down in a chair, he took some deep breaths to try and keep himself grounded. He glanced around the office and focused on Des's old computer, his eyes following the block that pinged back and forth across the screen. It never landed directly in the corner. He could feel himself getting worked up again.

He had to try something else.

He bit his lip as he took out his phone, and pressed the contact of the one person he wanted to talk to.

"Hey," Belle greeted after two rings.

"Hi," he mumbled.

"What's up?" He could almost see the worried look on her face.

"Um..." He sighed, messing with his glasses. "Nothing. I just wanted to hear your voice."

"Okay...well, I finished a new audiobook."

"Really?" He folded up one of his legs on top of the other.

"What was it about?"

Zach felt himself calming down each second that Belle went into detail about the fantasy world that she experienced, talking about how the narrators made the icy forests of the world come to life, along with how the dual POV made the romance feel that much more real. Zach found himself asking for the book title by the time she was done, and he was delighted to say that they had a couple of copies in stock. With a promise to pick up a copy for her as well, they hung up, and Zach felt like he could breathe again.

He hated it when he got like this. In high school, Zach had been stressed about classwork at times, but after the pool incident, his stress manifested into anxious thoughts, and those turned into moments of panic. He was fortunate that he had mostly conquered his fear of swimming after Joon had started coaching him throughout the rest of that summer, but that didn't make the fear of drowning go away. It turned out that he didn't need to be in the water to feel like he was trapped with no way out.

He knew what it felt like to be too comfortable with how things were and to have things ripped out from under him. It had happened when his mom left, when he got pushed into that pool, when he hadn't secured a job before graduating.

Maybe he'd gotten too comfortable again.

Maybe it was a trap waiting to snatch up the one bit of joy he had been feeling.

When he walked through the front door after his shift, Zach still felt on edge. It had been a while since he heard a couple fight like that, and when they did, it was usually an omen for worse things to come.

"I thought Amaya was with you?" Jed called from the living room, making Zach almost jump out of his skin.

"She's still at Belle's," he said softly as he toed off his shoes "I'm picking her up later."

He could see his father's jaw clenching from where he was. "You know I think it's quite odd that I haven't met my son's girlfriend or my daughter's boss yet."

Zach shrugged. "Belle is busy, besides she's just about the sweetest person ever, so there's no need to worry."

"Then you'll have no problem inviting her over for dinner this Sunday?"

"What?"

"I want to meet her," Jed said definitively.

"Why?"

"If there is someone this involved in my children's lives, I have a right to meet them."

"Can't you just trust my judgment?"

"No."

"Why not?"

"Because I'm not gonna let you make the same mistakes I did when I was your age."

Zach glimpsed at the spot on the wall where his parents' wedding photo used to hang. "Dad—"

"End of discussion."

Zach snapped his mouth shut. "Fine."

"Good. This Sunday," Jed said as he stood up from the couch, going over to the front table to grab his keys, "I'm going to pick up Corey. Keep an eye on the chicken in the oven." And with that, he was out the door.

He'd definitely gotten far too comfortable if he didn't see this coming.

It took a lot of deep breaths to keep Zach from screaming like a banshee. Instead, once he got up to his room, he took out his notebook and began to write.

Things I Wish I Could Say Out Loud
(To Be Shredded after Writing)

1. You don't need to know everything going on in my life

2. I wish you would just trust me for once

3. Why don't you understand how fucking stressful of a human being you are to be around?

4. Why couldn't you make Mom stay?

Chapter 27

Zach loved his family, but the idea of introducing all of them to Belle made his stomach turn into a knotted mess as he paced around his room.

Kit was the only girl that he'd ever had at the house before, and she had already been introduced to his extended family through birthday parties and such. She had even carpooled with him and his dad after school to the library for a short period of time when her Jiji got sick in elementary school. Having someone Zach was romantically involved with in the house made his mind frizz out with panic about what could happen.

Would his dad be kind and not treat Belle like she was like his ex-wife?

Would Gigi and Mimi be too nosey and make Belle uncomfortable?

Would Belle feel comfortable being around his family or feel bad about not having hers around anymore?

While she assured him that she'd be okay, he knew that she

was notorious for putting on a brave face, and he didn't want her to have to fake being happy around his family when he didn't have to be fake around her.

"You're going to make a rut in the carpet if you keep that up."

Zach looked up from his feet to see Amaya standing in his doorway, still wearing the jean dress she'd worn earlier. "Why are you still in church clothes? Don't you hate dresses?" he asked. Most Sundays when they came back from church, Amaya would be back in sweatpants before he could even get his shoes off at the door.

She shrugged. "I don't hate them, I'd just rather be in sweats. Besides, you think I want to deal with the scolding if I don't wear something nice? Already cleaned my room to cover my bases."

Zach groaned and started to pick the random piles of crap off his desk and floor.

"You good?" Amaya asked.

"I'm fine."

"No, you're not."

Zach shoved a bunch of old note paper into his tiny trash bin. "I will be when this dinner is over."

"Don't worry, Belle's great."

"I know that, but Dad has a tendency to run people off."

"Like Mom?" He could see Amaya bite her lip out of the corner of his eye, but he ignored it. "Mom left us, Dad didn't."

Zach scoffed. "Yeah, but he didn't exactly give her a reason to stay."

"We should have been enough reason," she said tearfully.

Zach sighed as he looked at his younger sister. It was hard to remember sometimes that she hadn't been that much younger than him when their mother left. She remembered her just as much as he did, while Corey knew next to nothing about her. He probably wouldn't recognize her if he saw her.

"I mean, yeah she left Dad but did she have to leave us too? She could have left him and, I don't know...if it's his fault she left, then why didn't she try to take us with her?"

Zach couldn't say. While their father was overprotective and controlling at times, he was damn well there for everything. He was there for Zach's attempts to go to the National Spelling Bee, and even when he came in tenth place at State, he took him out for lunch at Papa's after. When Amaya did her first gaming competition, he was in the front row, cheering his head off when she won. He volunteered for Corey's first field day at school and ran alongside him during their big foot race. Their dad was there for all of it, while their mother had missed it all, even when she had been around. Zach knew they worked about the same amount when it came to their jobs. He hadn't been blind to the way they would switch off responsibilities growing up, but while their dad made it a priority to get off work to be at their competitions and performances, their mother didn't. Even when it came to birthdays and holidays, their dad would try to savor the moments, while their mom would rush through them. Looking back on it, it felt like she was going through the motions of parenting rather than being a parent.

Amaya was right. If their father was truly a problem, she would have taken them too.

"I mean, why haven't we heard from her at all?" she said, brushing her hair back from her face. "Look at Owen's dad; he left and he still sends his son a damn Christmas and birthday card every year and takes him on vacation. If she really cared about us then…then she would have done something. Wouldn't she?" She shoved a tear off her face.

Without another thought, Zach pulled her in for a tight hug.

"I must look really pathetic if you're hugging me," she mumbled into his chest.

"Don't flatter yourself, you always look pathetic."

Amaya's arms tightened around him. "Hate you."

"Love you too."

She wiped off the rest of her tears before looking up at him. "Don't worry, everything will be fine." She left the room, leaving Zach alone with his thoughts.

For once, he really hoped that Amaya was right.

Zach didn't stop pacing once he came down the stairs until he heard the doorbell ring.

"I got it," he said as he rushed over to the door and pulled it open, only to frown when he saw that it was Gigi. "Oh."

She frowned, putting her hand on her hip as she looked him up and down, "Well, nice to see you too."

Zach paused his lips. "Sorry. Hi Gigi," he said, kissing her cheek and taking her dish of sweet potatoes from her.

"Hello, Zachary. You look more nervous than your father when he came to my house the first time."

Zach bit back the urge to remind her how that ended up meaning nothing in the long run. He just moved into the kitchen to put the dish down next to the lineup that Mimi had made. The smell of warm collards, mac and cheese, and ham filled the air, making Zach relax a bit. At least he knew that the food would be fine.

"There's my baby," Gigi cooed as she went over to place a kiss on Corey's cheek.

Corey cringed, quickly wiping away the lipstick once she pulled back. "Why do I still have to wear a tie?"

"Because it makes you look dashing," she said, straightening it.

Zach chuckled at his brother's discomfort as he straightened his own bow tie in the front hall mirror. Zach was always wearing button-ups and more formal clothing, so it was nothing for him to wear this kind of stuff throughout the day.

The doorbell rang again, and he bolted over to the front entry, breezing past Amaya. The smile he had dropped once he opened the door and saw Owen standing there. He glared at the teen. "What are you doing here?"

"Amaya invited me."

"Why?"

"Uh..." Owen shifted on his feet, making Zach smirk.

"Zach, let him in," Amaya called behind him. "Dad already makes him nervous enough."

Zach scoffed. "If I terrify him, what makes you think he's gonna do better with Dad?" He turned to Owen. "Seriously, you need to work on that. I don't even work out and you act like I can turn you into soup."

He heard Amaya scoff behind him as she moved to pull Owen into the house. Zach chuckled to himself as he closed the door behind him, only to jump when someone else knocked. He bit his lip as he slowly opened it back up, revealing Belle standing there with raised brows, ceramic dish in one hand, Appa's leash in the other.

"Hey," He greeted softly.

Belle nodded. "Hi. I'm guessing you didn't see me come up behind Owen."

His heart dropped and he winced. "No, I didn't. Sorry."

She looked him up and down before standing on her toes to kiss his cheek. "You're lucky you're cute, and I believe that you can be that clueless."

Zach nervously chuckled as he bent down to pet Appa. "Hey, buddy."

"Are you sure it's okay that I brought him?" she asked, flicking the fabric of Appa's leash in her hand. "You said your dad doesn't like dogs and I really want to respect that but it's been a really bad day and I—"

"Don't worry." Zach stood back up. "I told him Appa's an ESA and that you needed him around today. It's fine." While Jed didn't want a pet, he accepted people's need for service and support animals, especially after he worked at a library event where speakers spoke on the importance of both. Apparently, his father was more open-minded than Zach thought he was.

Belle smiled before propping up the dish. "Oh, I brought dessert. I hope that's okay, I've never done a meet the family thing before."

He chuckled as he took it from her. "It's more than okay." He shifted the pot in his hands. "I can't believe you walked here with this."

She waved him off. "It was nothing."

"Regardless, I'm driving you home, 'kay? Enjoy your passenger princess perks."

Belle smiled and kissed him softly. "Okay."

"Zachary Nicholas Roberts! Bring us the girl already." Gigi called from the kitchen.

Belle nervously giggled but Zach quickly grabbed her hand.

"I promise they are not that bad, and I apologize in advance for everything my dad says."

She just smiled wider and gave him a reassuring squeeze before he brought her into the den of hyenas sitting with their too-wide smiles on their faces, except for his father, who was already scrutinizing Belle, making Zach stand in front of her slightly.

Zach cleared his throat. "Alright. Everyone, this is Belle. Belle, this is everyone who will no doubt introduce themselves eventually."

"Hi," she said, letting go of his hand to wave at them. Nobody said anything, but they waved a bit before Belle pointed down to her companion. "Oh, this is Appa. I hope it's okay that I brought him," she said looking directly at her father.

Zach could see the small signs of disgust on his dad's face, but Jed just shrugged and said it was fine as Corey immediately ran up to Appa and started hugging him. Appa licked his face and hands in return.

"Hi, sweetie. We have heard so much about you," Mimi said as she wiped her hands and came around the counter.

"Really?" Belle asked.

"Yes, my goodness, Zach can't stop talking about you."

"Mimi!" Zach hissed.

"Hush, baby," Gigi said with a wave as she came over, noticing the dish in his hands. "Oh, you didn't have to bring anything."

Belle shrugged. "It's just strawberry shortcake. It's something I used to make with my Grammy. Zach said you all like strawberries too, so..."

Gigi let out a yelp that you would only normally hear her use in church. "A woman after my own heart."

Mimi smiled and coaxed Belle to come over. "Come on, sit down at the table, sweetie. You boys bring in the food." The older women took Belle and Amaya into the dining room, Owen quickly following with the ham. Zach glanced up at his father, who grabbed the ceramic dish of sweet potatoes just as he told Corey to go wash his hands.

"Zach..." Jed hissed as Zach came over to put down the dessert. "That dog is a lot bigger than you made him out to be."

"Dad, please," Zach fretted. "Appa is a great dog. He might shed and drool a lot, but Belle has been through a lot of BS and I don't need you saying anything about the thing that helps her cope with it the most," he explained looking at his father, more seriously than he ever had before. "I'll clean up the fur later okay, just let him be, please."

Jed sighed but nodded. "Alright."

Zach smiled. "Thank you." He grabbed the mac and cheese and went to the dining room, praying everything would be fine now that that was out of the way.

The dinner started off pretty smoothly, with everyone just working on filling their plates with as much food as possible. Belle was quick to compliment both grandmothers on their cooking after tasting it, which immediately made them giddy with glee. They got halfway through their plates before they started their interrogation.

"So, Zach says you're from New York City?" Gigi asked as she cut up her ham.

"Yes," Belle answered.

"Is it as fascinating as all those movies make it seem?" Mimi smiled, eating a forkful of greens.

Belle tilted her head back and forth. "Sometimes. Most of the time it just feels like you're just constantly moving and working. It's a very 'go, go, go' environment."

"What did you do for work there?" Jed asked after cutting up Corey's ham and collards and handing the plate back to his youngest.

"Content Marketing. Basically helping companies create online content to market to a wider audience. I worked on different projects to incorporate different products into social media posts."

"Like the stuff you do on your YouTube channel?" Owen asked while making his own forkful of food.

"Yeah."

"You have a YouTube channel?" Jed asked.

"It's so cool, Dad." Amaya grinned before Belle could answer. "She has like six hundred thousand subscribers, and she's showing me the ropes so I can set up my own gaming channel."

Jed raised his brow. "You plan on making a career out of that?"

Amaya shrugged. "I don't know. But it sounds like fun, so why not?"

Jed said nothing for a moment, letting the scraping of silverware on plates fill up the silence before he spoke again. "So you make money from YouTube?"

"It's one of the ways I make money, yes. My main job is my stationery shop that Zach and Amaya help me with. I show the process of owning my own business while showing how I make some of the products. That reminds me. Appa."

Appa crawled a bit closer to his owner and Belle reached into the bag that she had attached to him, pulling out two sets of crocheted squares. "Zach told me that you two love personalized kitchen stuff so I made these pot holders for you."

Both grandmothers looked like their hearts were melting at the sight of them. "Well, aren't you the sweetest thing?" Mimi gushed with her hand over her heart as she took them and passed Gigi her pair. Zach had to hold himself back from throwing a smug look at his father, but inside he was very excited and happy that Belle seemed comfortable with his family. Mimi turned to him, brow raised. "Zach, I can't believe you've been keeping this girl all to yourself. You're gonna have to learn to share."

He chuckled. "You'll have to take that up with Kit. She already has her booked for Self Care Saturdays and Movie Night Mondays," he said mockingly.

When Zach turned to Belle, she was glaring at him with a smirk on her face. "I already said you could join us."

"And spend the entire time just being your snack lackey," he scoffed. "No thank you."

She reached over and grabbed his hand. "You wouldn't only be there for that," she said before squeezing his hand. "You would also be there for us to shout at when the ex tries to win back the main girl because he thinks a wink and a smirk is all it takes for forgiveness."

Zach rolled his eyes. "Oh, thank you so much for the honor," he teased. "Call me when you start a book club, then I'll get involved."

Her smile widened. "Alright." She took her hand back and started gathering more food on her fork. "Meetings are on Thursday. Stop at Toe Beans to get some cakes and lattes on your way there from work."

He closed his eyes and sucked his teeth. "Can't believe I fell for that."

"I can," she giggled. "And you're in charge of buying the

books."

"Of course I am," he said with a mocking nod. "I feel like you're only with me for my employee discount."

"Hey, that is not the only reason I like you." She turned back to her food and made her final bite. "It's just one of your best qualities."

"Oh, right."

"Ahem."

Zach finally remembered that they were seated with the rest of his family who were looking at the two of them with amusement written across their faces. "Sorry," he said before looking back at his plate.

"No, please don't," Gigi chuckled as she leaned back in her seat. "I like a good debate. Makes me nostalgic for the good ole courtroom days."

Zach chuckled and started messing with his food again, enjoying the last bit of his grandmother's home cooking on his plate.

"Quick question though," Amaya began after a minute, looking straight at Belle. "Why *do* you like Zach?"

"Amaya," Jed scolded, but she just shrugged.

"What, it's an honest question."

Belle laughed it off, but Zach saw her free hand dig into Appa's fur under the table. The Australian shepherd put his head in her lap as she answered, "Because he's fun to argue with." She looked over at him. "But he's also kind, and smart, and funny, and compassionate, and caring and..." She smiled at him. His heart flipped in his chest. "He just makes me really happy." Zach reached over and squeezed her hand, which she returned before looking at his father. "You raised a good man, Mr. Roberts."

Zach looked over at Jed, expecting a contradictory side-eye look, but all that he saw in his father's eyes was pride. "I know I did."

Zach smiled. While he didn't need his father's praise and approval, it was nice to have every once and a while.

"Belle?" Corey asked.

She smiled over at him. "Yes, Corey."

"Can I play with Appa?"

"You're not going anywhere until you finish your vegetables," Jed said sternly before Belle could reply.

Corey frowned. "But I don't want them."

"Well, your Mimi worked hard on them so you're gonna eat them." Jed turned to his daughter. "Amaya, go clean up the dishes."

Amaya glanced up at Zach but said nothing as she started picking up some of the empty dishes.

"I can help," Belle said, already starting to stand, but Gigi waved her back.

"Sweetie, you are the guest," she said.

"Oh, I really don't mind."

Mimi sucked her teeth. "Nonsense. You young ones sit here while we go do the dishes. Jed."

His father sat back in his seat and Zach could see that Amaya was struggling not to laugh as well. "Mom, I just told—"

Mimi just glared at him. "Jedidiah Cornelius Roberts. Dishes now."

Zach let a little snort slip through but focused his attention on Corey, who was still playing with the vegetables on his plates. His brother was not much of a picky eater, but when it came to cooked vegetables and animal cookies especially, he was never keen to eat them. He would be there for a while if they didn't do anything.

Owen scooted over in his chair. "Hey, Corey."

The boy looked up to him.

"Remember how we talked about how everyone needs vegetables?"

"Yeah."

"Did you know that even dogs like them?"

Corey scrunched his nose. "Dogs don't eat vegetables, they eat meat."

"That's true, but sometimes they eat vegetables as a treat," Owen informed him. Corey continued glaring at him. "It's true."

"He's right," Belle interjected. "Appa loves to eat carrots and peanut butter."

"Because those taste better than collards," Corey pouted.

"Well, if you eat your vegetables, your dad will probably let you have some of the cake I brought."

Corey looked between Belle and his tiny pile of collards before sighing and getting some on his fork. "Fine."

Zach found himself smiling at Belle while he caught a glimpse of Amaya doing the same with Owen. Zach would not tell Amaya this anytime soon, but Owen fit well with their family, and it seemed like Belle was fitting in just fine as well.

"You know, you didn't need to drive me back," Belle said as she sat in the passenger seat of his car.

"Well, I didn't feel comfortable having you walk that far back in the dark," Zach admitted as he made another turn towards the cottage.

"I've walked further than that in the city."

"That does not comfort me either," Zach said with a shake of his head, making Belle giggle.

"Your family is really sweet."

Zach nodded. "They can be at times. Other times they can annoy the crap out of me." He bit his lip. "But I still love them."

"I don't think your dad approves of me very much," Belle said after a bit of silence.

"Who cares?" he said immediately.

"I care."

"Well, don't. Dad has been wary of all of us getting into relationships since the divorce. Owen and Amaya had been best friends for years before they started dating, and Dad is just as mean to him now as he was back then."

"Then why are you so mean to Owen?" she asked. He had to imagine her furrowed brow as he kept his eyes on the road.

"Because it's the older brother's job to terrify the little sister's boyfriend. It's one of the few things I look forward to when I'm at home," he chuckled.

"Seriously?" she guffawed.

"Yeah, I take my job as an older brother very seriously," he said with a firm nod, making Belle laugh louder. Zach wished he could record the sound to play at another moment when he needed it.

"Yeah, you do," she affirmed once she finally stopped laughing. "It's one of the things that I like about you."

"Good to know." He turned on the street that led toward the

cottage. "So do you mind if I stay over tonight?"

"Mhm." Zach glanced over in time to see the mocking look on her face. "Well, that depends on what you think is gonna happen if you stay over."

"Well, I know what I would like to happen," he said nonchalantly. "We could watch a little *Avatar*, maybe read another chapter of *River Misfortune*. End the night with my face between your legs." She scoffed a laugh before he asked, "Would you be amicable to such an agenda?"

"Who knew someone who looks so proper could be so horny?"

Zach chuckled as he glimpsed at her and he couldn't help but ask, "So, if I put my hand between your legs right now, it would be dry as fuck?" She not so subtly crossed her legs, making him smirk. "That's what I thought," he smiled before moving his hand over her legs.

"Hey, both hands on the wheel," she said, pushing his hands off her leg.

Zach wouldn't be deterred. "Hey, I'm a good driver. Even with one hand."

"Zach, I'm serious."

Zach quickly glanced over at her. It took him a while to realize why she was so adamant. "Right, I'm sorry." He immediately put both of his hands back on the wheel and kept his eyes on the road. Being in the car might be second nature to him at this point, but it was still terrifying for Belle.

It was hard to think of how much walking she did to avoid having to be in a car, and he was pretty sure it wasn't healthy for her to keep avoiding cars, even though she was getting plenty of exercise doing things her way. Maybe he could help her in some way or another. "You know, maybe I could take you driving one of these days."

"Why?"

He shrugged. "To help you get, I don't know, reacclimated to it."

Belle said nothing.

"That accident wasn't your fault. Maybe it will help you to practice driving around town a bit, to get you comfortable behind the wheel again. If we don't go at peak hours, it'll be like driving through the middle of nowhere."

"I'll think about it," she said softly, before glancing up in the mirror to look at Appa resting in the back seat.

Zach hoped that she would take up his offer. He honestly thought she was the bravest person that he'd ever met, and he really hoped that he could help her not live with that fear anymore, but, for now, he would change the subject. "So, did you get Kit a birthday present yet?"

"I made her a little set of New York-themed Pompompurin shirts," she told him and he could hear the smile in her voice. "Since she's so obsessed with New York, it's the next best thing for me to give her that's not a trip to New York."

"What's Pompompurin?"

"You'll see." This time, he could hear the smirk in her voice. "What did you get her?"

"A dress that she wanted from the farmer's market, and a bunch of vinyls for her record player. She hasn't gotten herself any new ones recently so I found some from her favorite artists."

"How do you know they're her favorites?"

"She's my best friend," he said with a shrug. "And her Spotify is public."

"Ah," she nodded as they pulled up next to the cottage.

He turned off the car and looked at her. "So, can I stay the night?"

"Sure," she giggled as she unbuckled her seatbelt. "But let's be clear." She turned to him. "I don't want your head between my legs."

He sighed, but if she wasn't in the mood, he was going to force her to be. "Got it."

"I want it buried in my ass." She smiled cheekily before opening her door. "Come on."

She let Appa out and practically skipped to the door.

Zach scoffed with a smile as he turned off the car. "Man, I love that woman."

He didn't realize how much he meant that until he was lying in bed with her that night, watching her sleep after they were both fully sated and in their PJs. She let out a snore once in a while, and he just smiled, thinking about how he wouldn't mind sleeping next to her every night or waking up with her every morning.

He wanted to spend every day of the rest of his life with her.

Because he loved her.

Excerpt from "Project Void" by Zach Roberts (3rd Draft)

"It should be smooth sailing from this point onward, Captain," Ty said as he put the last of the location parameters in the ship's navigation system.

Captain Wan let out a deep chuckle as he patted Ty on the shoulder. "Excellent. And the shields?"

"Still intact."

The Captain let his hand drop as he looked out at the dark path before them. "Ty, I've got to hand it to you, you've kept this crew together in ways I could not have foreseen when you were a cadet."

Ty scoffed. "I wasn't that bad."

"You bragged about being able to pilot a solo craft without any training whatsoever because you thought you were just that good. Next thing I knew you almost crashed into a mountain. If the autopilot hadn't kicked in, you would be dead."

"Alright, not my finest moment," he admitted with a shrug. "but I improved."

He nodded. "You have. And with your talents, I foresee great things for you."

Ty contained his smile, and stood at attention with all the professionalism he could muster, even though hearing those words from Captain Wan's own mouth meant everything to him. He simply said, "Thank you, Captain."

Chapter 28

Birthdays were a big deal to Zach. He felt like they were the one day that you could remind someone how much they meant to you.

When he was younger, he and Amaya would call a truce on each other's birthdays; they would be the only days when the two would be completely nice to each other without raising suspicion. Zach would help his father take down as many Christmas decorations as possible to make sure that Corey's birthday felt special since he was born two days later. He, Beau, and Mateo had a competition to see who could be the first to celebrate the birthday boy, then the winner would get bragging rights until the next birthday in their group.

He took birthdays quite seriously, and today was Kit's.

Zach chuckled as Belle and Kit sang along to Taylor Swift in the backseat while Joon bopped along in the passenger seat. They had been listening to Kit's twenty-second birthday anthem since they had picked her up at Town Hall after her shift, and while he wasn't a Swiftie like Belle or Kit, he could appreciate the song, especially on days like this.

All Kit wanted to do for her birthday was go out for ice cream with her friends, and they were helpless to say no to that request. Zach drove them over to the ice cream parlor that Kit had been wanting to go to since the start of the summer: The Little Creamery.

When he pulled into the parking lot and turned off the song, Kit immediately protested with, "Hey!"

"We're here," Zach shrugged.

She popped out of her seatbelt and ran out of the car faster than Zach thought was possible, and the rest of the group quickly followed. The Little Creamery had a line that led out the door. Even in the evening, Maryland's summer heat was beaming down, and the need for something cold was high. The staff seemed to be as quick as lightning; they were in the door only a minute later and had a full view of the rainbow lineup of flavors. They asked for probably too many samples.

"Joon, you are not getting vanilla on my birthday, we are here to celebrate with something different," Kit argued as the man tried to order.

"Fine," Joon said with a roll of his eyes, "but I shouldn't even be having this much dairy, you know."

Both Kit and Zach narrowed their eyes at him before Zach said, "You literally don't give a shit about being lactose intolerant."

Joon nodded with a shrug. "True."

Belle paid for their not-dinner dinner before the rest could get out their wallets, and they made their way to one of the red and white booths. They all took a full spoonful of their little sundaes and moaned.

"This is heavenly," Kit said as she dug in for a bigger bite of her almond-brittle caramel swirl. "Why haven't we been coming here all summer?"

"Because we would've been three times the size by the end of June," Zach said as he took another guiltless bite of the creamsicle flavor he'd purchased, the perfect amalgamation of his favorite flavors.

"But it would be worth it," Kit said through a mouthful.

"And love comes in all sizes," Joon nodded before scooping some of the vanilla coffee onto the waffle bowl he'd ordered.

Belle chuckled as Joon stuffed it in his mouth. "What happened to 'I shouldn't be eating this'?"

"Shut up, a man can change his mind," he snarked through the mouthful.

Zach chuckled and went to take another bite until he caught a glimpse of red hair in the distance. "Oh for fuck's sake," he groaned when he realized it was who he thought it was. "We're not even in town."

"What?" Belle asked.

"Baxter."

Kit scoffed. "You've gotta be shittin' me."

The smug bastard was standing in line with a blonde girl hanging off his arm. How he kept getting girls to fall for his false bravado, Zach would never understand.

Belle looked between the trio. "We could go."

"No, no." Kit turned back around to face the table. "We are not gonna let Baxter run us out of here on my birthday," she said with ferocity. "If he comes over here, we're gonna eat our ice cream and ignore him, or get kicked out for me shoving my cone in his face."

Belle bit her lip as she scooped up more of her ice cream. "Let's hope it doesn't come to that."

They tried to stick to the plan, but, of course, fate had other plans as Baxter sauntered over with too much glip in his smile a minute later. "Oh, would you look here?" Baxter said.

They said nothing, just kept scooping their treats into their mouths.

"Hello! I know y'all aren't deaf."

"Did you guys hear something?" Kit asked the table.

Joon shook his head. "Nope."

"Must have been the wind," Zach said before turning to Belle. "Sunshine, can I have a bite?"

She gave him a look, "You don't even like cake batter."

"I wouldn't mind tasting your cake," Baxter said over Zach's shoulder.

Zach turned to face the man slowly, a glare growing on his face. "What did you just say to her?"

Baxter just shrugged. "Hey, I calls it as I see it."

"So do I. You're a fucking douche, and you owe her an apology."

"Why?" Baxter scoffed. "A girl like her should be happy that—"

Zach almost stood up until he felt Belle's hand on his shoulder. He turned slightly to see the look of a lioness overtake her face.

"Okay, listen because I'm only gonna say this once," she informed him. "I don't mess around with troll dolls who can't tell their head from their ass, and I'm definitely not going to waste my time with someone who believes he's God's gift to women when he is clearly the reject of Hell. So, if you don't mind letting us get back to our evening, I'd really appreciate it."

Baxter stood there mouth wide open for a while until the blond girl he came in with called his name.

"Have a good night," Belle said cheerfully as he walked away.

The four of them burst out laughing as soon as Baxter was far enough away from the table. "That was the hottest thing I have ever seen." Zach chuckled as he turned to Belle, who had a blush rushing up her cheeks. "I didn't know that you had that in you."

She shrugged. "Kailey and I dealt with far too many fuck-boys in our college days. Reject of Hell was her signature anti-pickup line."

Kit laughed. "God, I have a feeling that we would have loved her."

Belle smiled before grabbing and squeezing Kit's hand. "I think she would have liked you all too."

It wasn't much long after that that they were done with their ice cream, and Kit managed to snag a pint of almond brittle to bring home with her for a birthday treat for herself. They walked out of the shop, talking about possibly going up to the lighthouse when they heard someone running toward them.

"Hey!"

Zach groaned. *Couldn't this fucker take a hint?* When he turned around, Baxter was marching toward them. "Why won't you go away?" Zach asked as they all stood around the car. "No one gives a shit about what you think."

"Everyone cares what I think," Baxter scoffed as he gave Zach a biting glare. "It's you no one gives a shit about. You always said that you were too good for this town and that one day we would be working for you, but you are just as sorry as you were in high school. You'd talk a lot of crap but you can't back it up with anything. You're back in town begging for scraps like a little bitch."

For a moment, Zach felt like he was back in high school, dealing with Baxter and his friends bumping him into lockers and snatching stuff off his lunch tray. Baxter had always been good at hiding what he was doing for teachers, so even when Zach thought about reporting it, he knew that there would be no proof that he could show it to anyone.

But he wasn't that helpless teen anymore. In fact, he was far from it. And he wasn't going to take any more of Baxter's bullshit.

"Why the fuck are you so obsessed with me?" Zach scoffed. "Why are you still here, Baxter? Did Hollywood not turn out the way you planned?"

Baxter shifted on his feet, bolstering Zach's confidence. "I'm on a break."

"From what?" Zach scoffed. "Your insurance commercials where you get the shit beat out of you by an owl?"

The redhead's eyes widened. "How did you—"

"Gigi ran into your Grams the other day. They talked."

Baxter glared, his face turning red, though Zach didn't know if it was from embarrassment or anger. Besides, he was enjoying this far too much, so he continued. "You wanna talk about me, but you don't have a leg to stand on. You're the one here begging for attention because they don't give a damn about you in Hollywood. You really must not have anything better to do because you are so fucking obsessed with trying to make me feel like crap," Zach taunted, taking a step closer. He wanted to look Baxter in the eye when he said what he needed to say. "Your mediocrity might work here, but you couldn't last a minute in the real world so you came back here because this town is nothing more than a place where people settle for what they got, and for some pathetic reason they settle for you. They don't want anything else because they just want this stupid view on a postcard."

Baxter said nothing, looking sufficiently embarrassed, but Zach couldn't help but get one more dig in.

"I might talk a lot of crap but at least I have the brains to back it up. But you will always be pathetic."

Zach got into the car without waiting for a response. The rest of the group did the same. Honestly, Zach felt pretty good saying all that as he pulled away from the parlor. He smiled as he turned the radio back on, letting Kit's anthem blast through the speakers once more. But he was surprised when Kit didn't start singing along again.

"What happened to the free concert?" he chuckled.

He looked into the backseat and saw that Kit wasn't smiling. "Not in the mood."

"I thought we said that Baxter wasn't going to ruin your birthday."

"Not everything is Baxter's fault," Joon mumbled.

"Then what—"

"You really think we're pathetic?" Kit asked.

Zach almost felt the car swerve beneath him. "Wait, what?"

Kit glared at him through the mirror. "We're pathetic because we couldn't make it out of this town?"

Zach glanced between his mirror and the passenger seat, confusion riddled across his face, "I wasn't talking about you guys, I was talking about him."

"But have you ever considered that some of us like it here," Kit yelled at him. "That we want to be in this town?"

"Why?" Zach scoffed. "This town is—"

"This town is our home. It's where our family is. You forget that all the damn time. It's like you can't wait to get away from us when family is supposed to stick together."

"Well, families don't always do that," Zach hissed. "Mine is fucking proof of that."

No one said anything for a moment as Zach made his way down the road into Lillet.

Joon turned to him once they got to Main Street. "Is that why you're so bad at texting us back?"

"What?"

"You don't respond because you don't want to be around us. You don't think we're family at all."

Zach pulled over when they got to Main Street and tried to face them. "No guys that's not it."

"You know what? Forget it," Kit said unbuckling her seatbelt. "Message received. Let's go, Joon."

They both got out of the car. Zach quickly followed.

"Guys, wait!" Zach called after them, but neither of them turned around. "You guys?" They definitely didn't hear him that time, because the air was rushing out of his lungs so fast that he could barely hear himself. He slumped back against the car, the divots of his keys digging into his fist.

What the fuck did he just do?

Any satisfaction that had come from that interaction with Baxter couldn't outweigh the pain he was feeling in his chest. He didn't know how long he stood like that, but he only snapped out of it when Belle came around the car and held out her hand to him. "Give me the keys."

Zach looked up at her. "What?"

"I'll drive."

"What?"

"I'm driving." She reached forward to grab the keys, but he pulled his hand back.

"Are you sure?"

"I mean, it's as good a time as any." She shrugged. "It's not a peak traffic hour so..."

He shook his head. "Seriously, Belle you don't have to—"

"Zach. I don't want you driving in this state. So, please, let me drive."

He bit his lip. Belle had her accident when she was a grief-stricken mess. Of course, she wouldn't want to be in the passenger seat of a car where the driver was in their feelings. He sighed and slowly handed over the keys before getting into the passenger seat. When Belle got into the driver's seat, she didn't put the keys in immediately. She spent five minutes checking and rechecking the mirrors, the chair, the seatbelt, and the controls of the car like she was going through a checklist.

Zach didn't say anything as she went through the motions a fourth time. Whatever it took for her to feel comfortable, he would let her do it.

She took a deep breath before she finally put the key into the ignition. She jumped a little when the car came to life, but she straightened up and put her hands on the wheels. She pulled away from the side of the street and got back on the road.

The rest of the car ride up to the cottage was silent. Far too silent for Zach's liking. It didn't feel like the comfortable quiet that he got used to when he was around Belle. When she finally parked the car, she let out a long breath.

"Great job, Sunshine," he said softly, giving her a sliver of a smile as he did.

"Thanks," she breathed out before turning to him. "You okay?" Belle asked as she unbuckled her seatbelt.

He shrugged. "I don't know." He'd known that one day he might say or do something that would turn off Kit and Joon, but he'd never guessed that this would be it. "I just wanted to get Baxter off my back," he muttered. "I didn't mean to hurt them in the process."

Belle reached over to squeeze his hand. "Well, Zach," she started, "you usually don't say things you don't mean."

His head banged his head against the headrest. "Fuck." He sighed. "I finally stand up to my childhood bully and I end up alienating my friends in the process." He looked over at her and saw the pity in her eyes. "My fucking luck, right?"

She bit her lip. "You need to apologize."

"No kidding." He snapped at her. He immediately regretted it. "Sorry. I'm sorry." He rubbed his hands over his eyes, knocking his glasses askew. "I wouldn't even know how to start."

"Well"— Belle reached over and straightened up his glasses—"sorry is as good a place as any."

"Yeah," he nodded, but he doubted sorry would be good enough for them, and he didn't know what else he could do to make this okay again.

"You want to stay over?"

"Nah, I promised Corey that I would read him to sleep tonight but thanks for the offer." He glanced at her with the biggest smile he could muster. "Go, I'll be fine. Promise." He turned to unbuckled his seatbelt but grabbed his hand.

"Hey." He looked back at her and she tried to give him a reassuring smile as she cupped his cheek in her hand. "Go home. Get some rest. Figure it out in the morning."

"Alright."

Belle leaned over and kissed his cheek. "Text me when you get back."

"'Kay."

"Bye."

"Bye."

With that, Belle left the car and went into the house.

I love you.

It was on the tip of his tongue. He could've said it right then, but after that shit show, it wasn't the right time to tell her that.

As the door closed behind her, his phone pinged. He took out the phone hoping it was a message from Kit or Joon, but his eyes widened when saw an email notification with the words "Retna Publishing" in the title.

He opened it and his eyes immediately scanning the message.

They appreciated his application.

They were impressed by his resume.

They wanted to interview him for a position in their New York City office.

Excerpt from "Project Void" by Zach Roberts (2nd Draft)

"Where are we?" Crya said, her voice shaking as she did.

"I don't know," Ty said as he took a look around the crash site. The surface was rocky and dense, though the front of their escape pod had managed to dig right into the ground.

"Do you think everyone else made it out?"

"I don't know," he said with a huff as he tried to move himself out of his seat to lean forward. There was a small speck of light in the distance, but nothing close enough to illuminate wherever they had landed.

"How are we gonna get out of this, Lieutenant?"

Ty looked over to his friend and frowned. "I don't know."

Chapter 29

Zach had never been good with apologies.

He could admit when he was wrong, but he never knew how to articulate a sorry beyond the word. He was a much better writer than a speaker but he felt like it would be weird if he spent two minutes standing in front of someone typing and editing an apology on his phone before he said it. Even so, that had been what he was doing throughout his shift that day while he sat at the counter.

The Book Haven had been pretty quiet all day. Only two people had actually bought books and even then, it was only picture books. Not even the impulse buy section had intrigued either customer. Jaime had texted him about the summer reading rush at Storybound, and he couldn't relate to how overwhelmed they felt after. Zach was still mulling over his spat with Kit and Joon, not to mention the interview request that he had gotten two days ago. He had sent that application weeks ago as a shot in the dark and now he had his first interview request ever, but he didn't even know if he wanted the job anymore.

It would be a lie to say that he hadn't been excited by the prospect at the time. The fact that he'd even gotten an interview request after months of rejection made him feel obligated to see it through. A month or two ago, it would have been an easy decision to go with a bag packed to last him a couple of weeks. Now, saying yes felt like it would cause a domino effect that could tear a building down.

Beau and Mateo had already been messaging him about his current situation with Kit and Joon, and how he needed to fix it, and he didn't disagree, but what do you do to make sure a lifetime of friendship doesn't go down the drain? It was almost as hard as trying to figure out how to tell the girl you've fallen in love with that you might move away.

"Hey, Zach?" Des said, knocking him out of his spiraling thoughts.

"Yeah?" Zach put away his phone and frowned at the solemn look on Des's face. "What's with you?"

Des let out a long breath as he leaned onto the counter. "Look, there's no easy way to say this. I've been approached with an offer for the store, and I've been considering it."

Zach felt his heart drop through the floor and damn well into lava as it burned in his chest. "What?"

"Look it's not ideal, but rent's starting to go up and sales have been going down. If things don't change soon, I'm going to have to close down."

Zach shook his head. "But, this is your dream."

It's my dream.

Des nodded. "It is. But dreams don't pay the bills. I haven't made a final decision yet, I just wanted you to be aware in case something happens."

Zach nodded slightly, trying to keep the tears from welling in his eyes.

"Look, you've always been a valued part of this store," Des continued, "and the last thing I want is for you to hold yourself back for something that might not make it if this place falls apart."

Zach nodded again. "I get it. I mean, I have an interview offer on the table so—"

"Really?" Des smiled, though it didn't take up his face like it usually did. "That's great. You deserve to work somewhere that can pay for your skills."

"What skills? All I do is read and write."

"And that will take you far in life, don't forget that." Des patted Zach on the shoulder, but it provided no comfort for him whatsoever. "If you need time off for the interview, let me know. I should be able to manage things around here by myself for a while."

"Sure." Zach bit his lip to keep himself from taking his growing frustrations out on Des, but he wanted nothing more than to yell at him to not sell his second favorite place in the world.

"Hey." Des stood up and took off his beanie, letting his bald head shine. "You can head out for today. Not many people have been in, so I can handle closing on my own."

"You sure?"

"Yeah. Get out of here. Go live your life." Des waved him off and went over to mess with the magazine rack.

What life?

Zach got up and quickly made his way back into the office. He shoved all of his things in his bag, and rushed back out the door without another word, trying to keep what little composure he had left together.

When he finally got to his car, he just sat in the driver's seat with the keys hanging off his finger while the idea fully sank in.

No more Book Haven.

It was one thing if The Book Haven wasn't there to be his safe space, but if there was no more Book Haven, what would Des do? Des was one of the first people who had helped Zach fall in love with reading. He'd modeled for Zach that there was a chance for him to make his own living being a book nerd, but if Des couldn't do it, what chance did he have?

The drive home felt too long and too short at the same time.

Zach walked into the house still a bit dazed. All he wanted to do was go lie down, but he didn't even get his shoes off when he heard, "Zach!"

He jumped and turned to see his father, Mimi, and Amaya sitting in the living room. The mixed looks of worry, anger, and guilt across their faces made him panic.

Please don't be more bad news.

"Come over here." Jed gestured to the empty spot on the couch next to Amaya.

Zach slowly made his way over, taking note of how Amaya didn't dare look up at him. "We having a family meeting or something?"

"Or something," Jed said through gritted teeth.

Zach glanced at Amaya as he sat but her gaze stayed buried in her lap. "Where's Corey?" he asked instead.

"Sleeping over at Gigi's."

He nodded. "What's up?"

Jed just stared at him, before he pulled an open condom wrapper out of his pocket and slammed it down on the table with a bang, making all of them jump. "Amaya, do you wanna tell me why I found this in your trash?"

Zach's eyes widened as he looked over at Amaya, who finally brought up her eyes to look at their father. "Why were you going through my trash?" she whimpered.

"Don't try to change the subject. I thought I raised you better than this. What in the world were you and Owen thinking?"

She shrugged, shaking her head. "We just...did it. Obviously, we were safe."

"That doesn't matter. What matters is that you did it in the first place. Where did you get this anyway?"

Amaya glanced over at him. "Zach's room."

Zach grimaced.

Fuck.

Jed turned to Zach. "Why do you have these?"

Zach raised a brow. "For sex."

His father sucked his teeth, but Zach just scoffed. "Dad, I'm an adult. I have a girlfriend. I have sex. You should be proud of me for having them. Aren't you always telling us to be prepared for things?"

Jed's glare deepened more. "That doesn't mean you need to have these things lying around for your siblings to see."

Zach turned to face his father and informed him, "They weren't lying around, they were in my bathroom cabinet, and we all know how much Amaya loves using my bathroom, so, of course, she found them." He glared at Amaya. "But I definitely didn't tell her that she could use them."

The fuck were you thinking? he tried to convey with his face. He didn't want his teenage sister having sex any more than their dad did. He knew that she was growing up, but he didn't want her to be this grown-up yet.

Amaya played with her hands in her lap. "Well, I was talking to Belle the other day about relationships, and said that intimacy can be a great way to strengthen them."

Jed scoffed as he looked at Zach. "Of course, your little girlfriend comes in here and messes with my baby girl's innocence."

Zach turned his glare to his father. "Don't you dare try to pin this on Belle," he snapped. "Maya needed someone to talk to, so she talked to Belle, and there's nothing wrong with that." He looked over at Amaya again but with a softer look this time. "But I will say that I'm ninety percent sure that Belle was talking about emotional intimacy. She's big on talking to people about their feelings."

A blank look spread across Amaya's face. "Oh."

"Yeah, oh," Zach quipped. "There's more than one way to be intimate with someone. Please use that AP Psych class next year to learn about that. And for the love of God, stop going into my bathroom while I'm still here!"

Jed groaned, rubbing his hands over his face as he sat back in his chair.

"You shouldn't be so hard on them," Mimi interjected finally. "I remember what you was like with their mother back in the day."

"And look how that turned out," Jed said, making her mouth snap shut, before he turned to Amaya. "Owen is not allowed in this house anymore, and you're not allowed at his."

"What? Dad, that's not fair." Amaya cried.

"If this is what you two are doing when no one else is home, I really don't care. I'm not letting you screw up your life."

"Can you allow us to have a life at all without you digging through our shit like you own us?"

The family turned to Zach, and he realized he said that out loud. Definitely not the time for his inner thoughts to become his outer voice.

The way his father straightened up like he was back in his linebacker days was enough to scare the Hell out of anybody, but Zach was so used to it to the point that it didn't faze him. "Zachary Nicholas Roberts, you better watch your mouth."

Zach scoffed. "Or what? You'll send me to my room. Oh, the horror."

Jed stood from his seat. Zach did the same. He was done with bullshitting the day away. He was so fucking done with this day that he really didn't give a shit about anything his father thought at this point.

Mimi stood up as well, trying to hold her hands between the two of them. "Alright, I think we should just calm down."

"Nuh-uh, my son doesn't get to speak to me that way in my house," Jed said, stepping around the coffee table. "I don't know where you got this disrespectful attitude from, but it ends here."

Zach's fists clenched against his legs. "I'm just saying—"

"You best help yourself and say nothing. I'm not one of your little friends that you can mouth off to. You may have come back from college and think you grown now, but you're not. You are still a child, my child at that, and my children know better than to disrespect me."

"So you don't have to respect our space but we have to respect you?"

"As long as you live under my roof, you respect my rules. End of discussion."

End of discussion.

Just when Zach thought his father might be trying to change, he went right back to his old ways. Those seemed to be his father's favorite way to shut down any conversation but Zach wasn't going to hold his tongue back today. He was at the end of his rope.

He was on the outs with his best friends.

His safe space could be shut down.

It was like the story of his life was unraveling at the seams, and he couldn't catch the pages in time to try and put it back together.

He couldn't let it fall apart any more than it already was.

He wasn't going to let this be the end of his story.

He looked right into Jed's eyes and said, "You know what? If that's the case, maybe Mom had the right idea then."

Zach didn't stay to see his father's reaction. He walked around the table, bypassing Mimi, who stepped in front of Jed as he started to yell at Zach. What Jed said, Zach neither knew nor cared. He just snatched up his bag as the sounds washed over him like static while shoved open the front door. He jumped into the car and tried hard to ignore the sight of a sobbing Amaya standing in the doorway as he pulled out of the driveway. He whirled the car around, put his foot on the gas, and careened out of the neighborhood.

Excerpt from "Project Void" by Zach Roberts (1st
Draft)

"That's not gonna do anything." Crya scoffed, offering no help like usual.

"Nothing's gonna do anything if we don't try," Ty
insisted as he tried to put the fuel cell back into the
panel.

"Why bother? We're stuck here and help's not
coming so why don't you just give up?"

Ty shoved back from his workspace and walked
right up to her face. "Because I didn't work this hard
to just lie down and accept defeat. Maybe I'm not
fully capable of getting this craft airborne again, but
I'm not gonna sit here like I can't do anything," he
spat at her. "The fact stands that if we don't get it together and do something, we're not going to make
it home. That's not who I am. No one in this crew is
gonna give up because that is not the kind of people they are."

Crya bit her lip, hard enough to let purple blood
drip from it "Well, what kind of people are we?"

Ty stared at her for a minute before using his
thumb to wipe the blood from her chin. "People that
believed in something."

Chapter 30

Zach wasn't a rebel by nature. He lived by the book when it came to school, work, play, and everything in between. He rarely deviated from doing what he was told, and rarely complained.

But all he wanted to do right now was tear up every rulebook he had ever seen and scream into the void, praying someone would hear him.

The drive away from his house was a blur but somehow he managed to find his way to Linley Cottage. He yanked the keys from the ignition and opened the car door, but he didn't go to the front door. Instead, he walked over into the meadow, staring at the town below him like he was on the edge of the world looking in at everyone else living their lives. He took deep breaths as he tried to push down the water threatening to fill his lungs, and he sank into the grass, not caring if his khakis got caked in dirt. How could one place bring so much joy and pain at the same time?

He didn't know how long he sat there, his legs curled into his chest and his head on his knees, but he flinched when he heard the sound of grass crunching beneath shoes behind him. He turned sharply, ready to face off with someone, but he relaxed once he realized it was just Belle.

"Thank God, you're here," she said, running over and plopping down on the ground to hug him. "Amaya's been texting me like crazy wondering if I've heard from you or not."

"Makes sense," he said with a shrug as he wrapped his arms around her and pulled her over to straddle his lap.

She pulled back, her arms still loosely hanging around his shoulders. "Are you okay?"

"I'm..." He chewed on his lip before letting out a sigh. "No, I'm not okay."

Belle got up and moved to sit next to him, clutching her hand in hers.

"I'm just really fucking tired of dealing with bullshit today." He looked over at Belle. "Is Amaya okay?"

"Besides the fact that she says she's holing herself up in her room, yeah. She said your Gigi is coming to get her so she can spend the night there."

Zach nodded as she threw her legs over his so she was sat perpendicular to him. "What happened?"

He said nothing for a while, just caressing her hand before he finally rehashed what had happened when he got home. Every once and a while, Belle would squeeze his hands reassuringly to urge him to continue when he lost the words. Once he finished, Belle just sat with the story, leaning her head on his shoulder for a moment before she spoke again. "Have you and your father always been like this?"

He shrugged. "In some ways. When I was younger, I practically worshiped him, he was like Superman to me. But when I got older, and it was clear that I wasn't gonna be like him, if I was gonna butt heads with anyone in the house, it was gonna be him." He bit his lip. "It's not even like I hate him, you know? I just wish he was different."

There were many days when Zach wondered what life would have been like if he had been born into a different family, like Kit's or Joon's. When he'd gone over to their houses growing up, it had felt like everything was calm and orderly. Sometimes, he resented how easy his friends had it compared to him. Their parents stayed together, stayed with their children, and encouraged them to pursue the things they loved. In turn, he didn't feel that same comfort at their houses after a while. He hadn't felt that calm anywhere else besides The Book Haven until he'd met Belle.

She made him feel calm like the world wouldn't swallow him up and spit him out. He felt at peace when he was with her. He flipped her hand in his, starting to trace the lines on her palms. "Have I ever told you about how my dad got to Lillet?" She shook her head and he continued, "He actually grew up in an okay neighborhood. Not the worst, not the best. Mimi was a single parent, but she made it work, and my dad and my uncle Jeremy did the best they could to stay out of trouble. At least that's what Mimi says. My uncle volunteered at the local youth center while my dad studied at the library when he wasn't at football practice, and they just kept their heads down."

Zach took a breath. "My uncle got killed on his way home from the center one day." Belle squeezed his hand harder, but he went on, "They never told me the full story, but you could pretty much tell from how they said everything that it wasn't an accident. Mimi moved them here and Dad has never thought of leaving or letting us leave for that matter."

The wind started to pick up, and Zach found himself glancing towards the sky. They weren't far away enough from any major cities to be able to see any real stars in the sky, everything was drowned out by light pollution, but the full moon was shining bright on its own, ever the constant source of light.

"I know objectively that this place is not a bad place to be," Zach continued, "but when I'm around him sometimes, I feel like I'm suffocating. Like when I would see Baxter after he threw me in that pool. I feel like I can't breathe, like I can't move without him trying to take control and I'm just really fucking tired of it. I think my mom was too."

"What do you mean?"

"I heard them fight before the night she left. She got a job offer in another state and wanted us to move there, but Dad had looked up the area and he thought it wouldn't be a good place for us to grow up. Here we had friends and family. If we moved, we would have no one. Dad didn't want that for us... but Mom wanted it for herself so she left."

Sometimes, he wanted to applaud his mother for taking her life into her own hands and making it something she wanted. Sadly, it had come at the cost of her children, but given her complete absence from their life after, it seemed that wasn't too high a price for her.

He felt Belle lean her head on his shoulder, and he wondered how anyone could discard their family to get ahead like his mom had done. One thought of Amaya and Corey, and he knew that he couldn't live the rest of his life without seeing them ever again.

Just like he couldn't stomach the idea of leaving Belle behind for a job in New York.

His parents let a fucking job come between them; he couldn't let that happen to him and Belle.

"I got an interview," he said, glancing at Belle.

Her eyes widened and she picked up her head to look at him. "What?"

"I got a job interview," he repeated. "It's for one of the publishing houses in New York."

"Oh, that's great," Belle said in a soft tone. She looked down at their hands. "You gonna take it?"

"I should see it through, shouldn't I?" He shrugged. If The Book Haven was going out of business, he would need a job more than ever. "I know it's not a guaranteed thing but it's something."

"Yeah, I guess," she murmured as her grip on his hand loosened. He kept his firm.

He couldn't let Belle go. She was the only thing he had left. "You could come with me," he blurted out.

She looked up at him. "What?"

"You could come to the city with me for the interview, and if I get it, we could move there together," he prompted, a smile blooming on his face as he thought of it more. It was the perfect solution. Belle already knew New York like the back of her hand, and once he settled into a rhythm with the job, he could still help with the shop in their off hours.

"Zach—"

"I mean we could find a nice apartment with an extra bedroom for an office space and then we could—"

"No." Belle's face firmed up. "No." She shook her head. "I... I can't go back there."

"What do you mean you can't go back there?"

"I just... I can't go back there. I'm not... I'm not ready." She pulled her hand out of his, brushing her hair back from her face as the wind picked up again. "But you know what, you can go if that's what you really want and—"

"Belle, I don't know if that's what I want—"

"Yeah, it is. You wouldn't be bringing it up if it wasn't and it's fine." She stood up, brushing the dirt off her sweatpants. "I mean, you said you were only gonna be here for the summer, so I shouldn't have expected anything less. I know I'm easy to leave behind anyway, so—"

"Belle, just hold on." Zach interrupted as he quickly got to his feet. "I don't want to end this. To end us."

She bit her lip. "You don't?"

"No, no Sunshine," he fretted as he grabbed her hands. "I might go but...I wanna go with you." He took a breath. "I just think that...we can both escape," he said with a nervous chuckle. "We can get out of this town, and start something new."

Belle shook her head. "I don't want something new in New York," she said, pulling her hands back from his. "This, this here in Lillet, this is my new start."

Zach's jaw dropped slightly as he tried to find the words to say. "Belle..."

She took a step back. "Look. I'm not going to leave this place when for the first time in my life I'm actually happy."

"Belle, I really think—"

"I know what you think," she said with a scoff. "You think that you want to go somewhere where no one will know your name and no one will know your baggage. Where you can disappear into a crowd of thousands and...I'm telling you it's overrated." Belle ran her hands through her hair. "I know that's what you think you want, but I'll tell you right now that it's not all it's cracked up to be. It fucking sucks, and I have no interest in going back and reliving that." His lips trembled as her words sunk in. "I'm sorry," she said as she turned away from him.

No. This is not what he wanted. He stepped forward to try and grab her hand again. "Belle—"

She took another step back. "Just go, Zach. Go be free and clear in New York, if that's what you really want." She started to walk back to the cottage.

"Wait," he called as he started to go after her. "Stop," he pleaded. "Don't walk away from me, Belle."

She swiftly turned back to face him. "I'm not walking away from you, you're running away from me."

He desperately shook his head. "No, I'm not Belle," he said through trembling lips. "You're not listening to me." He took another step forward. "I want us to run away together."

She scoffed. "You're not listening to me," she said through gritted teeth. "I want to stay here." The pained look on her face hurt Zach so much, but he couldn't look away. "How can you not get it? You can't have it both ways, Zach," she said, fidgeting with her fingernails as she always did when she was frustrated. "You keep saying that you want a life of your own that your dad doesn't control, but you can't come over here and ask me to change my life for you. Especially when I can't be that sure about us."

For a moment, his mouth couldn't form words, but he eventually asked, "What do you mean by that?"

She scoffed a laugh. "Come on, Zach. You've had one foot out the door this entire summer, and I'll tell you right now, it fucking hurt to see it," she cried, a tear slipping down her face. "For a while, I didn't even entertain the idea of being with you because I knew you were prime to leave at any time, and it was scary to think about what this could be if we did try, but I did it anyway because I was tired of being scared and I wanted to be selfish for once and have you for as long as I could." She bit her lip again, playing with the cuff of her sweatshirt. "That's what really hurts about this. You have a piece of so many people's hearts in your hand, and you just want to pretend that it doesn't matter, that if you run away, nothing will happen, and that people will just go on as if you were never here. But you are here, Zach, and they want you here." More tears fell down her face, and all Zach wanted to do was wipe them away, but he kept his hands to himself. "You have people who want you in their lives so badly that they will let you walk out so you might come back again just for a moment. You have a home here, Zach. Not everyone has that."

Zach fidgeted with the loose thread of his pants pocket. He desperately wanted Belle to realize that she did have people who wanted her in their lives; Kit and Joon enjoyed having her around; his family adored her; he loved her.

He loved her and he wanted her to be in his life, now and forever. "Do you want me here?" he finally asked.

Belle shook her head as she shoved tears off her face. "It doesn't matter."

"It matters to me, Belle."

She took another step back. "No, it doesn't. It can't. I'm not gonna give you a piece of my heart just so you can shatter it when you go." She took a deep breath. "I can't let my life revolve around someone else just to lose them again." She shook her head as she pulled her sleeves to cover her hands. "I can't keep putting the pieces back together. I just can't, so..." She gestured toward the Mustang. "Just go ahead and leave, alright?"

She walked away, back into her little cottage at the edge of the world, without one glance back at him.

"If there was a way to make things right, you know I would do it in a heartbeat."

Larry from *Laces Between Spaces* by Annalise Dale

Chapter 31

Zach was supposed to be smart. Really fucking smart. For years, that was the only thing he really knew about himself; he was smart, got good grades, and was destined to succeed.

But life made him question these things every day since he'd graduated. He just felt dumb now. He didn't know what the hell he was doing. He didn't know how he was going to get a job, how he would move on from The Book Haven closing, or how to mend things with Kit and Joon. He felt like a smart person should have all the solutions to these problems.

Maybe he wasn't as smart as he thought he was.

He entertained the thought of getting in his car and driving away, but Zach was smart enough to know that he damn well wasn't going to let a woman like Belle get away from him, and he knew for a fact that he wasn't going to let her feel like he didn't want her more than any job offer.

He wasn't going to be like his parents. He was going to own up and be the person he damn well wanted to be.

He marched himself right over to her door, and knocked.

She didn't answer.

He knocked again. And again. And again until he heard footsteps coming up to the door, revealing a red-eyed Belle standing there. As great as Zach was at writing, he had never been one to be able to easily say all the right things out loud, but looking at Belle, he knew one thing he wanted to relay in a heartbeat. "I don't want to leave you."

Belle bit her lip. "But you do want to leave town, and I don't." She shoved the remnants of tear lines off her face. "I told you, Zach. It's fine, just—" Belle went to close the door, but Zach held it open.

He shook his head. "No, it's not fine, Belle. I…" His tongue brushed over his chapped lips as he tried to find the right words. "I want to get out of my dad's house. I want to live my life without him making me feel like I'm always destined to have a target on my back. I want to leave that feeling behind, but I don't want to leave you behind."

"Zach…" Belle pleaded through her trembling lips. "I said you can go. Why are you being so stubborn about this?"

"Because I love you!"

Belle's eyes widened as she took a step back. He could see her hand trembling where it was clinging to the front door. All he wanted was to hold it in his, but instead, he sighed and said, "This is not how I wanted to say it, but I need you to know that I love you. I love your laugh, your smile, your pouty face when things aren't going your way. I love how you try to make every aspect of your life magical. I love how you are not afraid to be yourself and how you always try to look on the positive side of things, even when you're not feeling your best. I love you, Belle Thomas, okay?"

She shook her head as she took a step back, letting go of the door. "You don't mean that."

"Yes, I do," he asserted. "I'll shout it from the fucking rooftops if I have to, but like you said, I don't say things I don't mean."

Belle shut her mouth. "Look"—Zach took a step forward, his toes barely over the threshold of the house—"You say that I have pieces of people's hearts in my hands. Then you should know you have a big fucking piece of mine. I'm not sure of much right now, but I know for a fact that I love you." He laughed like a madman as a tear fell down his face. Any composure he had left that day was completely gone, but he didn't care. "I love you, Sunshine, and I don't want to have one foot out the door anymore," he admitted. "Not when it comes to you." He took another step closer. "I'm not gonna leave you behind, Belle. No matter how much you ask me to. Because you are my safe space, Sunshine, and you make my world so much brighter."

She glanced up at him through teary eyes, tugging at the sleeves of her shirt again. "What if you don't have a choice?"

"What do you mean?"

"What if you don't have a choice, but to leave me behind?"

His heart shattered in his chest, but he held himself together. "Belle, we both know I'm stubborn as hell. So, there is nothing that could stop me from coming back to you. Because you are worth fighting for." He took another step into her space. "Sunshine, you are not easy to leave behind."

She took another step back. "But, I am."

"No, you're not."

"Everyone I love leaves me!" She yelled through a sob. "It doesn't matter if they choose to or not. I'm always the one who gets left behind! And…" The tears rolled down her face faster. "And I'm always left alone. I'm always gonna be alone, I…I don't wanna be alone," she stuttered out as she curled in on herself. "I don't wanna be alone. I don't wanna be alone."

Zach couldn't hold back anymore. He surged forward, and wrapped his arms around her, bringing her face against his shoulder. He caressed her back as she sobbed. If he was one of those strong guys in romance novels, he would've picked her up and carried her to the couch. Instead, he closed the door behind them, and slowly guided them over into the living room. He sat down, bringing Belle with him, and gathered her into his lap as she kept crying into his shoulder, "I don't wanna be alone. I don't wanna be alone."

"You are not alone, Sunshine," he whispered into her hair, carefully taking off her glasses and tossing them on the coffee table. "I might not know how to make you feel otherwise right now, but you're not. You are so fucking loved and I will do everything in my power to make sure you know that, okay?" He adjusted himself so he was lying back on the couch with her lying on top of him. "I love you so fucking much."

Zach let her tears soak through his shirt as Appa came over to join them, putting his head on Belle's back. Zach rubbed his hand over the dog's head, feeling himself calm down with every stroke of his fur.

Eventually, he felt Belle's cries die down and her breathing slowed against his shoulder. He kept rubbing her back and pulled her in as close as possible. Within a few minutes, he felt her slump against him, tiny snores coming through her nose. He looked down, caressing her face with his hand, wiping the tear trails away as much as he could. "I'm not leaving you behind, Sunshine." He kissed her forehead. "Never."

Love isn't practical.

It's not rational in the least.

Giving your heart to someone who could break it is terrifying.

But the idea of finding the person who will cherish it, and protect it with all their being is worth the risk.

The Limits of Love by Trina Ali

Chapter 32

Zach never went into things without having a plan.

Without one, he would just spend the day worrying about everything that could go wrong. So, to save his peace of mind, he always made a plan. Even when he had a spontaneous thought, he made a checklist before he pursued it.

But for the first time in his life, he didn't have a plan, and he was fine with it.

Zach must have drifted off at some point because when he opened his eyes, little rays of sunlight peeked through the window. Belle was still asleep against his chest, while Appa slept next to the couch on the thick blanket Belle made him. Zach found himself running his hands over Belle's head, pondering the things she had said offhandedly before.

I'm used to doing it on my own.

I can handle everything on my own.

I'm used to being alone.

He may complain about his family, but at least he had one to come back to at the end of the day. Belle didn't have anyone. She was alone, and he didn't want her to feel that way anymore.

He sighed as he turned his phone back on; the notifications came rolling down the screen like a waterfall. Instagram updates, random app reminders, and tons of unread text messages. Not just from family, but Kit and Joon, and some of their family as well. His father must have reached out to others before Belle found him. It was overwhelming to see just how many people were reaching out, but he was starting to see Belle's point. He was in people's hearts even if he didn't see it. He made it a point to respond to Amaya's texts, letting her know that he was okay, and replied to Mimi and Gigi as well. He didn't even entertain the idea of opening his father's texts, and he was too scared to read everyone else's messages. The only thing he wanted to focus on at the moment was taking care of himself and Belle.

He slowly rolled Belle onto the couch as he moved from under her, covering her with a blanket quickly after. Appa woke up as soon as his feet touched the floor. The shepherd rubbed against him. "Hey, buddy," Zach murmured as he nuzzled his hand into Appa's fur. He could see why Belle was always cuddled up with him for once.

He let Appa out and watched him scurry around until he did his business and came immediately returning to Belle's side. Zach took that as a signal to do his own thing while Appa watched over her. He went into the kitchen and started to find some things to make a semblance of breakfast with what Belle had. He wasn't the best in the kitchen, but after years of being his grandmothers' and Joon's sous chef, he knew how to make a holdover meal.

He decided on omelets and toast with some of the homemade strawberry jam that Belle made. The art of cutting up vegetables and ham, rolling the eggs in the pan—and cleaning after—gave him some peace of mind as he tried to figure out how he and Belle would move forward from here. It was soon after he finished filling Appa's food and water bowls and called him over to eat that he heard the couch shift behind him. "Hey," he greeted as he turned to face Belle.

"Hi," Belle said softly as she sat up fully, looking at him through groggy eyes.

Zach walked over, grabbed her glasses, cleaned them with his lens cloth, and put them in her hands. "Hope you don't mind me messing up your kitchen a bit."

"It's okay," she said as she put on her glasses. He walked back to the kitchen and took an omelet for himself as his toast popped up. Belle eventually made her way over to the small table and sat in her seat, just as Zach put a bowl of cutup strawberries in front of her, alongside the plate he'd already made for her. After he made his own plate, he turned off all the burners and went to sit in his seat.

"You know," Belle started as he picked up his fork. "You didn't have to stay and..."

He lifted his head and gave a fierce look that immediately made her mouth snap shut. "I told you that I'm not gonna leave you alone, Sunshine." He shrugged as he cut his omelet with his fork. "Stop trying to fight me on that."

Belle bit her lip but nodded as she picked up her fork to pick up one of the strawberries. She took a small bite of it before sitting up in her chair a bit more. They ate in stale silence. After last night, it made sense that neither of them were keen to converse, but it was something they needed to do. When Zach finished his omelet, he put down his fork. "I think we have a lot that we need to talk about."

She nodded as she dragged hers over the plate, letting it

scratch the surface. "I think you're right."

"It hurt you to say that, didn't it?" he teased and luckily, that did put a smile on her face. He let out a breath before he began, "Look Belle, you were right when you said that I've always been primed to leave this summer. That's a fact. Being in town was supposed to be temporary, and I didn't want to find any reason to stay." He shrugged. "But there are a lot of things that I do love about living here. A lot of people that make me love living here."

She twirled her fork in her hand. "I don't want you to feel obligated to stay here because of me."

He shook his head. "Stop that. I know what you're trying to do. I'm well versed in trying to push people away, Belle." She bit her lip and pushed around her eggs. He sighed and grabbed her free hand in his. "Look, I'm not saying that you're not a huge factor in me wanting to stay, because it is, but...there actually is a lot here that I would miss: Amaya, Corey, Gigi, Mimi, Joon, Kit, Des—"

"Not your dad?"

"I'd miss him. To a degree." *Just not at the moment.* "I'm just really tired of dealing with him trying to keep us in this town. I know he cares, but his way of caring doesn't feel like when he and my mom used to cover me in ten layers to go out in the snow, you know. He feels like a prison warden controlling what times I'm let out in the yard. I pretty much need to ask his permission to do anything, still. It feels like I need his go-ahead to go out with my friends or do anything that's not at home, and now he's saying he has the right to go through our things and..." He scoffed. "I can't live there anymore."

If there was one thing he and his father needed right now, it was space. Maybe one day, they could patch up what was left of their relationship, but for now, they needed time apart.

"So home is up in the air, and The Book Haven might not be an option anymore—"

Belle's gaze snapped up from her plate to meet his. "What do you mean?"

Zach sighed. He probably wasn't supposed to tell anyone about it, but he needed to talk to someone. "Des told me that he was considering selling the store yesterday."

Belle's jaw dropped. "What?" She shook her head. "No, he can't do that. That's our place."

"I know right?" He yelped. "I mean, Des was one of the few people that made me feel like I could have a career when it came to books." He sat back in his seat. "I remember one time, he read one of my short story assignments that I had hanging out of my bag when I worked there in high school. I was mortified at the idea of someone other than my teacher reading it, but he told me it was good and that I should try expanding it into a full novel."

"Did you..."

He knew what she was asking. "I plotted it out, but I struggled with finding more to say. We were supposed to write a sad story, so I wrote something along the lines of how I was feeling when my mom left." He shrugged. "I couldn't find a way to give the story a happy ending because, at the end of the day, I'm pretty sure she's never coming back." He sighed. "And that's not really the story I want to write about. I write stories where young Black boys can read and know that things are gonna be okay. That we don't have to spend our entire lives in fear."

A story of a Black teenager in a position of power who can hold everyone together and they all make it home with their souls intact. He wished that could be his reality, but for now, he was happy living vicariously through Ty. It was probably the same feeling that Belle's viewers got when watching her videos:

something that made them feel like they could have a life like that. A life free from drama and the pressure of the rest of the world.

That didn't mean the pressure went away.

"But right now, I'm fucking terrified about what could come next," he admitted.

She squeezed his hand bringing his attention back to her. "I get it. Trying to figure my life out after Grammy and Kailey passed was terrifying. But I did."

A small smile crept up his face. "You're a lot braver than me, Belle."

She shook her head. "I didn't feel brave then. I just felt really tired, and I was so sick of living in that moment, so I had to find a way to move on to the next one." She shrugged. "I think you just need to figure out what that next moment is for you."

"Well, at this moment," he pondered for a moment before looking at her with a smirk. "I wanna finish eating," he said, picking up his toast.

Belle giggled, nodding a bit more before taking a bite of the eggs. "And after that?"

He smiled. "You need help with packing orders today?"

They spent the rest of their morning, packing orders while listening to a *Last Airbender* playlist. They were nearly at the end of the series, but they had held off on watching it recently, as the final restock of the summer collection had come in and Belle was prepping for the fall release. They made a good dent in the orders before they had enough to fill up Zach's car.

With a kiss on her forehead and a promise to be back, Zach

went to drop off the orders. He stood in the post office line with the wagon behind him. Making multiple trips felt ridiculous and, no matter how weird he might have looked as a grown man using a wagon, he wasn't going to knock its convenience at the moment.

"Zach!"

He only had a moment to turn around before his legs were fully encased in Corey's arms.

"Hey, buddy," he greeted as he patted his little brother's head. "What are you doing here?"

Corey let him go and looked up at him. "Gigi said we needed to drop off things."

His eyes widened just as Gigi walked through the door. Her eyes narrowed as soon as her eyes landed on him and her free hand went on her hip. "Zachary Nicholas Roberts!" For a second, Zach braced himself for a smack on the head, but to his pleasant surprise, Gigi hugged him instead. "The hell you think you doing scaring us half to death like that?" she said, holding him tighter.

He wrapped his arms around her and squeezed her back. "Sorry, Gigi."

"Oh, I'm not the one you need to say sorry to." She nodded her head toward the door. "She's in the car."

Zach bit his lip as he looked between the door and the packages in the wagon.

"I'll take care of these," Gigi said as she took the handle from him, before nodding at the door again. "Go."

He nodded and headed outside Gigi's SUV, the shadow of someone sitting in the passenger seat catching his eye. He knocked on the window, and the figure looked up at him. He barely had time to back away from the door before Amaya shoved it open and tackled him in a hug. He wrapped his arms around his little sister, holding her closer as the sweatshirt he borrowed from Belle began to feel wet.

"I thought you left us," she cried into his shoulder.

The fact that he had been the one to make her feel like that broke his heart. "I know," he said, rubbing her back. "I'm so sorry, Amaya."

She pulled back and looked at him through her bloodshot eyes. "You can't leave, Zach."

"Maya…" he sighed.

"I'm serious," she pleaded. "I don't think I can handle it if you left us too."

"Hey, look at me." He slightly tilted up her chin so she was looking him in the eye. "I could never leave you or Corey behind. Never," he insisted. "But things have to change."

"You right about that."

He turned back toward the post office to see Gigi coming back out, holding Corey's hand. She looked him up and down. "Now, I think we all need to talk."

Zach sucked his teeth. "Gigi, I don't feel like dealing with Dad right now."

She shook her head. "No, not your Dad. You two and me. If Marian and I are gonna hand your father his ass then I need to know everything that happened."

Zach opened his mouth to agree, but his eyes flickered to the road that led back to Linley Cottage. "Gigi, I can't do that right now," he said.

Her eyes narrowed. "And why not?"

He sighed. "Belle and I…" He adjusted his glasses. "We fought last night."

Both Gigi and Amaya gasped before glaring at him. "You

what?" Gigi yelped.

"We're okay now," he clarified. "But we still need to talk about some things."

"You'd better because if you break that girl's heart, you've got another thing comin' to ya." She jabbed his shoulder to emphasize her point.

He chuckled nervously, slowly backpedaling toward his car. "Yes, ma'am."

She waved him off once she noticed his movement. "Now go on."

He nodded and quickly ruffled Corey's hair before turning back to Amaya. She was looking at him like he was a timid bunny, ready to bolt at any moment. He smiled softly before kissing her forehead. "Love you."

She smiled back. "Love you too."

When he pulled up back to the cottage, Belle was outside, tossing the ball for Appa to chase before heading back to a gingham blue blanket she'd laid out near the cottage, one of her Carry glass cups and a charcuterie board on it. When he closed the car door, she looked over at him and smiled. "Hey," she greeted.

"Hi." He walked over until he was standing next to her, and gestured at the space on the blanket. "Mind if I sit?"

Belle patted the spot right as Appa came back with his ball. Zach gently coaxed it out of his mouth before throwing it into the field and sitting down next to Belle. "Saw Amaya at the post office."

"How's she doing?" Belle asked as she picked up her cup and

took a sip out of the glass straw she'd placed in it.

"Okay, I guess." He shrugged. "She's just scared." He accepted the cup when Belle offered it, and took a sip from the rim of the glass. "Gigi says we need to have a meeting about what we're gonna do about my dad."

Belle picked up a small triangle of sandwich from the tray. "Have you told them about the job offer?"

"No." He placed down the cup and picked up a piece of orange from the tray. "I don't know what I'm gonna do about that," he sighed.

If The Book Haven was really on its way out, he might actually have to start looking for work again, this time without the safety net of the store ready to provide a safe landing. Not to mention, he still had so much in Lillet that he wanted to stay for and fix, and a move to New York probably wouldn't be the best for mending bridges.

"Do you want the job?" Belle queried, rubbing Appa's head as he lied down next to her.

He shrugged. "I want a job. I want to be doing something, but I don't know if working in publishing is what I want to do anymore," he admitted. "I mean, I like helping people find amazing books, and I don't necessarily need to work there to do that, but without The Book Haven..." He groaned and took off his glasses before burying his head in his hands. "God, my brain hurts."

"Hey." Belle pulled his hands from his face. "Lie down," she instructed, slightly pushing him back.

"What?"

"Just do it," Belle insisted as she lied down on the blanket.

Zach sighed but lied down next to her.

"What do you see?" she asked.

"Where?" he questioned as he put his glasses back on, trying not to let the glare of the sun that bounced off them blind him.

Belle gestured to the sky. "In the clouds."

Zach squinted. "Um...cotton balls."

Belle shoved him lightly, making him smirk. "Come on, use your imagination. I know you have it," she teased before pointing to a cluster of clouds. "Look, that one is an elephant. See the trunk?"

"Yeah, I guess." He could see a bit of curve in the clouds that could be a trunk. He glanced over at another cluster before pointing at it. "That one could be a tree."

"See, there you go," she said. He could hear the smile in her voice. "And that is an orange that fell off the tree."

"And that's a squirrel chasing after it," Zach teased.

Belle snorted and turned her head onto Zach's shoulder. He automatically wrapped his arm around her and pulled her closer so she was almost lying on top of him. They looked at each other, and he could feel the usual magnetic pull between them as he leaned forward and kissed Belle, smiling as she reciprocated it.

"I don't want to break up," Belle mumbled after they pulled apart.

"We're not breaking up, Sunshine," he said softly. "We're gonna figure this out." He caressed her face with his other hand. "We're gonna sit here, look at these clouds, play with Appa, and we're gonna talk it through. That's what people in a relationship are supposed to do, right?"

Belle shrugged against him. "I wouldn't really know. I don't have many good ones to follow."

"Neither do I," he snorted, and Belle smiled. "But I know we're not gonna be like our parents. And I'm definitely not gonna let you go."

"And I don't want you to."

He kissed her on the forehead. "I love you, Sunshine." She snuggled into him as a response.

He didn't need her to say it back if she wasn't ready, but he wanted to show that he meant it and that he would be there for her regardless.

He wasn't going to let her be alone anymore.

"Love can't fix everything, but it will damn well help you when you feel at your lowest."

Lake from *River Misfortune* by Dorian Moses

Chapter 33

When Zach thought about who he truly wanted in his life, the list of people was actually longer than he thought it would be.

His family was a must. He never wanted to be one of those older brothers who moved out and never spoke to their younger siblings ever again, except for holidays. His grandmothers weren't going to let him leave them behind. He'd already gone to Gigi's for their family meeting, both Amaya and Belle sitting in on the talk as Corey was distracted by Appa. Belle and Appa were a new bit of family that he really wanted to keep, he honestly doesn't want to think about doing anything without either of them. He also knew that he really wanted Kit and Joon in his life.

Zach was used to thinking of himself as the forgettable type of friend. Someone that you cling to for a moment only to leave behind when your time together was up. He didn't want to alienate friends like Beau and Mateo or Kit and Joon. He wanted to be their friend for as long as they'd have him, and if he wanted that then he needed to mend a few bridges. He was fortunate that they both agreed to meet him at Toe Beans when he texted. It was probably because he never prompted the text chains, so they decided to take this one seriously. They sat at one of the tables in the back as Umi and Mr. Tae manned the counter. He slowly walked toward them and their conversation dried up once he entered their line of sight, making his stomach shrivel a bit. "Hey," he greeted with a wave.

They nodded at him. Zach stood for a moment, not knowing how to start this type of conversation.

"You can sit," Joon said, raising a brow at Zach.

"Right," Zach nodded, cringing as the chair scraped against the floor as he sat down. "I'm sorry," he blurted out.

Joon and Kit looked at him in surprise.

"I'm sorry that I haven't been a good friend to either of you. I think we all know that I'm not the most emotionally available person."

"Understatement much?" Joon said.

Zach groaned as Kit punched Joon's shoulder. "Let him speak. We of all people know how hard it is for him to apologize," Kit reminded Joon as she sat back in her chair. "Let him get it out before he gets more constipated." She gestured for him to continue.

Zach took a deep breath, putting his hands on the table before saying, "All I wanted this summer was to come back to lick my wounds before moving as far away as possible. I was scared of staying here and having more things fall apart."

The two had twin expressions of raised brows and quirked-up lips when Joon asked, "Like what?"

"My family," Zach shrugged. "You guys." Zach's eyes flickered between the two of them. He blinked roughly to hold back the tears that he felt welling up. "You two have always been there for me, but there's always a part of me that thought there might be a day where you two just leave me behind so..." He bit his lip as he looked down at his hands. "I wanted to be the one to do it."

He didn't dare look at their faces; he didn't want to know how they reacted to that.

"Zach," he heard Kit gasp out, "we would never leave you behind."

Zach glanced up and saw the serious look on Kit's face. "And I'm not just saying that," she stressed. "You're family, and I know that word can get tossed around a lot but..." She reached out and put her hand on top of his. "You are my brother. You annoy the shit out of me some days, but you always have my back." She smiled, tears welling in her own eyes. "Remember that time when you stayed up with me on FaceTime to help me write my final essay for that advanced English class that I was sure I was gonna fail? You made sure I passed."

Zach felt his lips turn up a bit. "I would never trust anybody to edit your essays but me."

Joon leaned forward in his chair. "And that time you took a train ride down to my campus to be in the audience when I sang at the talent show just so I would have someone in the crowd cheering for me."

Zach nodded. "And you rode with me back so you could try out that fro-yo bar near my campus. You forced me to sit in the bathroom with you after all the lactose caught up with you."

Joon's smile widened. "Worth it. And you actually stayed. That alone proves that you know you're stuck with us."

Zach chuckled as he turned his hand around and squeezed Kit's. "I'm sorry I hurt you guys too," he admitted. "I was just so sick about how I still felt nervous around Baxter and I...I just had to say something."

The two nodded in unison before Kit said, "Hey, we're glad you stuck it to him before I had to punch him again."

"But that's no excuse for ruining your birthday."

Kit shrugged. "It's not the worst birthday I've had."

"Yeah, what could be below that?"

"Last year."

"Oh...right." A mother's death was much worse than ignorant words from a best friend.

"Hey." She squeezed his hand again. "I'm serious. You're not the worst person in the world."

"Just the hardest to get along with," Joon interjected, making them all laugh.

"Besides we've all got our own shit to deal with, and sometimes it makes us say things we don't mean, but siblings fight, don't they?" Kit asked, looking between the two. "Seriously asking as an only child, here?"

"Yes, they do," Joon answered with a chuckle. "My sisters and I can go at each other's throats, but I will fight anyone who tries to come for them." Joon put his hand on top of theirs. "And we would do the same for you." Joon lightly punched Zach in the shoulder with a scoff. "You are our brother for life. Never doubt that."

Zach shook his head as he looked between the two of them. "I won't." He took a breath. "But still I want to make it up to you two, so how would you feel about a trip to New York?"

They both gaped at him. "What?"

"I need to go for a job interview, but I thought that while

we're there, we could explore the city a bit, maybe go to those iconic movie scene locations you've always gushed about, find some vintage shops and—"

"Are you serious?" Kit squealed. Taking a group road trip by themselves had always been one of her dreams growing up.

"Yeah, I gotta leave on Wednesday, so you guys wanna come with me?"

"Yes." Kit jumped up to hug him, but then pulled back. "Wait, I can't. I have work."

"No, you don't. Here's a benefit of you two working for the OWWA. Your grandmothers are letting you play hooky in exchange for finding everything wrong with New York, so I am forced to stay here and be with Belle. Gigi and Mimi want to be great-grandmothers ASAP."

Kit shook her head. "They did not say that."

"You know they did. Besides, Beau has scouted out a really great karaoke bar that he thinks you'll like," he said, turning to Joon.

Joon scoffed a laugh. "There's no way we can get a hotel or flight that quick."

"Gigi has a plethora of timeshare hours she's happy to let us use, and train tickets have already been booked."

"Oh my God, we're having a road trip. We're actually doing it," Kit squealed with her hands over her mouth.

"Happy Birthday."

Kit practically leaped over to hug Zach, and he happily accepted it as Joon got in on it as well.

Zach wanted to capture this moment for later so he never forgot how good of friends he'd always had.

That afternoon, while everyone in the house was at work or at summer camp, Zach went home to collect a few things. He grabbed his suitcase and threw in a few clothes that would hopefully last him until he came back.

"So you thought you were just gonna sneak through the house while I was gone?"

Zach's whole face scrunched up when he heard his father's voice. He hadn't seen a car in the driveaway, but sometimes his dad did come home for lunch. Zach continued packing regardless. "I didn't think we needed to see each other right now."

"Where have you been?"

"At Belle's," Zach sighed. Nothing would be solved if they didn't talk, and it was probably best to do it now, rather than wait until he got back.

"You planning on staying there?"

"For now." Zach shrugged as he turned to face his dad. "I think it's best that you and I have some space between us." He examined his father's appearance, and almost didn't recognize him. Jedidiah usually kept himself very composed and polished, something he taught Zach from a young age.

Look and be respectable every day, even when the world isn't respecting you. Don't give them a reason.

That was something Zach always kept in the back of his head when going out, and his father exemplified it all the time, wearing suits and button-ups for almost every occasion. At the moment, he was in sweats, and his beard and hair were sticking up in every direction, nowhere near maintained as it usually was.

"Was going away for college not enough for you?" Jedidiah haggardly asked as he stepped into Zach's room a bit more.

"Not when I couldn't go a day with you calling me," Zach mumbled as he folded up another shirt.

"I worry."

Zach scoffed. "I know you worry, Dad. All you do is worry and in turn, all I do is worry." Zach threw another of his shirts into his suitcase before looking back at his father. "I worry about everything that can go wrong and I never think about what could go right. You got me so worried about things that I ran away from the one place I've always known as my home so I wouldn't be afraid of you controlling every aspect of my life."

"I don't control your life."

"You don't because I don't let you, but if I didn't go away to school or have my own job at The Book Haven, you can't tell me that you wouldn't try to make decisions for me instead of letting me do something on my own."

"Why let you struggle when I've already found something that works?" Jed argued.

"Because I'm not you!" Zach yelled, before taking a step back to compose himself. "Just because something works for you doesn't mean it works for me," he said as he messed with the fidget cube in his pocket. "I love libraries, but I don't want to work in one. I love my family, but I don't want to stay in the same house as you all forever. I don't want to push Belle away because I was afraid of losing someone else I love." He shook his head. "I can't let your fear run my life. Not anymore."

Jed pursed his lips. "I didn't know you felt like that."

Zach shrugged. "Well, you've never been the touchy-feely type of parent, I...I used to talk to Mom... about that kind of stuff. Or try to, I mean. She always said it was a stupid thing to worry about."

"It isn't."

Zach shifted on his feet. "I didn't mean to talk about you and Mom like that." He flicked the switch on the cube again. "I know you tried to make it work with her."

Jed looked up at Zach sharply.

"I saw those moving plans in the trash after she left. You actually considered it?"

Jed nodded. "I love...I loved your Mom," he said softly. "I made so many mistakes in our relationship, but I loved her, and I thought it could be a good olive branch. Give her what she wanted so that we could be a family but..." Jed sighed. "In the end, it wasn't enough." He rubbed the back of his head. "I tried to get her to come back here for you guys. Even if she didn't want to be with me anymore, I thought she would at least be there for you all."

Zach scoffed. "I'm pretty sure we both know that she's never coming back. And I can't keep being mad at you for her leaving, but it's easier for me to go at you for that because she's not here. The truth of the matter is she left, you stayed. You raised us, she didn't, and...thank you."

Jed shrugged. "I'm your father. It's my job to take care of you."

"I know, but not everyone sticks around to be a parent, and you did," Zach said with a smile. "It means something. And no matter how much I get mad at you for things, I still love you," he admitted. "I just need you to give me some space."

"Alright," Jed said with a nod, letting a smile flicker up his face before he stepped into the room a bit more. "So, New York?"

"How did you—"

"Your grandmothers told me. Sat me down and practically whooped my ass with facts. Said I'm explicitly forbidden from not letting you go."

Zach scoffed a laugh. "What happened to your roof, your rules?"

"I value my life too much to say that to your Gigi," Jed said as he came over to the bed and started folding some of the other clothes that Zach laid out.

Zach almost guffawed, but reeled it in. "I got an interview. Thought I should at least see it through."

"And if you get it?"

He shrugged. "Don't know. Haven't thought that far ahead yet. I invited Kit and Joon to come with me, and we've made it a work-slash-birthday trip, so it should be fun regardless of what goes down."

"No Belle?"

Zach put a suit in a bag as he shook his head. "She has a restock to work on and...she's not ready to go back yet. I have to respect that." Zach noticed the skeptical look on his father's face. "Our relationship is not for you to judge."

Jed nodded again as he put the clothes he folded in the suitcase. "I know." He turned to his son. "She really is a lovely girl."

Zach smiled. "She's my everything," he admitted. "We've already talked about it. It's my decision to go. I'll do the interview and figure out what happens next from there."

"If you say so."

"Hey," Zach said firmly. "You taught me to use my head and do what's right. Can you just believe that you raised me well enough to take care of myself? Please."

Jed sighed as he put his hands on Zach's shoulders. "Doesn't make letting you go any easier."

Zach nodded. "But you need to do it eventually. You can't keep all three of us in this house forever." Though Zach couldn't speak for Amaya and Corey, he knew that he needed a life outside of the house. Outside of his family. He needed to figure things out for himself.

His father sighed before he turned back to the bed and zipped up Zach's suitcase. Jed held it out for his son. "I'll see you when I get back."

Zach nodded as he took the bag and headed toward the door, feeling relieved yet terrified at the same time.

He stopped for a moment.

He put down his suitcase, walked back over to his father, and threw his arms around him in a hug. When his father's arms wrapped around him too, he felt himself relax just a bit more.

"I love you, Dad," Zach mumbled into his father's chest.

Zach felt Jed kiss the top of his head. "I love you too." They pulled back and Zach saw a single tear fall out of his father's eye. "Now go. Live your life. Just know I'll always be here for you."

Zach nodded once more before turning to grab his bag and leaving his childhood bedroom, feeling lighter than he had in a long time.

When Belle volunteered to drive them to the train station at BWI in Zach's car the next day, he was equal parts excited and scared; excited that Belle was feeling comfortable enough to get back behind the wheel, yet terrified that this was the farthest she was going to drive for the first time in a long time. Maryland drivers were horrible sometimes. *Put on your signal if you're going to cross over three lanes of traffic, asshole.*

They left the radio off, filling the dead space with a bit of conversation at the red lights, but overall the three of them just let Belle focus. Kit and Joon knew how important it was for her to do this too.

They made it to the airport with plenty of time to get ready and get a good spot on the train. When Belle parked the car, she let out the biggest sigh and sat back in the car, practically trembling.

"You did it, Sunshine," Zach smiled as Belle hugged herself.

"I did," she cried. A few tears fell down her face that she quickly wiped away.

They all got out of the car, and the trio got their luggage together before they said their goodbyes to Belle.

"Now don't forget to get some cash as soon as you get there, believe me, it's gonna make things easier." Belle reminded them as she hugged Joon before turning to Kit. "Also don't forget to check out Mikey's Pizza. And when you're at the street market, FaceTime me. I want to see what they have in stock."

"Absolutely," Kit squealed before squeezing Belle so hard that the boys had to pry her off. Joon gave her a quick hug before dragging Kit over to the loading line, leaving Zach and Belle alone. Zach took note of the sad look on Belle's face and quickly grabbed her hands in his. "It's not goodbye."

She nodded. "I know."

"And while I'm out of town you'll..."

"Work on the restock and talk Des out of giving up his life work with that killer presentation we made and convince him to give social media a shot."

"Think you can do it?"

"Oh, I know I can," she smirked. "I can be very persuasive when I need to be."

"Oh I know you can be," he said, tucking a loose hair behind her ear. "You sure you're gonna be okay?"

"Of course, I'm used to being on my—"

He pulled her into his chest before she could finish the sentence. "You are not on your own, Sunshine," he said, caressing the back of her head, before pulling back a bit. "Don't make me have to come back here and remind you of that."

She smirked. "What are you gonna do, spank me?"

He raised a brow at her. "Would you like that?"

She shrugged.

"Damn vixen," he murmured, before attacking her neck with kisses, making her giggle and squirm in his arms.

She giggled right before Kit yelled, "Hurry up, Zach! We got a train to catch!"

The two pulled back from the hug, and Belle smiled up at him with a resigned look on her face. "I'll see you later."

Zach nodded and turned to join Kit and Joon, but quickly turned back to Belle, cupping her cheeks in his hands before kissing her. She kissed back, pulling him close, and he savored the feeling. They pulled apart, and Zach caressed her cheeks with his thumbs and reminded her, "I'm coming back to you. Don't doubt that for one minute, Sunshine."

She nodded. "Okay."

"Okay."

"I love you."

She nodded and let him go. When Zach got over to the entrance, Joon had already gone in, but Kit just stood there, smirking at him. "What?" he asked.

"I told you the rom-com gods were smiling down on you."

"Still not a thing," he insisted as he turned around to wave goodbye to Belle. She returned the gesture with a small smile on her face before walking back toward the car. Zach pushed Kit forward into the terminal, anticipation building in his chest, but he knew one thing was certain: he had every intention of coming back to Belle.

"a productive week in my life: making friends with the delivery girl, getting out of my comfort zone, matching with my dog"

45,304 views · 3h ago

Hi, My Lovelies,

This week, I'm taking you behind the scenes of a work week in my life. This week was filled with testing new manufacturers, packing orders, and delivering tons of them. Not to mention, some new little outfits for me and Appa. Also, a lot of personal stuff happened for me this week, like getting back behind the wheel of a car for the first time in a year. Honestly, I can't believe I did it but I'm happy I did so I can drive more orders down from my house myself. Hoping to do a Q&A soon about owning a small business so please leave your questions down below. See you all again soon.

Love, Belle

@TylaFlower · 2h ago

How do you always just exude main character energy? That's all I ever want to do in life and you're my major inspiration.

> @LoveBelle · 20 min ago
>
> Aw, thank you so much! Believe me, it's more possible than you think.

@luvbug1236 · 1h ago

Oh please tell me that those bandanas are coming to the shop soon! I need those for me and my dog

> @LoveBelle · 24 min ago
>
> Maybe? ;)

@RetView · 28s ago

I can't believe how sweet you are. But you're so right, delivery people deserve all the treats

@TiaDoll · 29 min ago

OMG I'm so proud of you for getting back behind the wheel

> @LoveBelle · 23 min ago
>
> Thanks, lovely! It was hard driving again but I'm happy that I have people in my life who make me feel brave again.

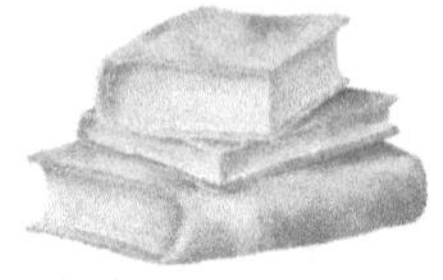

Chapter 34

New York was loud.

That's all Zach could think about as the train finally rolled towards the city.

As they made their way out of the train station, they were ushered into the chaos of getting a taxi to the hotel. They passed through the streets, looking at bunches of trash, streets filled with cars, and lots and lots of people.

"It's so magical," Kit gushed as she looked out the taxi window.

"Oh yeah, the hot steam coming out of the grates in hundred-degree weather is so refreshing," Joon scoffed as he shifted to get a bit more room for his legs. Zach had opted to sit in the middle, and he was already feeling cramped; he could only imagine how Joon's lengthy body felt.

"Hey, I'm trying to keep an open mind," Kit sneered at him before taking out her phone to take pictures.

Joon leaned over as much as the seat belt would allow him. "Aren't we supposed to find everything wrong with this city, so Zach doesn't stay?"

Kit waved him off. "We're here for a couple of days, I have plenty of time for that. Let me have my rom-com moment."

When they finally got to their hotel room, the idea of living a rom-com life while they were there turned into more of an unattainable dream.

"Why is this literally a broom closet?" Zach asked as they walked in. The matching brown carpet and walls weren't the usual Hollywood vision of New York, but they couldn't complain too much with a last minute booking.

"Never mind, the list begins right now 'cause this ain't it," Kit said, shaking her head and keeping her bag off the ground. "I thought you said Gigi's timeshares were good."

"They are. Usually. Booking last minute probably wasn't the best idea, but it could be worse."

As the two other two walked further into the room, Zach took a picture of the room and sent it to Belle, alongside a message of how size supposedly doesn't matter. She immediately sent back an eye-roll emoji and a crying laughing emoji, which made him chuckle. He walked over to the window in the middle of the wall opposite the door, and looked out at the busy streets below them. He immediately felt overwhelmed by the amount of motion that he saw; bikes, taxis, trucks, and pedestrians, all moving in this exclusive choreographed dance that he didn't have the pleasure of knowing.

"So what do we do first?" Kit asked as she stared down at the people.

"Well, I think we should just head to your birthday destination."

Kit dragged them back out the door so quickly that they barely had time to pick up their wallets.

Walking through the streets of New York felt like walking through a sardine can. Kit hung onto both Zach and Joon's arms, which she usually did for fun, but at that moment, it was so they could stick together and not get lost. They managed to navigate their way with their GPS, but with all the other pedestrians and cars that were more than willing to hit them when they crossed the street, Zach had many worries about what a commute would be like.

They spent the next hour going through Kit's itinerary of movie locations close to the hotel, taking pictures of her recreating the scenes in a meticulous fashion. It was honestly the most organized he had ever seen her. After that, they went to the street market that Belle suggested. Zach and Joon were turned into clothing racks holding all of the potential buys as Kit FaceTimed Belle, and they gushed over almost everything they saw. She ended up walking away with two oversized bags of stuff, and Zach was sure that he was going to see the two of them talk about it more once they got back home.

They made a stop at Mikey's, and Joon gave them a full critique of the pizza before leaving a Five-Star review on Yelp before they headed to a bookstore for Zach to check out.

It was a smaller one, which Zach appreciated more now, and he took it as a chance to see what they could do differently at The Book Haven. He took note of their social media card by the front door and the different displays that made it seem like books were coming out of the walls, and it truly inspired him to see how such a small store could still be so whimsical. He took a few pictures and sent them to Belle before he started browsing the shelves. He nearly walked away with nothing, until he noticed a familiar title.

The Limits of Love, Belle's favorite book, but with a different cover than the ones she already had. He chuckled at the sight of it before putting it under his arm and looking around some more.

That night, the trio dressed up a bit before taking a taxi to the side of town where Beau and Mateo resided. The streets were lined with people dressed in clothes resembling the K-Pop videos that Sunny gushed over all the time.

When the taxi stopped, they were let out in a more lowkey area. Zach appreciated that until he realized it made them really easy to spot. He barely got out of the car when he heard someone call his name, and he turned to see Beau running up to him. He tried to step back. "Wait, no hugs. No no... oh."

"You're finally here. I'll hug you as much as I fucking want," Beau cheered as he wrapped his arms around Zach, who reluctantly let Beau squeeze him to his heart's desire as Zach let the fact that they were actually in the same city again sink in. As soon as he let go, Beau turned his attention to Zach's companions. "Joon and Kit, it's so nice to finally see y'all in person," he said before pulling them both into a hug as well.

Zach looked over and saw Mateo lurking by the building entrance. Zach sauntered over to him.

Mateo looked him up and down. "Zach."

"Mateo," Zach delivered in the same monotone voice.

Mateo scoffed and stepped forward. "Come here, you bastard."

The two grumps hugged, and Zach had to admit that he was happy to be back around a fellow pessimist. Once the other three joined them, they made their way into the karaoke club that Beau had been gushing about since they moved to New

York, Vocal Adrenaline. They walked through a hallway covered with LED strips that gave everything a purple glow before walking into a private room with a yellow and orange theme

They were given a menu, and Kit, Joon, and Mateo had fun trying out fun-sounding drinks like "Teeter Totter" and "Purple Slide." Zach opted for coke, as he did not want to show up to an interview hungover, regardless of whether he wanted it or not. Beau sat next to him sipping on a virgin Pina Colada before they started up the songs.

Zach joined Kit in a rousing performance of "Style" before they all practically bowed down to Joon's rendition of "There's Nothing Holding Me Back."

Kit, Joon, and Mateo were mid-"Total Eclipse of the Heart" when Beau turned to him. "So, you really think you gonna join us up here?"

"Maybe," Zach shrugged, taking a sip of his drink. "It's all a little..."

"Too loud."

"Yeah."

"I like it loud," Beau said with a smirk, before looking over at Zach. "But you don't."

Zach scoffed. As usual, Beau was able to read him like an open book. Zach sat back against the sticky pleather booth and sighed, "I just thought that it all made sense." He put his drink down. "People here are very much go go go, and that's me right?"

"Eh."

Zach turned to face him completely. "Is it not?"

"You like going when it's on your terms. You'll adjust when you need to, but you would much rather move at your own pace," Beau chuckled as he reached over to pick up his drink once more. "I think you're designed for small-town living and big-city visiting."

Zach sighed, "Why do I have a feeling that you knew all of this a long time ago and you were just waiting for me to catch up?"

Beau chuckled around his straw. "Because even though you're very smart, you don't always know everything."

"People have been telling me that a lot lately."

"Well, if you only had a crowd of people telling you how great you are all the time, you would never improve, and I have to say, this"—Beau gestured to Zach's whole demeanor—"is an improvement. Like, look at you, you're actually smiling. You actually might have to worry about smile lines now."

"Shut up." Zach shoved his friend off as the trio finished their tune.

"No, because it's our turn, and we're doing Alicia Keys." Beau put down his drink and grabbed Zach's hand. Zach said nothing as Beau dragged him forward. For once, he was actually enjoying himself.

Things to Ask in the Interview

1. How many books do you expect team members to review in a week?

2. How much paid time off is there?

3. How do you define a successful book?

4. How do you intend on diversifying your author portfolio?

Chapter 35

New York summer felt like a different beast compared to Maryland.

Summer days in Maryland could fluctuate between being hot enough for short-shorts and having to wear a jacket, but what Beau had told Zach, it was just this hot all the time in New York. He was lucky that he had packed a short-sleeved button-up to go alongside his khaki pants and well-loved brown loafers, otherwise, he would've been boiling as he walked down the street toward the Retna Publishing building that matched the rest of the gray towers surrounding it. Once he got in front of the building, he took a good look at how high it went into the sky. There weren't many buildings like that in Maryland, and he didn't know if he liked that or not.

He checked in at the front desk before being pushed up to one of the middle floors. When he stepped out of the elevator, he was brought into a sea of cubicles, ringing phones, and people running back and forth between desks and offices. He got a badge from the receptionist on the floor and went to sit in the waiting area, where a number of other recent college graduates were sitting, probably getting ready for the same interview. Instead of looking down at his phone like most of them, Zach took the time to take notice of one particular thing, only two people of color were on the floor.

He glanced around again to make sure that he didn't miss anybody, but he came up with the same number. He looked between the other candidates and saw that he was the only person of color waiting.

Neither of these facts gave him hope.

"Zachary Roberts."

Zach looked up as somebody waved him over. He followed them to one of the conference rooms where a white man with a combover sat with the window at his back.

"Hello, my name is Clark Adams. Thank you for coming in today," he greeted as he stood holding out his hand for Zach to shake.

"No problem." Zach shook his hand.

Clark chuckled. "I would beg to differ," he countered as they both sat down, "Your application says you're from Maryland."

"Yes, but some of the best publishing houses are around here, so it's no trouble to come up here to check them out."

Clark nodded, and Zach felt like he had passed a first test of sorts. "Alright then, let's get started."

When Zach was a junior in high school, his school sponsored a career fair where recruiters from colleges and companies came to give the students a chance to work on their resumes and practice interviews. It was there that Zach had talked to a recruiter from Walker U, who had talked so passionately about their creative arts programs that Zach had been more than inclined to apply by the time fall came around.

Talking to this guy felt like talking to a robot, and not the robots in Marvel's movies who came back with witty remarks and told you to eat your vegetables. The kind of robot that gave the most generic answer to a question without actually revealing what they thought, all in the most cheery tone imaginable. Zach thought Belle's cheery voice was adorable. With this guy, it felt like being initiated into a cult.

"So, are there any other questions for me?" Clark asked once Zach finished answering his last question. "Because I gotta be honest, you are one of the best applicants we've seen so far."

"Really?" Zach said with a raised brow.

"Truly, I think you'll fit in very well with the culture around here." Zach worked very hard to keep the cringe off his face; who would actually say that out loud? Regardless, he let the man continue, "We're looking to diversify our staff and talent this year, but it's hard to find someone we can actually work with."

Zach sat up more in his chair. "What do you mean by that?"

Clark shrugged, "Well, some authors want to stir the pot a bit, make waves when all we need them to do is write the book. We know what our audience wants, and if the authors can't provide that then...you know."

"Right." Zach nodded with a fake smile plastered on his face. "Yes, I was looking at your website, and I noticed that you don't have many Black authors on your author's page. Or many authors of color in general." Zach saw the man's smile drop a bit, but he persisted. "What are you doing to increase that number?"

Clark shifted in his seat. "Well, I think we have one who we are about to add to the agency."

"One."

"That's right, but I'm sure we'll get more in the future," he said, waving off the thought.

The biggest thing Zach was concerned about was how far in the future would that be.

When Zach finally got back to the hotel room, he ripped off his tie and promptly fell back on the edge of the bed. He didn't get to rest for long before Kit and Joon came busting back into the room with arms of grocery bags and other trinkets.

"Oh good, you're back," Kit said as she put the bags down. "So what did they say? Actually, before that, we need to give you our presentation."

Zach barely had a chance to sit up before the hotel TV lit up with a PowerPoint presentation that reeked of an elementary schooler's first time getting access to the app. Zach had to chuckle at the image of his fifth-grade graduation photo on the title page next to the title, "Protect this Kid."

"Welcome to our TED Talk on why Zach should stay in Lillet," Kit said as she stood on one side of the TV with Joon on the other.

Zach chuckled as he rubbed his hand over his face. "Guys."

"No, let us talk because we've got a lot to go through," Joon interrupted as he messed with the laptop, changing the slide. "We will be starting with the pros of why you should move to New York because there are very few. One pro that we will give you is that there is no Baxter here. Easily explained, moving on." Joon went to the next slide that showed the three of them eating pizza the day before. "The second pro is the restaurants that are around here. Excellent. If you moved here for the food, we would not blame you." Joon nodded, before looking at Kit,

"And that's it with the pros. Let's get to the cons with Kit."

"Guys," Zach interjected.

"Number one con: people," Kit said as if Zach hadn't spoken. "There are lots of people here, and you don't like people, so for that alone, you shouldn't come. Next, to also counter a previous pro, is that the food is expensive as hell, so while you could move here for the food, you couldn't afford it because all of your money will be dedicated to living in a broom closet." Kit looked Zach dead in the eye. "Not to mention, none of them are Papa's or Toe Beans."

Joon nodded. "Very true, and I'm not gonna send you coffee grounds through the mail."

"Guys," Zach guffawed a laugh, finally getting them out of their presentation mode. "I'm not moving."

"What?" The two asked in unison.

"I'm going back to Lillet with y'all. To stay this time."

"Really?" Kit asked with a wobbly lip.

"Yeah. So thank you for the TED Talk but it's not needed—" Zach started to say, only to be cut off when Kit tackled him with a hug. "You really would've missed me that much, huh?"

"Just a little," she whispered as Joon came over to get in on the hug, and Zach let them stay there. He was lucky to have people in his life, besides his family, who wanted him around. Even if he hadn't known how much they really did at first, he definitely knew now.

He pulled back from the hug. "And now if you'll excuse me, I need to make a call." He stepped out of the room and made his way over to the elevator bay of their floor, leaning against the glass window that looked out over the four-way intersection below them.

"Hey Gigi," he greeted once the phone connected.

"Hello Zachary, how's New York?"

He glanced down at the busy streets. "It's...something."

"Alright, I'll ignore that tone in your voice if you tell me what you really calling for."

Zach chuckled. He should have known Gigi would be able to see right through him. That's why he was hoping that she would be open to his request.

Later that night, the trio ventured to Beau and Mateo's apartment. It wasn't as big as it had felt over FaceTime, but it was homey, with the blanket thrown over the worn couch, coffee cup trolley in the kitchen, and their skateboards leaning next to the door. The little table of pictures next to the front door also added a personal touch. Zach smiled when he saw one of the three of them from graduation a couple of months ago. If that Zach saw him now in New York about to head back to his hometown after turning away from a job he'd always wanted, he would probably try to strangle his future self. Hopefully, he would have come to his senses once he saw how happy the future him was.

"Thanks for letting us come over," Zach said to Beau as the trio walked further into the house.

"No, thank you for letting us witness your reaction to the finale of the best cartoon in history," Beau smiled as he went over to boot up the little flat screen that had followed them throughout college. Zach had felt a little guilty at the idea of watching the finale without Belle being there but she insisted watching it in a group would be more fun and that she could easily video conference in to join the party. "Mateo is making some fancy drinks for an article he's working on for Focus, so you get to be the guinea pigs, and there should be room for you to work, Joon."

Mateo and Joon worked in the kitchen while Kit and Beau sat on the sofa, throwing out different Zach stories from different ages at his expense. He didn't love the fact that he was what bonded them at that moment, but he was just happy that all of his friends were getting along.

Testing both virgin and very non-virgin drinks at the kitchen counter, the group started a game of truth or drink, in which Zach learned that Joon had done drag once in college, and Kit had had her first kiss with her debate team rival from high school. Zach and Joon tried to tease her about the rom-com possibilities, but she swore that she would never actually date someone as annoying as him, and they dropped the matter as Joon finished cooking his fiery noodle soup.

"Beau, I might have to leave you to marry this man," Mateo moaned around his soup spoon.

"Not if I leave you first," Beau retorted.

Zach was working to get a large bite of noodles on his chopsticks when his phone rang. He pulled it out and smiled when he saw Belle's name with a sun emoji on the screen requesting a FaceTime call. He quickly connected the line.

"Hey," Belle greeted as she appeared on the screen, sitting in her living room with her hair flowing around her face.

"Hi, Sunshine."

"Aw," the other four in the room cooed.

Zach rolled his eyes before pushing back from the counter and walking over to the couch. "How was your day?"

She shrugged. "Oh you know, a lot of drawing, a *lot* of packing."

"You and Amaya have fun with that?"

Belle giggled as she adjusted her hold on her phone. "Actually, your family came by to help."

Zach's eyes widened. "Wait, they did?" he asked, straightening his back against the couch. "I swear, I didn't make them come over there."

"I know you didn't," she scoffed. "Amaya told them about the restock, and she knew I was gonna need a lot of help so she called in the calvary. She showed your dad and Owen where to find things and—"

"My dad came? And he let her and Owen be in the same room together?"

Belle nodded. "Yeah. He was actually very helpful when it came to keeping things organized. Gigi and Mimi kept us fed while Corey occupied Appa."

Zach scoffed a laugh. "Of course he did."

"It was actually really nice. I'd forgotten what it was like to have people who just want to come help because they like you."

"I told you they love you. If we ever fight again, they're gonna be on your side, I guarantee."

"Well, I come with stationery, baked goods, and a dog. Who wouldn't want me?"

"You fought with Belle?" Joon yelled at Zach from the kitchen.

Zach groaned. "For two minutes!" He explained as he looked at his friends, but that didn't diminish the glare on Kit's face.

"How dare you go after someone as innocent and as pure as she?"

Zach scoffed. "First of all, she ain't innocent, nor is she pure. She's a vixen and damn menace who is gonna get a spanking if she don't stop giggling," he hissed as looked back at Belle on the phone, her hand covering her mouth as she tried to muffle her laughing. Once she calmed down, he looked back to the kitchen. "Second, we worked it out, so go back to your food, 'kay?"

Kit narrowed her eyes a bit more before she turned back to her food. Zach rolled his eyes as he turned back to Belle. "See what I'm dealing with in your honor? You don't have to worry about a thing, Sunshine."

Belle nodded as she smiled again. "The only thing that was really missing was you."

Zach nodded; he would have loved to be there to witness all that, but hopefully, they would have more days like that in the future. "I'll be home soon, Sunshine. Don't you worry about that."

"Okay, let me see this infamous Belle?" Beau asked as he sat down on the couch next to Zach. "Oh my God, darlin', you are gorgeous."

Belle giggled. "Oh, thank you. And you're Beau?"

"That I am. It's a pleasure to make your acquaintance, but I must ask how the hell did Zach convince you to date him?"

"He can actually be really sweet you know," she said with a shrug.

Beau shoved himself into the camera frame more. "Are we talking about the same Zach?"

Zach shoved him away. "Shut up!"

"What are you gonna do if I don't?" Beau said with a raised brow. "Spank me?"

Zach narrowed his eyes at his best friend before looking at the kitchen. "Mateo, get your man."

"I thought we agreed to share custody of him?" Mateo said as he started cleaning their glasses.

"Yeah, but it's your weekend."

Though Mateo groaned and rolled his eyes, Zach saw his lip quirk up a bit. "Fine, I'll deal with him later."

"Yeah, you will," Beau teased, only to be cut off by barking from the phone. "What was that?"

"That's her dog, Appa," Zach answered.

"Our son," Belle corrected, but Zach shook his head.

"I'm not calling him my son."

"Um, he and I are a package deal, so you better get used to it."

"Bring out the dog," Beau ordered as he took the phone from Zach's hand.

Zach scoffed a laugh, but couldn't help but smile at the scene before him as Mateo came over as well to look at Appa. Seeing all of his favorite people together was not something he'd known that he needed to see until now. The fact that all of these people who had come into his life at different points were able to come together and bond felt like an anomaly in space. It was something he'd wished for through his writing when he wrote the ragtag crew Ty traveled with. Finding people who he could navigate life with and not worry about the outcome felt like the type of ending you would only find in a book, but now he had it in real life, and he couldn't be happier about it.

The five of them were able to sit down in front of the TV and queue up the finale episode of Avatar to play, and Belle watched and reacted with them over FaceTime. When Aang finally bent all four elements together at the same time, the room went wild. Zach saw the glee on Belle's face and in that moment, he felt just as giddy as her while they watched the final showdown with Ozai.

Beau and Mateo later texted him while he was on the train home saying they got a noise complaint from it, but they assured him it was more than worth it. Zach chuckled and looked over at Kit and Joon in their seats across from his. Kit was reading a book, while Joon was watching videos on his iPad. He was happy to have these wonderful idiots in his life.

And Belle.

He was very happy to have Belle in his life.

"People are like shoes in some ways. Some you'll outgrow. Others won't match your lifestyle after a while. But the ones that are tried and true, the ones you can rely on in a pinch, they'll be with you forever."

Crissy from *Laces Between Spaces* by Annalise Dale

Chapter 36

The feeling of serenity that Zach felt coming back is something he'd never thought he would feel towards Lillet.

Their rideshare car let him and Joon out in front of Toe Beans after dropping Kit off at her place. They went inside and he smiled at Umi as Joon announced, "I'm home."

Umi barely glanced up from where she was rearranging the display of treats upfront. "Go knead the bread."

Joon glared at his sister. "I just got off a train and that was your job today."

"So?" Umi shrugged. "Go wash your hands."

Joon turned to Zach with his hand out. "Give me my money. I told you she wouldn't take over for me."

Zach scoffed as he took out his wallet. "Can't believe you were right." He slapped a ten in Joon's hand.

"Especially since he's rarely right about anything," Umi said as she went over to the register.

Joon rolled his eyes. "It happens more than you think Umi because you're not the only smart one in the family."

"But I am the only valedictorian." She glanced over at Zach. "But I will admit that Zach is worthy of losing too."

Zach turned to Joon. "Is she complimenting me?"

"Yeah, while insulting me."

He shrugged. "I'll take it."

Joon looked between the two of them before snatching up his bags. "I hate both of you."

Umi glanced at Zach before typing into the register. "So, a cold brew and an orange scone?"

Zach's jaw dropped. "Okay, how could you possibly know that? You never take my order."

"Joon's binder," she shrugged.

"His what?"

She turned to the place where they stacked the employee manuals, pulled out a light blue one that stood out from the white ones surrounding it and handed it over. "Joon writes down everyone's usuals in there."

Zach scoffed a laugh as he flipped through pages that detailed most of the town residents' orders by family, and a few individuals who didn't live in the town proper. "So that's his secret."

"Not really," she said as she started making Zach's order. "He has them written for us to use when he's not here, but he just remembers all of this." She set down his coffee and went to grab his scone. "Seriously, whoever gets him is gonna be lucky as hell. Don't tell him I said that."

"Don't worry, I won't."

Not yet at least.

Umi placed down the scone and narrowed her eyes at him. "Now—"

"I know," he said, picking up the cup and scone. "Family doesn't pay. See you later, Umi."

He walked out of the store without another word and headed over to The Book Haven to have his meeting with Des.

When he got home an hour later, he was riding high. He walked into the house with a skip in his step and smiled when he saw his dad sitting in the living room with his crossword book. "Hey," he said, putting down his keys and taking off his shoes. "Where is everyone?"

"Mom took them to the pool," Jed said as he put down his book. "How was New York?"

"Loud."

"How was the job?"

Zach grimaced as he put down his keys. "Not for me."

"Why not?"

Zach sucked his teeth as he sat down in one of the armchairs. "Let's just say I have no interest in helping them meet a quota."

"Ah," Jed nodded. "So you're staying?"

"Yup."

"And you're going to be working at?"

"The Book Haven."

Jed groaned as he rubbed his forehead. "Zach—"

"Dad, this is not up for discussion," he said sternly. "You may think I should go somewhere else, but that store means everything to me and to Des. Which is why I'm taking over the shop's social media."

Jed looked up. "The shop has social media?"

"It does now. I just met with Des about it," Zach said with pride. "Belle's gonna help me get started with it before I take over, and she's building the store a website too, so we can get online sales. Des was very reluctant, but he's willing to give it a shot."

"Good for him."

Zach straightened up in his chair. "I heard you went over to Belle's to help her out with the shop."

"I did." Jed nodded. "You were right. I can't believe how much that woman is doing."

"Told you she needed help."

"She's a hard worker, though. Got a good head on her shoulders, great with Corey," Jed said before he winced. "I could still do without the dog though."

Zach shrugged. "Well, he's part of the deal, so you're gonna have to get used to him coming around too."

"Well, feel free to bring them over to the house more often."

Zach held his breath for a moment. This is the part of the conversation that he was most nervous about, but had to happen. "About that," he started, folding his hands in his lap. "I'm moving out."

Jed's eyebrows rose up his face. "What?"

"I'm moving out."

Jed leaned forward in his seat. "And where exactly are you gonna go?"

"To Gigi's," Zach informed him. "She's letting me stay in Mom's old room. Says I can do it up however I want."

Jed leaned back against the couch, letting these new facts sink in before looking back at his eldest. "And that's what you really want?"

"Yeah. Because if I stay here, we're just gonna drive each other crazy, and that's not what either of us needs. If I want to stay in Lillet, then this is what I need to do," Zach said firmly. "'Cause I really do want to stay here. I want to work at Book Haven and hang out with Joon and Kit. I want to spend every day with Belle and tell her how much I love her. I want to have more time with Amaya and Corey and Gigi and Mimi...and you. But if I'm gonna do this, I need to do it on my terms, and I need you to be okay with that."

Jed frowned. "I'm not trying to drive you away. I just wanted to keep you safe."

Zach scoffed. "I'm a Black man in America, Dad. I'm never gonna be safe. I'm never gonna be able to be able to do whatever I want without fearing the consequences, or fearing that something bad will happen when I look at someone the wrong way. Neither of us have that type of control." Zach held his head up. "But I can control how I let it affect me. I can say that I'm not going to let those fears consume me, and you shouldn't let it consume you either. I just want to live my life as much as I can the way I want to."

Jed said nothing for a while and just stared at Zach with warm eyes.

"What?" Zach finally asked.

"You really are a man now."

"I'm getting there," Zach said with a shrug, before taking another deep breath. "One more thing. Please don't do to Corey what you did to me."

Jed raised a brow. "What?"

"I can already see it. He's terrified of making the wrong move or saying the wrong thing because you keep drilling into his head that if he's not perfect, something bad is gonna happen. He's six. That's the last thing that should be on his mind," Zach stressed. "Life is gonna happen regardless of how safe you think everything around us is. Just let him be a kid and think the world is filled with talking dogs and flying horses because soon enough he's gonna be my age and moving out and there is nothing you can do to prevent what happens next." Zach shrugged. "Just let him live carefree for as long as he can."

Jed nodded. "Alright."

"And maybe think about getting some help."

Jed's head tilted. "What do you mean?"

"Dad, you've got control issues and you need to work on them," Zach explained. When his dad went to argue, he continued, "Mom already left. I almost left. I know you went through a lot with your father and with Uncle Jeremy's death"—Jed looked away, but Zach got up and sat down on the couch next to him to get back in his eyeline—"but if you don't want it to be Amaya or Corey running away next, then you need to do something. If not for us, then do it for yourself, so you can stop worrying about everything all the time." Zach chuckled. "Believe me, life gets easier when you let yourself chill for a moment."

Jed looked over at his eldest, biting his lip. "I'll think about it."

Zach nodded. That was good enough for him right now. He and his father would probably never be on perfect terms. He wasn't hoping for a complete 180 with his father's attitude from one conversation, but if he could save his younger siblings the stress of what he'd been through, it would all be worth it.

Excerpt from "Project Void" by Zach Roberts (4th Draft)

"I want to go home," Captain Wan said, tears threatening to spill out of his eyes as his finger hovered over the detonation button.

"But it doesn't mean anything if we lose ourselves along the way," Ty pleaded as he took another step closer. "If we lose who we are, then we can't expect for home to feel like home when we get there."

The Captain glanced between his Lieutenant and the button once more. The glow of the enemy's ring shined on his hand, but Ty kept his focus on the captain.

He took another step forward. "Home isn't a place, it's a feeling. You have to remember that, Captain. Please."

The Captain glanced down at the ring, then back at his Lieutenant. Ty felt his lungs burning as the seconds felt like they were turning into hours, but let out a breath when the Captain yanked the ring off his finger.

Ty snatched it and threw it into the vaporizer. The small explosion that followed the ring's destruction was the most relief he'd felt in a long time. He turned back to Captain Wan with a small smile on his face. "Welcome back, Captain."

The Captain huffed as he slumped back in his seat. "Good to be back, Lieutenant."

Chapter 37

Zach had only called one place home in his twenty-one years of life.

Even then, he considered his family's house as more of a home base than anything else; somewhere he could go where he didn't have to worry about what life was going to be like when he got there. To find someone who felt like home was something entirely different.

Zach felt the tension leave his body as he drove up the hill to the cottage. After he parked, he pushed the car door open so quickly that he thought that he'd almost knocked it off its hinges. He quickly ran over to the front door and knocked.

The familiar sound of barking filled the air, and the door opened to reveal Belle's smiling face.

"Hey," she said.

"Hi," he replied.

The two of them just stayed like that for a moment, drinking each other in as if they had been apart for months instead of three days. Zach felt at peace when he looked at her. He knew.

"I'm home."

Belle's lips wobbled as she scurried forward and wrapped her arms around him. She held him tight as he quickly returned the hug, kissing the top of her head.

"I'm home, Sunshine."

Appa came over and knocked against their legs, begging for attention. They finally broke apart.

"Hey, buddy," Zach said enthusiastically as he bent down to pet Appa's head. "How are you? You've been taking good care of your momma for me?" He dug into his bag and pulled out a small peanut butter cookie. "Here, I brought you a treat."

Appa immediately gobbled it up as soon as it was in his mouth space. Zach chuckled, before noticing the fond look on Belle's face. "What?"

"Are you actually becoming a dog person now?" she giggled as she ushered him into the house.

"I'm becoming an Appa person."

"What if I wanted to get another dog to name Momo?"

"Then I will support you and prepare myself to be perpetually covered in dog fur."

She giggled as she walked over to the kitchen. "So, how was it?"

"Loud. Obnoxious. Beau and Mateo took us to this hidden karaoke bar and Kit and Joon got drunk off their asses while singing their hearts out to Taylor Swift."

"Please tell me you have a video of that?" she asked as she brought out a pitcher of lemonade with strawberry bits floating in it.

"Oh, you know I do. And while I was there, I got you an early birthday present," he said, digging through his bag.

Belle shook her head as she put the pitcher down. "You didn't have to do that."

"I know. I wanted to do it," he said as he finally pulled out the book and showed it to her.

"*The Limits of Love*?"

"It's a new cover you don't have."

She smiled for a moment until she noticed the little tabs sticking out of the book. She flipped it open and gasped when she saw the little notes in the borders of the pages. She looked up at him. "You annotated a book for me?"

He noticed that tears were welling in her eyes. "Yeah, on the train ride home. Don't worry, I got you a clean copy as well." He smiled. "I kinda see why you like annotating now. It's like another journal to look back on. See the kind of person you were. Why you love the book in the first place." He leaned back and took a good look at Belle. "You helped me see that."

"With what?" she sniffled.

"You helped remind me that there is more that I loved about Lillet than hated about it. That the things I love here are worth staying for. New York can't compare to here, but it turns out the city did have what I needed. Or had, I should say," he shrugged.

Belle's brow quirked up. "What do you mean?"

"It's where you're from. Maybe if we got lucky, we would've bumped into each other at a bookstore, or Appa would've run me over on the street there—" Belle laughed but Zach contin-ued— "but I'm glad it happened here," he said as he reached out to grab her hand. "Cause now I get to stay in a place I love, with a job I love, and be with the woman I love." Zach quickly wiped a tear that fell from her eyes. "It's a lineup of perfect coincidences that resulted in the best thing ever." He shrugged. "You know?"

Belle scoffed a laugh tearfully. "Now, you're quoting *The Limits of Love* to me?"

"Like I said, it's actually a really good book."

"I love you too," Belle blurted out. Zach's eyes widened as she went on, "I know didn't say it before you left and...I really wanted to, but I was really scared and I didn't know if—"

Zach stood from his chair and quickly pulled her in for a kiss. His lips caressed her strawberry-tasting ones. "Sunshine..."

"Yeah?"

"You know that most days I love your rambling, but I'm gonna need you to shut up for the next thirty minutes, 'cause I have plans for you," he said as he moved to nibble at her neck

"What kind of plans?" she giggled as he dragged her into the bedroom and practically threw her on the bed, closing the door behind them.

He pushed her onto the bed and crawled on top of her. "You've been giving me all this lip lately," he said before nibbling at her own. "You need to be punished."

She raised a brow. "Do I?" she moaned.

"Yes." Zach flipped her over and spanked her ass, making her giggle. "You do."

Belle's giggles quickly turned into a moan as Zach pulled off her jean shorts. "Mmm..." she breathed out as Zach took off her underwear. "Zach."

Zach bit his lip. "You're so fucking pretty like this, Sunshine," he declared as he placed a soft kiss on her ass before lightly smacking it again, making her yelp and giggle at the same time. He quickly stuck a finger in her, pumping in and out as he smacked her ass, making it redder with every tap. He savored her sounds like they were his new favorite song, memorizing her moans like they were lyrics that he wanted to hear over and over again.

He turned her over so her back was on the bed and began to methodically undress her, pulling off her sweatshirt and unhooking her bra when she arched her back as his other hand found her clit. Once he brought her to the brink, he pulled out his finger, leaving her breathless on the bed.

As she tried to reclaim her lungs, Zach got off the bed and leaned forward to press a small kiss on her pussy, making her breath out a laugh. He started pulling off his shirt as he walked over to her bedside table. Belle rolled over just in time to see him take the condom out of the drawer. "I thought you didn't like the strawberry condoms," she teased, lying on her stomach, smirking up at him.

Zach chuckled before leaning down to peck a kiss on her lips. "I'll get over it."

Belle smiled as she slowly got on her knees, quickly undoing his belt and shoving down his pants and underwear to free his half-hard cock. She took the condom out of his hands and put it on before lying back, her head resting on her pillow.

Zach didn't get on immediately. He just stood there, drinking in the curves of her body and the smile on her face as he took off the rest of his clothes.

"What's with the delay?" she asked impertinently.

He leaned over her, propping himself up with his hands. "You are so loved, Sunshine," he declared, leaning down to kiss her before he pulled back, leaving a whisper of space between their lips. "And you deserve so much."

Belle reached up and cupped his cheek in her hand. "So do you." She pulled him down, kissing him again. He crawled on top of her, not breaking their kiss as pressed his cock into her pussy.

"Mmm..." she moaned when he got all the way in. Zach just let her lie there as he did all the work, kissing and biting her neck as he did.

"Oh my God, right there," she gasped out when they were both close to their climaxes. "Yes, yes!"

He bit her neck harder as he came, but quickly moved his hand in between them to keep Belle on edge until she was gasping out in his ear. He kissed her neck once more before he rolled off her to the other side of the bed. He tied off the condom and threw it in the waste bin in her room before he gathered the comforter, put it over Belle, and got in next to her. She cuddled up to him immediately, burying her head in his chest.

Zach smiled as he caressed her back with his hand. "I love you so much, Belle," he muttered into her hair.

She smiled against his chest. "I love you too, Zach."

He kissed her head and pulled her closer if that was possible. He had no intention of ever letting her go.

Amelia,

It's been 51 days at sea.

I can no longer see the shores of Lillet, but
your siren song still plays in my ear.
I dream of holding you in my arms,
keeping you close, and it is that dream that
will always bring me back to you.

You are my lighthouse.
You are the beacon that brings me home.
Every time.
I long to see you again and when I do,
I will never let you go.

That is my vow to you.

Yours for Eternity,
Oliver

Chapter 38

Zach didn't believe in fate, and he didn't believe in magic.

He did, however, believe that everything happened for a reason.

Whether it was a good reason or not, the jury was still out, but everything happened so something else could happen.

He didn't get a job in New York so he could learn that everything he needed was in Lillet.

He didn't get his job back at The Book Haven at first so he could be open to taking a job with Belle.

He took a chance on taking a job with Belle so he could find his bookish soulmate.

In some way, everything had worked out the way it was supposed to, and he could finally let himself relax.

Kit had managed to convince Zach, Joon, and Belle to come out to a concert with a local blues band that she helped organize for an end-of-summer blowout. Fewer people turned out than the Fourth of July celebration, but there were still sizable groups of families and friends hanging around the park and enjoying the live music. One of the elementary school dads brought a cotton candy and popcorn machine, and a little dance area had been made in the middle of everything. The four of them had decided to have a little picnic in the park. Belle had brought a charcuterie board and homemade strawberry lemonade, while Joon made some nigiri and pan-fried noodles, which made everyone very happy.

"Between the two of you, you could make one of those businesses where you set up a picnic or dinner for someone else to enjoy," Kit said, picking up another piece of nigiri with her chopsticks.

Joon nodded. "I can see it." He glanced over at Belle. "What do you think?"

Belle smiled after taking a sip of her drink. "Can we make it cat and dog-themed?"

"Absolutely."

"What happened to our pop-up book and coffee truck?" Zach asked, holding the cracker sandwich he made next to his mouth.

Joon shrugged. "Sorry, got a better offer."

"Fuck you."

"We are years past the possibility of that."

Zach scoffed a laugh and shoved Joon over, making them both laugh that much harder. As Belle picked up her camera to grab some footage of the band, Zach glanced over at the other side of the park to see where the rest of the family had made their own camps. Gigi and Mimi were sitting with the rest of the OWWA, chatting about whatnot, while Amaya was dancing with Corey, Owen, and Sheila. Their dad was standing to the side with Des. Zach knew his father was glancing over at him every once and a while, but he gave Zach his distance. He'd moved the major things out of his room and into Gigi's house, and it was already doing wonders for their relationship. They talked more about what they needed to do going forward, and Jed had, by some miracle, agreed to start going to a therapist. He'd even dialed back to one call every other day, and there were already plans to have Sunday dinners at the house after church, to which Belle and Appa were also invited. Jed was trying, and Zach appreciated it.

"Now," the lead singer of the band said as they started adjusting their instruments. "It's time to slow things down. So grab someone and shake a leg folks."

The band started playing a slow ballad, and Zach vaguely remembered the scene of the two main characters in *The Limits of Love* dancing in the park. He stood up and held his hand out to Belle, who just looked up at him confused.

"I thought that you didn't dance?" she asked.

"I will for you," he said with a shrug. She smiled, taking his hand before he dragged them over to one of the more open areas of the grass and put his arms around her waist while she wrapped hers around his neck. "Always for you Sunshine."

She pecked a kiss on his lips before resting her head on his chest. Zach hugged her closer, kissing the top of her head. When he turned them back so he could face the blanket, Zach glanced at Kit, who was taking video on her phone of them with a giddy look on her face. "For your wedding," she mouthed.

Zach rolled his eyes, but chuckled regardless, holding Belle all the closer, swaying back and forth to the slow song, feeling lighter than he ever had before.

Zach knew at that moment, everything he needed was right

there in Lillet.

And that's where he was going to stay.

"End of Summer Vlog - Blues Concerts, Beach Days and Berry Pancakes"

58,093 views · 2h ago

Hi Lovelies,

I don't know what the weather is like where you live, but it's starting to cool down a bit here in Maryland (finally), so let's celebrate the end of summer together with some of my favorite things. What's your favorite thing about Summer? Tell me in a comment down below!

Love, Belle

@TiaDoll · 2h ago

Your videos always make me feel so cozy! I can't wait to see your fall videos this year.

> @LoveBelle · 2 min ago
>
> Oh, I already have so many plans for fall. Me and my friend are planning on camping and watching fall rom-coms in the tent while we plan her perfect love story. So ready for that!

@AlwaysAlthea · 1h ago

I just took a trip to the beach and made a picnic like the one you made a couple of videos back. It turned out so good! Thanks for inspiring me!

> @LoveBelle · 30s ago
>
> Thank you Lovely! If you have any pictures of it, please send them to me on Instagram, cause I would love to see them!

@SmartAsh · 5 min ago

Love the video, but quick question - who's the cutie you're cuddling with?

> @LoveBelle · 4s ago
>
> The person who made me feel like I wasn't alone anymore *heart emoji*

Acknowledgments

I can't believe that the day is actually here where I get to write an acknowledgments page. Little me would be so happy to see a book she wrote in the world and I wrote this book for her! Never give up on your childhood dreams my friends!

First off, I want to thank my Mom and Dad for always encouraging me to do this. Being an author isn't an easy career choice but my parents knew this was my dream, so they always encouraged me to keep going. Thank you for your constant reminders of how I should be writing and keeping me grounded when my doubts start to kick in. Mom, thank you for listening to my rambles about my characters, even though you're not a big fan of their tragic backstories. Dad, thank you for helping me figure out the business side of things and reminding me to invest in myself as much as I invest in this book. You two have been my number one fans since day one and I'm ever grateful that you are in my life. Squad for Life!

Cass, thank you for being the first one to read from this book and giving me the initial boost I needed to keep writing.

Ellie, thank you for your feedback and for being Zach's original biggest fan! Your support means everything and thank you for helping make the e-book a reality.

Britney, thank you for your amazing editing prowess that helped me make this opposites-attract romance actually feel like an opposites-attract romance.

Aida, thank you for making the cover that perfectly captures the essence of Zach, Belle, and Appa so well. You made my babies come to life!

Sally, Kelli, and Cameo, you lovely people have kept my spirits high and your reactions remind me why I love sharing my writing with others. Thank you for your comments, emojis, and ever-present love for Appa!

Anna, you freaking rockstar! Thank you for all your grammar know-how and help fine-tuning this story. You've taught me to appreciate the comma and semicolon and for that, I will always be grateful.

Zach and Belle, thank you for being my first book babies. I hope your stories inspire others and help them find all the books that we wished we could have seen when we were younger.

Finally, thank you reader for giving my book a chance, it means the world to me. I hope you consider leaving a review so other people will be encouraged to check out this book for themselves.

About the Author

JJ is an author with a penchant for love stories, whimsical settings, and cozy vibes. She loves creating stories where readers will know that everything will be okay by the end of it. She was interested in storytelling her whole life and dabbled with writing fanfiction and short stories before taking the plunge to write her debut novel, The Belle of Linley Cottage. She currently lives in Maryland and spends her days writing, reading, and watching Disney movies.

Visit her website (authorjjwrites.com) and sign up for her newsletter for bonus content and sneak peeks of future books

Follow her at @authorjjwrites on social media to stay up to date on what's to come.